THREE DECADES OF FATE.
ONE INSTANT BETWEEN
LIFE AND DEATH . . .

1958. In a Miami café a Cuban agent passes information to the C.I.A. After the Bay of Pigs, the informant—now wanted by the U.S.—goes into hiding.

∎

1966. On the streets of a faded northern city a boy watches a rookie policeman shoot his father. The dead man was Castro's agent. The cop would start life over again in Florida. The boy would never forget...

∎

1986. Fort Lauderdale is overrun with drug traffic and pleasure seekers. The rookie cop is now a veteran, the boy is a rising kingpin of the underworld, and their war within a war is just beginning. A missing undercover cop, a beautiful party girl, and a network of espionage have plunged J.B. Richards and Onyx Montilla into a deadly duel—to bury the past in blood.

∎

Also by
Cherokee Paul McDonald

The Patch

Published by
POPULAR LIBRARY

GULF STREAM

CHEROKEE PAUL McDONALD

POPULAR LIBRARY

An Imprint of Warner Books, Inc.

A Warner Communications Company

A
BERNARD GEIS ASSOCIATES
BOOK

POPULAR LIBRARY EDITION

Cover illustration by Ken Joudry
Cover design by Jackie Merri Meyer

Popular Library books are published by
Warner Books, Inc.
666 Fifth Avenue
New York, N.Y. 10103

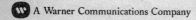 A Warner Communications Company

Printed in the United States of America

First Printing: August, 1988

10 9 8 7 6 5 4 3 2 1

For Russell J. Smith,
always my friend.

With special thanks to Charles Scribner Sr.,
and John J. ("Boca Jack") Furtado,
two gentlemen
of distinction . . . and vision.

Cast your bread upon the waters,
for after many days you will find it again.

—Ecclesiastes 11:1

ONE

It was the face of the small boy that stayed with him.

The explosive, terrifying event took only seconds to unfold and change his life forever, yet that moment was filled with images that became fragmented parts of his life's memories. The face of the small boy, however, was a clear and detailed picture that lived in his mind always. The wide-eyed expression stared at him; the eyes, shiny black in their accusation, were always questioning.

He had just killed a man on a bright sunny day in the heart of the city. He had shot him with his revolver, watched him stiffen and spin around and crumple to the hard sidewalk while thick red blood bubbled from his victim's mouth. As a young police officer, working on foot, he alone had seen the confrontation. He had seen the guns and had somehow immediately fathomed what was taking place, and had acted. Having shouted, he had drawn his service revolver, shouted again, and then fired.

He had killed a man, heard the roar in his ears and felt the heat from the sun. The color of blood, and the face of the small boy who had watched him blurred. He had heard the boy cry out, not knowing what the small voice asked, and then he had the fleeting impression of someone, a woman, pulling the boy by the hand into the crowd of people that was gathering. And then the boy was gone.

After the disastrous Bay of Pigs invasion in 1961, President John F. Kennedy asked one of his aides, "How could I have been so stupid?" The dynamic young president was, perhaps, a bit hard on himself because he had been advised by the "best and the brightest." He was given all of the intelligence data that could be gathered, and a scenario was drawn for him that promised success. Years later, volumes would be written about how flawed most of that information was, and about how impossible it would have been for the meager invasion force to grab a toehold on the beaches of Cuba and stay there long enough for the Cuban people to join them in an overwhelming uprising that would topple Castro. Much of that flawed intelligence data had to do with the fantasy that the Cuban people would, if given the chance, rise up against their charismatic leader. Intelligence data cuts both ways, and the insidious mechanism that cloaks bad intelligence with the good has a label: disinformation.

Felix Ortiz had happily contributed to the disinformation gathered prior to the Bay of Pigs invasion. Born and raised in Cuba, he had worked on the fringes of the Batista government as a domestic operative, but he was, in addition to being cunning, fast, and ruthless, very politically aware. He had watched what was happening in the mountains, in the streets, and in the small bars. He perceived a change in public opinion. Long before it was too late he gave himself into the service of Castro's people, bringing them information and, in turn, supplying the Batista forces misleading intelligence. Felix was light on his feet; he had lived for many months on the razor's edge, and was surprised and quite pleased when he wasn't summarily executed by Castro's new government after Batista and his group were forced to flee.

There was one catch, however.

Felix was told that he wasn't trusted; that he would be closely watched—always. He was urged to accept an assignment out of the country.

Felix Ortiz relocated to Miami before the Bay of Pigs invasion, and it was not uncommon to see him once in a while in Washington, D.C., smiling and nodding his head and speaking rapidly but quietly to some faceless gray suit with a hat and a briefcase. Felix was comfortable in the *Estados Unidos*; he liked the freedom, he liked the cars, and he liked the fact that his young son lived there. Felix's baby boy had been born in 1958, one year before the fall of

Batista. The child was less than one year old when Felix managed to move him from Cuba to the United States. Castro's people were aware of the baby but let Felix spirit him out for their own reasons. Felix did not know where the boy's mother was by that time, nor did he care. He felt secure in the knowledge that the son he loved would stay in the care of a woman even he called *mi tía*.

When in Miami, Felix would sit in the shade of a small sidewalk café, sip bitter coffee, and wait for his orders. Once briefed, he would dutifully pass on his knowledge on the pulse of the Cuban people to the same gray suit, hat, and briefcase. The gray suit was always pleased to get what Felix would give him, and rarely saw the need to check it through other sources.

After the invasion forces suffered humiliating defeat at the hands of a well-informed and strongly entrenched Castro, Felix felt a definite chill in the air around Miami and D.C. He made himself very small for a while, and then, two years later, when Kennedy was assassinated in Dallas, Felix Ortiz made himself *desaparecer*.

But Felix couldn't make himself disappear completely. He had to stay in contact with those who gave him his orders from Cuba. He found that even they seemed to lay very low for a while after Kennedy's death. He also had to stay in contact with his son. Felix Ortiz spent almost three years on the run, knowing he had to get out of the U.S. and back home to Cuba for a hero's welcome, but he realized that he could never leave without his son.

Felix was hunted, and there was a personal involvement in the hunt. The faceless gray suit wanted Felix Ortiz very badly. He wanted him alive, for a time. The faceless gray suit had almost pathologically loved his young president, and had worked very hard to gather important intelligence for the invasion. He was young and devoted to his mission. He had been one of the principal sponsors of the Cuban operative known as Felix Ortiz. Then the invasion came and the assassination, and the realization that Ortiz had been a double agent. The faceless gray suit knew he, and many others, had been had. It didn't help his career, and it didn't help his disposition.

In the summer of 1966, when the innocence and naïveté of America lay spread-legged and in blissful ignorance of her impending rape by a tumultuous and merciless decade of events that had already started with the first military advisers being assigned to a mystical place called Vietnam, Felix Ortiz managed covertly to contact the woman who cared for his son. They would come from New York, and they would meet him in the featureless brick mountains of a tired northern city. Then, by bus and by car, Felix Ortiz would take them with him to Miami, where the term Little Havana was already very appropriate. From there, he was sure, his supervisors in Cuba would figure a way to get him, and his son, who was now eight years old, home.

The faceless gray suit who pursued Felix Ortiz so continuously was William Buchanan. He continued to wear gray suits and carry a briefcase. He still worked for the CIA, and he still smarted every time the Bay of Pigs was mentioned. But now, he knew, he was finally close to getting his hands on Ortiz. He knew that the CIA wasn't supposed to dabble in domestic enterprises—that was handled by their "sister" service, the FBI—but in this case Buchanan knew there was no way he would let any other agency get to Ortiz first. He would justify his action by saying that the hunt was domestic but the product was foreign.

Buchanan had watched and waited. He knew where the woman was, and that the small boy with the pure black eyes was the son of his quarry. He did some telephone tapping; he did some illegal mail interception; he did some leaning on frightened Cubans who didn't want to be forced to go home, and he hurried to the tired northern city where Ortiz would meet his son. He took with him a new squeaky-clean agent who was ready to follow Buchanan without asking too many questions.

In the summer of 1966, in a downtown area of a tired old northern city, twenty-two-year-old rookie patrolman J.B. Richards walked around a corner on his way to a neighborhood drugstore where he knew he could use the telephone to call home. He was on duty, in uniform, and he felt funny about conducting his personal business during that time, but he wanted to check on his young wife and their baby girl. He walked around the corner—and became embroiled in an action that would haunt him for years.

"Hold it right there! Freeze . . . we're federal agents!" yelled a young man in a gray suit to a smaller man nearby.

"Give it up, Ortiz, you know who I am!" yelled his partner, an older and heavier version of the first. Both had small revolvers pointed at the third man.

Only a short distance from the other two, stood the third man. He was small and thin, with a very Latin look to him, black shiny hair, and brown skin. He wore work pants and a leather jacket, and as Patrolman Richards watched, the Latin pulled out a small automatic pistol, dropped to one knee, and started firing rapidly at the two agents.

Richards reacted with a sure knowledge of what he was seeing. Somehow he knew the first two men were, in fact, Feds. He could see that the Latin was bent on their destruction. One of the agents, the young one, cried out, jerked backward, and fell to the pavement, holding his hip. The other, ducking with one hand in front of his face, as if to ward off flying insects, jumped to the side, hit the fender of a parked car, and fell in a sitting position with his back against the tire. Neither of the agents had fired their weapons. Richards wasn't sure if the Latin had fired four or five shots, but he pointed his service revolver at the darker man and squeezed the trigger twice rapidly. He felt the gun buck in his hands, and he saw the Latin stiffen and spin around, his eyes wildly darting this way and that. Richards felt the heat from his gun on his hands as he saw the man finally crumple heavily to the sidewalk, the blood in his mouth a vivid red.

Then the heat from the sun, the roar in his ears, and the face of the small boy standing on the other side of the street clouded Richard's vision.

The small boy had been very excited. He had missed his father, with whom he had spent so little time, and he had asked his aunt over and over again why his father couldn't be with him. His aunt had told him it was because his father did secret work; that his father was a hero. When he had seen his father across the street, he had started to yell, but his aunt had shushed him quickly, and somehow he felt her fear. He looked again at his father, and then heard two men yelling at him. He watched as his father whirled to face the men, and then he felt his aunt hugging him tightly. He could hear loud firecrackers going off and people screaming. He stared at his father and then at the big policeman who pointed his ugly black gun at his father and fired it twice. The explosions were very loud. The boy watched as his father spun around, and he could see that his father's eyes were wide open, looking everywhere . . . but not at him.

The little boy screamed as loud as he could, "Look at me, Daddy! Look at *me!*" But his father didn't see him. He watched as his father fell to the sidewalk, his eyes staring, and he was crying and confused as he felt his aunt pulling him violently through the crowd, away from the noise, and away from the father who wouldn't look at him.

The last thing the boy saw as he was pulled away was the pale face of the big policeman with the light-colored hair and the ugly gun. The policeman was staring at him.

The first few weeks after the killing of Felix Ortiz were a time of confusion and pain, of disillusionment and anger, and of hard growing for young Patrolman J.B. Richards. During the first hours he was a hero, pounded on the back and smiled at, lauded and congratulated. Back at the station house, with the detectives, people brought him coffee and asked him to tell the story over and over again. He longed for a few moments of quiet, but was visited by the brass instead. A seedy assistant chief winked at him and told him he "did a nice job on that beaner," and the chief of detectives told everyone who would listen that J.B. had pulled the Fed's fat out of the fire.

One voice of sanity managed to break through—that of J.B.'s very senior partner, Theo Novak, who had gone home ill the morning of the shooting. That afternoon, while J.B. had been in the detective division giving statements, Novak had come in looking for him. The cancer that would soon kill the old street cop made him look drawn and feverish. He watched J.B. carefully for a moment before taking him aside. Then he said quietly, "You did what you had to do, kid. You did the right thing, but it ain't somethin' that deserves this circus, right?" He looked around the room slowly, then went on, "Sometimes you have to kill, and you did, and you'll have to come to your own terms with it. With time, you will. In the meantime, be careful. I mean, watch your ass with this thing." He had smiled his thin smile and finally said, "The Feds are involved, the brass smell somethin' big, and before it's all over you're gonna have to watch your ass, right?" Then he had gone.

It took only one week for everyone's mood to change.

J.B. was called in to a meeting with the brass. As he walked in he nodded at the older federal agent, the one who hadn't been wounded, but the man just stared at him. J.B. began to feel uneasy. He was told by the assistant chief that after examining the shooting, and talking it over with the federal agents involved, the administration had decided that J.B. had rushed his actions, and that he had acted without determining what the situation was. J.B. started to protest, saying that he could see the agents were in trouble, but the assistant chief put up one pudgy hand and stopped him. Yes, he was told, they saw his view of the incident, but they believed J.B.'s view was limited. He wasn't aware of the big picture.

And what was the big picture? J.B. had asked.

The federal agent, Buchanan, gave J.B. a brief outline of Ortiz and why the government wanted him. He told J.B. they had planned to confront Ortiz and take him alive, so they could turn him around and play him back. Although Ortiz was popping off his little automatic, and despite the agent's young partner getting shot, the situation had been under control. Buchanan thought it regrettable, but really what J.B. had done, being a new kid and all, had been to barge into something he shouldn't have messed with, and he wound up killing a man that the U.S. government dearly wanted to capture alive.

J.B. listened in stunned silence, and when it was all over he knew he was finished with police work, finished with being a street cop in a dirty, tired old northern city. He was angry and hurt and confused. At the same time his old partner, Theo Novak, had taken a turn for the worse, and J.B. was having trouble understanding why he was there, doing the job.

The period after the killing of Felix Ortiz was a time of confusion and pain, of disillusionment and anger for the young boy who had watched his father die. His old aunt had managed to get them to Miami where they eventually found a place to live with friends. Somehow they survived those terrible lonely years. The boy grew up on the streets of the Hispanic neighborhoods of Miami: tough streets, streets filled with machismo and honor and a driving hunger for the good things. By the time the boy was a young teenager his aunt had died and he was a veteran member of the Hispanic criminal element—he had been a party to some burglary, some numbers running, some street scamming. Even in a hard world he soon acquired a reputation for being very hard; the other predators respected him and gave him room to work. He became very passionate in his desire to succeed. Those that spent any time with him saw the intensity in his eyes—and something else—a penetrating hate. They made room for him in the gangs. They knew if a job was important, and the yield good, he was the one to be counted on. There was one problem with him, however, that made some of the more established groups cautious about using him too often: He had a thing about cops.

Even if he was routinely stopped and questioned he would become very edgy with the police officer. Some of the street types who worked with him at such a time were uncomfortable with his reaction because they knew that hassling a cop would invite trouble. They knew it was best just to "yessir" and "nossir" a cop, but they would watch him come close to actually picking fights. They would watch the policemen react, and they would just shake their heads, not understanding the undefined anger that ran through their partner.

The established Hispanic criminal elements kept a close watch on him. His thing about cops worried them. Who needed the hassle?

The boy managed, by street smarts and an inner toughness, to survive his teenage years, but then his luck changed. On a hot and sticky summer night he and two others pulled an armed robbery of an all-night drugstore. The word on the street was that there was more money under the till than in it because the manager of the store had a numbers thing going on the side. The robbery went smoothly until the manager started to fight with them during the getaway, screaming that he would call the police. He was shot in the face, and died before he hit the pavement in the dirty alley behind his store. Weeks later, one of the three robbers was arrested during a drug rip-off, rolled over on the drugstore killing for consideration, and all three robbers went to trial.

Again the boy hung tough, and the prosecutor could not prove to the jury, absolutely, just who was the trigger man. The boy's public defender asked for, and got, a separate trial, and finally the boy pleaded guilty to lesser charges. In 1979 he was sentenced to seven years and was sent to Raiford. He served a little over two years and, because of the groaning prison system and his luck again, he was released on a paper-thin parole.

One thing came of his short jail time, though: He learned beyond any shadow of a doubt that he hated being jailed. He was not an institutional man. He had survived in good shape, but it had frightened him and degraded him, and he swore to himself that he would never go back. He would not go straight, but he would carry out his criminal activities in a cooler, more professional manner. He would lay low for a while, then be more careful in his dealings.

By that time he was a career criminal, with many connections in the Hispanic criminal element, the traditional families from New York, Chicago, Cleveland, and Canada, and even the local "Dixie Mafia." He became a manager at a small Latin club, kept his nose clean and his eyes open, and eventually made cautious contacts with some of the local narcotics players who might have an occasional job for him. He was introduced to a man named Kolin, who convinced him that if he moved a little north, to Fort Lauderdale, life might blossom for him. He saw Lauderdale as an "open" town, with less firmly entrenched groups, and saw the possibilities there for what he wanted to do. He looked toward the small islands of Bimini only forty-eight nautical miles across the Gulf Stream, and he smiled. Bimini had a north island, traditionally and firmly inhabited by Bahamians, and a south island, which in the seventies was largely taken over by Colombians—and Cubans.

It was 1986, and he was twenty-eight years old. He ran, on the side, small amounts of cocaine, because it was light and a quick operation that provided instant money. He also ran loads of grass. It was bulky and awkward and a pain to carry and off-load, but it was also more low-key and not as important to the police as it used to be, and it too made money.

He had taken his aunt's name instead of his father's, at her insistence. His first name was not a common one, but one that his father had given him and loved. Maybe it had something to do with his shiny pure black eyes.

He was an up-and-coming drug smuggler working the Fort Lauderdale area. He was a professional, and he had already shown how ruthless and deadly he could be. He didn't know he had been watched for many years . . . watched by some of the men who had employed his father a lifetime ago. Soon he would be approached by an echo from the past, an echo from that struggling island that lay just ninety miles from Key West. That echo would wrap him in a challenge and mission that would change his life forever.

His name was Onyx Montilla.

Within six months after the killing of Felix Ortiz, veteran Patrol Officer Theo Novak was dead. He left behind a wife, two daughters, and a young son.

J.B. Richards resigned as a police officer for the tired old Northern city.

After talking it over with his wife, J.B. decided he liked being a cop but that he needed to work in a smaller, simpler atmosphere, someplace that respected the old values—someplace nice.

J.B. said his good-byes to Theo Novak's widow, promising to stay in touch with young Ted, Theo's son, with whom he already had unofficial "uncle" status, and headed to Florida with his wife and baby daughter. After some searching he was hired by the city of Fort Lauderdale as a patrolman. He served for some time on the palm-lined, sunny streets. Because he was quiet and neat and did his job well, with rarely any problems, he was rewarded with the assignment that he had longed for and requested.

J.B. Richards, patrolman, worked in the marine unit of the FLPD, and he loved it. He drove his small police boat on the beautiful waterways, waved at the recreational boaters, had coffee with the professional fishermen, and stayed mellow. He had worked the streets in the cold, in the heat, in the rain, and in the darkness. He had handled domestics and suicides, child abuses and wife beatings. He had been beaten, spat upon, and sued. He had tried to help while he watched his fellow man struggle through his sad and sometimes brutal charade. He had tried to help while society vomited on his shoes.

And he had killed. J.B. Richards had been around too long to be a hot dog cop, out to save the world, but at the same time, he still believed in the job he did too much to spend his time hiding in the doughnut shop. He listened to his police radio and answered calls when assigned, helped out when needed, and gave the city what they paid him for. At the same time, he understood and worked with the knowledge that life went on in the streets and on the waterways of the city even when he wasn't there patrolling his beat. When his shift was over he took himself home and devoted as much energy and caring to his family as he did to the public he served. He was a veteran, a professional, aware of his own limits and of his own value.

In 1986, twenty years after that sunny day on the streets of the tired old Northern city, only once in a while, did the face of the small boy flicker, like a subtle chill, in J.B.'s mind.

TWO

The Gulf Stream moves from the south Atlantic, sweeps through and around the Bahama Islands, flows past the shelf off Florida and continues up the East Coast, where it then keeps pushing northward. The water is warm, and carries all before it in a majestic and inexorable flow. It is both a mystical and scientific body of water; it can be seen and touched.

A mountain stream, cold and clear, follows a downhill path through the rocks, taking millions of years to erode and undermine and change direction. The Gulf Stream is different; its borders undulate and wave and change every hour, and its water, though clear, is always noticeably warmer than the waters of its mother, the ocean.

The warmth of the Gulf Stream affects the lives of all those who dwell in her, and the lives of all those who live on the land she touches. Temperate climates and a strong food chain are only part of what she has to offer. . . . The Gulf Stream seems as permanent as the sun.

Against the golden beaches of south Florida and the islands on the other side, the Atlantic Ocean sometimes appears green, peaceful, and sometimes angry. Then the jade green turns into a gunmetal gray. There is a richness to the ocean's colors, and it is captivating to look out every day to see if she is relaxing, or if she tosses her foam-topped tresses here and there in disharmony, crashing against the beaches and pounding against herself in a howling wind.

Yet when compared to the richness of colors in the Gulf Stream, the ocean appears faded.

During the summer, when the ocean stays calm most of the time and the pure sun radiates down upon us all, the Gulf Stream is a thing of sheer and intense beauty. If the color blue were played on a flute, the melody would be entrancing, but if that blue were played by one of the world's great symphony orchestras, the intensity of the Gulf Stream's blue—rich, deep, royal, sparkling—would be heard.

Life thrives in the Gulf Stream with a gritty enthusiasm. Many of the tropical birds, indigenous and migratory, circle overhead, flit by proudly, or balance precariously on some passing palm frond. The fishes in the southern hemisphere live in the stream, as do many of the water mammals.

The beautiful, open, larger-than-life Gulf Stream hosts hunters too—those powerful, sinewy, silent creatures that move with such grace through her depths, searching for prey. The predators also share her warmth, and find good hunting in her folds.

The predators that glide on her surface are equally powerful and sinewy, but they are not always as silent.

Stiletto roared out of Port Everglades.

She let her long pointed nose rock up and down a couple of times as she cleared the slight swell pushing in past the north and south rock jetties at the entrance to the port. Then she settled down and as the RPM's on her twin 450 horsepower engines were increased, she eased between the first set of cage markers, and then between the next set of buoy markers. The throaty rumble of the four exhausts were proof of her power. *Stiletto* was thirty-two feet long, with layered fiberglass tapered to a fine bow and blunted at the stern. She was black and gray in color. Her windscreen was small, finely cut, and raked a bit, and she moved through the pale green water like her namesake.

As *Stiletto* approached the third whistle buoy, her bow was turned slightly to the right to a heading of 120 degrees, and she trembled in anticipation. Her throttles were pushed smoothly forward, her twin engines began to roar, her bow came up and then dropped nicely, and within seconds she was planed out, doing close to fifty knots, heading for Bimini. The wet ocean spray turned to fine white lace around her bow, and she crossed the line from waters of pale green to that of deep blue in minutes.

She was in the Gulf Stream.

Standing at the helm of *Stiletto*, his hips pushed back into the bolster seat and his hands wrapped around the padded steering wheel, a set grin on his face, was Onyx Montilla. His mirrored sunglasses were already covered with a fine salt spray, but he left them on as he looked directly into the first pink-orange-red of a spectacular sunrise. He had gathered his passengers and left Fort Lauderdale before dawn, and now, as always, he felt exhilarated as he guided *Stiletto* through the water.

Montilla's passengers stood shoulder to shoulder beside him, their hips also pushed back into the bolster seat, their legs also spread, their knees flexed to absorb the slight pounding. The man in the middle, an attorney, clung grimly to a small handrail mounted above the cabin hatchway. He was pale, and his carefully combed and sprayed hair was already blown in disarray. He wore new deck shoes, white slacks, and a pale blue short-sleeved shirt. He had a heavy Rolex watch around his left wrist, and a fine gold chain around his neck. He was very uncomfortable, frightened of the speed of the boat and the roar of the engines, frightened by the vastness of the ocean, and slightly nervous about the whole idea of this trip with Montilla.

The attorney had represented Montilla a couple of times through the years on minor criminal matters, and eventually had gathered some knowledge of Montilla's drug smuggling activities. He invested some of his money in a couple of Montilla's deals, liked his profits, and found that smuggling was an exciting business. Of course, Montilla was involved with grass, but everyone knew that the real money and kick came from cocaine. The attorney found coke to be fun and socially appealing, and he did it as much as he thought was fashionably safe. After reviewing his position with Montilla, the attorney had recently decided to take the lead in their deals. He knew how to get cocaine, and he talked Montilla into investing some of his money in a sweet little cocaine deal.

The attorney, squinting into the almost unbearable sunrise, frowned as he remembered that deal. He had been the victim of a reverse sting operation, and besides losing his money and Montilla's, and getting himself arrested on conspiracy charges, he felt stupid. He cleverly, cautiously, or so he had thought, made some noises here and there about wanting to purchase a couple of kilos of cocaine, and he let it be known that he had the money. He was introduced to the young man who was in the boat with them now, and another man, and eventually they were able to meet with some dealers who showed them some pretty fine coke. He was pleased with the whole situation until he showed the money. That was when the men with the coke pulled out badges and arrested everybody. He was booked at the same time the young man in the boat was, and when he bonded out later, he saw that the young man was still there, arguing with the booking people. The attorney had gone home, chagrined and feeling stupid.

Montilla had been furious at first and had broken all communication with the attorney for over a week. Then suddenly, last night, he had contacted the attorney and invited him to ride along this morning over to Bimini to "take a look at the other side."

The attorney Fred Hadley was so glad that Montilla had contacted him, and so intrigued by the thought of roaring across the Gulf Stream to Bimini, that he didn't think about being frightened until after they were out in the ocean. Then he remembered that he hadn't told his partner, his wife, or his mistress where he was going. He looked to his left, at the grinning and obviously thrilled face of the young man who had been arrested with him in the coke sting. The man had stayed in touch after he had bonded out of jail, and left a number where Hadley could leave messages for him. When Montilla had invited the attorney along for this ride he had asked about the young man, and the attorney had told Montilla he would invite him too.

Montilla had been pleased. Now Hadley looked to his left again, and hung on.

The young man on the left of the attorney was Ted Novak, and this was his first exciting adventure since going undercover as a narc with the Fort Lauderdale Police Department. He had been a cop for only two years and he still had that fresh, squeaky-clean look, even though he was older than the typical rookie. He looked younger than he was, so much so that even younger officers often referred to him as "young Ted," or "kid." He hadn't acquired that "cop look." His face was friendly and open, and the hardness around the eyes that veteran cops get hadn't appeared yet.

Ted was older than most rookies because of his mother. He had always wanted to be a cop, like his father Theo, but after his father's death his mother had opposed his going into any form of police work. He finished college with an English degree, and then had worked as a teacher in the public school system from 1980 to 1984. He spent much of his free time during those years watching the police shows on television and reading as much Wambaugh as he could get his hands on. He structured sentences and graded papers, but his heart was never really in his work, and after his mother died of a heart attack he quit. He had done what his mother had wished, but now she was gone. He left his two married sisters in the North, and followed his "Uncle" J.B.'s path to Fort Lauderdale, where he was hired to do the job he had always dreamed of. He was now twenty-nine years old and very proud to have been pulled from the uniformed ranks to go undercover in the "Venice of America" and the Caribbean basin. He felt the salt spray on his face, watched the eastern sky catch fire, heard the steady droning roar of the engines on *Stiletto*, and grinned. Absolutely ten-four, he thought, wish ol' Uncle J.B. could see me now.

Chance had put him out in the Gulf Stream with Montilla and the attorney, and although he was new, he had already learned how to take advantage of circumstance. Ted knew he had no business being where he was, heading for a foreign country, without carrying any identification.

He hadn't even called in to let his sergeant or his partner know where he was going. He had agonized over that decision. But the attorney had said this "quick deal" with Montilla was a chance to redeem themselves. The deal came up, and he figured he had to go for it.

Just over a week ago Ted had been introduced to Hadley by a confidential informant, supposedly because he knew some dealers with cocaine for sale. Then he had been "arrested" with the attorney to maintain his credibility, and everything had gone down nicely. During the deal, the attorney had hinted that the money wasn't all his, and Ted was glad for the opportunity to find out who really was involved.

Ted Novak glanced quickly to his right, past the attorney, and he stared at the hard-looking Montilla at the helm of the boat. He knew Montilla had been part of the money that had been used in the coke deal, but Ted didn't yet have a clear picture of how. Montilla had been friendly to him when introduced by the attorney, and had hinted that there might be a possibility of making up their loss in the future.

Ted hung on to the handrail in the racing *Stiletto*, and told himself that chance had put him in this situation, and that all he had to do was ride it out to its conclusion. If he had called in, he knew he would not have been allowed to make the trip. He would just have to report his findings later.

As Ted watched the bow of *Stiletto* cut through the incredibly blue Gulf Stream, he saw half a dozen porpoises break water about fifty yards off the port side, felt the wind rushing past him, and thought, *God, life is beautiful.*

Montilla did not take *Stiletto* straight into the cut between north and south Bimini. Instead, he swung right when they were close inshore and then he raced south. In a few minutes they came upon the concrete ship forever aground in the shallows south of Bimini. Anchored nearby was an old weathered wooden island fishing boat. Standing at the stern of the boat was a very large Bahamian, who waved as *Stiletto* approached.

Montilla swung *Stiletto* close, and the big islander jumped nimbly from the old fishing boat onto the engine cover of the racing boat, and then down into the cockpit. He stood behind the three of them now, and gave them a toothy grin.

Ted Novak looked him over. He was well over six feet, and at least two hundred and twenty pounds. His skin looked like black rubber, except where it had been creased with bluish cut scars. His hands were big, and his hair was cut very short. He wore ragged shorts and a fishnet shirt with no sleeves.

Hadley cleared his throat, and said, "Onyx, who is this? Why haven't we gone into Bimini?"

Montilla smiled and said easily, "This is my friend Cuda, who has worked with me in the past." They all shook hands. "I brought him aboard here because there has been a change. We have a chance now to meet some of the people that bring some stuff up through the chain, and they have told Cuda that they will meet with me on a boat, south of here, down past Cat Cay." He smiled again. "Don't worry, amigo. It will be fun, and you will get to see how some of this business of ours works. *Si?*"

The attorney nodded and swallowed, worried. Novak grinned. He was thinking of the report he would compose back in Lauderdale.

They had left the deep blue waters of the Gulf Stream, and as they raced south along the Bimini chain they cruised over emerald green water with patches of reef and pure white sand. The water was so clear that in their great speed it appeared as though they were flying. It looked like the water had no surface—there was just the fiberglass bow of the boat, and fifty feet below, the coral reef. Honeymoon Bay, Gun Cay, and Cat Cay disappeared on their left, as did the smaller islands in the chain. They stayed over the green flats, the deep water off to their right. The sun moved higher in the sky, the air became warmer, and the day turned into a Caribbean basin calendar photo. It was still early, as it had taken them just over an hour from Lauderdale to Bimini.

The attorney looked back over his shoulder, past the bulk of Cuda, at the horizon, where he could just barely make out the small gray ripple of the last island they had passed. Suddenly he felt the boat slowing, and he watched as Montilla pulled the throttles all the way back, looking all around as he did so. The throaty rumble of the idling engines was a blissful silence after the thunder that had enveloped them. They drifted in the sun across the smooth green surface of the water, their pointed shadow rippling fishlike below them across the coral reef.

Montilla hopped up onto the bolster seat, tucked in his legs, swung around, and jumped down into the cockpit area. He stretched and looked around again. "Hey, amigo," he said to the attorney, "the other boat isn't here yet. Pull that cooler out from the cabin and let's have a cool one."

While Hadley struggled with the cooler, and Cuda stood on the engine cover, urinating over the side, Novak climbed over the seat and joined Montilla in the cockpit. He stretched, and looked up into the flawless blue sky. He looked at Montilla and smiled, saying, "That ride over here across the Gulf Stream was sure worth the price of admission."

Montilla studied him for a moment, and said, "You think so, my friend? Good. I'm glad you are enjoying it."

The attorney got the cooler into the cockpit, Montilla handed out the cold beers, and everyone took a grateful pull, even Ted, who didn't care for beer in the morning. They were just relishing their first swallow when Montilla gave an almost imperceptible nod of his head, and Cuda moved with catlike speed and strength.

Novak saw him coming but couldn't move out of the way fast enough, and then Cuda had him by the neck and crotch and he felt himself lifted up. He spun once and hit the water with a loud splash. As he came up sputtering, he noticed how cold the beer felt against his wrist as it spilled out of the can, compared to the water in which he was already dog-paddling. He pushed his hair out of his eyes and said, "What the hell . . ." as Montilla grinned and jumped over the bolster seat. Novak watched helplessly as *Stiletto* was put into gear and idled off a few yards.

Hadley thought at first that some kind of joke was being played on the young guy, but then Cuda grabbed him too and spun him around, pinning his arms behind him. The attorney turned his head and watched as Montilla climbed back into the cockpit, and moved closer to him. Montilla held a fishing knife in his hand. The attorney's eyes widened, and he started to speak but stopped when he felt the point of the knife at his throat. Cuda grabbed his hair then, and pulled his head back. Hadley swallowed hard, and his Adam's apple moved grotesquely.

"No one . . . makes Onyx Montilla look like a fool, my friend, not like you did with my money. Don't you think the people in my world laugh at me when they hear how I gave so much money to a gringo lawyer who loses it so easily? I can't have that, señor . . . no, I can't have that." Montilla moved his face very close to that of the sweating attorney, and said quietly, "And what now, señor? Now that you've so stupidly been busted . . . huh? You, a smart attorney, with a coke charge hanging over you . . . I know you're jumpy now . . . I know you'll give me away if the cops pressure you."

Hadley started to say, "I'm sorry . . ." when Montilla cut his throat savagely, jumping back to avoid the bright red blood that spurted out. The attorney felt the pain, then a numbing wetness, and realized he was in the water, staring up into a lovely blue sky. He struggled feebly, and his ears filled with a far-off rushing sound, before he felt an enveloping blackness.

Ted Novak watched as the attorney was thrown overboard, and the first cold chill of fear drilled into his groin. This can't be happening, he told himself, this can't be real. But as he watched he saw Cuda and Montilla looking at him, then Montilla climbing behind the wheel of the racing boat. They pulled away from him, the engines pounding. He paddled in a circle, frantically, and in his limited horizon he saw only water and sky. What were they going to do . . . leave him there to swim home?

He heard the throaty rumble of the engines then, and got his answer.

Montilla's face was grim as he added power and pulled *Stiletto* around in a big circle, increasing her speed. He looked over his shoulder, checked Novak's position, and straightened her out. He put the point of the bow right on the swimming figure and pushed the throttles all the way forward. *Stiletto* leaped toward her target.

Ted Novak knew what was coming. He tried to swim as hard as he could, first to the right, then to the left, and each time he saw that Montilla only needed to make a slight correction to fix the aim. The sinister black and gray pointed bow was on him in seconds, and at the last moment he kicked as hard as he could, down and away.

Montilla deliberately pulled hard on the steering wheel and *Stiletto*'s hull dug in and she turned, missing Ted by less than a foot. Ted came up sputtering, engulfed by the boat's violent wake, and then he was swimming again, almost as angry as he was frightened.

Again Montilla brought *Stiletto* around, again he pushed the throttles forward, and again, at the last moment, he turned away from the man struggling in the emerald green water.

Cuda laughed out loud, enjoying the cat and mouse game.

Montilla let the engines idle now, and eased her on around so the shiny hull rocked gently a few feet from Ted, who was breathing hard, but still strong. Ted looked up at Montilla, confident behind the wheel of the racing boat, and gasped, "Why . . . ?"

Before he could say more Montilla called out, "So, my friend. Here you are, soon to be shark bait, and I am going to give you a chance to live."

Ted waited, treading water.

"My attorney was greedy, and anxious, and stupid . . . yes? And to tell you the truth, señor, I had already begun to worry about him. But then, last week, he gets busted after trying to buy coke . . . coke which *you* were supposed to set him up with." There was a pause, and the only sound was that of *Stiletto*'s engines, bubbling easily while the hull rocked in the water. Montilla called out again, "I think you might be a cop, señor. I'll be able to find out eventually, but for now I think you might be a cop. If you are not, then I think you somehow ripped off my poor attorney." He stopped, wiped the sweat off his brow, and looked all around the sky, shielding his eyes as he did so. Then he turned back to Ted, who was still dog-paddling in the warm water. "Either way I am most unhappy, señor. Now. . ." He pushed the throttles slightly forward and the boat moved. ". . . Why don't you tell me what you really are, señor, so I can let you back into this boat and take you home, yes?"

Ted's mind was racing, going over the possibilities, looking for an answer that might be the right one, but he already knew in his heart that there could be no right answer. Montilla would destroy him. He gambled, having nothing to lose. "I'm not a cop! I'm a small-time cocaine trafficker! Shit, I got busted, too!" He kicked his feet and moved his arms, keeping his head and shoulders above the water. "Listen, even if I *was* a cop, which I'm not! But if I was a cop, don't you think killing me would bring you lots of trouble, lots of heat?" He spit out some water and waited.

Montilla cocked his head, looked around again, and shrugged. "I don't know, señor, heat I've had before. . ." He looked around the horizon again and stiffened. Cuda looked too, and saw, far away, a small airplane circling lazily. Montilla looked back at Ted, and made his decision.

Again the power of the engines was increased, again the knifelike bow was brought around in a pounding circle, again to be lined up dead on the figure kicking and thrashing in the water. This time Montilla did not turn the wheel. This time he held her steady.

Ted watched the boat approach, took several deep breaths, and waited. At the last moment he kicked as hard as he could, down and away.

Montilla felt *Stiletto* shudder slightly as the big stainless steel cleaver props dug into the man in the water, and then they were over him. He and Cuda both looked back over their shoulders at the bubbling, spreading crimson stain in the water. He slowed the boat, looked all around, saw only empty sky and ocean, and took a long pull from the beer that Cuda handed him. Then he turned and idled back to where the bodies were.

There would be no surprises later. No one would miraculously wash up on some beach and be saved. Not today.

He waited patiently in the sun, silent, until he saw the

first signs of barracuda and small sharks gathering. He heard Cuda grunt and point, and saw the supple brown back of a big hammerhead moving toward them, the ugly head slowly swinging back and forth, the dorsal fin just cutting the surface of the green water.

"He be da' big mon' to be this close, hey," said Cuda. Montilla just nodded, pleased.

He turned to Cuda and held out his hand. Cuda looked at him and grinned, shrugging his massive shoulders.

Montilla took off his sunglasses, and looked long and hard at the big islander.

Cuda hesitated, saw the look in the smaller man's eyes, and sighed. He smiled as he handed Montilla the dead attorney's Rolex watch.

Montilla looked at the watch, pursed his lips, then shook his head and threw it as hard as he could, out away from the boat, and into the water. "Hey, *mi compadre,*" he said easily, "you know I'll pay you enough for today. Don't get greedy."

Cuda looked into Montilla's black glittering eyes, and said, "Okay, mon . . . dat be okay."

Montilla watched him closely for a few seconds, then pushed the throttles forward again, pointed the bow north, and headed back to the concrete ship.

After Montilla had dropped Cuda off and pointed *Stiletto* west, toward home, he thought about what he had done.

Marijuana was still good business. There was still consumer demand, and the better quality grass could always turn a profit. Sure, cocaine was the drug everyone wanted to do and everyone wanted to deal in, and there were designer drugs out West, and "black tar" coming out of Mexico. Now there was crack too, selling like crazy on the streets and in the schools. He shook his head. All of those popular drugs carried the heat with them. The cops were on the cocaine cowboys like mad, and the new stuff got more media coverage and made the cops try even harder. Reefer was still there, still making all those good folks high, still selling like crazy. It was bulky and smelly and awkward and a pain to work with, but it still made money—and the heat was not so bad on it.

So he, Onyx Montilla, worked in the stupid marijuana smuggling business. He provided sportfishing boats that off-loaded from the freighters and brought the bales across the Gulf Stream and into the Lauderdale area. He provided the boats and the crews and the waterfront homes where the stuff was off-loaded. After that the reefer was somebody else's problem.

He turned the wheel of *Stiletto* slightly to avoid a large piece of wooden hatch cover with a silly seagull standing on it, and grunted. In this day and age, after all that's happened in narcotics smuggling history, here he was smuggling bales . . . just like they did in the wild days of the seventies. The people who financed and controlled the group he worked for were dinosaurs, he decided. They were still plodding along with bug lumps of burlap-covered weed and they were still humping. Grass was safer, they said: Earn more, fear less.

Shit, he said.

Sure, he was doing it. He was making some pretty good money, even though he had all of the expenses of the boats and the crews and the houses. He made enough money to live well. And besides, the women needed it these days. He needed it. But he was in control.

Still, he thought, marijuana is not where it's at. Onyx Montilla should be a full-time cocaine smuggler. Making the really big bucks, having the power. Women needed cocaine more than marijuana. He could control that drug, too. Onyx Montilla could run with the fast guys, and he could handle it. Sure, he used the drug, but *he* knew what he was doing, he knew he would always stay on top.

He thought about what he had done today, about the killings. Fred Hadley had lost some pretty heavy money, and had made Montilla look like a fool. Montilla thought the attorney had been showing too much interest in the business lately, trying to suck in, and anyone could take one look at him and know that if the cops put the heat on he would sell out in a heartbeat.

That other one, Ted, he was just another Fort Lauderdale

opportunist ... looking for a score. Montilla's face hardened into a scowl as he thought of him.

What if he was a cop? Was it smart to kill him now?

He watched a big sportfisherman pounding across the stream heading east for a moment, knowing they were too far away to really get a good look at *Stiletto*, and thought, *Hell, I really don't care if he was a cop or not. There's no way they could make me on him, or prove a damn thing.* He paused. *They say the coke will make you believe you are invulnerable and incredibly capable. Did I make the decision to kill a guy who might be a narc because I'm using too much coke?*

He flexed his hands and arms against the wheel, drawing strength from the power of *Stiletto*, and said out loud, "I'm in control!"

Either way, the guy was a nobody, and the lawyer was a fool, and now they were both out of the picture.

The killings did not bother Onyx Montilla. He had killed before to get, or keep, what he wanted. He could not know that what he had done on this day would link him again to his past. He could not know what effect this victim would have on his future. If he had known, he would have been pleased.

The horizon was broken here and there with miragelike shapes, and Montilla looked at his watch. He was almost home. He moved his shoulders, and changed his stance a little.

I am Onyx Montilla, and I have been laying low and being careful and keeping a low profile long enough now. Now maybe it's time for me to go after what I know can be mine.

He grinned, and said out loud, "No, I will not go back to the *carcel*—but I will surely go to *infierno*."

It was just before high noon when the pointed bow of *Stiletto* knifed its way through the port entrance, and Montilla headed for one of the fashionable waterfront restaurants for lunch.

THREE

Fort Lauderdale Police Marine Patrol Officer J.B. Richards used one strong hand to keep his twenty-two-foot police boat from bumping too hard against the hull of the small rental boat he had stopped in the Intracoastal Waterway, just on the north side of the Seventeenth Causeway Bridge. The rental boat was packed full of well-oiled but still painfully sunburned bodies. All of the faces stared at Richards wide-eyed as he spoke to the man at the helm of the little boat.

"I'm sorreee," said the man, his hands held up into the air, "I have no English."

Richards rubbed his free hand across his face, hard. Great, he thought, a boatload of Canadians out for a day of fun in their rental boat. He looked at the incredible mixture of milky white skin and fiery red skin and shook his head. Then he looked at the man at the helm and said, "Don't have any English, huh? Well, how about this, sir? Do you understand Bastille . . . hmmm? Or jail maybe? Because that's where you're going if you don't slow this stupid rental boat down when you're passing by these marinas here, okay? Even though this is a small boat, your wake . . . understand wake? Your wake can damage other boats against the docks around here."

The man at the helm looked at the cop who had come alongside him in the police coat. The cop was big, over six feet, and heavy, although he didn't appear to be fat. His uniform was crisp and neat and fit his big frame well. The cop had a full head of dark blond hair, and a broad face with an angular nose that looked like it had been broken at least once. His skin was fair, the hair on his sunburned forearms very blond. His hands were big and rough, with scarred knuckles and calluses. The man at the helm watched as the cop took off his sunglasses, letting them hang across his chest on a string. The skin around his eyes was creviced with deep lines that accentuated the ice blue color of his eyes. A formidable man, this cop, but the man at the helm of the small boat saw something else in the cop's face—an openness and a hint of an easy, good nature.

He had a feeling that the cop, although very official looking, was probably a decent sort. He put his hands on his hips, and looking very indignant, said, "Well. You don't have to get excited, Officer. Of course I speak English, I just didn't understand what you wanted at first. I'll slow down if that's what you think I should do."

Richards looked at the man, smiled in spite of himself, and said quietly, "Yes, sir . . . that's what I think you should do." Then he pushed the small boat away from his, turned his back on the occupants, and idled away, south under the bridge, and into the port area.

J.B. Richards had been with the Fort Lauderdale Police Department for almost twenty years. During that time he had spent the earlier years working in the patrol division, driving a squad car, and doing all the usual police work. Because of his size and temperament, he was assigned to the tactical squad, or TAC, detailed now and then to walk the beach area during the spring break invasions, or the New Year's Eve craziness. He didn't mind the work, except he missed the water and felt that every year the college kids he dealt with appeared to be younger and younger. He had been assigned to the marine patrol for the past ten years and it was exactly where he wanted to be. J.B. Richards was known as a good cop, quiet and professional. He left the fireworks and histrionics to the younger cops, and gave the people of Fort Lauderdale a solid, steady performance for their pay.

Even though Richards had lived in the area all those years, he was still fascinated by the water, and he loved being out on it. Many times in the early morning, or in the quiet dusk, he would sit in his small police boat, two or three miles out in the Gulf Stream, off Fort Lauderdale's lovely beaches, and shake his head in wonder that he was actually being paid to be there.

Most of the other older men in the department had already forgotten that Richards had worked briefly as a cop up North, and of course the younger officers had no idea. In fact, there were many young officers on the job who didn't even know who Richards was. He was content with his low profile. It pleased him to know that even the brass weren't very familiar with his name. The Fort Lauderdale Police Department was not a large unit anyway—there were only about five hundred members—but J.B. Richards had learned to go about his business without being too noticeable.

There was no doubt, however, that he was still a cop. When he was on duty he paid attention to what was going on. He worked hard at being helpful to the citizens and out in the boating world, he was often needed. He didn't make many arrests, but he did give out a lot of warnings and admonitions. He carried himself professionally, but in a relaxed manner, so those who came into contact with him on the job usually left feeling good about the cop.

J.B. Richards waved at a deckhand on one of the large tugboats tied up at its wharf at the north end of the port and slowed his speed even more. He thought about his family and his job. He grinned as he thought of young Ted Novak.

Ted was the son of J.B.'s old partner, Theo Novak. Old Theo had taken a lot of ribbing when it was learned that he and his wife were going to have another child so long after the first one. Theo was thirty-nine and his wife thirty-five when Ted was born. The other children, both daughters, were twelve and fifteen years old at that time. Theo had just shrugged and grinned and accepted the noises about Ted being a "surprise gift" or an "afterthought."

Ted was nine years old when his father died of cancer, and he knew even then that all he wanted to be was a cop, just like his dad and his Uncle J.B. Ted had been hurt greatly by the loss of his father, and then J.B. had moved to Florida, taking his family with him. J.B. had stayed in contact with his mother, and as a child Ted was able to spend some summers at the Richardses' house.

J.B. knew that Ted's dreams had been put on hold for some years in deference to his mother's feelings. Ted felt responsible for his mother, and to her, because he was the only one left living at home during high school. He went to college and became a teacher to please her, but he always dreamed of a career in law enforcement.

Richards shook his head and smiled now, thinking of Ted. At his mother's funeral, Ted had spoken with J.B. One month later he moved into an apartment in Fort Lauderdale and he had an application in for the police department. He loved it, that was for certain. He was enthusiastic and aggressive and liked by the other guys as well as the brass.

J.B. frowned as he remembered how excited Ted had been when he was offered the job as an undercover narc. The glamour, the excitement, and the fun appealed to him. J.B. had been hesitant, and a little worried. They had several long talks in which J.B. tried to tell Ted that being a narc wasn't all fun. The drug world was a cesspool—a high-gloss, well-oiled, snappy-dressed, toy-filled cesspool. The people who played and worked there were some of the lowest forms of life that existed. Ted listened but wouldn't be put off. It was too much of a good chance for him to advance his career and at the same time do something really challenging.

Richards held on to the steering wheel of his boat as the small craft was rocked by a huge wake thrown by a big sportfisherman coming in from the outside, still in an area where the speed could be kept up. The salty wind blew his blond hair off his forehead, and he tasted the spray on his lips.

Richards knew a lot more about the narcotics smuggling world than young Ted understood. He had never been undercover, but he had been out on the water in Fort Lauderdale during the middle and late seventies, and he had seen it all. He had sat out in the middle of Port Everglades all through the night with U.S. Customs, waiting for the load boats. He had chased boats in the Intracoastal, watching while the occupants hurled things over the side or jumped overboard themselves. He had pulled up freshly sealed fiberglass decking to find bags of cocaine hidden below, and he had spent backbreaking hours humping bales when a load boat had been taken down, packed to the gunwales with marijuana. He had seen the methods change from the huge yachts stuffed so full they were almost awash, to the pretty sailboats with two boys and two girls aboard, waving and looking fresh and innocent. He had seen the macho racing boats, the "go-fast boats," used for a while by the hotshots. He had witnessed the closely coordinated combinations of all of the above, radio-controlled from an airplane, and counter-surveilled by a girl with a strong pair of binoculars and a two-way radio, sitting in an ultra-expensive condo overlooking Port Everglades and the whole area of Fort Lauderdale-Hollywood waters.

Richards knew that most of the marijuana arrests and seizures were nonviolent. There would be a chase, but rarely gun shooting. Cocaine smugglers, however, were a different breed of criminals. They were unpredictable and therefore more dangerous. He knew they rarely shied away from violence. He had seen them in action, and knew what Ted was up against.

Richards had also seen the money and the power games. He had seen hours of work go down the tubes because of a court decision. He had seen attorneys wearing enough gold to pay a cop's yearly salary come into the marine patrol office to claim a seized boat. He knew of cases that were worked to a certain point, and then a quiet "hands off" would be given, or the case would simply cease to exist. He knew the consumer market for all of the drugs was still there, and he knew that many of the legislators had their fingers in the pie, no matter what they said about the drug epidemic on television. He knew that the original blockade runners and drug smugglers had been shouldered out and replaced by giant machinelike groups that ran the business like a huge corporation. And he knew that within the last couple of years even governments had become involved in the drug trade. There was just too much money involved.

Richards had watched with dismay, as had many working cops, as the Miami area police forces were devastated by repeated arrests of their own officers—cops who couldn't resist the temptation of all of that easy money. And he had watched over and over again, when some young person, caught with a small amount of some stupid drug, would wind up fighting for his life, or at least some years of his personal freedom, in a court system that was hardened to his pleas—a court system that at the same time could be so sickeningly lenient to a group of investors and participants in a multimillion dollar drug ring.

J.B. had conceded to Ted that he was slightly bitter about what he had seen, and that he was worried about Ted working in that arena. Ted had laughed and slapped J.B. on the back and said something about J.B. just getting overly cautious with the years. J.B. had responded by asking Ted where he learned to dress like a narc—where were his socks? A T-shirt under a rumpled cotton sport coat? Italian shoes all the time? Ted had laughed.

Richards heard the roar of powerful engines coming into the port entrance now, and he turned to see a sleek black and gray ocean racer cutting its way into the port, just starting to slow down, and weaving in and around the moderate traffic of fishing boats and sailboats.

Stiletto passed close by the marine patrol boat.

J.B. could see the operator of the racing boat was dark and fit, with a muscular frame, about five ten, one hundred ninety, with close-cut black hair, and a neatly trimmed black beard that covered his square jaw. The man appeared to be of Latin descent. He was wearing a couple of impressive gold chains around his neck, and large, mirrored sunglasses covered his eyes and cheekbones. The man glanced at the police boat, then looked away, unconcerned.

J.B. found himself staring at the boat, and at the driver, even after they were behind him and heading for the bridge. He felt uneasy, but he didn't quite know why.

Later that afternoon, as his shift ended, J.B. Richards docked his police boat behind the marine patrol office at the end of Southeast Fifteenth Street, secured the lines, and climbed out, taking his gear with him. He was a little tired, and a little bored, and he had to admit to himself that he probably felt tired simply because he was bored. Just over forty-two years old and a twenty-year veteran of police work, he was out driving around on the waterways of lovely Fort Lauderdale, looking at the girls and trying to enforce the No Wake laws. He was laying low, and he knew it.

He sighed, and walked toward the office.

The ambush was set up perfectly, and it was only because he saw a flash of movement that he managed to be ready just in time. An orange and white furry blur went for his right pant leg as he passed behind a small boat on a trailer. Two quick swipes were made with small paws, and then his attacker was off, bounding ahead of him, up the steps at the rear of the office.

"Hey, Salty, what are you attacking me for? I'm the guy that feeds you around here," said Richards. The small cat just looked at him and licked her paws, waiting.

A little over a month ago Richards had been cruising slowly down one of the small canals off Cordova Road in the heat and quiet of the afternoon when he heard a small keening sound over the noise of the idling motor. He had looked to his left and spotted the little cat, paws bloody from trying to climb up the barnacle-covered seawalls, struggling feebly in the brown water. He had carefully moved the police boat as near as he could, reached in, and pulled out a thoroughly saturated and exhausted cat. He had wrapped her in a towel, taken her back to the office, and then to a nearby veterinarian's office. The small cat was given some shots, cleaned up, and pronounced fit. J.B. had been given the bill, which he paid out of his own pocket. He had briefly debated taking the cat home, thought of the four small dogs already residing there, and informed the marine patrol sergeant and the other officers and aides that the cat would live at the office. Most of them had taken one look at the sad little thing and offered that she probably wouldn't live long enough to be much of a nuisance anyhow.

They were so wrong, he thought now as he fed her and rubbed her soft fur while she purred between bites.

He stood and stretched, and said out loud to the empty office, "Yeah . . . that's good ol' J.B., always ready to salvage some stray, no matter what her potential."

The valet held the door of the Mercedes 450 SL and watched appreciatively as a woman climbed out, swinging her long perfect legs and standing, smoothing the back of her tight white skirt as she did so. The valet was not alone. Every man in the area of the driveway of the waterfront restaurant, and many of the women, watched closely as the girl, her back straight, walked toward the front doors. The doors were opened and held for her, of course, and she stepped into the cool shadows within. She wore thin white sandals on her feet, and the white skirt was topped with a sleeveless yellow blouse, with the collar up. The girl was in her early twenties, stood just over five four, had rich honey-colored hair worn long and full and swept back away from her forehead, and had a perfect tan. As she walked through the restaurant, heading for the dockside bar out back, her body moved with a controlled, supple grace that confidently stated her femaleness and her sexuality without being blatant or brassy about it. Many were the looks of appreciation and raised eyebrows, and those who saw her wondered what man possessed her.

The girl stopped and looked out onto the wooden deck of the bar and dock area. She saw *Stiletto*, and looked across the small tables and groups of people, looking for Onyx. She felt hesitant, aware of a strange desire to stop searching for him, hoping not to find him, right now. She wished for a few more moments of being alone, of being just herself instead of Montilla's woman.

A young, tall, good-looking man brushed against her, his warm skin rubbing the skin of her right arm briefly. The young man turned, pulled his sunglasses down on his nose a bit, and smiled into her eyes. She smiled back, for a few seconds, then dismissed him with a shake of her pretty head. He turned away, still smiling.

She took a deep breath, looked again for Montilla, and thought about what she was doing there. She knew she represented the classic story of the ugly duckling. As a child, and as a young teenager, she had been gawky and awkward, with unruly hair and long legs that never acted as they should and always looked too skinny. Her eyes had been too big for her face, her lips too full, and she had spent many hours looking at her straight body in the mirror, wondering if her breasts would ever grow. Then at seventeen—or was it eighteen?—she had looked at herself one morning to find that she had turned into a woman, and almost immediately she discovered that men wanted her and would try very hard to possess her.

The girl could not remember her father, but all too clearly she remembered watching her mother drink herself to death, working at one hard job after another, never having enough money, always having to move from one small apartment to another. Her mother had died sitting in front of a rented television set. She had just given up two weeks before the girl was to graduate from high school. She had promised herself then that she would not live like her mother, but she soon learned that trying to change things was very, very difficult.

She took jobs—at the mall in a dress shop, in an office, answering phones, at a rental car agency. The money was never enough. She took other girls as roommates to help share the rent and groceries. Her roommates ran up the telephone bill, skipped the rent, and stole things when they left. Her roommates' boyfriends made advances, usually not nicely. It was a hard time for her. She was always broke, always working so hard with nothing to show for it.

She began to feel alone and desperate.

One night, after coming home again with a paycheck that wasn't enough, after having another roommate move on, after fighting off clumsy advances from her new boss, she sat in the bathtub and cried. She cried until the water lost its heat and got cold, and then she just sat in the cold water, shuddering. Finally, dripping wet, she stepped out of the tub and stood in front of the mirror, looking at herself. And she made a decision.

She picked through her wardrobe of inexpensive but pretty clothes, carefully did her makeup and hair, and got herself ready. Then she got into her dingy old Toyota and went out into the night, alone.

She really didn't know where she wanted to go, or what exactly she would do when she got there, but off she went, determined to do *something*.

She drove by a recently opened club she had heard about, the "new" place to be. It was just on the east side of the Oakland Park Boulevard Bridge. It was called Antonio's. She was embarrassed to let the valet park her car, so she left it in a bank parking lot a block away and walked, hearing several wolf whistles along the way. The doorman took one look at her and let her in without the five dollar cover charge, and she made her way to the crowded bar. She heard someone nearby order a "Cape Codder," so when the bartender asked for her order, that's what she told him. She paid for her drink and lost herself in the music and the people. Even though she was lonely she had turned away from several young guys who made passes at her, though she wasn't quite sure why. And she kept ordering drinks.

She was into her third, or was it her fourth, when she felt someone at her elbow and turned slightly, expecting another young stud with a smile and a Rolex to be standing there. Instead, it was an older man, small and trim, with gray hair and a dark blue three-piece suit. He was ignoring her, speaking softly to the bartender, who listened carefully to what the older man had to say. When the man finished and the bartender turned away, the girl was still staring at him. Finally, the man smiled a friendly smile, and in a soft voice said, "Hello there, pretty lady . . . having fun?"

The girl looked at him, cocked her head, and for all of the crazy reasons—the alcohol, the mood, the loneliness, the anger—she lifted her chin and said defiantly, "Fun? I'm not here to have fun, mister. I'm here to find some rich old fart who'll support me because I'm beautiful and smart and dynamite in bed." Then she turned away from him, horrified and embarrassed.

The man was staring at her. He had a smile on his face, and she felt her face redden, not believing what she had just said. She swallowed, and turned to him to say something, anything. He gave a little bow, reached into a pocket and came out with a card and handed it to her. As she took it, he said gently, "Yes. You are indeed beautiful, and yes, probably smart too. But you carry your anger too close to your skin, and you've had just a little too much to drink." He looked into her eyes, smiled, and said, "Listen, I'm one of the owners of this place, so why don't you give this old fart a call in a couple of days. Maybe there's a place for you here."

She looked down at the card in her hand as he walked away: It said: Sam Golden, Financial Consultant.

She had waited a week before calling Sam Golden because it had taken her that long to get up her nerve. She had been mortified by her behavior. She couldn't believe the way she had spoken to the man, a perfect stranger. Certainly she was no virgin. She had had boyfriends even in high school, and afterward, but none of them had been right for her and she had known it all along. She was a healthy female animal, comfortable with her sexuality, and knowing that it had never really been tapped. But she also knew she wasn't worldly. She hadn't had the opportunity or the experience of dining at fine restaurants, of mingling at cocktail parties or participating in the subtle male-female combat of relating in the genteel world. The men in her life so far had been boys really—hunks, of course—but boys all the same. They were always in a hurry, and never fully aware of the complex female entity that she was. She was not pleased with the way she had acted during her first night out to better herself. Actually, she felt she had acted like a cheap tart, clumsy, and dumb to the max.

Because she sensed a kindness in Golden, and because she wanted a chance to show him that she wasn't that person he had met at the bar, she did finally call him. He had invited her to come back and speak with him about a job at the club. She agreed, and was hired as a receptionist. She took the job anticipating Sam to be all over her expecting his favor returned. But he had left her alone, and had always been very polite to her when he was there. He always asked how things were going. She could tell he cared. A couple of weeks after she was hired and feeling settled in, she asked him if he always saved fair damsels in distress after they had made fools of themselves? No, he had told her, not always, only when the damsel was so obviously special. He started courting her then. That was the only word for it, and after a short time she was spending so much time at his condo that he asked her to move in, which she did. Sam became her lover and her teacher; her uncle and her friend. He was gentle with her and kind to her, and he always treated her with respect. She grew to care for him deeply, appreciating his gentleness and his sharp mind, learning from him, becoming a lady on his arm just as he carried himself as a gentleman. For a time they made an interesting couple, he older, sharp, well dressed, and confident, and she young, vibrant, and beautiful.

As more time went by, Sam took the girl increasingly into his confidence, teaching her about his financial dealings, briefing her carefully about some of the partners in the club. The girl learned that everything having to do with the club was not always what appeared on the surface. Some of the men involved were hard men, and some of the money that Sam moved around came from sources that Sam only darkly hinted at. She had asked him once, over breakfast, if he was a criminal, or part of the Mafia, or a drug smuggler. If he had been surprised, he didn't show it. Instead he sipped his tea, smiled, and said, "Yes." Then he went on to explain that he was just a money person—an economist, a financial adviser. He just moved the money around, that's all, and he didn't participate in any of the activities that his partners did.

In time she worked with him, helping him with the paperwork, carrying documents, meeting with attorneys and other businessmen. He liked her mind, was pleased to have her as an assistant, and held back very little from her. She still worked at the club, but only occasionally, and it was there that she met a man named Kolin, one of Sam's partners, and a younger man—a hard man—Onyx Montilla.

She came back to the present with a jolt. Someone had

laughed loudly, and it had startled her. She was standing in the artificial shadows of a waterfront lounge, looking for Montilla. She shook her shiny hair off her shoulders and sighed.

And now Sam Golden is dead, she thought, killed just because he happened to be with one of his partners when someone decided to hit him, shot down in a hail of gunfire meant for the other man, but dead just the same. She pinched her nose, remembering how everyone had moved in on her afterward, like sharks circling her for the kill.

Montilla had come to her rescue like a white knight, to help, protect, and guide her. She remembered that he had always respected her in the past, and that he had always told her that she needed someone with fire like him.

Montilla helped her to hide Sam's secrets from the police and from some of Sam's former partners. He had told her that the police would nail people to the cross for those secrets, and that the former partners would kill for them.

Montilla owned her now.

He was a Cuban, and although he was very close-mouthed about his background, she learned quickly that he was every inch the passionate Latin male. She had to admit that he excited her physically. He was tough and quick and unpredictable, with a dangerous streak that attracted her.

She lived with Montilla now, and enjoyed all the luxuries he could provide. They skied in Vail, they cruised to Cozumel, they dined in the best restaurants. She had the clothes, the cars, the jewelry, and all the other toys. Montilla always had cocaine available if she wanted it; to his surprise she did not. Grass bored her, and cocaine frightened her. She liked herself too much to use it. Montilla would offer her coke and she would just shake her head. Instead, she took a spa membership and joined an aerobics class. Montilla liked showing her off to his cronies and to the boating community of Fort Lauderdale. He gave her toys, protection—and threats—and she gave him herself.

She saw him wave now, casually, from a place near the end of the bar where he stood with two or three other men. She smiled at him and moved toward the bar, trying to feel comfortable.

She was surprised to hear a phrase from a song repeating itself in her mind. The phrase was "subtle whoring," and she wondered as she moved toward Montilla if it could possibly apply to her.

The girl shook herself slightly as she stood beside Onyx Montilla and kissed him on the cheek. Sometimes she felt like a stray cat.

"Hey, my friends," said Montilla with a grin. "Let me introduce my lady to you." He looked at her slowly, from her feet to her lovely hair, and he said softly, "She won't tell me how she got the name, or if it means how she feels or how she looks, but it is, in fact, her name. So . . . meet Silky."

How long would the pain last?

How long would the fire across his leg and in his lungs continue to burn? In his pain he understood that the transition to death should be quick.

But it was the pain that held him now. He had heard about the tunnel and the bright, comforting light, and his ears were roaring as if he were there.

Through his pain he felt himself in an alien environment. He was frightened, knowing he was thrashing around in a world where his body could not adequately perform . . . where to stop fighting, even for a moment, was to lose.

What little he could see through squinted eyes was harsh. . . . There was searing blue above him, punctuated by a blistering hot orange centerpiece, and all around him was a metallic surface.

His face caught fire now, similar to the fire that washed his leg and clenched his lungs. He burned, and shook himself in wonder as he realized how cold he was.

Suddenly he felt movement around him and his chill deepened as he sensed a patient and predatory circling. Something deep inside whispered to him to be still, but when he tried to comply, he found himself enveloped by the cold, and his lungs burned even more. He had to move, he had to stay on the surface, but with each stroke he sensed the quickening interest of the predator that moved with such timeless and sinister fluidity. The shark was coming closer, cutting through the cold green metal with ease and purpose.

A voice came then, a scream really, and with it came strength and will and longing.

He screamed at the bright orange light, his head back, his lips pulled away from his teeth, his hands flailing against the cold green water.

How long would the pain last?

How long would it be until he died?

FOUR

J.B. stopped at the grocery store on his way home, and was burdened with a gym bag that held his police equipment and a large bag of groceries as he struggled out of his old pickup truck and headed for the front door of his house. He noticed his wife's car wasn't in the driveway yet, saw his son's dirt bike half in and half out of the always cluttered garage, and pulled the door open.

His younger daughter Erin stood in front of him. At least he thought it was his daughter Erin. The teenage girl wore a fluffy blue terry cloth robe and had her blond hair wrapped in a large towel. He could see her eyes glaring at him, but the rest of her face was covered with a thick, goopy white paste.

Erin's thin hands were balled into fists and resting on her hips as she said, "Perfect timing, Dad, really. I mean, you got here just in time to keep me from doing something rash to your other children, and I must stress that word children because if you were around here when they get home from school you'd see how they act. I mean, mature individuals like you and me and Mom have to put up with the most pitiful displays of immaturity I've ever seen."

J.B., still burdened, managed to get the door closed, and asked, confused, "Well, what . . . ? And your face . . . ?"

One long, carefully painted fingernail pointed at the goop-covered face as Erin said indignantly, "My face? You're wondering what's going on with my practically . . . well, most of the time . . . flawless face? The *sun*, Dad . . . yes, the sun has totally fried my face. Well, I guess it's my fault, but not completely because stupid Bevvy Freeman is having another dumb fight with her nerd boyfriend and she called me and I talked with her on the phone while I sat out by the pool and I guess we talked for a little too long and the sun felt so good and when I finally hung up and looked in the mirror my face was stoplight red and if I just let it be it will dry up like one of those desert scenes where they test the atomic bombs and stuff. So I had to apply this cream which is aloe based and *great* for my skin—but which can't stay on *too* long—and now your other daughter, Kathleen, who just because she's a little older than me thinks she's a woman while I'm still a little girl, is in the bathroom and won't come out even though I've asked her politely several times. And your charming son Ricky took a picture of me like this when I didn't know he was going to and he did it with that stupid Polaroid camera of his and he says he's going to take it to school with him tomorrow unless I do his pathetic homework for a week and he knocked over the magazine rack when I was chasing him and he won't help me clean *that* up. If Mom was here none of this would be happening and can you make Kathleen get out of the bathroom so I can take care of this face?"

J.B., reeling, managed to put down his gym bag, move past his daughter into the kitchen, and put the groceries down. He sighed and rubbed his face as he asked, "Do you remember, Erin, that we have *three* bathrooms in this house?"

Now Erin sighed, as if it was such a difficult thing to make her sweet, poor old dad realize the severity of the situation. She spoke slowly and clearly as she said, "Dad . . . that hallway bathroom, because of the way the two side mirrors swing out, has the best light . . . Mom's isn't bad, but that hallway's the best . . . and I *need* the best light to look at my skin and see how much damage has been done. Dad, think about it: Do you want your youngest daughter to have skin that looks like a week-old apple?"

J.B. was contemplating this as his daughter Kathleen came out of the bathroom that had the best light. She smiled sweetly at her sister, who gave her a nasty look and scampered into the bathroom, not quite slamming the door behind her. Her older sister picked up her purse from one of the end tables.

"Dad," she said softly, "could I have some money for gas and a Coke or something later? I'm going out for a while to an Honors Club meeting."

J.B. looked at his daughter, always amazed at how lovely she was, with her big eyes and long shiny hair, and said, "First of all, how about, 'Hi, Dad,' or 'How was your day, Dad?' . . . and second, I thought you just had one of those club meetings yesterday, and third, how much gas does a Volkswagen burn anyway, and fourth, button the top button on that blouse."

Kathleen smiled, came to him, stood on her tiptoes, and kissed him on the forehead. "Hi, Dad. That was drama club yesterday. I think my little car needs a tune-up or something and that's why it burns so much gas. The top button *is* buttoned, Dad . . . that's as far as it goes."

"Well, then . . . that's as far as *you* go, Kathleen, unless you pin it up or something."

"Oh, Dad . . . that would look so queer, really."

"Queer schmeer, that blouse is too open. I can't believe they sell clothes like that to kids. What if your mother saw you wearing that blouse like that?"

"Dad, Mom bought this blouse for me."

J.B. looked at her, sighed again, shook his head, and reached for his wallet. Kathleen took the ten dollar bill, kissed him again, and left.

J.B. watched her go, and then went into the kitchen to make some coffee. His son Rick, all elbows and knees and feet and shaggy brown hair, walked into the kitchen, biting his lip and pulling on his tear-away football jersey, which looked as if it had been torn away several times.

"Hi, Dad," he said, distracted.

"Hello, Rick . . . what's the problem?"

"Uh . . . have you seen a snake? Like three feet, a little more, dark blue in color?"

J.B., who suddenly wished he could take wing and fly away, said, "No. Have we lost one?"

"Yeah . . . I caught it down by the canal yesterday, and I had it in a box in my bedroom and now it's gone and it's an indigo or a blue runner and I hope it's okay and all."

J.B. leaned forward, resting his forehead on the face of the microwave oven, and said, "Rick, I suggest you find that snake before your mom gets home, or we're all in trouble."

"Okay, Dad."

The front door opened and J.B. heard the rattle of car keys hitting a countertop, footsteps on the tile floor, and then his wife Jane came into the kitchen, blowing her curly hair out of her eyes. She put her purse down on the table, made a face, and said, "Boy. Those afternoon drivers out there are all crazy. All I was trying to do was to get from the mall to here and I'll bet I had three near misses and some horrible man in a big truck wouldn't let me turn and then when I did he started yelling but I ignored him . . . and am I glad to be home."

J.B. had been pouring a glass of white wine while she talked, and he handed it to her now. She smiled, kissed him lightly, and sipped the wine. Then she said, "Hi, honey, I'm home."

J.B. smiled too, and they shared a moment, just looking at each other. They were comfortable with their long-lasting and rich relationship.

The moment ended in a terrified cry.

"Daaaaaddddyyyyyyy!"

Rich ran past them, helter-skelter through the living room, yelling, "Don't hurt him! Dad! Don't let her hurt that snake!"

Jane looked at J.B. in alarm and bewilderment, but he just held up one hand and said with a small laugh and a shake of his head, "Things are just normal here in the Richardses' house."

* * *

That evening, while Silky took a long shower and got herself ready to go out to dinner with Onyx, he waited for her with habitual impatience. He sat in the living room and stared at the television set for a few minutes, thought about doing a couple of lines of cocaine before they went out, and finally shuffled out into the kitchen area to get something cold to drink. It was dusk, the light was fading fast, and as Montilla turned away from the refrigerator, wine cooler in hand, he looked out through the window at the dock located at the rear of the house. The house was situated on one of the isles off Las Olas Boulevard, and each house was close to the water. *Stiletto* was tied at the dock. He noticed that the tide was almost full high, and then his eye caught the shape of a man standing on the dock.

Montilla stared, his stomach tightening and his jaw clenching. Some stupid son of a bitch was standing right there on his dock. He started toward the rear door, then hesitated. Cops? he wondered. He looked again, saw no one else, then moved quickly through the house and looked out the front windows.

Nothing.

Then he hurried to the back again, grabbing a small automatic from a bookcase as he went by.

He eased out the backdoor, and staying in the long shadows thrown by the dying sunlight, he moved cautiously toward the dock and the man standing there. He had not moved.

When Montilla was about twenty feet away, he took a good look at the man, who appeared to be a Latin in his mid-thirties, fit and tough. He wore a jacket and tie, and looked relaxed. Montilla felt the weight of the gun in his hand as he took another step forward and started to challenge the man.

"So . . . Onyx Montilla-Ortiz . . . finally you see me here at your dock and you come out to me with a gun in your hand. My patrón told me it would be so."

The man spoke English, but with a heavy Latin accent. Montilla wasn't stopped by the accent, however, or the man's sure confidence—it was the use of his father's name that disconcerted him. He eased forward a little more, his breathing shallow, and asked, "Who are you . . . and what do you want here?"

"Who I am is not important to you, señor," said the man quietly, "but the name of my patrón. That is what is important."

Montilla waited. "All right. Tell me who is your important patrón, and stop playing this game with me."

The man's eyes brightened then became masked again as he said, "Listen to me, Montilla-Ortiz. My patrón, Maximiliano, he wishes to speak with you, alone, tomorrow morning in our side of Miami. *Comprendo?* You are to know he will speak with you about your father, and about something that is *muy importante . . . sí?*"

"How do I know that this Maximiliano knew my father?" asked Montilla, his heart pounding.

The man slowly pulled something out of his jacket pocket, his eyes flicking constantly from Montilla's eyes to the gun in Montilla's hand. He put what he was holding on the dock and walked back several feet. Montilla moved forward quickly and picked up a piece of paper with an address in Miami printed on it. With it was an old black and white snapshot, browned with age.

Montilla held his breath and looked at the photo. His father wore no shirt and a smile, his dark hair windblown. On his shoulder sat a tiny baby, naked. His father's hands were on the baby's hips. The background was made up of a thin strip of sandy beach and water. Montilla took his eyes from the photograph and looked at the man who had brought it for him. He said evenly, "I will meet with your patrón, this Maximiliano, but if you know this much about me, señor, then you know it would not be wise to try to give me trouble."

The laugh, when it came, was rich and sharp and genuine. The man grinned and laughed some more. Then he said quietly, "Oh, we know you are a tough hombre, señor Montilla-Ortiz. No. We will not be playing games, all right? You must be there. *Al diez de la mañana.* When you leave here I will be watching you, to clear your tail, *sí?* I will be driving a dark blue station wagon, I will make sure you see me, then I will stay behind you." The man looked all around, slowly, then continued, "If I see something that is not right, someone following you . . . then I will pull in front of you and cut you off sharply. If that happens you are to go somewhere else, forget the meeting, and we will try again some other time. *Sí?*"

Montilla nodded.

The man watched him for a moment, an amused look on his face, then turned and walked off the dock and across the backyard, toward the street.

Montilla stood on the dock, staring at the photograph and searching his childhood memories for any hint of the name Maximiliano.

A few minutes before ten the next morning, Onyx Montilla parked his car a block away from the address in the old section of Miami where he would meet Maximiliano. He had not seen the blue station wagon since Lauderdale, and the drive down had been uneventful.

Silky had a hair appointment this morning, and then she was supposed to go to the gym for one of her exercise classes. He had surprised her by giving her a wad of money and telling her to make a day of it—do the nails, the face, the whole thing. He had not mentioned anything about Miami or the meeting, and if she guessed he was trying to keep her busy for the day, she said nothing.

Montilla stopped for a moment on the quiet sidewalk, enjoying the sounds and smells and sights of Little Havana. He watched the people he saw carefully, but none seemed to be paying him any attention. He started moving toward the address again, thinking about the job he had going today.

It required him to be back in Fort Lauderdale that afternoon. Montilla brought in load boats and off-loaded them for a fairly large smuggling group. They called the shots, primarily, and he did what they wanted and made his money. Like any subcontractor, he had the opportunity, occasionally, to score a little on the side. During the last couple of months he had built up a small surplus of bales of marijuana from the larger loads. These were bales that were lost or damaged, according to the big tally. He paid

Cuda to store them on Bimini, and every once in a while he had them brought into Lauderdale for straight profit. He usually did not use his own boats or people for these little side deals, but contracted the jobs out to smaller teams or groups. Today a buddy of one of his regular captains, using a small boat owned by that same captain, would be bringing in over five hundred pounds. Montilla waited at a crosswalk, watched the traffic, then crossed the street. On the other side he stopped, bent down, and pretended to tie his shoe while he looked behind him. Still nothing. He moved on.

He had to be back in Lauderdale by three in the afternoon because the guy driving the boat in from Bimini was completely inexperienced in the game, and Montilla wanted to watch him. He had been told to enter Port Everglades right after three. It was the middle of the week so there wouldn't be much boat traffic: It would look as if he had been out locally and was just heading home. He was supposed to bring the boat to a dock at the rear of a house on the same isle as Montilla's house, but farther out, closer to the Intracoastal Waterway and the New River. Montilla planned to be nearby.

He wondered how long this meeting would take, and he thought about the almost sleepless night he had had, waiting for the morning. The meeting on the dock, and the photograph, had awakened intense feelings in him that he had spent years trying to bury. Now a man named Maximiliano was going to forcibly dig them up again.

He arrived at the address and faced a plain stucco wall with a weathered wooden door on rusty hinges. The number of the house was set into the wall in small tiles. He let his fingers rest against the small gun in his back pocket as he pressed the buzzer near the top of the door. Almost immediately the door was pulled open. He stepped inside into silence.

The man who had waited for him on his dock was there, smiling. He motioned with one outstretched hand toward a stone path that ran alongside a very small but pretty house. Montilla noticed the absence of street sounds or traffic. Inside the walls it was peaceful; the only sounds came from the birds and insects flying around the many cultivated plants and flowers. Montilla walked around the side of the house to the back where the stone path opened into a tiny but fine courtyard also surrounded by the stucco wall. More plants and flowers abounded, most noticeably a flowering bougainvillea and a small jacaranda. Vines covered parts of the wall, and wind chimes and bird feeders hung from tree branches and latticework that partially covered the yard.

Sitting at a small wooden table, in a straight-backed chair, was a dark and lean man who appeared to be in his early sixties. His neatly cut black hair and full mustache were touched with gray. His nose was sharp and hooked, and overhung a small mouth with thin lips. His eyes were very brown, and alive, watchful, moving. He wore a simple linen suit, a knitted tie, and pale shoes. On a chair beside him was a leather briefcase, and the inevitable straw hat. He put down the tiny cup of coffee he sipped from, smiled with his mouth but watched with his eyes, and stood up. He nodded, gave a small bow, and said quietly, "Thank you for coming all the way here to see me, Onyx. I am Maximiliano."

Montilla shook the offered hand, felt its quick dry strength, and sat down in the chair that the other man motioned to. He looked around and saw that the man who had let him in had disappeared, probably into the house. He turned back to his host, and waited.

Maximiliano gestured toward the small coffeepot, but Montilla shook his head negatively and shifted slightly in his chair.

"So, Onyx Montilla-Ortiz. I'm afraid I have you at a slight disadvantage, as they say. You see, I know a lot about you, about what you are doing, and why, and you know so little about me. I know you are very busy, um... doing your thing. Is that how one says it? I know that what you do is important to you, and I know the only reason you are here is because I had my man mention your father and bring to you the *photographía* . . . yes?"

Montilla waited, silent.

"So," Maximiliano continued, "I will tell you some

things now." His eyes brightened, and the hand he lay on the table was balled into a fist. "First, about your father. He was brave, and smart, and he played a dangerous game for us a long time ago.. He helped us win a great victory when we were still so young and vulnerable, and then we tried to bring him home and we lost him."

Montilla's eyes were riveted on the other man now, and his breathing was very shallow.

"Your father was coming home, with you, to enjoy the fruits of his clandestine labors in our behalf. I know you were there when they killed him."

The quiet courtyard seemed frozen for a few seconds while Montilla's mind took him back to that sidewalk so long ago, to the image of his father spinning and falling, but not looking at him. Maximiliano waited until Montilla took a deep breath and nodded slightly before he went on.

"After that, Onyx, you came here, and you grew up in the streets, fighting, always fighting, always trying to better yourself and at the same time you have been fighting the same political structure that your father fought."

Montilla spoke now, almost sullenly. "Politics do not interest me. I don't get involved in any of that nonsense."

"Of course not," said Maximiliano gently, "but what I am saying is that your enemies are the same as the enemies of your father."

Montilla shrugged.

"So, Onyx Montilla-Ortiz. You did the armed robberies for a short time, and the stealing of the autos, and all of that street badness. Then you were brought in on some narcotics smuggling deals, and since then you are a smuggler, yes? You smuggle large amounts of marijuana for a syndicate-type group, and they pay you well."

Montilla stared at the other man, and said through tight lips, "So what are you, some kind of narcotics cop? If you know so much, then come and get me, and quit messing with memories of my father."

Maximiliano took a breath, sipped his coffee, and looked around the courtyard for a moment. Then he nodded slightly and said, "Well, I am not some kind of narcotics cop, but sometimes I do similar work. I am an investigator, a collector of information. I work for my government . . . but wait!" One of his strong hands gripped Montilla's forearm as Montilla got ready to stand up, his face angry.

"Wait for a few more moments, mi amigo, okay? And let me explain further."

Montilla forced himself to relax, and he watched the other man carefully.

"Good," said Maximiliano quietly, "good. Now. We know that your group makes good profits because they get the drugs they smuggle from representatives of the Bahamian government." He saw Montilla's mouth tighten, and he hurried on. "Of course it is such a splendid thing really. The government of the Bahamas 'seizes' narcotics being smuggled through their waters and airspace by groups who have not paid them off, they release the boats and aircraft, and the operators, and they keep the drugs. Then, because they have no overhead, they sell them at a cheaper rate than normal to your backers, and everyone is pleased, yes? And it's been working so nicely for them—and you."

He paused, and Montilla waited.

Finally Maximiliano went on. "Now I will tell you why I had to meet with you. It is to offer you a proposition . . . a deal. I would like you to smuggle drugs into the *Estados Unidos* for us, at the same time you smuggle for them." He held up one hand, palm out. "Hear me out Onyx, yes? Now, you smuggle those heavy and bulky loads of the marijuana for that group, for the money. We want you to carry with you, at the same time, kilos of fine cocaine. You will do it for the money, and you will do it for us."

Montilla's heart was beating strongly now, and he felt a film of sweat form on his forehead. He licked his lips and asked, "Why me? And who are you? And who will I be working for?"

Maximiliano smiled. "Why you? Because of your father, because of your blood, because of your pride, and because of your experience and capabilities. You can do it, and you will enjoy the profits, yes? And you will be doing a fine thing for us, the people of your homeland, even as your father did."

"People of my homeland?"

"Yes, Onyx Montilla-Ortiz. You will be doing this for the memory of your father, for a chance to hurt those same people that killed him in front of you. You will be doing it for me, and for my government. The government of our people's leader."

He stared at Montilla now, his eyes bright. "You will smuggle the poison—cocaine—into this country . . . for Fidel Castro."

God, he was angry. He was angry at himself mostly because it bothered him to be surprised, caught off guard and rendered impotent so easily. But it had happened and he knew the only way he could have prevented it was to have said no in the first place.

It was funny, he thought to himself, how lucid he could be for a few moments, and then fall back into unconsciousness.

What really angered him was his own inability to let go, to just relax, to stop fighting. He knew there was peace waiting for him, because he felt very sleepy and comfortable, and somehow he knew that all would be soft and quiet once he just closed his eyes and slipped away.

But no. He just kept fighting, working, burning, screaming. He wouldn't be still, he wouldn't let the peaceful slumber take him. The pain will go away as soon as you let go, he told himself. Why prolong the inevitable in struggling agony?

His head fell back, and he saw that the taunting orange light had moved from the center of the searing blue over near the edge, dipping itself, undulating, into the pulsing green metallic surface. He looked around him, slowly, realizing that he was now alone, and remembering that he had not been alone before. The circling presence had gone, but his fear remained, eclipsed now by his anger.

He would try again.

He would stop fighting. He would just relax his body and his mind and let himself sink into the waiting sleep. The pain would end then, and the fear. It would be so easy, and so much better. Just stop the feet first, good ... now the hands. All right ... now just sink down ...

Dammit!

Why did he struggle? Why was he still fighting?

The questions rang in his mind, and at the same time his ears told him there was a new sound in his world. There had been such an empty sameness since he came here, gentle sounds if any, and now there was something else.

Rhythmic pulse, deep and vibrant, not hurried. Steady.

It came closer, still steady ... not louder but somehow stronger. He sensed the sound had nothing to do with him, and he determined it was not important.

He put his head back again, and sobbed. This time when he let go he would really do it ... he would really force his body to stop fighting ... he would really go to sleep.

He knew he could to it, and he knew it was time.

If only that sound would just go away.

FIVE

J.B. Richards sat in his police boat, drifting in the basin of Port Everglades, and glanced at his watch. Almost three o'clock—less than an hour to go, he thought. It was the middle of the week, things were quiet, and he was impatient for the shift to be over. But most of all he was worried about Ted Novak.

Ted had not shown up at the Richardses' house for dinner, as he had been scheduled to do, nor had he called, which wasn't like him. It now seemed as if no one had seen or heard from him in almost two days, including the men he worked with in the narc office, or his sergeant. Quiet inquiries were being made. The lieutenant from the narc office, knowing of their friendship, had called J.B.

and asked if Ted was having girlfriend problems or anything.

J.B. ran his fingers through his hair and pointed the bow of the boat north. He waved at the Causeway bridge-tender, idled under the span, and then let her drift between Fort Lauderdale Marina and the Pier 66 complex.

He thought about the lieutenant's question, and about his older daughter's reaction when J.B mentioned to his wife that Ted might be missing. Kathleen had turned pale and ran from the room. What the hell, he thought, Ted and Kathleen have known each other since they were kids.

He leaned back in the seat behind the steering wheel, listened to the burble of the engine's exhaust, and wondered when Ted would show up.

J.B. was musing when he caught sight of a yellow Wellcraft Scarab, a twenty-seven footer, occupied by one man. The boat was heading north under the bridge, just as J.B. had done a few moments before, and would pass right by the police boat. It was moving too fast for the area, pushing a good bow wave and enough of a wake for J.B. to take action if he chose to. J.B. sat up a little straighter and took a closer look at the boat and the operator.

The boat wasn't new, but it was in pretty good shape. The chrome wasn't pitted out, and the engines did not smoke. She was riding bow down though, as if she wasn't trimmed right, and she was covered with salt spray. The operator was a young man with curly black hair and what was, just a short time ago, very pale skin but which had recently been severely sunburned to a painful red color. He wore a sleeveless T-shirt, and shorts. He did not look at the police boat or at J.B.

J.B. put his boat in gear and eased alongside the Scarab as it continued north, past the yacht club and the shallows on the west side of the channel. He could see that the small ports in the cabin area, forward, had been painted out with black paint. He could see the wooden cabin doors were closed and locked with a small padlock. He could see two or three of those red plastic five-gallon jerry cans sitting in the aft section of the cockpit. He looked again at the way the boat moved through the water—"plowing" they called it—the bow down, pushing the water in front of it instead of cutting through it.

J.B. pulled his boat into neutral and let it drift behind the Scarab. He rocked gently in the channel, thinking about what he had seen. The salt spray meant the boat had been outside, the jerry cans hinted that she had been refueled somewhere, the painted-out ports indicated a reluctance, along with the padlocked doors, to display what was inside, and the angle of the bow showed that she was carrying something heavy up front.

J.B. rubbed his chin and grinned. *Shoot*, he thought, *that thing must be the picture-perfect poster of suspect smuggling boats. If that's not a go-fast load boat cruisin' through my waterways in broad daylight then Rambo works for the KGB*. He hung back, waiting to see if the Scarab would ease to the right and follow the Intracoastal north past Bahia Mar and then under the Las Olas Bridge, or if it would turn left and head west on the New River. He put the police boat in gear and followed along.

The guy driving the Scarab never once looked at him. J.B. had seen this tactic before. The driver would think, "Oops, it's the cops . . . don't look at 'em, don't catch their eye." He watched the boat turn west toward the New River, then make a slight dogleg and head into one of the canals bordering the Las Olas Isles.

Las Olas Isles, mused J.B. There was a time in the seventies when even a rookie cop could throw his badge into the air in the vicinity of the isles, and it would come down and stick onto a house full of dope.

J.B. rubbed one hand over his face, and realized he should be going home soon, not jumping on a suspect load boat. What was he trying to do—set the world on fire? He looked at the Scarab again, looked at his watch, and muttered, "Rats."

He contacted the dispatcher on his channel and asked if there were any patrol units in the immediate area of the Isles. She checked, and indicated that it was shift change and there weren't many units available close by. J.B. acknowledged, and decided to follow the Scarab to where the guy planned to dock it, then brace him.

J.B. kept the police boat about fifty yards behind the other boat, and once he was in the canal, which was bordered on each side by expensive homes with pools and docks, he observed that the driver of the Scarab seemed unsure of where he wanted to go. He kept putting his boat into neutral, then moving ahead, constantly looking at the docks to his left.

As J.B. began moving closer so he could speak to the guy, he saw that the driver of the boat had apparently found what he was looking for because he pointed his boat toward it. The guy was heading for a dock near the Las Olas end of the isle. Another boat was already tied up there—a sleek, black and gray ocean racer with a name on the side: *Stiletto*.

J.B. realized that he had seen the boat before, tried to place it, then pulled alongside the Scarab and called over, "Hey, Cap'n, how about shuttin' her down for a minute? I'd like to check your registration."

The driver of the Scarab whipped his head around and stared at Richards as if he hadn't even known he was there.

"Sure, sure, Officer. Just a second."

As Richards put his boat into neutral and reached out to fend the two boats off, the driver of the Scarab suddenly turned the steering wheel and pulled back on the port throttle while he pushed the starboard throttle forward. This caused the Scarab to turn violently to port, partially skidding and partially jumping around in a 180 degree turn. The stern of the Scarab smacked the side of the police boat solidly and the sound of cracking fiberglass could clearly be heard. Richards was almost thrown off his feet as the wake from the Scarab rocked his boat violently from side to side. He fought with the throttle and wheel as he tried to turn his boat in a small, fast circle, but it was difficult because he had only one prop. He watched as the Scarab went to full power, racing out of the small canal, throwing a huge wake that rocked all the boats tied up along the docks. Just as he got his police boat around to pursue, J.B. took a quick glance at the dock where *Stiletto* was tied up. Standing there, with his arms at his sides, his hands balled into fists, was the Latin guy Richards had seen the other day on the *Stiletto*—mirrored sunglasses, black beard, and all. It registered, but J.B. dismissed it immediately and concentrated on the chase.

When the yellow Scarab got to the end of the canal, instead of turning back east where he could have gone north in the Intracoastal or south to Port Everglades and then back out into the ocean, the driver turned west, toward Tarpon Bend in the New River. He had several miles of river ahead of him, but eventually it decreased in size until it was just a small canal. The Scarab could be driven miles inland on the river until it became very narrow, looped south and then east again, and eventually intersected the Intracoastal again south of the city, but it was not a well-known route, and the driver probably wouldn't know it unless he was a local. As Richards watched the Scarab turn west, he thought, he's just trying to put enough distance between us to bail out and make it on foot.

The police boat was a North American C-22, which had a single three-fifty with a Volvo out-drive. It could do approximately forty-five, tops. No match for a twin-engined Scarab that could do sixty-five. But this Scarab was loaded with something, and Richards sensed that the driver was not that experienced with boats and probably wouldn't know the area well. So it would be close.

The Scarab had a good lead and went into the "S" curve at Tarpon Bend about one hundred yards ahead of the police boat. Coming east through the bend was a large sailboat, and when the captain of the sailboat saw the speeding Scarab coming toward him, he began blasting his horn and waving excitedly. Richards tensed as he saw the Scarab swerve wildly to the side and breathed a sigh of relief when he saw only the large wet wake crash against the hull of the sailboat. As Richards roared by, the captain of the sailboat was waving him on, yelling, "Get the bastard!"

Richards watched as the driver of the Scarab turned to look back at him and then faced forward again. The Scarab did not slow at all as it weaved in and out of the other boats.

Almost as if he was just remembering it, J.B. reached

for the radio transceiver clipped to his shoulder and shouted into the mike, "Marine Three . . . I'm in pursuit!"

"Go ahead, Marine Three," came the calm voice of the dispatcher.

"I'm chasing a yellow boat west on the New River . . . we're coming up on the tunnel area now!"

"Ten-four, Marine Three. All units, Marine Three is in pursuit west on the New River approaching the tunnel. Any unit that can assist, come to channel three."

As he struggled to keep his boat under control and keep up with the wildly fleeing Scarab, J.B. was heartened to hear land units from all over town responding to the various bridges that he would eventually come to if the chase lasted that long.

"Marine Three . . . we're coming up on the Third Avenue Bridge now, can you get the FEC trestle closed?"

The Florida East Coast Railroad trestle was the first railroad bridge they would reach, and it was characteristically low, and could cause the Scarab to slow down or stop.

"Ten-four, Marine Three . . . we're calling now."

"Alpha five-three . . . I'm at the Third Avenue Bridge now and I have him in sight. Man, he's goin' like a bat out of hell!"

"Bravo five-four. We'll be at the Marshall Bridge."

"Alpha five-one . . . I'm at the Andrews Avenue Bridge. I see 'em, I see 'em! He's goin' past the Andrews Bridge now. Forget the FEC trestle—he'll be through in a second. Try the Seaboard trestle!"

"Ten-four."

Richards's arm ached from the tight grip he had on the wheel. So far he had not touched the throttle other than to open it all the way. He could see that the Scarab was having trouble in the turns, the boat was sluggish and not responding as it would if it were empty. As he roared past the Marshall Bridge, Richards could see two land units and the uniformed patrolmen waving him on. He knew units from all over would be rushing to the river, moving west as long as the pursuit did and, if the driver bailed out, there would be K-9 teams and the airplane and every officer that could be spared would beat the bushes until they caught this guy. Yeah!

"Marine Three . . . we're coming up on Little Florida now . . . still westbound!"

"Ten-four, Marine Three."

Little Florida is the name given to a spit of land that juts out from the north side of the New River, just west of where the old Seventh Avenue Bridge used to be. It has the general shape of the peninsular state, hence the name. It causes the river to make a sharp turn to the south, then curve radically around again to the west.

Richards watched as the driver of the Scarab veered sharply to the left, entering the south leg of the turn. The Scarab laid over and the stern skidded around violently, throwing a huge wave against the seawall. When the Scarab driver realized that he was going to have to turn back to the right, he panicked. First he twisted the wheel hard around, and when that appeared to have no effect he chopped back on the throttles. Richards saw the Scarab driver's arm pull back on the throttles just in time, so instead of climbing over the engine covers and crashing into the cockpit of the Scarab, the police boat skidded to the left and jumped into the air, over the wake of the Scarab. Richards looked down into the cockpit of the yellow boat and saw the driver standing there, looking up with his mouth open.

"Yeeaaahh!" yelled Richards as his boat came crashing down in an explosion of spray. He was exhilarated. Even as the Scarab accelerated west again on the New River, J.B. knew he would catch the other man. He knew because he had felt this way before in other chases. When he *knew*, he just knew the son of a bitch was his.

"Marine Three . . . we're still westbound, passing under the Davie Bridge!"

"Ten-four, Marine Three . . . the Seaboard trestle is in the down position."

"I'm twenty-six!"

Now all the land units began converging where they knew it must end. Once the Scarab got to the trestle there was no place to go, and at the speeds of the chase so far he would never be able to maneuver back around once he spotted the trestle.

As the Scarab made the turn past the the two big marinas just east of I-95, Richards was thinking the same thing. He watched as the driver of the Scarab pushed harder on the throttles and looked back over his shoulder to see if the police boat was still there. As the two boats approached the I-95 overpass over the New River, the police boat started gaining on the Scarab. Other boats were still being forced to take evasive action, and people on the docked boats all over the river were yelling and shaking their fists.

Just west of I-95 is the Seaboard trestle. When in the down position there is less than three feet between it and the water. As the Scarab came around the curve under the overpass, the driver saw the trestle and screamed, "Shit!" He saw at a glance that he couldn't go under it or around it, and he knew he could never stop in time to make a smooth turn and go back. He had only one option. Without pulling back on the throttles, the driver of the Scarab turned the wheel slightly left and pointed the bow straight at the muddy bank along the south side of the river, just east of the railroad tracks, toward its jungly, marshy, overgrown land. There was a huge plume of brown spray as the yellow boat punched its way out of the water and ten yards up onto the mud flats. Before the boat even stopped moving, the driver was out from behind the wheel and over the windshield. As Richards pulled back his throttle and threw his boat into a skidding turn, he saw the Scarab driver jump off the bow of the yellow boat and into the heavy shrubbery alongside the railroad tracks.

"Marine three . . . he's baled out! He's on the south side of the river, running toward the highway! He's a white male in his twenties, dark curly hair, sleeveless shirt, green shorts!"

"Ten-four, Marine Three. All units . . . subject fleeing southbound, on foot."

Richards drove the bow of the police boat up onto the mud just behind the Scarab. The entire area was consumed by the roar of the twin engines that the driver had left running when he fled. Richards jumped from the bow of the police boat onto the stern of the Scarab, climbed into the cockpit, and switched off both engines. As he bowed his head in relief he saw that his hands were jumping on the rubber-padded steering wheel. "Sheeit," he said to himself.

"Papa One . . ."

"Go ahead, Papa One," said the dispatcher, answering the radio call from the police airplane.

"Yeah . . . uh . . . Roger, Papa One. We're overhead now, and, uh, we see the suspect running south along the railroad tracks. He's . . . uh . . . on the dirt road on the west side of the tracks. It looks like he's trying to make it to that marina complex near the highway. If he . . . uh . . . makes it into there he's gonna be hard to spot from up here, and hard to find."

"Ten-four, Papa One. All units . . . suspect on west side of tracks, running south toward the marina complex."

"No, no!" muttered J.B. as he jumped off the bow of the Scarab and into the bushes and started climbing up onto the tracks. "Not now! We can't lose this sucker now!" As he reached the railroad tracks he could see it all clearly—the long dirt road running south toward the highway, the marina complex less than a half mile away, and the figure of the Scarab driver, running his heart out to get to the complex before any ground units got there ahead of him. Richards started running after the figure with a slow, loping gait, knowing he could never catch the guy on foot.

Then, from the highway, something caught his eye and he stopped. It was a dust cloud, rising fast behind a rapidly approaching vehicle with flashing red and blue police lights. Richards watched the dust cloud and said, "That car is flying!"

He saw the running figure hesitate, then speed up, then start to run off the road, then slow down. He watched transfixed as the bronze police unit with the flashing red and blue lights zeroed in on the Scarab driver. The unit appeared to be going almost a hundred miles an hour. Because it was on a dirt road it seemed to float as it swayed back and forth gently. The car was approaching the running figure with relentless certainty, and it appeared that the car was going to run down the Scarab driver and keep on going into the river. As Richards watched the car coming on he knew there was only one cop in the department who could, or would, drive a car like that, and he said quietly through dry lips, "Holy shit!"

When it became certain that impact was inevitable, the Scarab driver made a couple of hesitant lunges this way and that. Then he just stood there, paralyzed, like a rabbit caught in a spotlight. The Scarab driver watched as the hood, headlights, and grill of the police unit became his whole world and he felt frozen in place. Long after it should have been too late, the driver of the police car applied the brakes and swerved the wheel. The car gently turned sideways on the dirt road, slowed, and skidded along, still at a high rate of speed. Richards could hear the car skidding along on the dirt and gravel. Just as the sliding car approached the standing figure and Richards expected to hear the *whomph* of impact, a huge white cloud of dust covered the police unit, the standing figure, and the entire roadway. Richards started running toward what he knew would be a messy scene.

"Papa One ... uh ... we think one of the units has the suspect. Uh ... we're not sure ... visibility is bad ... uh ... hold on a minute."

"Ten-four, Papa One."

As Richards neared the police car, he saw the cop he expected climb out and slowly walk around to the right front fender where the Scarab driver was standing. The car had stopped literally inches from the man, who had just reached out and placed his hands on the hot hood. As Richards came running up, puffing from the exertion, he saw the Scarab driver look at the cop's face and try to speak, but nothing came out.

Richards came up beside the Scarab driver, caught his breath, and looked at the strained expression on the man's face. Then he looked to the cop who was standing there with his arms folded across his chest, on top of his rather pronounced belly. He looked at Richards with bloodshot eyes and said, "He's all urine."

"Thanks, Skids," said Richards. "But man, I thought you were gonna run right over this guy!"

"What? And chance throwing out my front-end alignment? No way."

"Marine Three . . . Marine Three. Is the suspect in custody? Can I clear the air?"

"Ten-four, Dispatch. Suspect is in custody. You can clear the air and thank Papa One for us. We'll need a supervisor here, and see if Customs can send one of their guys out here to the scene so we can search the boat."

One of the Miami office Customs agents was just leaving the Broward County Courthouse when the call came through; he immediately responded to the scene. The patrol sergeant had a pair of bolt cutters in the trunk of his unit, and now Richards leaned on the bolster seat and watched as the Customs man cut off the small lock on the Scarab's cabin doors. The agent stuck his head into the cabin and whistled. Then he pulled back and looked up at Richards with a grin.

"Hey, just like the old days, huh?" he said as he climbed up out of the way. "You done good."

Richards bent down under the bolster seat and looked inside. Heavy square burlap-covered bales were stuffed tightly into the cabin area. He reached in with one hand and dragged the closest bale out onto the deck; using a pocket knife, he cut open one side. The Customs man reached in and pulled out a handful of dry, greenish brown weed and held it to his nose. He handed it to Richards and said to the sergeant, "It's not real fresh, but it's pretty good stuff."

The sergeant just grunted.

J.B. made arrangements with the sergeant for one of the lab detectives to come out and photograph all of the bales in place, then photograph them individually as they were hauled out of the Scarab. A sample of each bale would have to be Valtox tested to show chemically that it was in fact cannabis, and then each bale would be weighed and marked as evidence. It was a slow, laborious job, but police agencies all over the country had learned the hard way just how easy it was to lose a smuggling case in court on a technicality. There were too many places a good attorney could attack the search and seizure method and the evidence procedure. The Customs man left, and Richards walked over to talk with the Scarab driver before he was taken in to be booked.

He learned very little.

The arrested man was polite, and gave his name and an address in Ohio. When Richards asked him about the boat he just shook his head and smiled. He told Richards he didn't know who owned the boat or anything about it, just that he had been asked if he would drive it around today as a favor to a guy whose name he did not know. He said he did not have the key to the cabin and that he had no idea what was in there. He saw the look in J.B.'s eyes, and said, "Look, Officer, I'm not tryin' to be a smart ass about this. It's just that I'm more afraid of them than I am of you. Do you understand?"

Richards looked at him for a few seconds, then nodded his head and walked away.

Before he could leave the area, J.B. was approached by a tall and lanky reporter from the *Fort Lauderdale Herald*. The press had already arrived on the scene, but J.B. didn't really feel like talking to any of them.

"J.B. Richards? I'm Kuhler...Dave Kuhler, from the *Herald*...I spoke with you some months back about liveaboards on the New River."

Richards shook the offered hand and nodded, preoccupied.

"Listen, I know you're busy here, and I've got most of what I need for my story. Nice grab, by the way, and I guess you didn't get anything from the driver, right?"

J.B. shook his head.

The tall young reporter paused, then said quietly, "I don't know if he told you or not, but Ted Novak and I have become friends. He thinks the world of you...he's very excited about being a narc, and he's a great source for me...I mean, because we're becoming friends it is giving me a different perspective on cops as people, you know?"

J.B. smiled. "I'm glad to hear it, Dave ... I just hope you don't abuse the friendship for the sake of some story."

Kuhler smiled too, sighed, and said, "Yeah. Well, you just don't know me well enough yet."

He walked off, and J.B. left. He thought once more about Ted Novak and about the crazy, dangerous games played in the drug smuggling arena.

SIX

Lieutenant Jed Tallert sat back in his chair, put his feet up on his desk, crossed his hands behind his head, and looked at J.B. His eyes gleamed under his bushy eyebrows, and his little half grin gave his face a boyish look, which was accentuated by the tinges of gray at the temples of his full head of reddish brown hair. His uniform was spotless and fit his trim body well, and all the brass insignia on the long-sleeved brown shirt shined brightly. The feet he had placed up on his desk cowboy style, were sheathed in a pair of polished black boots.

Richards looked into Tallert's shining eyes and at the half grin and thought about how many people were fooled by looking at Tallert and concluding he was just a country bumpkin. Yeah, he wore cowboy boots and raised sheep-dogs and chewed a plug now and then. But despite his habits and boyish looks, Tallert was as tough as pure steel. Richards had known Tallert for several years, and he knew Tallert had a sharp mind that missed little and a command-ing presence he didn't need to broadcast. Richards was glad he was working for Tallert because he was fair, and that was about the best anyone could ask for. Richards knew Tallert didn't take any lip from anyone—the brass or the troops. The lieutenant took care of his people, and that was worth its weight in gold.

Tallert shifted his weight in his chair and said, "Well, I listened to the whole thing, start to finish, and other than the usual unnecessary radio chatter from some of the units I'd say it was handled all right. Toward the end I kinda got the impression it was a good thing that Officer Bedlam was in the area, though . . ."

"Yessir. It was a good thing Skids was there. I'm not sure what would have happened if that guy had made it to the marina complex."

The lieutenant removed his feet from the desktop and shuffled some papers in front of him. Then he looked up and said, "I called you in here to talk with you about the chase, but since I left the message for you someone else told me they wanted to see you, and we agreed he could meet you here . . . so we'd both know what was goin' on."

J.B. just nodded, puzzled. There was a short knock on the door, and then Narcotics Detective Scott Kelly walked in. He gave a little salute to Tallert, who just grinned, and he shook J.B.'s hand firmly.

J.B. watched him while he grabbed a chair and sat down.

Scott Kelly was a legend around FLPD. He had been deep undercover on the street for years, doing everything from making street buys to setting up million dollar cocaine traps. He had recovered stolen explosives by meeting the thief in a fake buy, and he had harassed organized crime figures with the tenacity and strength of a pit bull.

Scott Kelly was all cop. And then one night, when the adrenaline was flowing and the sweat dampened the brow, he was shot down in the middle of a blown cocaine buy. He was not expected to live. Then he was not expected to keep both legs. Then he was not expected to ever walk again. Because he was in excellent physical condition on the night he was shot, and because he had immediately put himself into a brutal therapy schedule, he was able to prove all of the doctors wrong. He had lived, and he was not a cripple. During his long fight to recover, however, Scott Kelly had fallen from favor with the chief. When he finally walked back into the station, eight months after being shot, expecting to get back into the narc slot he had been blown out of, he found that things had changed. The organized crime unit and the narcotics unit were now under the administration of new captains who held the ear of the chief. They said Scott Kelly was old news, washed up, possibly a liability to the department. He was told he could no longer fill the narc slot. He could work in administration, in records, or in the Comm Center. Or he could quit.

He had come very close to quitting, but because he needed to provide for his family, he had accepted their offer. It had burned him inside badly, but then he had found inner strengths he didn't know he had. Sooner than he expected, he was told he could get out of administration and go back to work as a narc in a limited capacity, if he still wanted it. Maybe this opportunity arose because the old chief had retired and a new chief was trying to move people around and thereby gain a measure of control over the department.

Scott Kelly had not hesitated, and now he was a narc again, laying low, doing his thing, and very happy to be back in the saddle. When J.B. looked at him now he saw a man in his late thirties, with brown hair flecked with gray brushed back off his forehead. His good-looking face sported a thick mustache, also flecked with gray, and his eyes seemed to say they had seen it all but still held out hope. He was very tanned, and J.B. could see that he still worked out regularly; he didn't have a huge body like those huff and puff guys at the gym, but his well-muscled arms and tight stomach indicated just how seriously the man took his health.

Kelly frowned a little and said, "Tell you why I asked Lieutenant Tallert here if I could meet with you, J.B. It's about that boat you nailed today. And it's about Ted Novak."

Now he had Richards's full attention.

"About the boat," he said carefully, "I . . . uh, sort of by myself, have been watching for it for a couple of days now. I'm pretty sure I know who owns it, and I think I can tie it into somethin' I've been working for a while now." He took a deep breath and looked up at the ceiling. "Ted Novak was assigned to work with another narc because he was new. Everyone knows we're always shorthanded over in our office, so even though it's not supposed to happen Ted was sent out on his own, just local stuff, just to kind of get the feel of things."

Richards was aware of the use of the past tense, and it chilled him.

"He's a little older than the ordinary new narc, but as you know he still has that innocent look about him. They hooked him in with an informant about a week ago to pull off a cocaine sting, where the bad guy comes with the money for the coke that our guys show, and then he gets busted for conspiracy. It's worked pretty good for us in the past. So, Ted got busted along with the bad guy, an attorney named Hadley, and it looked swell." He took another deep breath, looked at Richards, then at the floor, and said, "The same informant who put us onto the attorney who wanted the cocaine came back to us with a whisper from someone he hears from on the Bimini side of the Gulf Stream."

J.B. was very still now, waiting.

Kelly went on. "This informant who is a dirt ball himself, of course, tells me now that Ted and the attorney went for a boat ride with a guy named Montilla, and they didn't come back . . . and they're not coming back."

The three men sat silent in the room. Kelly's words hung heavy about them, roared in their ears, and clamored in their minds. The unthinkable had been said out loud. It had to happen . . . everyone said so. Somewhere along the way one of the local narcs was going to bite off more than he could chew because of all the running over to the islands and down to Miami and the Keys in pursuit of the bad guys, and then that narc was going to turn up missing. The worst situation had occurred. Ted Novak may very well have been murdered by a smuggler, but for the present time, officially, he was just AWOL—unaccountable. Each man in the room knew in his heart how slim the chances would be of ever recovering the body, or of bringing the killer into a courtroom on a murder charge.

After a few moments, J.B. pinched the bridge of his nose, cleared his throat, and said softly, "The worst thing, of course, is that we may never really know, right? We may never know for sure what happened to Ted."

Kelly's silence was the answer.

Tallert spoke up then. "Well, Scott, even if you just have an informant's story on this, at least you have a lead to start working on, right? Cases are made by digging and digging away, we all know that. You've got a name now, someone you can start really looking at closely, and even if you never make him on Novak's death, if that's what happened, you can still make life miserable for the bastard that did it."

Scott Kelly nodded and said quietly, "Well, yeah. That's what I was going to tell you about. My info says that boat that J.B. nailed is owned by a young guy that works for this Montilla character. The young guy is the captain of one of the sportfishermen that Montilla uses to bring in loads of grass. Most of it is hearsay and speculation right now, and we've got a long way to go before we can make a direct link between the boat and grass that J.B. seized today, and Montilla. But there's somethin' there, I'm sure. And it can be worked."

J.B. sat stiff in his chair, punching one of his fists into his other palm. There were two red spots high on his cheeks. His eyes had a faraway look as he said, "Oh, it can be worked all right. If there's a link between the load I got today and Ted's disappearance, you can just ease off it, Scott." The other two men saw the hatred in Richards's eyes as he said quietly, "I'll take care of it myself."

Tallert started to speak but stopped when Kelly held up one hand and said quickly, "Hold it, J.B. Listen for a moment, okay? I hear you, man, I know what you're saying, but it might not be that easy. My old narcotic agent bones are telling me this is a big thing we've stumbled across, I don't know why. I counsel caution, and patience. Listen, I'm sittin' on this info. You guys are the only ones who have heard what I've got so far." He hesitated. "I have my reasons for playing this close to the chest for right now. When I got back to that narc unit I didn't find the tight-knit professional bunch of guys I had been working with . . . it's a mess now, to put it mildly. The captains are looking for newsprint, and the lower brass are all playing Lauderdale Vice—and I mean playing. Letting a new guy like Ted go out into the cold shows you how screwed up things are right now." He stopped and rubbed his brow, as if tying to rub out the creases worn there. "Believe me, there's a possibility that Novak's been murdered, and there's no way I'm gonna let anyone slide on it. I think we can work it, quietly for now, and move forward toward an arrest. I asked Lieutenant Tallert for this meeting to go over my info with you, and to see if maybe you'd be interested in working this thing *with* me. You'll be doing your regular work out there on the water, in your police boat, and I'll be doing my thing in the gutters of this lovely little town. I'll pass on to you what I learn, and vice versa, right?"

Richards just nodded, his face grim.

Tallert rubbed his chin, and said to J.B., "I think Scott's idea is a good one, J.B. Work with him on it, see where it goes. Take more time to concentrate on the smuggling scene. Oh, I know it's an old story now and all that, but maybe it's a good time to stick your foot out into that Intracoastal Waterway and see who, or what, trips over it. I'll make sure you'll be left alone, and you can give it some time to see what develops. It's worth a shot anyway."

J.B. left the office a short while later. His head was pounding, and he felt a great weight on his chest. He walked out across the rear parking lot of the police station, his pace slow, his breathing shallow. One thought drummed repeatedly in his mind.

Who the hell was Montilla?

He was alive.

Ted Novak came to this realization with excruciating clarity as a searing bolt of pain traveled up his right leg, from the ankle, through his knee, into his groin, and then up into the rest of his body. He licked the sweat off his upper lip, and tried to figure out what had caused the pain. It came again, he almost passed out, but then he realized that the pain came because he had tried to move his leg.

He was alive. But how?

He stared up at a plain white-painted wooden ceiling and tried to remember what had happened. He remembered the attorney's blood, so wet-red in the sun. He remembered the roar of *Stiletto* as it charged toward him. He remembered screaming, struggling, rolling, and diving to get away from the hull and the hungry propellers that would surely follow.

Coral reef. That's what it was. A part of the reef, called a coral head, like a tall column of coral reaching for the surface. He remembered that as he rolled and dove for the bottom, his head and left shoulder had hit the coral column and he had instinctively grabbed on to it. Then one of the props ripped into his right leg, while at the same time glancing off the coral, which broke away in chunks.

He couldn't know that when Montilla felt the prop hit the coral column he thought he was feeling the solid bite the props would make as they tore through Ted's body. He couldn't know that in the swirl of water and blood and coral dust Montilla didn't see his face break the surface, if only for a moment, to suck in the sweet air.

Death and sunshine had bounced off the propeller-tormented surface of the green waters and Montilla had seen the blood and the predator fish moving in and he concluded that the job was done.

He had been wrong.

Ted now became aware of movement, and noise, and then he lost consciousness again.

When he came to, it was because the movement he had felt earlier had increased, his body was trying to roll back and forth, and each way it moved brought the pain. He continued his speculation on how he could still be alive.

He remembered the silence around the reef, broken by his hungry gasps as he would bring his face slightly out of the water to take air. He didn't know how long he waited, but finally he left himself break the surface with his head and shoulders, put his head back, and sobbed as he took huge breaths of air. The constant pounding of the powerful engines of *Stiletto*, which sounded like hollow thunder under the water, was finally gone. He remembered looking around then, all around in a circle at the unbroken surface of the green sea... registering that *Stiletto* and Montilla were no longer in sight. He remembered being cold while his right leg burned as if on fire. He remembered choosing a direction, pointed to by some inner compass, and striking out toward land, any land, no matter how far. In his pain now, he thought about the surge of strength he had felt then, knowing he was still alive and swimming away to save himself.

It became a hazy blur then, a brutal montage of metallic cold water and brassy, burning sun, and his gulping sobs of pain.

He turned his head, slowly, and through swollen eyes he made out the edges of the bunk he was on. He saw rain gear hanging on pegs on a wall. Bulkhead? There was another bunk across from him, piled with clothes and food wrappers and first aid gear.

He was on a boat, some kind of old wooden boat, rocking and pounding through the ocean. He raised his head to call out, and the pain came through him like a fist, making everything hazy again.

The next time he awoke, it was dark, and he was afraid. He lay there, feeling the boat rocking, hearing the steady drone of what sounded like twin diesels, and he tried to think back to when he was in the water and had given up, knowing that he could swim no farther, that he would sink into the clinging ocean forever. Did he remember loud voices? An argument? Did he remember being dragged roughly up out of the water and across a wooden gunwale? He wasn't sure. He knew only he had been in pain, he was still in pain, he was alive, and he was going somewhere on an old wooden boat.

The captain of the boat looked again at the source of his problems in the forward cabin. He scowled at the pale figure tied into the portside V-bunk, his right leg covered in bandages. He muttered, *Madre de Dios* and made his way back to the helm, where the mate held her on their southbound course through the light chop. One of the crew had spotted a figure struggling in the water, in the middle of nowhere. As captain, he had ordered the boat turned off its course and the deck crew pulled the injured man out of the water.

He noted the depth-meter reading, the drone of the RPMs, and he thought about the argument that had followed the rescue. The mate had said that the man's injuries were too severe, that he suffered from exposure and would surely die. Why should they keep him aboard to die on their fishing boat when he could die in the water as was obviously his fate? The captain had shrugged his shoulders. Then the mate had reminded the captain that they were illegally fishing the Bahamian waters, and that there was no way they could explain their being there if they tried to get help for the man. Although *their* government knew and even encouraged them to go into the Bahamas for the fish, no one else would be pleased to know they were there. So what could they do with the injured man, who appeared to be from the *Estados Unidos*? He told the captain it was a mistake to stop and pick up the man from the sea.

The captain turned to the mate, looked at the others, and asked, "If it was God's will that this man die in the water, then why did we come along now, on this course? And which of you will pick him up and throw him back into the sea?" He watched while they furtively crossed themselves and looked down at the deck.

So it was decided. The injured man was aboard, and they were headed for home. Soon they would be in the straights, and by the next evening they would be off the coast. The captain would take the boat into the harbor and report to the officials what had happened.

He let the salty wind blow through his hair as he watched the darkening sky and thought, *So, mi amigo, Fidel, I will bring you this injured and mysterious gringo, and you will be pleased, or you will not. And then what will you do? You will shoot me, or even worse, take away* mi pequeña barca.

The day after his meeting with Lieutenant Tallert and the narc, Scott Kelly, Richards stood in the bow of the police boat as Fat Harry moved the boat alongside an old cabin cruiser passing under the Causeway Bridge. Also in the police boat was U.S. Customs Officer Hank Zaden. Fat Harry was really Officer Harold Tommasen of FLPD. He was in his fifties, had a full head of shaggy gray hair, and a huge stomach. He was a big man with a natural desire to eat all good things at all times. It was said that during the manatee mating season Harry was reluctant to go swimming for fear of unwittingly sparking an amorous urge in a traveling sea cow. He was an experienced street cop who had worked his way out into the boats and who could be counted on when things got rough.

Hank Zaden was young, dark, and handsome, with a muscular build and straight black hair and a black Fu Manchu mustache. He was a career Customs officer whose father had retired from the same service. He was dedicated and smart, and he believed in the job he did. Normally he worked with another Customs man as his partner, but that partner was in Miami on a court hearing, so Zaden was riding with FLPD.

As the police boat got closer to the cabin cruiser, Richards called out, "Hey Cap'n, put her in neutral. We'd like to see your registration."

The operator of the boat, a skinny young man with dark blond hair, waved at Richards and yelled something down into the cabin. Immediately two more young guys came out onto the deck. Neither wore shirts, and their shorts were dirty. They all looked tired.

"Look at the scuff marks on the hull. Looks like they been layin' up against somethin' for sure," said Zaden to J.B.

"Yeah, and they've got a bladder tank for extra fuel roped to the transom," said Richards as he reached out to fend off the two boats as they came together on the north side of the bridge.

As Tommasen secured a line from the stern of the cabin cruiser to the police boat, and Richards did the same at the bow, Zaden stated, "U.S. Customs Officer . . . where are you coming from?"

The operator of the boat stepped over to the rail and said, "West Palm Beach, sir."

"Do you have the registration?"

"Yessir, right here."

Zaden handed the papers to Fat Harry who copied the info down into his notebook and checked the hull numbers to make sure they matched. As Richards moved back toward the stern, Zaden said, "We're gong to board you, sir," and stepped over the rail of the police boat into the aft deck of the cabin cruiser. J.B. followed behind.

While Richards took identification from the three men, Zaden went below and checked out the interior. He came up in a few moments and covertly shook his head. As he and Richards climbed back into the boat, Zaden said, "Thank you for your cooperation . . . and have a nice day."

The operator of the cabin cruiser took the papers back from Fat Harry and said with a smile, "Always happy to cooperate with the law, Officer."

As the two boats drifted apart and the cabin cruiser began making headway north on the Intracoastal Waterway, Fat Harry said to no one in particular, "Slimy sonsabitches."

Richards looked at the info Harry had taken off the registration and said, "Well, the damn thing's registered in Palm Beach, and they were clean, but did you see that big industrial vacuum they had in the main cabin?"

"Hell, yeah," said Zaden, "those guys are dopers for sure. We just missed the load, that's all."

"Well, every dog has his day," said J.B. "We'll see 'em again."

They watched as the cabin cruiser went out of sight toward Bahia Mar, then they settled down to see what else came along.

"They're out there, but they're just making spot checks, that's all," said Lieutenant Billy Erricks, Fort Lauderdale Police, organized crime division. "They're working blind, stopping anything that looks good. Hold your people off until this evening, that's all." He gripped the phone tighter and looked around the office to make sure no one was listening. "Yeah, I know this is a busy time for you. No . . . how the hell was I supposed to know they were gonna be out there? I know . . . I know. It's the same thing with that Scarab the other day. Just a fluke. Listen, my outfit is the only one that's supposed to be working this stuff . . . Okay, okay. I'll find out what's going on as soon as I can. In the meantime, tell your people to hold off." As he hung up the phone he said, "Crap."

As Onyx Montilla hung up his phone, he also said, "Crap."

SEVEN

Using a small towel Richards wiped the early morning moisture off the driver's seat of his police boat. The engine had been idling for a few minutes and he had stored all of his gear. As he slipped the lines and idled away from the dock, he took a deep breath of the sweet morning air and smiled. There was just a faint gray haze to the east and many stars were still visible overhead in the dark sky. He had folded the canvas Bimini top down so that it wouldn't slow him with its sail effect. He slid under the Causeway Bridge with an outgoing tide and cruised slowly past the tugs along the western edge of the port. He hugged the seawall as he traveled south; it provided a natural backdrop and cover as he approached the middle of the dock area. He eased alongside the rusty hull of a medium-size island freighter and took a look out to the east, between north and south jetties, toward the ocean.

From his position in the port, J.B. could see the entire inlet clearly. To his left, or north, were the huge high-rise condominiums, concrete monuments to man's desire to find beautiful places in this world and then crush everything beneath tons of steel and concrete, stacking people on top of one another in steadily ascending dwellings. With the exception of a very few lucky individuals, most of the people living in the buildings had a view of either another large building or the blinding glare of the sun reflecting the ocean from twenty stories high. Richards had heard the locals talk of the jetties before the condos came along. He tried to imagine the cool green pine forest and the clean, clear water, and the sun-browned kids running across the rocks or diving into the warm water. He had heard the old fishermen tell how, in the quiet of the early morning, you could hear the crash of the great silver tarpon as they leaped out of the water after mullet. He looked now at the huge buildings with their electronic security gates and parking lots as big as football fields, and sighed.

To his right, or south, was the Hollywood side of the port. South jetties had remained relatively untouched through the years. In fact, the state had purchased one of the last remaining natural strips of beach in the area and had turned it all into a state park. It was the best thing that could have happened to it. With the exception of a small navy facility and a branch of the Nova College research facility, the only other buildings there belonged to the U.S. Coast Guard complexes just south of the navy. There would be no more buildings in the area. It was now a park and would retain its natural beauty. Beyond the coast guard was Whiskey Creek, so named for the rumrunners of old who used the area for off-loading operations years ago. It was an area with a romantic history, and a violent one. The coast guard had actually hung a rumrunner at the old station after he killed one of theirs, and in later years a guy named Murph the Surf got rid of a couple of young but potentially incriminating witnesses in a most permanent way in Whiskey Creek. Then came the Intracoastal Waterway again, winding its way south toward Biscayne Bay and, finally, the Keys.

On the west side of the Intracoastal, still on the south side of the port, was the docking area for the cruise ships. Richards noted that there were two there now, each showing just a little smoke from the main stacks, ready to shove off later in the morning. Navy ships tied up on the south-side of the quay. The area was empty now except for a sinister-looking black nuclear sub that was barely visible in the dawn light. Farther west were the red and white striped power company stacks. These were visible from a long way offshore and were commonly known as the candy stripes to the boat people in the area.

Behind Richards were all the port buildings and facilities, more wharf area, and several large tankers and freighters. To his left was the Causeway Bridge and the motel/marina complexes on both sides of the waterway. As the sun rose, the condos on the north and the navy radio tower on the south turned a golden copper color for a few seconds, and then started to show all the various colors visible in the first pale wash of daylight. Richards saw several white gulls wheeling and circling around one of the channel markers, and a squadron of pelicans, majestic in their flight formation, gliding overhead. He watched while the water in the port turned from almost black to lead gray to pastel green and brown as the sun rose. It looked like it would be a beautiful day, but suddenly he remembered Ted and felt a chill.

He saw a large new sportfisherman come up into view from the south, just outside the first buoy. She was a beauty, with a tuna tower, gleaming outriggers, and lots of radio antennae and radar gear visible topside. Richards whistled softly to himself at her beauty, watching the boat turn slowly, the bow pointed directly into the port right at him. He noticed that the running lights were still on, indicating that she had been running in the dark. With the huge orange fireball glow of the sun rising behind her, the sport-fisherman entered the port. Her bow looked a dull eggshell color while her stern appeared to be on fire; its burnished copper rigging had sparkling highlights all over. Richards noticed that she appeared to be bow down just a little, but not too much so. When she turned north toward the Cause-way Bridge, he noticed that fish pennants were flying from the riggers. He put his boat in gear and idled toward her to get a better look.

As he got closer Richards could see two men sitting in

the fly bridge steering station, apparently intent on their approach to the bridge. He pulled up close to her stern and saw the name painted in gold across the transom: *Sausea Girl*. She was indeed a beauty, a fifty-three-foot Hatteras, with Lee riggers and full electronics. There was a ginpole on the starboard side of the cockpit, and a full set of gleaming gold Internationals in the rod holders. The pennants snapped briskly in the breeze; he noticed they were billfish, marlin, and sailfish pennants. That's odd, he thought; if they were out all night fishing they wouldn't have caught marlin and sails . . . broadbill maybe, or what's left of them since the commercial boats started doing their thing along this coast. Well, they might have caught them over in Bimini and they're just getting home, he thought. But then, where was their yellow quarantine flag?

The captain of the *Sausea Girl*, a young man with thinning red hair, sunburned and freckled skin, and wearing dark wraparound sunglasses, had not yet noticed the police boat trailing him. He had a headache, he was tired, and he just wanted to get to the stash house dock, tie her up, and go home. He looked over at young Arnie sitting next to him, and suppressed the urge to speak his mind.

Arnie was a mistake, all the way. He was the brother of the captain's girlfriend, and the girlfriend knew that the captain of the *Sausea Girl* did more with the lovely sportfisherman than just troll for the tigers of the sea. She knew that he occasionally brought in loads of contraband for big bucks. She knew because he spent much of his earnings on her. The captain had been working on boats, and on the water, for his whole life. He was an experienced professional. Arnie, on the other hand, had trouble finding the pointed end of a boat, and he had a big mouth.

But the captain had been talked into taking Arnie with him. His sister had said he needed the work, needed the money, needed the chance. She had convinced him that her brother would prove more than helpful.

Arnie was a disaster. He could not take orders, and he masked his ignorance in bravado and gutter language. He did things without thinking, and he became defensive when corrected. So far, it had been a very trying trip for the captain. He was anxious to just get to the dock, make arrangements for Arnie to get his sizable pay for his incompetence, and go home. The captain looked at the bridge, wondering if he wanted Arnie to spread the outriggers and drop the antennae so they could pass underneath without having the bridge open for them. He thought of the one thing about Arnie that really made him a liability.

Arnie was scared; scared of the police, the Customs people, the coasties, the DEA, the FBI, the FDLE, and probably the VFW. He was just plain paranoid about getting caught with the load. He talked long and loud about how he would spend the money he would make from the run, but he was paranoid all the same.

Richards was still trailing behind *Sausea Girl*, trying to figure out what it was that just wasn't right about her, when one of the men on the fly bridge turned and looked down and saw him sitting there behind them in his police boat. He saw the one guy grab his partner's arm and point toward him. Both appeared surprised to see him there. Richards waved and watched as the captain pulled the yacht out of gear. He couldn't hear what the two men were saying but it was obvious they were having a heated discussion, pointing and shaking their heads. Finally one climbed down into the aft cockpit while the other stayed at the wheel on the fly bridge. They had turned the boat to the left so that it was now making a slow circle toward the west, then south, with Richards following behind.

Richards noticed that the door to the main cabin was closed, and that all the windows and ports were closed and covered with curtains, He could not see into any part of the boat. He picked up the mike to the P.A. set and spoke: "Hey, Captain, how about letting her drift right there for a minute so you can talk to me, okay?" When he said this he saw the captain wave at him, apparently relaxed, while the other one yelled something up the ladder.

There was another argument, then the captain waved again and smiled and hit the flat of his hand on the clutches, showing that he was in neutral. The big yacht slowed and then started to drift easily into the turning basin of the port. Richards pulled alongside, being careful not to bump the bow of his boat into the side of the larger boat, as the captain watched him. The one in the cockpit watched him too, and looked all around the port, his eyes wide. This one now came to the rail and Richards could see that he needed a shave and his eyes were red. He smiled nervously as he grabbed the rail of the police boat and said, "Mornin', Officer . . . did we do something wrong?"

"No, no, you didn't," replied Richards. "I just wanted to check your registration."

The one in the cockpit turned and yelled, loudly, at the other one, "He says he wants to check the papers on the boat!"

The captain left the controls and stood by the aft rail of the fly bridge, and J.B. asked, "Where are you guys coming in from anyway?"

At the same time both men answered, "Elliot Key" and "Merritt Island." Then they both said the same two again, only each said the other place, then they both stuttered to a stop, the captain with a look of disgust on his face.

"Well . . . which is it?" asked J.B.

Neither man said anything. Richards looked at them hard and said, "Have you guys been to Bimini?" while he moved his police boat farther alongside by pulling on the side rail of the Hatteras.

With this the captain said, "No" while the other started to say, "A couple of days ago . . ." and then stopped and looked up at his partner, a look of dread on his face.

Richards knew something was not right, but he wasn't sure where to go from here. He was standing alone in his police boat, tied alongside the Hatteras, and they were all drifting peacefully along in the turning basin of Port Everglades. He wasn't sure if he could, legally, board her or not at this point. He again asked for the registration and the captain said, "Uh . . . listen, we just borrowed this boat and we're not sure where the papers are. Do you really need to see them, or can you just let it slide this time?"

J.B. looked up at him and then at his partner. He looked at the closed cabin door, at the sailfish pennant snapping in the breeze, and said, "No, I think you'd better pull her over to the marina docks just on the other side of the bridge and tie her up. Then I'll stand by while you look for the registration. Who knows? Maybe you guys stole this boat. There's a lot of that going around these days."

When he finished, Richards slipped the single line holding him fast alongside the cockpit area of the Hatteras. As he did so, he saw the man who had first come down into the cockpit look around wildly. The man's eyes were bulging and he hit himself on his hips twice with his open palms. Then he yelled "Shit!" and dove over the side of the *Sausea Girl* away from the police boat, into the water, apparently heading toward the docks where a rusty old freighter was tied up about a hundred yards away.

As this happened, the captain yelled, "Goddammit, Arnie . . . you asshole!" and turned back to the controls on the fly bridge. Richards saw the man look back over his shoulder at him, his face grim, as he pushed the clutches in gear and jammed the throttles forward. He began turning the wheel hard left, to bring her around and head back out toward the ocean, out of the port. Richards, in the meantime, pulled his boat into reverse and backed hastily away from the wildly slewing sportfisherman. He grabbed his mike and spoke into his radio for the first time, just getting his call sign out when he heard a piercing scream and looked to see the captain of *Sausea Girl* leave the wheel and step to the aft rail of the fly bridge and look out over the stern. Richards looked too and saw the normally white frothy foam wake turn crimson. He knew than that the captain had not given his partner enough time to swim clear before turning hard left. The boat, with both props turning hard, had skidded over the guy in the water, pulping him, and spreading parts of him all around the stern of the boat.

With a horrified look, the captain gripped the rail and screamed, "Arneee! Oh, Arneeeee!"

Richards just stared, numb, as the crimson turned to pink, then to dirty brown, and the water was dotted here and there with pieces of cloth and small white bubbly things. As he moved the police boat closer to the sportfisherman, he saw the captain staring at him with wide eyes, then turning back to the wheel. He pushed the throttles forward again and turned the wheel furiously. It became apparent that something was wrong because the boat rocked around to the starboard side, even though the wheel was being pulled hard left. Richards guessed then that the impact of the body had caused the starboard engine to stall, and the force of the port engine full forward was causing the boat to slew around awkwardly.

The captain was obviously an experienced professional, but he looked as if he had been through a rough couple of days and was now in the middle of a nightmare. He began to panic because he did not seem to understand what was wrong with the boat. He kept screaming, "No! No! No!" and fighting the wheel. As he did so, the boat moved erratically toward the south part of the port. Richards followed along, advising the dispatcher of what was going on and requesting assistance. He watched as the sportfisherman finally impacted the seawall between the cruise ships and the big restaurant that was located out on the end of the dock. It struck the wall with the starboard bow, and as it did the captain pulled the throttles back, climbed over the windshield, down the forward part of the main cabin, and then out onto the bow. From there he jumped wildly into the air. For a second it appeared to J.B. that the man would be crushed between the bow of the boat and the dock, but then he saw him stagger into view, running unevenly toward the building complexes west of where he was. Then he was gone.

Richards advised the dispatcher of the description of the fleeing captain and the direction he was heading and asked for the port police to give assistance. When the dispatcher asked for a reference on the chase all Richards could say was, "Just fleeing a police officer for now. I don't know what the hell I've got here."

J.B. pulled the police boat alongside the port stern quarter of the Hatteras and tied her fast with a single line. Then he climbed aboard her, went across the cockpit, climbed up to the fly bridge, and shut her down. Some of the sailors and dock personnel nearby came over to see what the commotion was and assisted him in getting some lines out so the Hatteras was more or less secure for the moment.

As Richards climbed down from the fly bridge, he saw two Lauderdale units racing toward him across the docks with their sirens wailing. The first one skidded to a stop and out jumped one of the road sergeants. He was young and J.B. knew him but had never worked with him. The other unit stopped behind the sergeant and one of the older street patrolmen stood up outside the car just long enough to ask, "You all right?" When Richards nodded affirmatively, the cop got back into his cruiser and drove off to look for the suspect.

J.B. jumped over to the seawall and met the sergeant. The sergeant looked at the damaged bow of the Hatteras and asked, "Well . . . what have we got here?"

J.B. explained how the whole thing had gone down. When he got to the part about the guy being run over by the big boat the sergeant's eyes widened and he held up his hand to stop Richards. He then got on the air and asked for his supervisor and the dive team to come out as soon as possible. Then he let Richards go on. He stood there with his hands on his hips, biting his lower lip as Richards finished with, ". . . and I think if we look into the cabin we'll find some kind of dope load. Why else would they act like that? Unless the damn thing really is stolen?"

"Yeah. Yeah . . . I think you're right, J.B.," said the sergeant as he climbed aboard into the cockpit.

"What are you gonna do, Sarge?"

"Well, shit guy . . . let's look and see." The sergeant grabbed the main salon door and slid it open. Richards started to protest, concerned about search and seizure, but before he could say anything the sergeant turned to him, pointing, and said, "Holy shit."

Richards looked to where the sergeant was pointing and saw that the entire main cabin was filled with marijuana, the square bales placed so that the entire cabin was packed, leaving just enough room for a person to squeeze through. They both made their way into the main cabin and looked down forward. The entire boat was crammed full with bales. As they stood there in the hot stuffy cabin the sergeant turned to J.B. and said, "Richards, the driver of this thing may have gotten away, but you just got yourself one nice commendation. What a really beautiful fucking grab!"

J.B. looked back at him, wondering. He said nothing.

Divers soon searched in vain for a body in the area that J.B. had indicated. An inspection of the bow area showed that the Hatteras was not critically damaged, so she was moved to the police docks and unloaded.

It was a slow, backbreaking task of off-loading, marking, testing, photographing, and weighing the bales of marijuana. The brass that had arrived earlier realized that it was almost time for lunch when the hard work began, and so they had a good excuse to leave.

It was a tired, dirty, and dispirited Officer Richards who climbed wearily into his pickup truck and drove home late that afternoon. The heaviness he felt in his heart for Ted overshadowed any sense of accomplishment regarding the seizure.

When the old wooden fishing boat tied up at the wharf, other Cuban fishermen, dock workers, and military personnel were already standing huddled here and there, pointing and talking quietly. A coastal patrol boat had met the fishing boat offshore, as they frequently did, got some fresh fish from the crew, as they always did, and were told of the incredible rescue of the injured man.

The crew of the patrol boat had contacted the Captain of the port, and now he and the flotilla commandante stood on the dock, watching as the fishing boat captain made sure his boat was secure before climbing ashore to report to them.

They listened to his story, and then they reviewed with him his decision-making process. They offered no sign as to whether or not the captain had done the right thing by rescuing the man. After they had spoken with the captain, the flotilla commandante and the captain of the port waved him away and spoke in low but rapid tones with each other.

"This is, I think, a military problem."

"No . . . I think it is more something for our esteemed intelligence service."

"He needs to be hospitalized, and guarded."

"Yes, but he cannot be the responsibility of the port."

"Well, he's not a flotilla matter, either."

"Let's give him over to our brothers in the *Policia Nacional*. They can take him to the nearby prison, where I'm sure there is an adequate infirmary. Then he will be held in state custody, and those in the *Policia* will surely advise their brothers in the intelligence service . . . and then on up the line."

"Yes. That way we will have done what is necessary. We can both advise our superiors, and *they* can send it on up the line . . . as far as *they* think necessary."

"Yes."

Ted's body was then wrapped from head to toe in rough blankets. A towel was wrapped around his head, almost covering his face. He was carried from the bunk in the forward part of the boat out onto the open aft deck. He lay there, barely conscious, aware only of the bright morning sun, and the pain. He was aware of men speaking all around him, speaking in a rapid, guttural way, but he could not understand them.

He was lifted off the boat and placed on a stretcher that lay on the wet concrete of the dock. Soon a small convoy of two cars and two covered military-style trucks arrived. Armed, uniformed men piled out of the trucks, glaring at everyone and feigning disinterest at the body laying on the stretcher.

The men who climbed out of the cars huddled around the captain of the port and the flotilla commandante while questions and answers were fired back and forth, with many hand gestures and shoulder shrugging included. Finally one of the men held up his hand and gestured for silence. He looked at the figure on the stretcher, gave a quick nod of his head, and turned to walk back to his car. With this, orders were given, and several of the armed men shouldered their weapons, grabbed the stretcher, and loaded it into the back of one of the trucks.

The captain of the port and the flotilla commandante watched only briefly as the small convoy sped away, across the docks, through the warehouse area, up the hill, and out of sight around the first curve. Then they nodded to each other and briskly walked away, back to their respective offices to start making phone calls.

The captain of the small fishing boat had watched the convoy leave, and as he saw the last car disappear he turned back to his boat. There was still work to be done. He had not been told he would be detained; in fact, he had not been told anything at all. He knew very well that they could find him if they wanted him. He jumped aboard his boat and left.

Ted was not sure how far he traveled in the back of the truck. He could see only the canvas roof and two dark sweaty faces staring down at him and the tip of the barrel of a weapon. The ride was rough and he was hot, and every time the truck hit a bump a searing pain shot through his right leg and side. He passed out.

He came to while being carried, still on the stretcher, across some kind of open courtyard, then into a building and down a rough plastered hallway. He was aware of people staring at him, and he felt fear, not sure if it was his, or theirs.

He was taken into a room, and his senses were assaulted with many distantly familiar smells, smells that made him uncomfortable. He was pulled from the stretcher and onto a bed, roughly, and the blankets he was wrapped in were pulled off him. He lay naked and shivering until he became aware of a man in a white smock hovering over him. The man said something rapidly to someone else in the room, and then touched Ted's right leg. Ted passed out again.

Later, when he awoke, Ted found that if he didn't move his head, just his eyes, he could look around somewhat without causing himself too much pain. He was able to see drab plaster walls, painted in two-tone green. He noticed some type of I.V. bottles hanging by the side of his bed, apparently attached to his arms. The ceiling seemed to be very high, and hanging from it was an old wooden fan. High up on one wall was a window covered with iron bars.

Suddenly Ted was consumed with an intense wave of pain, which caused him to clench his teeth and close his eyes. At the same time his senses were lifted to a super-sensitive level, and he became a conduit for feelings that made up the atmosphere of his room, and of the rooms beyond, and of the whole complex of buildings where he was being held.

He felt fear, and anguish, and pain, and anger.

He felt frustration, and impotence, and sinister energies.

He felt despair . . . and yet he also felt hope.

· EIGHT

The day after the seizure of the *Sausea Girl*, the remains of Arnie went public.

On the north seawall of Port Everglades, behind a row of expensive homes, a small beach had been formed over the years by the circular tides in the turning basin. The people who live close by consider the sandpit to be their own private beach and call the police when someone stops there by boat. Early in the morning after the *Sausea Girl* incident, retired Colonel James Cawdelle was taking his morning hike around the small beach. He was old and leathery tanned. He carried a walking stick and took long purposeful strides as he poked around at the flotsam and jetsam that were washed up on the sand. When he walked up to the remains of Arnie, he stopped. The retired colonel had seen a lot of death all around the world. After determining just exactly what it was he was looking at, he turned and strode purposely up the beach to the nearest telephone to call the police.

But first he stopped by the seawall and threw up his breakfast.

"Arnold Brukker . . . age twenty-six . . . local address, no prior arrest record, unemployed," said Lieutenant Tallert as he handed a printout to Richards. "And I already got a call from Scott Kelly. He says the link isn't as direct as it was with the Scarab, but he's pretty sure that *Sausea Girl*, and her load, are part of somethin' that clown Montilla has goin'." He pulled his glasses down from his forehead. "Looks like you may have kicked our boy Montilla right in the ass again."

Richards said nothing but followed the lieutenant down the hallway to the legal adviser's office. Outside, the lieutenant turned and said, "The major said for us to come down here as soon as I found you. I don't know what it's about. They probably just want to pat you on the ass a little for the job you did."

They walked into the office, and when the secretary closed the door behind them Richards knew that whatever was going to happen he wasn't going to like it. As they walked in the major said simply, "Tallert, Richards, sit down, please."

Also in the room with the major were Tallert's, and subsequently Richards's, captain—a vain, stuffy man—and the fat little red-faced lieutenant who sometimes assisted the major on special projects. J.B. remembered that the fat lieutenant had ridden to the dock on *Sausea Girl*. Richards saw that the legal adviser, a real Ivy League type wearing a pin-striped suit, had given up his seat behind his huge desk to the major. He was sitting in a stiff-backed chair beside the captain and the lieutenant. The three of them were directly across from where Tallert and Richards sat down.

The legal adviser, Harper, shuffled a huge pile of papers on his lap. The captain, Fransetti, flicked some dust off his glossy shoe with a handkerchief and studied Richards coolly. The fat lieutenant, Whitney, was fidgeting around in his chair and positively beaming. J.B. could see the little beads of sweat on the man's brow as he puckered up his fat little face into what J.B. supposed was intended to be a copy of the major's dour expression. Jesus, thought Richards.

"Lieutenant Tallert," began the major, "we've got a couple of things we need to speak to Officer Richards about. First, is there any further word on the whereabouts of Officer Novak?"

J.B. just shook his head, and Tallert said, "No, sir. His apartment's been checked, and everything appeared to be in order there. He apparently left no message with any friends, and none with his office."

The major nodded. "All right. I understand that Officer Richards is the closest thing that Novak has to family in this area. So we would expect to hear immediately if he makes any contact with you."

Richards nodded. The major went on. "Also, so far we've managed to just keep this in-house and low-key. We have, this morning, put out a quiet lookout order for Novak statewide. The media doesn't have it yet, and for now Novak is just AWOL." He paused. "The narcotics unit is apparently running a pretty loose shop right now, and no one there can seem to pinpoint exactly what cases Novak was working on. Of course, he was new. Just get us the word if you hear anything from the home angle, all right?"

Before J.B. could respond, the fat lieutenant, Whitney, coughed and said, "Well, sir. It looks to me like Novak just took off somewhere. Probably off chasing some nookie down in the Keys or something, now that he's been assigned as a super narc and all."

No one said anything, and J.B. remembered that the troops on the street called Whitney "Lieutenant Witless," and he almost grinned when he remembered that the harbor patrol police aide, Liz Fox, told him most of the female officers called him Lieutenant Waddles.

The major started again. "We also need to discuss this *Sausea Girl* incident, and since you authorized Richards to break away from his normal duties, Lieutenant Tallert, I thought you should be here too. Some problems have come up. Mister Harper will explain further. Before we begin I just want you to know, Jed," he said familiarly, loosening up a little, "that I know Richards was just doing his job."

J.B. didn't like the sound of that. "But you know in the long run we have to try to protect the best interests of the city here."

Richards saw Tallert nod his head, sit back, cross one shiny boot over the other knee, and lay his head back against the wall. Whitney had puffed himself up to his full pudgy self when the major mentioned the "interests of the city," and he sat there now, looking at Richards sternly.

"Mister Harper, why don't you give Lieutenant Tallert a brief picture of what we've got here," finished the major. Then he too leaned back in his chair, unwrapped a cigar, and began playing with it.

"Yessir," said Harper. He placed the pile of papers on the floor, put his hands thumbs down into his vest pockets, and said, "Basically, what we have here is an agent of the city, Richards, operating city equipment—the police boat —out of the city's jurisdiction . . . illegally detaining a vessel with its two occupants, participating in the possibly accidental death of one of those occupants, illegally boarding said vessel, making an illegal search and seizure of the allegedly contraband material."

Richards had already heard enough and was just straightening up, preparing to hurl himself up out of his seat to protest when he felt the firm hand of Tallert on his arm. He sat back, not believing what he was hearing.

". . . and just generally ruining what could have been a darn nice grab." Harper bent down to pull a paper from the pile on the floor and Richards saw that Fransetti was calmly studying his nails. Whitney was staring at Richards as if J.B. had just been accused of urinating on the state flag.

Tallert, taking off his glasses, said quietly, "I know you're gonna explain all of this to us, right?"

"Yessir," said Harper. "I would have a hard time in court giving the judge a valid reason for Richards to stop the yacht in the first place. Oh, I read his report—about the fish flags and all, but it's weak, believe me, it's weak. Then we have the fact that the city limits line runs right down the center of the port. The city of Fort Lauderdale has the north half and the city of Hollywood the south. You guys know that. The area where Richards showed the divers to look for the body was in the south half. You know that means that Richards had *no* enforcement powers there at all."

"Well, with all the excitement," said Tallert, "maybe J.B. just indicated he was a little south. Really hard to tell, I would think. I bet if we went out and looked again we'd find that ol' J.B. here was in the city limits after all. Besides, if J.B. was out of jurisdiction that means those boys panicked and ran from just another citizen . . . not an agent of the city." Tallert said all this leaning back with his eyes closed. The major was looking down at the cigar in his hands, smiling.

"It's not that simple, Lieutenant," answered Harper. Richards saw Whitney sit up with his hands on his hips. He gave his fat head a shake as if to agree, and turned to Harper to see what came next.

"Whether or not Richards was in or out of jurisdiction will only affect the criminal proceedings, not the civil suit. I've already been contacted by an attorney representing the family of the deceased, uh, Brukker. He stated the family intends to sue the city for the death of their son."

"Now wait a minute!" said Richards, standing up in spite of Tallert's grip on his arm. "That's a bunch of bullshit and you know it. That stupid asshole just panicked, that's all, and then *his partner* ran him over."

The major, who was standing also, spoke. "Hey . . . hey . . . J.B. Sit down please and let Mister Harper finish. We're all on your side." Reluctantly J.B. sat back down, furious. Whitney's red face was staring at him, but when he glared back Whitney turned away toward the major.

Harper, letting out a sigh to indicate to everyone just how difficult it was to communicate with laymen, said, "Look. What you feel about this and what you saw really happen doesn't matter. What matters is that the family can and will sue the city and when they do their attorney will be able to show that if you hadn't illegally stopped the boat in the first place their son would not have been killed. That's all they have to show. Because you stopped the boat, the boy died."

With this J.B. leaned forward and put his head in his hands. He knew he wasn't responsible for that guy getting run over, he knew he was right in what he did. He just couldn't believe it was all being twisted around so. The others in the room, misinterpreting his gesture, began fidgeting around. The major stood up and took off his jacket, Fransetti walked over and carefully poured himself a cup of coffee from Harper's private stock. Whitney leaned back with his short little arms folded across his round belly and looked at J.B. with a triumphant grin. Tallert still had his eyes closed.

Harper began again, a little quieter now. "I should tell you, of course, that it's in the city's best interests to do all it can to refute those allegations. You will be represented completely by my office and other attorneys for the city. Somewhere down the line we'll probably end it all with an out-of-court settlement, and that will be that."

"Why not just fight it out all the way, Harper?" asked Tallert. "We all know that J.B. here was just doing his job, and I'm not so sure a judge would go along with everything you're saying if he heard the whole story. First of all, whoever comes forward to be the witness to the fact that the kid was even on that boat is gonna be indicted for conspiracy to smuggle, and second, I think the fact that the boat was loaded with grass is gonna have some impact on the court's mind."

Harper started to speak, but before he could do so, Whitney, feeling strong because he was obviously on the winning side, said brusquely, "C'mon, Tallert. Quit tryin' to get the heat off Richards. We can all see clearly that he fucked up and he's gonna cost us all, the city that is, a lot of money. Now *we* have to bail *him* out of a jam."

Richards thought seriously of getting up and punching that fat red face right back through the wall but Tallert, reading his mind, increased pressure on his arm and just shook his head.

"Uhem . . . yes, yes . . ." coughed the major. "Let's not get carried away, Lieutenant Whitney. We all have a problem here and we'll all work together to solve it, okay?" Whitney settled back into his seat, flushed.

Harper, irritated by all of the interruptions, began pacing up and down the room, looking at his watch. "Gentlemen, look, you all know that there is nothing simple about your job anymore. There is no right or wrong, there are no good guys or bad guys, there is just the law—or I should say there is just the court. Instead of thinking in terms of good grabs, you should be thinking in terms of staying clean in court. Doing things just because they are right is so . . . so . . . gauche."

"Mister Harper," said the major, "please don't lecture us. Just tell us where we stand now so we can get on with it."

"Yessir. Sorry, sir . . . I'm just trying to educate Officer Richards a little," replied Harper, vexed. Then he went on quickly. "What we have now is a potential lawsuit against the city, which I think will end with us paying out a hefty sum, no one under arrest, because Richards let the operator of the yacht escape, and a big pile of marijuana that will have to be destroyed at our expense."

Captain Fransetti spoke for the first time, thinking that what he would say could not be challenged and he would appear to be right on top of things as usual. "Well, at least we have a several hundred thousand dollar yacht in our possession that the city can auction off and make a few bucks on."

Richards watched Whitney's fat face shake in agreement as Harper spoke again.

"Not quite."

With this everyone stared at him, the major leaning forward intently, and Tallert sitting up and putting on his glasses.

"If a representative from a corporation claims the yacht, and an attorney will probably come out of the woodwork to do just that soon, we will not only have to return it to them because we cannot link it in any way with any *person* from that corporation . . . we will also be responsible for any damages or theft that occur while it is in storage."

Richards sat back now, deflated. Everyone else was exasperated except Whitney, who sat there looking as if he knew it all along.

"So really, gentlemen, there it is. You know my office is here to assist you in any way, and I'll be doing my best to make sure we come out all right on this. But we will all have to work hard to make sure we don't have these problems in the future." Harper bent down, picked up all his papers from the floor and stood there, waiting for the meeting to end.

As Fransetti stood up and studied himself in the reflection from the glass painting on the wall, Whitney said, "Yeah, Tallert . . . you really should try to keep a line on some of these patrolmen of yours when you break 'em loose from their regular duties." With that he stood up also and looked at the major, seeking support.

The major looked perplexed as he said, "I'm sure Jed knows how to take care of his people, Whitney. Any warnings along that line will come from me anyway, right?" Whitney looked down at the floor, his face red. "Anyway, Jed," continued the major, "have Richards here ease off a little on these boat grabs until we get on firm footing with what we can and cannot do." He jerked his upraised thumb toward the ceiling and said, "You know the boss is very concerned about this, and the situation with Novak. He wants to make sure we don't get jammed up in the future. We're not gonna pull J.B. from active duty or anything, we just expect him to lay low for a little while, okay?"

Tallert looked at Richards, then back at the major and said simply, "Yessir." Then they all turned and shuffled out of the office and down the hallway in different directions.

As Whitney walked away with Fransetti, he said loudly, "See, here's a perfect example of letting some patrolman take on too much responsibility without proper leadership."

Fransetti said nothing. Richards stopped and stared after the fat lieutenant as he waddled away. Tallert came back and stood beside him for a moment. Then, as he turned to walk back to his own office, Tallert said quietly, "What an asshole."

J.B. followed along behind him, agreeing totally.

Back in Tallert's office, Richards sat down heavily as Tallert took off his glasses and rubbed his eyes for a moment. "Look, J.B., you know you did good. You know it and I know it—so just keep on and don't let it get to ya."

"What about my orders to lay low?"

"Okay. So you just take it easy for a week or so. It'll blow over like it always does. Just go back out there and do your job, that's all you can do. I don't expect you to set the world on fire, but I don't want you to crawl into a hole either."

"Okay, Lieutenant, and thanks." He got up and walked slowly out of the office and down the hallway. He left the building and climbed into his old pickup truck and headed back toward the harbor docks. His mind was a jumble of mixed thoughts and emotions, and he had a splitting headache.

As Skids Bedlam would say, he felt like hammered shit.

In the quiet, tree-filled residential section south of Davie Boulevard and west of the New River where it curves to the south is a small elementary school. Behind the school stands a giant old oak tree. Its huge limbs created a cool cavern of shade that turned into a shadow cave in the early evening. Under the oak tree sat two cars. School was closed so there was no one else in the area. One of the cars, a solid black BMW with black smoked windows and fine gold pinstriping, was backed against the base of the old tree. It had Dade County tags, and a check would have revealed that it was registered to a Hispanic female with an apartment address. A closer check would have revealed that the female didn't exist, nor did the apartment. The other car was a red Thunderbird, with New York tags. It had several other tags bolted to the brackets, but New York was showing now.

Sitting in the black BMW was Onyx Montilla. He wore his mirrored sunglasses despite the time of day, and his shirt was open to the waist. Several gold chains hung on his hairy chest. He sat in his car, slumped down in the driver's seat, and looked over the window edge at Lieutenant Billy Erricks, FLPD, Organization Crime Bureau, who was sitting in the T-bird. Erricks was wearing sunglasses too, the dark aviator kind. He wore a shirt and a sport jacket. Montilla could not see his trousers but guessed he was wearing jeans as usual, with black Wellington boots. Montilla was tense, angry. Erricks was nervous.

Erricks was beginning to question the wisdom of this liaison with Montilla, and that of this involved affair. Erricks had not been a narc during the crazy days of the seventies. He had worked in regular patrol and then administrative duties, quietly working toward promotion, steadily advancing his career. He was one of those police officers who managed to avoid spending much time out there doing his job on the front line level but was always assigned to some peripheral post. He had been assigned to the narcs during the recent shake-up. A man of his rank was needed, and he was available. Besides, they really needed an administrator, not a street narc, and that's what he was. Having worked in Lauderdale during those crazy years, though, Erricks was well aware of all of the stories about narcotics smuggling and the money involved. He knew the ones about the ex-cops who hired themselves out to work for the smugglers in countersurveillance for big bucks, and about ex-cops who actually became big-time smugglers themselves.

By the time Lieutenant Billy Erricks was assigned to the narc job he was already divorced twice, with two children to support from the first marriage, and an incredible amount of bills from the second. Like most cops, he couldn't make ends meet without working details, extra time spent standing around malls or banks as a security guard, and he hated it. When he was assigned to the narcs Erricks was also bored. Bored and broke.

Having access to all the narcs files, he took his time and he searched until he found what he thought would help him out. He wanted someone who was involved in some kind of smuggling for the good bucks, but someone who, for whatever reason, was not real hot. In his search he had stumbled across the name of Montilla.

It had been an awkward courtship at first because Erricks was so obviously not streetwise. Maybe that's what made it work finally. He had spent several days following Montilla around, being highly visible so Montilla would know he was there. Then he had made his approach one evening while Montilla waited for a tire to be changed on his BMW. A meeting had been arranged and it was then that Erricks made his pitch. He would work countersurveillance for Montilla from his vantage point in the narc unit for a percentage of the loads that made it in. Otherwise, he threatened, he could use his info to send the hounds after Montilla. He had guessed that because Montilla was running grass instead of coke Montilla would be more interested in his services, not because of the money involved, but because of the sheer logistics of boats and houses and people. He had also based some hopes on the old stories of how the grass runners were just businessmen, mellow . . . not crazy like coke freaks.

Montilla had told him where he could stick those threats, and there had been a tense moment before he had grinned at the cop and said, "Sure . . . maybe we can work something out."

Now, sitting under the huge old oak tree, Erricks was wondering if the money was going to be worth it. His stomach was already in knots, and during the day he had had a flash while at work that had caused an instant headache. He and Montilla had only recently come to terms, so he didn't know for sure, but he had to ask himself if there was any connection between Montilla and that new narc, Novak. Erricks didn't know, and just the thought of it filled him with dread. He was in this for the money and the kicks, not to play hardball, especially at the expense of another cop.

"So what's goin' on, Erricks? I thought we had an agreement."

"We do, we do. It's just that this is off-the-wall shit. I

had no idea this was going to happen. I mean, who would have guessed?"

"Nobody's supposed to guess, Erricks. You're supposed to know. And you're supposed to take care of it when you find out, right? I mean . . . I am paying you for something, ain't I?"

"Yeah, Onyx, yeah . . . you're payin' me to cover for you, I know. But shit, this is something some lieutenant put together all by himself. Then he puts some broken-down old patrolman out there in a marked boat and he starts makin' busts. So he got lucky once."

"Twice."

"Okay, twice. But hell, you know my division is the only group set up to work against narcotics activities in the area. How do you think I've been able to keep a handle on things?"

"Well, you've got to do something about this asshole water cop. The guy's already cost me a lot of money."

"You know you're going to get that yacht back."

"Yeah, that's what my new attorney says."

"And you know I'm real sorry about that new kid you had working for you."

"Hey . . . fuck him. Those guys didn't work for me direct anyway. I guess that's what I get for subbing some of this stuff out. The boat's not directly hooked to me either, which is why I should be able to get it back. But that's not what's worrying me, señor. It's the loads I keep losing. It's costing me money, and it angers me. If I quit then you get no more golden eggs, right?"

"Yeah."

"And if I'm busted, you know you're going down with me, don't you?"

"Yeah."

"Okay, then. Use your administrative powers, or your ear of the chief, and get this loco pulled off the boats. Whatever you have to do . . . do it. I have enough shit to worry about without some cop tryin' to be the Lone Ranger out there in Port Everglades. *Sí?*"

"Okay, Onyx, I'll take care of it."

"Good. *Hasta luego.*"

NINE

Richards was sitting around in the U.S. Customs office, which was adjacent to the FLPD harbor patrol office. With him were Hank Zaden and his partner, Reggie Maguire. Zaden was tall and athletic while Maguire was thin, stooped, and pale. Zaden had women-killing dark good looks and piercing eyes; Maguire had a thin face, an uneven nose, large thick glasses, and brown kinky hair. The only similarity between the two was their intense desire to get a job done. Maybe Maguire didn't look as heroic as Zaden when they both boarded a suspect boat, but he wasn't afraid either. They both liked their work, and they went after it hard.

"My partner here says it's all a Communist conspiracy," said Zaden as he leaned back in his chair. "He says the Commies are poisoning the minds of the free people of the world with the killer weed and the nose candy, and when we're all stoned out of our gourds they're gonna waltz in here and take over the whole mess."

"That's right," responded Maguire, with his feet straight up above him on his desk. "We're gonna have coke in our breakfast cereal, in our ice cream, in our air-conditioning systems ... everywhere!" He swung his feet down and straddled his chair, facing Richards. "You know how those trucks come by spraying the bugs ... I'll bet they're sprinkling the magic powder as they do! We're talkin' the Grim Reaper in drag, okay? Dressed up like Tinkerbell! Somethin's goin' on in this country. There just ain't no way that much nose candy is being consumed by our citizens. You've heard the numbers, a half ton of cocaine here, fifteen hundred pounds there, and those are just some seizures! We only stop a tiny fraction of what comes in, okay?" He pushed his glasses up on his nose, a grin on his face. "So who's using all that coke? Or look at it this way —how many American nostrils have to be packed every day to keep up with it all? Huh? See what I mean?"

"I see that you're baked," said Zaden with a laugh. "You know it's just good old supply and demand. The people in this country demand the crap, and the dirt balls in the South supply it, gladly, with huge gold-filled smiles on their greasy faces."

Maguire spun a full circle on his chair, pointed at Zaden, and in his newscaster's voice said, "Earlier today it was reported that millions of blood vessels and brain cells were being systematically burned out, actually fried if you will, by the introduction of a poisonous dust that costs an arm and a leg, and appears to be one of the ultimate stupidities! Film at eleven!"

"Yeah!" said Zaden.

"Well listen, guys," said Richards, "we're the front lines, right? We're the blue soldiers in the drug war . . . you've heard of the drug war, haven't you? The president's wife was just talking about it the other day."

"Absolutely correct, J.B." said Maguire solemnly. "I have heard of the drug war. The entire Caribbean basin is supposed to be involved, big money is being spent, and by gosh, intrepid warriors like you and me and my Adonis-like partner are expected to hurl ourselves on any mood-altering hand grenades we come across."

"Sheesh," said Zaden.

Richards looked at Zaden and asked, "Say, Hank, has your partner been sticking his head into the evidence locker again? He seems to be operating without both paddles in the water."

Zaden nodded. "Yeah, it's a sad thing. But it's only since he's been working here in Lauderdale. Before that he was only whacko. Since he's been here, surrounded by this money-drugs-freedom-sincerity charade, he's really spaced out into the ozone layer."

"Sure, another nonbeliever!"

"I think the bad guys have gotten to his brain," said

Richards. "He's finally fallen victim to the insidious, dreaded assholes."

"That's right!" yelled Maguire. "They've finally caught up with the Prince of Justice and subjected him to unspeakable horrors. Say." He sat up now, his back against the wall, took off his glasses, and looked up at them. "Did I ever tell you guys about the time I had this lady out in Reno gargle my balls while she hummed Beethoven's ninth symphony?"

Both Richards and Zaden groaned, and as Richards put his head down on his folded arms Zaden threw his hat at his partner and rolled his eyes.

"What an absolute bonehead."

"Well, shit, man," said Richards, his voice muffled by his forearm, "he's your partner."

"Listen J.B.," said Zaden, a little quieter now, "my weird partner and I have been kinda waitin' to talk to you about something. Maybe we could get into it now—what d'ya think, Reg?"

Maguire put his glasses on, and nodded, his face serious.

Zaden hesitated, then asked, "J.B., what can you tell us about that narcotics unit you guys have over in the organized crime branch of FLPD?"

"Well, they've got a lieutenant and a couple of sergeants and some pretty good people over there. They're supposed to be the ones who work all the heavy narc activity in the city. You know we got a new chief not too long ago, so there were some changes made, and they're kind of unsettled right now."

"FLPD has always had a good reputation," said Zaden, "and you know that through the years our Customs guys have never had problems working together with your guys, but do you think they're squared away now?"

J.B. reflected a moment, not sure where the conversation was going. Then he said, "You guys have heard about our narc, Novak, who is missing, right?"

Both Customs men nodded affirmatively.

"There's a chance that he's been taken out, and before it

happened there seemed to be some loose work done, I mean, they didn't have their act together."

Maguire and Zaden looked at each other, and Maguire said, "Taken out? As in wasted? I thought he just went over the hill."

J.B. rubbed his face with his hands. "Yeah, that's what they've let it look like, but there's, uh, info to indicate something else may have occurred." He sat up straight. "Anyway, I guess you could say they need some time to tighten up, but overall they're a pretty good bunch."

Zaden fidgeted around a little and looked at his partner, who just shrugged. Then he said, "They've been acting kinda strange toward us recently, and we were wondering if something is going on that we need to know. I mean, if we did something wrong, or if they think we'll screw up one of their busts or somethin', then they should get with us and we could talk it over, ya know?"

"Yeah, but what do you mean? What are they doing exactly?"

"Well, like all of a sudden the information is only going one way. We get the word on some boat or a group working in the area and we send it out to everybody. I mean we're all after the same assholes, right? So anyway, lately it's been drying up from the FLPD side. We don't get anything good from your office anymore, or it's old shit or somethin' the whole world knows about. Not only that." He was leaning forward now, intense. "We aren't really sure, but we think there might be a leak somewhere." He stopped and just looked at J.B., who looked back and whistled softly.

"Yeah, J.B.," said Maguire, "maybe it's just a couple of wild coincidences, but we've had a couple of sure-thing traps all lined up and then they just evaporated. Twice now I've had a real good informant give me boat names and estimated arrival times. And when we passed the info on to FLPD, like we always do, we wind up sitting up all night only to find out the damned boats turned around *for no reason*, according to the informant, and went back to the islands. I mean, what the fuck?"

Richards didn't say anything at first. He just sat there

thinking about it. He knew he wasn't real popular right now with the guys over at OCB, but he figured it was just interunit rivalry because he had lucked into a couple of good busts and got some headlines. But he wasn't sure, and he didn't like the sound of this at all.

Maguire stood up and straightened out his uniform. As he buckled on his gun belt, he said, "We know this is real sensitive, serious stuff. For now, why don't the three of us here just keep it to ourselves. We are a federal unit anyway, so we sure as hell don't want to get involved in some local department's internal investigation. You know that Hank and I have worked with you now for a couple of years. We trust you, so we're gonna keep on trading info with you and we'd appreciate it if you'd do the same with us. We'll be really selective about what we give your narc unit, and see what develops. Who knows, maybe we're just being silly. . ." He turned and flapped his wrist at Zaden, saying, "You big silly," then went on. "But we feel like somethin' ain't working like it should, so we're gonna go slow for a while, see?"

Richards looked at Zaden, who was studying him intently. He knew these men. He knew they were straight and he knew they must have agonized over whether or not to let him in on their suspicions. He nodded and said quietly, "You guys know Scott Kelly, right?"

Zaden grinned, and said, "Hell, yes. He was good. Too bad he had to get shot up like that. He was the best narc FLPD ever had."

"Right, and he's back—just easin' his way back into the mainstream again." J.B. looked at them both, and made a decision. He told the Customs men everything Kelly had told him about Ted Novak and a guy named Montilla. When he was done the room was very quiet for a long time.

Then Zaden stood up and stretched, his fingertips almost brushing the ceiling. He strapped on his gun belt, and said quietly, "I'm glad Kelly's back on the job. We'll talk to him like we'll talk to you. About the Novak thing." He paused, his face tight. "If it happened like he says, then somewhere along the line this dude Montilla is gonna have to get religion."

J.B. got his gear, held up the keys to his boat, and said, "Hey, let's go fight some crime and/or evil."

As they walked out the backdoor, headed for the docks, Maguire said, "I had a crime and/or evil once, but I traded it in for a VW."

They had an uneventful night. Richards drove the police boat slowly up and down the Intracoastal Waterway while they talked and swapped war stories. It was just before midnight when they tied up the boat and headed for their cars to go home. As they walked across the parking lot, Maguire raised his arms to the sky and intoned, "O goddess of love and poontang, please see fit in your wondrous and pink heart to locate a sensuous, sensual, and basically horny female companion for this puny but dedicated fan of yours. I beg you, don't make me take matters into my own hand again tonight."

Ted knew he was drugged, he knew he was still in pain in spite of the drugs, and he knew he was being watched. During one period of consciousness he had recognized the smells that had assaulted his senses earlier. He was in a hospital, or some type of infirmary. During that time he realized he was being bathed, and he was swept away by the cool caress.

Now it was morning, or he thought it was morning; the light had that early, washed-out look to it. He was still in the small room with the green walls, and he was covered with a clean sheet. He still had I.V. bottles beside his bed, with the tubes in his arms. He felt very weak, and if he moved his right leg at all, pain shot through him. He lay there, listening to the sounds around him.

Three men came into the room, one dressed as a doctor, in a smock, with a stethoscope around his neck. The doctor stood beside him, lay his hand on his forehead, and grunted. His face was not kind. Ted watched as the doctor moved to the right side of the bed, and lifted the sheet away from his leg. The other two men leaned forward to see; the doctor grunted again, then let the sheet drop. One of the other two men was in some kind of uniform. He was short and squat and very dark, and his uniform did not fit him well. He said something to the doctor, who answered curtly and then walked out of the room. The man in uniform stared at Ted for a moment, and then turned and spoke at length with the other man.

Ted realized they were speaking Spanish. It was rapid, guttural Spanish, like the Spanish he heard on the streets of Miami. He realized that they were Cubans... and he wasn't in Miami. His Spanish was elementary, and he could pick out only a few words. He understood the United States. He knew *malo* meant bad. *Problema* was exactly that, but he had trouble with *arriesgado*. The conversation had to do with him, he knew, and he felt the two men were discussing a location, but he couldn't tell if they were speaking of where he was, or where they might take him. The short heavy man in uniform did most of the talking, and it seemed to Ted that the man's eyes lit up every time he said, *La Cabaña* or *Isla de Piños*.

Isla de Piños? Ted closed his eyes and tried to think of why he knew what that place was. The man in uniform used *acá* when he said it. Here? Ted's head started to swim, and he closed his eyes, knowing it was important to stay aware of what was going on. He heard the two men speaking, arguing? He heard *muy importante* and *valor grande*. He opened his eyes and looked at the two men again.

The one standing beside the stocky man in uniform was trim and fit. His simple suit was neat and clean. His lean face and black hair and piercing eyes had a distinct Latin flair, and his quick mannerisms and sure confidence showed power. The man saw Ted's eyes on him and slowly held up one hand as he stared at Ted. The other man sputtered to a stop. The lean one came closer to the bed, and still watching Ted closely, said in a strong but quiet voice, *"Señor, está usted un regalo, o está usted un caballo de Troy?"*

Ted looked into the man's eyes, then slowly shook his head. Why was he asking him if he was a Trojan horse?

The man turned toward the man in uniform, shrugged,

and motioned to the door. The left without speaking further.

Ted stared up at the ceiling, his head pounding. He was alive, in Cuba, and they were arguing over what to do with him. *Great,* he thought, *I don't even know enough Spanish to order a meal. I can't even get out of bed, let alone walk out of here, and if I did get out, where would I go?*

He closed his eyes. First things first, he thought. He knew he would need to get back in shape, then when his strength was up, he would start hollering for the State Department or somebody to rattle this cage.

Maximiliano walked behind the director of prisons, down the hallway, and out into the courtyard. He watched the squat body waddle along in front of him, detesting the man but respecting the poisonous danger he exuded. He felt the questions creeping into his mind again, and he fought to keep them at bay. The questions, he knew, would kill him. They would slow him down, make him hesitate, and then they would kill him. He watched the other man, the pompous uniform riding the pudgy body, and asked himself again if this is what all the years of fighting were for. Did this gross figure, sadistic and brutal, represent what he, Maximiliano, was too? Was this what they had all become?

He was startled when the other man stopped suddenly and turned on him, saying, "So. You think this is an American. You think this is an intelligence matter, and you think the American should be moved to one of your 'safe houses.' Well, I say to you, fine, when I have orders to release the man, if he is an American, then I will. You know as well as I that our leader is out of the country, showing support for the glorious revolutionary fighters in Nicaragua, and you also know that even though Raul is here and running things, a matter such as this cannot be decided by him." He put his small hands on his hips, squared his shoulders, and looked up at Maximiliano. "This man, who may be an American, has been brought here, *to me,* to be watched until a decision is made. I will not hurt him, now. I will make sure the doctor keeps treating his leg, and I will not let them begin any rehabilitation program yet. If he has great value, as you say, then our leader will tell me what to do with him. In the meantime, he stays under my care."

The director of prisons did not wait for a reply, but turned and walked away. He got into his Alfa Romeo and drove off, grinding the gears badly as he did so. Maximiliano watched him go, knowing the car was a gift to the man from Fidel Castro, given for his efficiency as a jailer.

Maximiliano walked slowly toward where his car and driver waited in a shady spot in the courtyard. So, he thought as he walked, Raul is running the country while Fidel is out slapping Ortega on the back, and we have to wait for a decision. And what will happen when Fidel really leaves us? Will Raul, first secretary of our Communist party and heir to the head of state, beseech heaven for answers to our questions then? Will he and Fidelito put their heads together and solve our problems? Will we be strong enough? Ah, our magnificent Fidel, did you think you would live forever when you created a government that is only you?

Maximiliano stopped beside his car, thinking about the wounded American lying in that tiny infirmary, watched over by a doctor more used to stitching together the bleeding products of the guards' enthusiasm than genuinely caring for a patient.

Can it be that the young man brought by a fishing boat is one of those he had heard about? A source on Bimini had detailed how the racing boat *Stiletto* had been seen in the area with four men aboard, yet when it returned there were only two. Could it be that the battered gringo lying in this jail is in fact one of the men that Montilla tried to kill? And if it is, he wondered if it could be used in some positive way for their cause.

He scuffed the toe of one shoe against the gravel in the courtyard and thought about Fidel's penchant for smuggling cocaine into America in order to use the money not only to help Cuba's staggering economy, but also for funding revolutionary fighters in other Latin countries. Maximiliano knew that the leader wanted him to use Cuban-Americans for this work. He found Montilla and recruited him. Now Montilla had stupidly decided to start killing people, and one of his intended victims had possibly washed ashore. He stretched out his arms, and then cracked his knuckles and said quietly before climbing into the car as the driver started the engine, "This sounds like a series of events that Gabriel Garcia Marquez would absolutely love."

"What did you say, sir?" asked the driver, but Maximiliano did not hear him as he sat staring out the window of the car.

J.B. parked his pickup truck in front of the harbor patrol building, climbed out, and walked across the lot and up the steps to the front door. As he reached for the knob, the door was opened from the inside and the unit's police aide, Liz Fox, stepped out. She frowned.

Liz Fox had been a beach bunny at one time, a surfer girl, a girl who posed in bathing suits with oiled and muscular men at the beach. She had known all about "where the boys are" before it was a film. She knew sun-filled days and good music and good fun. That had been years ago, but she was still surfer-blond and tanned. She had been through marriages and childbirth a couple of times, and had seen good times and bad. It was kind of ironic that she had finally found a home with FLPD, but she accepted it without much thought, and she did her job with a pleasant smile. She was well liked by those who worked with her. As an aide, she didn't have arrest powers but could fill in for the officers doing auxiliary jobs. Most of her time was spent in the harbor office, acting as secretary to the sergeant.

J.B. saw her frown and cocked his head in question.

Liz pointed over her shoulder with one red-painted nail and whispered, "Two lieutenants to see you, J.B.—Erricks, and Witless, uh, Waddles, uh . . . Whitney." There was fun in her eyes as she said, "One's too fat and colors his hair, and the other's too nosy and smells like cheap cologne and fear."

J.B. laughed, and said, "Been reading spy novels again, Liz? Cheap cologne and fear?"

"Go in and see for yourself," she said, walking down the steps on her way to lunch. "They've been waiting for you."

He waved and went inside.

Erricks and Whitney were indeed waiting for him. There was no one else in the office. Whitney began by saying, "You come strolling in here at lunchtime, Richards? What do you do, make your own schedule?"

"Yeah," said J.B. evenly. "I make my own schedule."

"Don't get smart right off the bat, Richards."

"Look, Lieutenant Whitney, I've got a lieutenant of my own, and a sergeant too. Why do I have to get smart with you?"

Whitney started to speak again but was interrupted by Erricks. "Whoa, hold it a minute, you guys." He looked at Richards and said easily, "Look, J.B., this isn't official or anything. I wanted to come out and speak with you man to man, and Lieutenant Whitney wanted to come along for the ride, just to get out of the air-conditioning for a while."

J.B. just looked at him, so he went on. "I just wanted to talk with you about some of the extra stuff you been doin' out here lately. I mean, you've been doing a hell of a job and you've made a couple of real nice busts and all, but the problem is I'm afraid if you keep it up it's gonna cause some confusion."

J.B. went to his locker, opened it, and started taking out his gear. He remained silent as Erricks went on. "The thing is, J.B., you know my guys are out there working their asses off on these narcotics smuggling groups in the area. They're collectin' info and flippin' informants and developing leads and all that. It's really a very complex, complicated business, and it requires a lot of finesse. You can't just go charging around in a marked police boat stopping every yacht you see coming into port, like in the old days. While you're doing that you could inadvertently screw up a planned deal that we have going. See what I mean?"

"Well yeah, Lieutenant, but why don't you have your

guys tell me what they've got going so I'll know what not
to mess with?"

"Hey, J.B., you know that sounds good, but there's
really no way we could keep you posted on everything we
have going on over there. Besides, you know how jealous
narcs are of their info, right?" With this he came up with a
little grin and hit Richards lightly on the arm. "So how
about it? Kinda leave things alone out there and let our
guys do their job. One other thing. If you come onto something and want to hit it, or if you think it's hot, or loaded,
or whatever, just get ahold of me. Really, I don't care what
time it is or anything. You think you got somethin' going
down, give me a call, okay? Here . . . here's my card, and
my home phone number's on the back. We're all on the
same team around here, J.B., right?"

His grin faded as J.B. took the card and asked, "What
team was Ted Novak on? Narcs can be jealous of their
info, but not care about a new guy, right?"

"That has nothing to do with this conversation, Richards," said Whitney importantly. "We all know that Novak
is . . ."

"Novak is missing," interrupted Erricks. He looked at
J.B., and J.B. could see real concern in his eyes. "You're
right to be angry about the Novak thing, J.B. I can only tell
you that I had nothing to do with that whole deal, and that,
yes, it *was* sloppy." He paused, and J.B. remembered what
Liz had said about cheap cologne and fear. "Anyway, J.B.,
let's keep working together on all of this, okay?"

Richards just looked at him, and as he turned to go
Whitney spoke up again. "And another thing, Richards.
Just because you have Tallert standing behind you doesn't
mean you can run your job like this is some kind of Club
Med, got it? Try to get here in the morning like all the rest
of us working cops."

Both lieutenants turned and left, leaving J.B. standing
there with his jaw clenched and his big fists bunched.

Hank Zaden opened the door adjoining the FLPD office
and the U.S. Customs office and asked, "What was that all
about, J.B.?"

Richards crumpled the business card in his hand. "That

was our friend Lieutenant Erricks from the narcotics division. He was just very politely asking me to leave the smugglers alone."

J.B. was loading his gear, letting his police boat warm up, when he turned to see Marine Patrolman Mike Kendall walking out onto the dock with a grin on his face and a coffee cup in one hand, an oily rag in the other. The man wore an FLPD jumpsuit with cloth FLPD insignia on the shoulders and a cloth badge on the breasts. The jumpsuit was spotted with grease, as were the man's arms. His sandy hair was in disarray and the laces on one worn boat shoe were untied. He looked more like a marine mechanic than a cop, and he seemed to be happiest when digging deeply inside the bowels of some ailing engine.

Kendall said, "Hey, J.B., saw you had visitors . . . didn't know you hung out with the brass." He took a sip from his coffee cup.

Richards looked at the cup. It was one of those made with a clear plastic sleeve that can be taken off. Kendall had removed it and had pasted a colorful collage of bits of photos from girlie magazines onto the cup. Then he had replaced the sleeve. Richards looked at the grease on Kendall and said, "Into the mechanics again, Mike? They should pay you double, or call you 'Officer Goodwrench.'"

"Ah . . . starter went out on number three. If we wait for the city to approve a work order, it'll never get done. I'm done now, and Sarge said I could have some time off in the morning, do some fishing."

Kendall was a very serious and talented blue-water fisherman, J.B. knew, so he said now, pointing to the cup with a grin, "Well Mike, which is more important—fishing the Stream or diving into some of that stuff you've got pasted all over your famous coffee cup?"

Kendall looked at the cup, shrugged, and said, "Gee, J.B., that's a tough one to answer. Either way, you get some on ya, and you come home smelling the same way."

Kendall decided to ride with J.B. over to the coast guard station to have a cup of coffee and talk with some of the mechanic-type coasties about swapping some noncritical engine parts. He wiped his hands with a clean rag, saw Liz Fox out on the back porch of the office, went to her, handed her the cup, grinned, and joined J.B. in the police boat. They waved as they idled off.

Liz stood there watching them go, holding the coffee cup between two fingers as if it were a dead frog.

TEN

The morning was quiet, and the light from the early sun was still soft. There was very little breeze, and the sky was completely clear. Small birds darted and flew around the citrus trees in the fenced yard at the back of the Richards house, adding color and movement to the scene.

J.B. sat at the kitchen table, sipping coffee, waiting for his daughter Kathleen to come out of her bedroom. Erin and Ricky were already off to school and his wife, Jane, was in the shower. Scattered around his feet, in various poses of totally contented repose, were four small dogs. The black one and the white one looked like poodles. They had been around the longest. The black one was a crazy mix that hid in terror when it thundered. The cinnamon dish mop that looked as if it had been chasing parked cars was the newest addition. J.B. wasn't sure how he came to own four ankle-biters at once, but there they were, and he had to admit it was quite the spectacle when the doorbell rang and all four started yapping and digging for traction on the tile floor. He absently rubbed the white one with his bare foot, and waited.

Kathleen came out of the bedroom brushing her long hair. She wore a skirt with white buttons on one side, and a fuzzy pink sweater. J.B. looked at her and smiled. She was so fresh, and healthy, and lovely. He saw again how the light appeared to be gone from her face, replaced by a creased brow of worry. It had been that way for a week now.

"Mornin', Dad . . . are you okay today?"

"Fine, Kathleen, just fine. And you? Sleep all right and everything?"

"Um . . . so-so, I guess."

He nodded and sipped his coffee. Then he said, "Well, you look great. I love that sweater on you."

She pulled at it, shrugged, and said, "I guess it's still too warm to be wearing a sweater, but I like it."

He watched as she went to the counter and mixed a glass of chocolate milk. She stood there, staring out the window, sipping the milk.

"How about letting me fix you a nice big breakfast, Kath . . . just what you need with your busy schedule. I'll do it up right, eggs—whatever you want."

She licked her upper lip, smiled, and said quietly, "Thanks, Dad, but I'm really not hungry this morning. I'll help you, though, if you want to make some for yourself."

"Nah. To tell you the truth I'm not so hungry either."

They were silent for a moment, looking at each other. Then he rubbed one hand across his face, sighed, and said, "Kath, we need to talk about Ted."

She turned away then, put the cup down on the counter, and hugged herself. She nodded.

"It's almost certain at this point that Ted is gone, and we will never see him again. We have information that he's been . . . killed." He had agonized all night over how to say it to her, how to give her the news gently. There was just no way to soften it. He knew the daughter he raised deserved the truth, and it was not his nature to dance around a difficult subject. He cleared his throat and went on.

"Ted is like family to us all. Losing him is like losing an older brother for you, like losing a son for me. Adjusting to this will be terribly hard for all . . ."

She had turned and was staring at him with tears in her eyes.

He looked at her standing there, his daughter, and his

mind filled with a racing kaleidoscope of her as she looked to him through the years, toddling across the lawn, sitting on a bike, modeling a new dress. He saw her standing there now, a woman, and he had to turn away for a moment and stare into his coffee.

She came to him, stood behind him and wrapped her arms around his broad shoulders. She rested her chin on the top of his head and hugged him.

"Dad, go back to your sources and tell them they are wrong. Ted is not dead, and we *will* see him again."

"But Kathleen . . ."

"But nothing, Dad. I can feel it. I know what I'm talking about. Ted may be in some terrible trouble, I know. He's hurting, I think, but he's alive." She hugged him again. "Ask Mom, okay? She told me about how her feelings for you grew through the years. She told me about how she just *knows* sometimes when you're hurting, or scared."

J.B. reached up and rubbed her shoulders with his big hands. He sighed, a smoldering pain in his heart. He nodded, and said in a soft voice, "I understand that, Kathleen, but I also understand that terribly hard world Ted was out there working in. I don't want you to hold on to some faint hope that will just hurt you more in the long run."

She came around and stood beside him then, and smiled.

"You've been working in that same terrible world all these years, Dad—and Mom still has you. And you're right. Ted *is* family; he's my big brother and we've grown closer than ever in the last couple of years. I know you're hurting about what's happened to him. And that hurts me." She bit her lip. "Dad . . . he's alive, and we *will* see him again."

J.B. saw the simple faith in her eyes. "Okay. I shouldn't say this, but I will. *If*, somehow, Ted is alive, then I will do whatever it takes . . ." He paused. "*Whatever* it takes to get him home."

Kathleen smiled, hugged him again, and turned away. She grabbed her purse and car keys, slipping into her shoes at the same time. Then she looked at him with her eyes brimming with tears.

"I know, Dad."

And she left, quietly closing the door behind her.

J.B. sat there motionless, and the small white dog moved closer to his foot and rubbed herself softly against it. He didn't hear his wife come into the kitchen in her bare feet, but the next thing he knew she was standing beside him wrapped in a fluffy terry cloth robe, a large towel around her wet hair. She lay one soft hand on his shoulder, tilted her head, and said, "I listened in at the end."

He looked down into his coffee again. "You heard what she said about Ted being alive? My plan was to break the news of his death to her, and then be big and strong and comfort her. Instead." He shook his head. "Instead she gives *me* hope. She tells *me* that it ain't over until it's over."

He stood up suddenly, and walked from one end of the kitchen to the other, punching one big fist into the other. Then he turned to her and looked at his pretty wife, and softened. He came to her and held her tightly, rocking gently back and forth. His big hands rubbed her back, and she could feel his warmth, and his strength.

Two days later, on a late Sunday afternoon, it was hot, clear, and a little breezy. Richards had been out on the waterways most of the day and he was thinking about heading home. It had been the usual boating Sunday, with all the crazy antics happening up and down the waterways, the canals, and the ocean all along Lauderdale beach. He had stopped many boats with warnings, and had written some tickets.

Before heading for the docks he decided to take one more look at the port entrance. There was plenty of traffic as he made his way through the turning basin and headed east. He could see several big sportfishermen and sailboats passing by the jetties. He waved to the crowd on one of the drift boats as he idled by her port side. He knew the heavy traffic would keep up for several hours. They stay out on Sunday, especially on a day like this.

As he made a wide turn to head back, he saw the black and gray racer idling out by the first buoy. He recognized

Stiletto. From where he was he could see two people in the boat, and he felt his chest tighten. *Stiletto* was the boat that Scott Kelly had told him belonged to Montilla. J.B. thought it a funny coincidence that he started seeing this particular boat everywhere at just about the same time Ted was having trouble. He noticed that the other person in the boat was a female. There were two radio antennae standing out on the sleek hull, just in front of the windshield. He guessed they folded down flush with the deck when not in use. He watched as the racer drifted into the inlet with the incoming tide. Even though there was heavy traffic the operator made no attempt to clear out of the inlet. He just drifted along, making all the other boats move around him.

Richards hesitated, then decided to talk with the operator of the racing boat.

As he approached *Stiletto*, J.B. could see that the female was wearing a skimpy bikini, and that she was beautiful. The girl looked healthy, with an athletic body and lovely long hair. He took his eyes off her and saw that the operator, the same dark Latin male he had observed in the boat before, was concentrating on speaking into a radio mike he held in one hand. He saw the man's eyes widen at the sight of the police boat so close to him. Richards watched as the man hung up the mike and closed the cabin hatchway. He pulled alongside and said, "Afternoon, Captain, are you broken down?"

Montilla looked at Richards through his sunglasses, trying to read the name tag on the uniform shirt. He wondered if this was the saltwater cowboy who was causing him all the grief. He leaned back against the bolster seat and said, "No . . . no, I'm not officer, why?"

"Well, I'll tell you why. You're drifting along here right through the channel, and I've watched several boats alter their course so they could get around you. I figured there was just no way a competent boat operator would clog things up like that on purpose. So I thought you might be broken down."

Montilla's jaw tightened, and he looked at the girl, who just watched Richards coolly. Then he shook his head and said, "Yeah, I guess I just wasn't paying attention. You know, I was just talkin' with some of the fishing boats on the CB and I drifted into the channel without realizing it. I'll get out of the way now if you think I'm a hazard."

Richards felt his chest tightening as he watched the man. He reached for his notebook, opened it, and copied down the registration number on the bow. The girl and the operator of the boat watched him in silence. He felt a trickle of sweat at the small of his back, and said evenly, "I really should check your ownership papers, but why don't you just tell me your name? Are you the owner?"

Montilla's eyes narrowed behind the sunglasses. He was torn. Finally, he shrugged and said, "The boat is owned by a corporation . . . used for business-related entertainment." He paused, staring at Richards. "My name is Onyx Montilla."

J.B. caught his breath, and the two boats rocked together in the channel. Seagulls wheeled, pelicans glided by, other boats weaved in and out, and airplanes flew overhead. The two men stared at each other, both of them feeling a collision of energies.

J.B. looked at the girl, then back at Montilla. He wanted to reach out and grab the other man by the throat, he wanted to choke him and beat him and ask him, Did you do it? Did you do it to Ted? Instead he took a deep breath, and said, "Look. Clear out of the channel . . . now. That way I won't have to write you a citation."

Montilla, aware of the man's chilling animosity, said, "Okay, Officer . . . no problem."

As Richards eased his boat away from *Stiletto*, he muttered under his breath, "See ya, shit head."

As he watched the police boat move away Montilla muttered under his breath, "Fuck off, *puta*."

Richards pulled around the racer, pointed the police boat toward the range markers in the port, and gunned the engine. The boat surged forward, went up on a plane, and weaved its way smoothly through the traffic, heading home.

When J.B. slowed down to pass under the Causeway Bridge he happened to look over his shoulder, and as he did he saw the black and gray racer rounding the corner into the turning basin. His chest still ached from the encounter, and he realized that he was gripping the wheel tightly. Once under the bridge and headed for the Fifteenth Street canal and the harbor patrol office, he looked again and saw that the racer was just passing under the bridge behind him. As he pulled up to the police docks and tied her off, he looked out toward the Intracoastal Waterway and saw *Stiletto* slowly sliding by, northbound. He could see Montilla staring in his direction through the mirrored sunglasses, and he thought, Now . . . what the hell?

He climbed out of the boat, and on the way to the backdoor of the office he was again ambushed by Salty. He picked up the orange cat and held her in one arm while he gently stroked her head. He stood for a moment like that, then trudged up to the office, did some paperwork, looked around for Zaden and Maguire, couldn't find them, got in his truck, and went home.

When he arrived he saw that his wife's car was not there. He went into the living room and noticed there was only one stereo playing, and the TV was off too. With the general peace and quiet that permeated the house he guessed he was alone, except for the four dogs jumping around at his feet. It took him only a minute to find the note from his wife propped up against the fruit bowl on the table.

> *J.B., Kathleen went to the movies with a girl-friend. I took Erin and Ricky with me to the mall. I made stew, there's some in the oven for you . . . just heat it up. Don't know how late we'll be, may see a movie too, or go for ice cream. Wait till you hear what Ricky did today. Be good. Love, Jane.*

Rats, he thought. Stew. After all these years he could not understand why Jane would not believe he *hated* stew. He wondered what Ricky had done, but decided it couldn't be too bad, or Jane wouldn't take him to the movies. At least he was fairly sure she wouldn't.

He made some coffee and sat in his recliner and looked at the *TV Guide*. The list of programs was as exciting and fulfilling as the coverage of the Republican convention. He threw it down in disgust. He got up and walked around, coffee cup in hand. He stuck his head into the refrigerator, poked around, and came out empty. He went outside and watered the edge of the flower garden by the driveway.

He couldn't get Montilla off his mind. Damn, he had been standing only a couple of feet away.

He said to his dogs, who looked up at him in wonder and approval, "Listen, I'll just go back for a little while." Before he left he scribbled on the bottom of his wife's note: *Might be home late, J.B.* Then he grabbed his gear, got back into his truck, and headed for his office again.

Montilla had tied up his boat at Lauderdale Marina's fuel dock, walked quickly through the parking lot, and watched as Richards drove away from the harbor office, which was only a couple of hundred feet from the front gate of the marina. He waited ten minutes, then satisfied that Richards had gone home for the day, jumped back into *Stiletto* and roared back out into the port turning basin. Once there he put her in neutral and let her drift, waiting.

Now he adjusted the radio, grabbed the mike, and began transmitting on the upper sideband.

"Sunfish, Sunfish, Sunfish...this is Hammerhead. Over."

He got no response at first, and tried again. This time he heard strongly, "Go ahead there, Hammerhead, you got Sunfish here...kick it back." The voice was strong, but sounded distorted, like Donald Duck, as sometimes would happen on the upper sideband.

Montilla decided he could read him adequately so he said, "Yeah, Sunfish...are your friends near you, or standing by on the other channel?"

"Roger, roger, Hammerhead. We're all just sorta' waitin' for the word. Have you got it?"

"Yeah, Sunfish, this is Hammerhead. Everything here is ten-ten, I say again...everything is okay. You and your friends can come home anytime."

"Roger. I'll yell at everybody. Figure an hour at least. At least one hour, have you got that?"

"Yeah, Sunfish, I understand one hour. Shout at me when you get to the crossroads. I'll stay on this channel. Hammerhead clear."

"Roger. Sunfish clear."

As Richards crossed Cordova Road on Fifteenth Street, headed toward the office, he saw the dark blue pickup truck that belonged to U.S. Customs turn onto Fifteenth ahead of him. He could see Zaden driving, and he could see Maguire too, but instead of being in the cab with Zaden, Maguire was riding in the open bed of the pickup, with his hands on top of the cab roof. Richards followed along behind and watched as Maguire yelled, *"Hoooeeeee!"* and waved his arms and blew kisses every time they passed a girl walking or riding a bike alongside the street. Several of the girls smiled and waved back, causing Maguire to clasp his hands to his chest and swoon in the back of the truck. As they pulled into the office lot Maguire jumped out of the back of the truck and onto the hood of J.B.'s truck, yelling, "I'm in love! I'm in love!" Then he climbed down and circled around the parking lot, swooning some more.

Zaden stood beside Richards and said, "Have you ever seen such a total whacko in your entire life?"

J.B. watched for a minute, then laughed. "If I have, I can't remember when."

"So what the hell are you doing here so late in the day, J.B.? Thought you were here early this morning?"

Richards told him about the situation at home, about being restless, and about Montilla. "I don't know, Hank," he said as they climbed the outside stairs to the Customs office, "but somethin' just isn't right. I feel like somethin's goin' on, but I don't know what. I think I'll go back out and just ride around a little, just for the hell of it."

"Well, listen, J.B. Mind if my demented partner and I go with you? We just put the Magnum away for the night. Still having fuel problems with her. Can't get the RPMs we need."

"Glad to have the company," said Richards as they got their gear. They walked out the door of the office and met

Maguire at the top of the stairs. Zaden grabbed him by the arm, spun him around, and said, "C'mon, lover boy, we're going for a boat ride."

"Oh *my*," lisped Maguire, rolling his eyes and swishing his hips as he walked down the steps. "Just what I *love*, a domineering sailor type." Richards and Zaden just looked at each other and shook their heads.

Later that day, back at his house, Montilla reached behind Silky and pulled the string on the bikini top, untying it. Before it could fall away from her breasts the girl held her arms close to her body and asked, "What about the boats coming in, Onyx? Are you sure we should be back here at the house, instead of out on the water, looking?" She knew that she really didn't care about the boats, or the deal, she just had a thing about other people counting on her—or rather them, in this case. Montilla reached out, grabbed the front of the suit, and pulled it away, causing her full breasts to bounce slightly.

"You," he said, pointing his finger in her face, "you worry about doing what you know how to do best. Leave the boat business to me, understand? Believe me, I've done enough of these gigs to know that when they say 'just an hour' you may as well figure at least two, especially with those damn sailboats. I'll worry about the boats, and you worry about how happy I am. Because when I'm happy you eat all that good food and go to all those nice places and wear all those nice clothes and drive that sweet little Mercedes, *sí?* So just get your pretty little ass into the bedroom and get it ready for me. I'll be there in a minute, and because I like you in spite of your big mouth, maybe I'll let you do a couple of lines of toot with me."

Silky looked at the floor, with a small smile on her face, and then she walked quietly into the bedroom. Once there she stood beside the bed, and felt a chill run down her spine. Montilla was becoming more and more abusive, almost harsh, and she knew she wasn't the catalyst. It had to be the cocaine, or maybe he was just growing tired of having her as his toy. She stopped analyzing the situation, sighed, and peeled off her bikini bottom.

Montilla picked up the telephone, dialed a number, and said, "Kids are coming home. Anything going on?"

On the other end of the line, Lieutenant Billy Erricks, with more confidence than he felt, said, "No, no, it's real quiet. Everyone has gone home."

Montilla hung up the phone, smiled, and walked slowly into the bedroom.

As Richards pulled the police boat alongside the big sailboat all the people on deck started yelling and waving. It was obvious that they had been out on the water all day. Probably a dozen people aboard, all young guys and girls in bathing suits. Some were sleeping in the afternoon sun, and those in the cockpit were singing and toasting the police boat happily.

"Wouldn't ya know it," said Maguire. "They've been partying all day and didn't even invite us along. What a shame, they don't know what they've missed."

"I think they do, Reg," said Zaden. "That's why they're all so happy." As he said this, one of the girls leaning on the stern rail yelled and waved. She was a big blonde with a purple bikini. When she caught their attention she turned her back on them, pulled her suit bottom to her knees, and shot them a pretty pink moon.

"Oh *yeah!*" yelled Maguire. "Do it, do it! Shit, man . . . do you believe that? What am I doin' on this rollerskate when I could be over there, standing in her drawers?"

They all smiled and waved as Richards turned the boat and headed back out into the port. He idled out to the entrance, then put it in neutral and drifted near the south jetties. They were still talking about the blonde when the dispatcher called Richards and told him to switch to the records channel for an off-duty unit. Richards did so and found himself talking to Fat Harry.

"Marine Three . . . this is off-duty Marine Two."

"Go ahead, Harry. What are you doing on the radio?"

"Hey, J.B., I take this thing everywhere I go. Dedicated like you, right?"

"Right, Harry. Whatcha need, old man?"

"Listen, J.B., if you look almost due north right now,

and about twenty stories up, you'll see me on the balcony of my wonderful in-laws' condo."

Richards, Maguire, and Zaden all looked up, squinting, and sure enough, there was a tiny figure almost on the top-floor balcony, waving at them.

"Okay, Harry, we see you. And we are impressed. Didn't know you had such class."

"I don't; I married it. Anyway, I think I've got somethin' for you."

"Well, go ahead, wondrous obese one."

"Okay. I been watching all the boats from up here through my father-in-law's big telescope and there's four boats out there I think you should take a look at when they come in."

"Four?"

"Yeah, four. I know the grand days of the portable radar sets scanning these waters are gone now, so I'm doing the best I can here. I watched these four come over the horizon over an hour ago, then they just stopped and hung around for a while. Then they started up again and they're comin' in single file, in a big line, with about ten minutes between 'em. Two of 'em are stick boats and the other two are sportfishermen, but the fishermen are goin' slow like they don't want to outrun the blow boats. With me so far?"

"Yeah. Go ahead."

"I'll tell ya, J.B. I think they'd be worth checking out. It just don't look right. Like they're waitin' for the all clear, know what I mean?" Richards thought of Montilla, saw Zaden's grim expression and knew he was thinking the same thing, and said, "Okay, Harry. Tell us which ones they are, and we'll pick 'em off."

"Yeah, well, listen, J.B. I can keep a good eyeball on 'em from up here, and if anybody on their team was listenin' to a radio scanner they would have already heard this discussion and done a one-eighty, but they're still comin'. Why don't you guys ease on back inside the turning basin, around the corner, so you don't spook 'em. If they see you they'll just turn around and haul ass back outside."

Zaden was nodding his head at Richards, who said, "You got it, magnificent whale." He pushed the throttle forward, turning the boat toward the center of the port. He drove as fast as the boat would go, rounding the corner in a blur of spray, and idled back against the seawall. Then he put it into neutral and said to Zaden, "The way I see it, we're not gonna get any help out here today, so it's us against them, right?" Both Customs officers nodded. "Okay, then, I'll get up alongside the first one that comes in and put you guys aboard. If she's dirty you should be able to tell soon enough. While you're doing that I'll stop the next one myself. You guys can take yours to the docks by the office, and I'll call for some FLPD street units to assist us. Then I'll order the one I stop to tie up alongside the same dock and you can board her after you've finished with the first one. Maybe I'll even have time to turn right around and go back out for one of the remaining two. What do you think?"

"Yeah. Sounds good. Let's get at least two of 'em stopped anyway. We'll have to play the other two by ear, have your dispatcher contact the coasties or Hollywood PD or something. Hell, a bird in the hand as opposed to one in the bush and all that."

Maguire grinned then, and said, "Say, did I ever tell you guys about the time I had my hand in this girl's bush and she whistled 'Fiddler on the Roof' through my fingers?"

"Holy shit," said Richards.

"Christ on a bicycle," said Zaden.

"Way out of tune," said Maguire.

Silky tried, and almost succeeded, to let the immediate physical sensation of their lovemaking wash away all her other feelings. Sexually, Onyx aroused her, excited her, and was capable of pleasing her with his rough and insistent, often aggressive sharing of her body. He could be such a basic male animal, hard and hot and quick, and she liked the way his rough, hairy, and muscular chest felt against hers. She liked his strong and knowing fingers, his searching mouth, she liked his musky sweat, and the salty taste of him.

He was very strong, and when he felt like it, during the unselfish times, he could last a long, long time . . . staying unyielding for her as she pushed herself against him and climbed the plateaus over and over again.

He was dangerous too, and unpredictable sometimes, and she admitted it caused a quickening of her breath, and a heating and moistening. He could hurt her as they came together. He didn't, but she knew he understood she was aware of the possibility, and this somehow heightened her senses and gratification.

She tried to purge herself of any and all nagging thoughts now as she lay back, her neck arched, her eyes half-closed. The small of her back was couched in his strong hands, the inside of her knees brushed against his warm shoulders, her fingers pushed through his hair and against his ears as he tasted her, knowingly adding to her warm wetness. Her breathing was deep, and she said, "Uh-huh."

Suddenly, in one movement, he swept his lips up across her belly, ran his hands out from under her to her breasts, arched his back, and entered her smoothly. She gasped and locked her long legs around his hips, squeezing him, and matching his strong rhythm.

The phone rang almost a dozen times before Montilla rolled away from Silky, cursing, and picked it up.

"Something's wrong," said Erricks.

"How do you mean, 'something's wrong'? What's wrong?" growled Montilla as he sat up on the edge of the bed. Silky rolled away from him, sat up, and started brushing her hair.

"One of the marine units was on the air a couple of minutes ago. They're supposed to be all off duty by now."

"Well, what are they saying? Are they out on the water, or what?"

"I don't know. I was on the phone and all I heard was the dispatcher giving a message to one of the marine units, and he acknowledged it. But I didn't get what the message was. After I was able to get off the phone I checked all the channels but didn't hear anything else."

Montilla was quiet for a moment. Then he said, "Hell, I saw the only cop they had on the water go home almost an hour ago. Maybe they just had a phone call for him or something. I know your guys take their radios with them everywhere. Just keep listening. It's probably nothing, but call me if you hear anything else."

"Okay, I'll keep listening. I didn't mean to jump the gun but I just . . ." Montilla had already hung up. Silky got up and went into the bathroom and closed the door. Montilla sat there for a minute, thinking, then he stood up and began getting dressed. "Hurry up in there, *chica*. We're going back out onto the water. Maybe that squirrel really did hear something."

There was perhaps an hour of daylight left as the black and gray racer passed under the Causeway Bridge, headed south. In the racer were Silky and Montilla. Montilla was tense and didn't know why. As he passed under the bridge he was just in time to see Richards's plan go down as smoothly as if someone was filming a smuggling movie. "Oh, shit," he said as he saw the two Customs men jump from the police boat onto the sportfisherman. He saw one of the Customs men pull his gun and gesture at the guys on the big boat. Then he could see the crew standing on the aft deck, hands in the air. He saw one of the Customs men on the fly bridge, waving to the cop in the small police boat, and steering the big sportfisherman deftly around the Idle Speed sign and toward the bridge. Montilla added power and turned the wheel to the left, hoping to slide over to the marina on the east side and blend in with the other boats there. At the same time he grabbed the radio mike and yelled into it, "Bonfire! Bonfire! Bonfire!" He then watched helplessly as the police boat roared alongside the sailboat that had been following the sportfisherman. The sailboat had just been making the turn from the channel when the Customs men had jumped on the sportfisherman. Seeing this, the crew of the sailboat had tried to turn her around but had stopped and Montilla could see them standing there with their hands up as the police boat moved alongside. He could see the cop standing at the wheel—was he the same cop from earlier?—one hand holding a revolver pointed at the crew of the sailboat.

"Estúpidos! Why don't they listen to me? They don't have to stop. They don't have to stop! That cop can't make them stop for no reason!" He pounded the rubber padded wheel with clenched fists. He turned his head and looked at Silky, who was standing on the port side of the cockpit, watching the action calmly. He just growled savagely when she said, "That's kind of hard to say, Onyx, since the cop has a gun stuck in their faces."

Montilla eased the racer past the action, hugging the east wall of the port, keeping as much distance as he could. He saw that the sailboat was under way again, with the police boat right on the stern. Just before he pushed the throttles forward he heard sirens, and looking back over his shoulder he saw several squad cars pulling up to the docks of the marina on the west side of the waterway. He gunned it then and blasted through the turning basin and out into the channel. As he headed toward the entrance to the port, he was heartened to see that the last two boats had received his "bonfire" message and had turned around to head for the open sea. Now where would they go? Gun Cay? Honeymoon Bay? Montilla didn't know for sure; the individual captains would decide.

Fat, red-faced Lieutenant Whitney stood on the dock, looking up at Richards, who was standing on the aft deck of the sailboat. J.B. was feeling pretty good. Both boats were loaded with bales of grass; they had six guys in custody, no one got hurt, and it went off just great.

"Well, Richards," squawked the fat lieutenant, "everything legal this time?"

"Yeah, Lieutenant, I'm pretty sure we'll be okay on this one."

"You're 'pretty sure' we're okay? You'd better be damned sure, Richards, or it's your ass this time, hear me?"

Before J.B. could respond Fat Harry pushed past the lieutenant, threw his heavy arms straight up into the air, and yelled, "Well! Alllrriiiight! What an honest-to-God fucking beautiful grab! Damn, J.B., what a beautiful job!"

He looked at the fat lieutenant standing there, face red, fists clenched, and said, "Say, Lieutenant, you should calm down a little. I mean, maybe all this excitement is bad for your heart, know what I'm sayin'?" Whitney just looked at him, spluttered something unintelligible, and waddled away.

Richards stared at the lieutenant as he walked over to where the Customs men were busy filling out paperwork, stuck his hand out and congratulated them. Richards saw Maguire look back toward him and shrug eloquently. He looked down at Fat Harry and said, "You came by just in time, Harry. I was just gonna tell that fat shit head to take a flyin' fuck at a rollin' doughnut."

"My pleasure, J.B."

Someone called his name, and J.B. turned to see one of the Fort Lauderdale *Herald* reporters standing there. It was Dave Kuhler . . . and J.B. remembered Kuhler had said he was a friend of Ted's. Dave was young and tall, almost gangly. He had curly light-colored hair, a soft voice, and an easy smile. J.B. had spoken with Dave before and liked him.

"Two boatloads of marijuana? In broad daylight? And you guys go out and nail them in your marked police boat?" Dave grinned. "What are you doing, J.B., turning back the clock to the seventies? We haven't seen big loads of grass like this in a long time. Hell, I didn't think there was even a market for it anymore."

Richards smiled and shrugged. "Who knows, Dave? There must still be a demand, or somebody wouldn't be going through all of this hassle to bring it in."

"Amazing," said Dave as he opened his notebook. "Is this grab today part of a bigger case your department is working with the Feds, or is this just one of those lucky deals?"

J.B. laughed. "Luck? This is the result of ever-vigilant cops out here putting their lives on the line in the face of incredible odds and . . ." Dave was now laughing too. He closed his book, nodded his head, and said, "Nice grab though, J.B., no kidding." He waved and walked off.

J.B. climbed down off the sailboat and shook Harry's hand. He slapped the big man on the back and said, "Harry, you are really somethin', man. You picked those boats off like a pro." Harry, who had been into a little wine while waiting for the hammer to fall on the load boats, brought his face real close to J.B.'s and whispered, "And guess what, ol' ancient mariner policeman? Your friend, 'the obese one,' done spied the name off the stern of the other sportfisherman that turned around mysteriously as you guys made your move. I've already passed it on to the intrepid coast guard, and they have a cutter out there on the Gulf Stream somewhere and they're gonna head for the Bimini chain to see if that little ol' boat don't show up over there. How's that?"

"Great, Harry, great. Oh! And guess who came by looking all distressed while we were making our heroic grabs?"

Harry looked all around him. Then, satisfied that no one was listening, he leaned closer and said, "Could it be a little greasy dirt ball in a gray and black racing boat, hmmm?" They both laughed.

Zaden walked up and shook Fat Harry's hand. Then he turned to Richards and said, "Real fine, J.B., I mean *real fine*. By the way, did you guys see that little prick out there in his macho machine?" Fat Harry and J.B. both grinned and nodded their heads. "Anyway, we've got some guys comin' to help out and that patrol sergeant from this area said he'd have a couple of his men transport these assholes into booking. Now all we gotta do is hump bales."

Richards turned to look at the two boats tied up at the dock. He felt good. Maybe they were hurting Montilla, maybe they could get more info from the guys they arrested, maybe...maybe Ted was still alive somewhere, and all of this would mean something. He sighed.

Now the real work would begin. Humping bales was tedious and backbreaking work. It was all evidence, and had to be treated like it. There would be volumes of paperwork, and no room for mistakes. Oh, well. He fished around in his pocket for a quarter to call Jane. It was going to be a long night.

ELEVEN

Montilla slapped Silky so hard she tasted blood on her lower lip, and she fell backward over a chair. She rolled over onto her knees and looked at him wide-eyed but did not cry. Somehow this angered him even more.

"You smart-assed bitch! You think you knew all along, huh? Stupid me. I should have listened to you, is that it?"

Silky stood, slowly. She ran her fingers through her hair, licked her lips, and said in a husky voice, "I didn't say anything, Onyx . . . and I don't know anything. You're angry because the cops hit you again, but it's not right for you to take it out on me." He stared at her as she hesitated, then she went on. "And something else, Onyx. You've been treating me worse and worse. You know I didn't want to stay here with you, and you know why I have. I don't like it, but I've felt like I had no choice." She touched her lower lip with two fingers as he watched. "But now, Onyx, now you've hit me . . . for no reason. You've hit me, and I won't stay here and let that happen."

His laugh was like the sharp bark of an angry dog. "You! You won't stay here and let it happen? What will you do, *mi chica?* Pack your Gucci bags, jump into your Mercedes, and drive off into the sunset? Huh?" He glared at her, then raised his arm, his hand in a fist. He shook it in her face. "I saved your ass when Sam Golden went down . . . saved you from his partners, and saved you from the cops who came sniffin' around, but I can just as easily give you away any time I want." He leaned forward, and she pulled her head back, her eyes on his. "Listen, Silky, you are mine! I can give you to the cops, I can give you to Sam's partners, and I can kick your ass if I feel like it! You're going to run from me because I hit you when I'm angry? Shit, you're breaking my heart." He dropped his arm and ran his hand up and down his chest. "Listen, pretty one. If you ever leave me it will be when I say, and it will be on my terms. *Comprende?*"

They stood there, staring at each other, and even as they tested each other's will Silky knew she had to back down. He asked, *"Comprende?"* again, and she nodded her head and looked at the floor. She watched as he slowly reached out and gently touched her lips with his fingertips. Then he turned away, and walked across the room toward the phone.

Silky walked slowly to the bedroom and closed the door quietly behind her.

The telephone rang as Montilla reached for it.

"Onyx, honestly, I didn't know. . . ."

"But *now* you do, huh, asshole?"

Erricks tried again. "Listen, Onyx, I know you're upset. I'll find out what happened. It's gotta be some off-the-wall thing again. I'll find out."

"You listen, mi amigo. You'd better find out how and why real fast. I'm losin' too much money because of these assholes, and it just can't go on. If you can't do the job, maybe I'll do it myself, or maybe I'll find somebody who *really* needs the money. Understand?"

"I understand, Onyx, I really do. This will be the last time. I'll take care of it."

Montilla's voice got softer as he said, "Yeah, you take care of it, Erricks, or the goose that's been layin' those golden eggs is gonna shit right on your fuckin' head." Then he slammed the phone down, hard.

Lieutenant Billy Erricks sat in his darkened office, holding the telephone receiver away from his ear, staring at it. He hung it up and let out a long sigh. He noticed his fingers were trembling. He bit his lip, feeling a knot form in his stomach. He had checked his own phone for a tap, in the unlikely event that someone would run one of the lines in the OCB office, and he had periodically checked the line to Montilla's and knew it was clean too. But still, he absolutely did not like having these conversations on the phone. It made him too vulnerable.

He rubbed his temples, and thought about the situation. He liked getting the money from Montilla, and he liked the intrigue to some degree. But he didn't like the way Montilla had been sounding since a couple of loads had been grabbed. Too threatening. Erricks grunted. He acknowledged he was corrupt, yes, but Montilla's threats of "handling it himself" sounded too much like he was planning to somehow hurt a cop. This Erricks knew he could not permit.

It took Erricks just two days to prepare. When he was ready he made an appointment with the major's secretary, gathered up all the reports he had finished, conjured up a most concerned expression on his face, and proceeded to initiate the in-house moves that would result in the goal he sought so earnestly.

He was with the major less than half an hour before the major called upstairs requesting an immediate meeting with the chief. Then he bade Erricks come along with him, bringing all the reports. Erricks displayed just the right combination of confidence and concern as he followed the major into the chief's office. He had to present the information and then be perplexed, as if there had to be some answer but he couldn't discern it. Then, of course, the chief and the major would pool their experience and administrative talents and eventually come up with the answer Erricks wanted all along. The only answer.

Erricks displayed reports, figures, personal knowledge, and sentiments passed on to him by other agencies showing that the uniformed police officers working against narcotics activities on the waterways of the city, in marked or unmarked police boats, were just not the right answer. He could show the confusion and overlapping work they were causing. He could show the lack of security they exhibited. He could pass on the lack of confidence expressed to him by agents of the state and federal units working in the area. This was especially important because it made FLPD, in his words, "Look bad to all the other professional units in the area." He even had a written report from Lieutenant

Whitney stating that the legal adviser had already found several problems with the legality of the most recent seizures, which were being played up by the media as a big deal, and would make FLPD look foolish when they fell through in court.

Erricks could show that the patrol officers in their police boats were probably trying to do their best, but because they were not really narcotics oriented they were hurting more than they were helping. They were good guys; they were just in the way. He was also quick to point out that a racing-type boat that had been seized by FLPD several weeks before—he neglected to mention that it had been seized by patrol units—was now, through the good efforts of the legal adviser, available for the department's use. It would not do to have a uniformed patrolman driving around in this expensive piece of machinery, as suggested by Lieutenant Tallert. No, it could be put to better use as an "undercover" boat, operated by a boat-qualified narcotics officer.

Most of all, the thing that made the major and the chief sit right up and take notice was that he could show that using the patrol officers in the police boats was not the most efficient way to stay within the budget. He backed this up with a report from the city manager's office and the opinion of the financial director who thought that having policemen riding around in boats all day was just a waste of taxpayers' money.

Now, this was heavy stuff.

The budget was being misused. The budget was being ineffectively used. The budget was clearly showing that a change had to be made.

The major looked at the chief and the chief looked at the lieutenant. Then they pulled themselves up in front of the all-powerful budget, and they made a decision.

J.B. grabbed his old rain jacket from his gym bag and climbed out of his pickup truck. He had parked under the trees behind the main station so that he could go into the supply room and get a new jacket and maybe a new flashlight while he was at it.

He closed the door and turned. Scott Kelly was smiling at him.

"Hey, J.B., glad I ran into you here. Wanted to pass a couple of things your way."

"Did you get more info on that Montilla guy? Do you know I had words with him the other day? Got anymore on Ted?"

Kelly laughed. "Yes, no . . . and no." He stretched, the muscles in his arms bunching and relaxing. He looked around the parking lot and said quietly, "The guy driving the *Sausea Girl* sat and spoke with me for a few minutes." He saw J.B.'s eyes widen, and he went on. "Yeah, well, like I said, I'm kinda workin' this whole thing on my own, ya know. Not really official, in the sense that I'm not making daily reports or briefing my bosses at this point, okay?"

J.B. nodded. Kelly went on. "Anyway, the guy is pretty broken up about his partner, Arnie, getting killed . . . told me the boat was owned by a dummy corporation that Montilla has a part of at least, and that as far as he knew, the load was organized by Montilla for some other group. He didn't know who the money was, but confirmed that Montilla at least got hurt by your timely intervention." He smoothed his large mustache with two fingers, his eyes far away. "The guy might turn into a good informant for me in the long run. We'll see. Tell me about your run-in with Montilla."

J.B. did so, telling Kelly how difficult it had been for him to remain professionally aloof. He did not tell Kelly about how he had felt a nagging familiarity about Montilla.

Kelly listened, his face grim, and then said, "Well . . . this has to be a time of staying tough and cool. We don't want to jump the gun and blow whatever chance we have of nailing that crud."

"I hear you," agreed J.B.

"And no, I don't have anything new on Novak. But there is one thing that's happenin' that I feel is strange. I had a call from a guy I used to work with in DEA—one of the good ones. He told me he was calling, reluctantly, in behalf of some other federal agent who wanted to meet with me, real soon he said. Wouldn't say which outfit this agent is with, and acted like he would forget the initials immediately if he heard 'em. I don't know, the timing makes me feel like maybe it has to do with this deal we're into." He paused, and shook his head. "Hope it's not one of those State Department guys again."

J.B. shrugged, and said, "You're getting out of my league there. I'm just a little ol' patrolman."

"Yeah, I know, J.B. I said that because some years ago the State Department blasted some of us real good because we were in a local task force and did some deals in the Bahamas, tryin' to bust some of their government types who were involved in the drug business. Seems our government has radar sites and submarine routes or some other secret bullshit going on with the permission of the Bahamian government, so they got all tense and nervous when we tried to slap their wrists for helping the smugglers."

"Ah, Truth, Justice, and the American Way."

"Right on. I'm just tellin' ya about the Fed agent in case it has something to do with us, okay?"

"Okay, Scott. And keep in touch."

"Yeah . . . and hey!" Scott Kelly grinned. "That was a fine grab you and Fat Harry and the Customs cats made the other day. You'll probably find a stack of commendations waiting for you in there!"

He waved and walked off. J.B. headed for the backdoor of the station.

Richards was approaching the supply room counter when he saw Fat Harry walking slowly down the hallway toward him, gazing dejectedly at a couple of letters in his hand. J.B. could see that they were on FLPD stationery, and one looked like a commendation of some sort. He hit the big man on the arm, and said, "Hey, Harry, what's with the long face, man? And what do you have there—been promoted?"

Harry looked at him for a moment, rocking slowly on his heavy legs. Richards could see that his face was flushed.

"Harry . . . what's wrong, man?"

Harry ran his thick fingers through his shaggy head of gray hair and said, "J.B., I just don't know anymore, man.

I just don't know. You're supposed to go see Tallert as soon as you can. Better go see him." While he said this he carefully folded the papers and slid them into his shirt pocket. Then he stuck his hands down into his pants pockets, looked down until his chin was on his chest, and said, "There is no gravity here at all, J.B. This place just sucks. No matter what you try to do, you're wrong, ya know?"

J.B. stood there in the hallway as Fat Harry walked away, head down. He had a sinking feeling as he headed to Lieutenant Tallert's office, knocked lightly, and went in.

Tallert looked up at him, pushed his glasses up onto his forehead, pointed to a chair against the wall, and handed him a letter. Richards sat down slowly and read all the fine words glorifying his recent actions on the waters of the city in combat against the evil and insidious drug smugglers. He read how he had gone beyond the line of duty, and how he had used his experience, skill, and courage in the good fight against crime. He was a credit to the department and he was to be commended for a job well done.

Richards looked up from the letter and said, "And . . . ?"

Tallert took off his glasses, set them down carefully in front of him, rubbed his eyes hard with the palm of his hands, and said, "And you're transferred off the boats and back into a patrol car as of this evening. You'll be working for Lieutenant Whitney, riding the south end of the city on afternoon-evening shifts. I understand they plan to let you ride with Skids Bedlam for a while if you want, just so you can ease back into it—since you haven't been in a patrol car for some time."

Now Richards understood Fat Harry's attitude in the hallway. He leaned forward with his elbows on his knees, looked down at the floor, and said, "Shit."

Tallert pushed his chair back away from his desk, got up and walked around to the front of it, and sat on the corner nearest J.B. He cleared his throat and fidgeted a little and went on. "I'm told by the captain, who was told by the major, who was told by the chief, that this is primarily a budget matter. Everybody is real pleased with the job you were doing out there, but the budget just can't justify it anymore. They're not doing away with the entire unit, thank goodness, it's still there, in name at least. They can't get rid of Mike Kendall, or none of the boats would ever run. They've still got Liz Fox, the aide, and they'll generally keep up the appearance of a unit." He paused. "Hell, here in the 'Venice of America' we *have* to have a marine unit. Anyway, about this budget explanation, the way I see it that's just a load of cow manure. I know Erricks over at OCB managed to bushwhack you guys, but I'm havin' a hard time believin' professional jealousy could go this far. And there's nothin' I can do about it. I got a call from ol' Milt Faust from FDLE this morning. Seems he was concerned because Erricks had come to him and they had had a big talk about you uniformed guys trying to catch the dopers. Faust was afraid that Erricks would take what he said wrong and somehow use it to hurt you. Which is exactly what he did. I know it ain't right, but like I said, there's nothin' I can do about it. As soon as the heavies start talkin' about 'the budget' their eyes glaze over. They start to look all sweaty and they just don't think straight."

J.B. looked up at Tallert and asked, "What about Harry?"

"They decided it just wouldn't be right to put him back in a unit so they transferred him to the court liaison office. He'll sit there all day and make sure the guys show up for court and all that."

Richards stood up slowly and looked at Tallert. He could see that the lieutenant was just as pissed off as he was. His head was swimming. He turned toward the door and said, "Well, I'd better get my gear together. I know I have a nightstick and a traffic book around here somewhere." He paused, then said quietly, "Tell you something else. I've got a daughter who tells me Ted Novak is alive somewhere, and I find myself believing her. And just so you'll know, I may be out of the boats for now, but that doesn't mean me and Montilla aren't going to have our few seconds of reckoning someday."

Just before he walked out the door he crumpled the letter of commendation into a little ball and threw it into a trash can beside the desk. After he was gone, Tallert let out a sigh. He slowly walked over and pulled the crumpled letter out of the trash, went back to his desk and sat down, and began smoothing the wrinkled paper with his hands.

Richards walked slowly into the locker room. Several men were already there, getting ready for evening shift briefing. They were talking loudly and banging their lockers shut but Richards hardly heard them. He was still stunned. He sat down and took off his boat shoes and put on the old beat-up black street shoes. They were scuffed and needed polish, but he couldn't bring himself to do more than pass a brush across the toes a couple of times. He picked up his notepad and went out the double doors and into the briefing room.

Uniformed cops were still milling around, grabbing hot-sheets and shooting the breeze. The briefing sergeant was still getting his papers together, so Richards walked up to the porcine figure of Lieutenant Whitney and said, "Excuse me, Lieutenant, I just got the word I've been transferred to your unit. I still have most of my gear and stuff out at the harbor patrol office, so after briefing I'm gonna run out there and get it squared away. It'll only take about an hour."

Whitney stood there with his hands on his hips. He stuck out his jaw and said, "That'll be an hour that the rest of these officers will be working their asses off out on the street, Richards. So why don't you make it a half hour? You may as well get used to being just one of the guys here, pal. You're no hotshot boat driver here, you're just a cop, and I'm your boss. Get squared away fast, and maybe you'll be able to cut it with us. Got it?"

Richards started to respond, but then stopped and said nothing. He nodded at the fat lieutenant and turned to walk away. As he did he looked at the old briefing sergeant. The sergeant had pretended to be busy with paperwork as the lieutenant was speaking; now he just looked up at Richards and rolled his eyes. Richards turned around and took a seat. As he sat down he heard one of the new men behind him whisper to the whole room, "Hey, who's that old guy?"

* * *

Skids Bedlam, who had offered to give J.B. a lift, was thirty-eight years old and looked at least a decade older. He wasn't fat, but he had a stocky, round-looking body, with a pot belly, and thick stubby fingers. He was going bald fast, and what hair he did have was light brown and slicked back along the sides of his round head. What most people noticed first when they looked at him were his eyes, which appeared painfully bloodshot at all times. He was kidded a lot about drinking on duty, and when he wanted to he could do a very accurate wino imitation. In fact, several of the more memorable conversations heard and witnessed on the street by fellow officers were serious, head-to-head confabs between Skids and a totally inebriated citizen involved in some police matter. Somehow the drunks always understood Officer Bedlam perfectly.

Skids Bedlam's real name was Marvin, but no one ever called him Marvin except for old Mrs. Meekin down in the records division, and that was only because the Bedlams and the Meekins had been neighbors many years ago and little Marvin Bedlam had been in the Cub Scouts and Mrs. Meekin had been the den mother. No one could remember when Bedlam was first called "Skids," but most agreed it was probably sometime during his high school years, or more likely, when he first got his hands on the wheel of an automobile. As a teenager he had rebuilt and modified several cars, including the family Buick, much to his father's chagrin, and he had won trophies driving stocks and dragsters. In the police department he had become almost legendary for his wild driving exploits. Most of the officers agreed he was probably stone cold crazy, but at the same time they all agreed he was the best in a chase, or if you needed a backup fast.

As they approached the car, Richards automatically went over to the passenger side and threw his gear down on the seat. Richards hated to drive at any time, and he knew that Skids drove all the time no matter what. He helped Skids check out the gear in the trunk and then went back to the front and sat down. As Bedlam got in and started the car he said, "Well, J.B., I asked for a good car and they gave me old seventy-one here. For a hog Plymouth she didn't run too bad the last time I had her out."

Richards didn't say anything but watched as Bedlam started the car and then sat there listening to the engine as he revved the RPMs up and down. He backed out of the space and then cruised slowly toward the gas pumps, cocked his ear, and said, "Hmmmmm," all the while listening to something in the engine that Richards would never be able to hear. Once at the pumps, Richards filled the tank while Bedlam lifted the hood and fiddled around with something. He seemed satisfied as they climbed in again. As they rolled away from the pumps, Richards remembered the time Bedlam had captured the Scarab driver on the dirt road by almost turning him into a hood ornament.

He reached down and snapped on his seat belt.

Ted Novak was failing.

He was getting weaker, losing strength while his body fought the raging infection that had set in around his wounds. His right leg and side were a mass of multicolored bruises and welts. Near his right ankle, on the outside of the leg, were several cruel cuts. Yesterday he had been doing fine, and had actually been sitting up in bed. He had even tried, in vain, to speak with the dour doctor. Later, when a pretty nurse, dark and small, came into the room, he had tried to speak with her also, but she had turned away. Even so, he sensed her friendliness.

Then, last night, the fever had come to him in a torrent. His mind tumbled and struggled with images and sounds; he was frightened and wondered why. In the middle of the long night during a few moments of lucid understanding of his surroundings, he had heard the doctor and nurse conversing in rapid Spanish, and he remembered where he was. It was then that he became afraid again, only to lose touch with reality when the fever came back.

It was morning now, and Ted slept as the young dark-haired nurse wiped his brow with a damp cloth. She was very tired, and looked forward to going to sleep. She thought about the time, just before the sunrise, in the quiet darkness of deep morning, when she had gently held him, the young American who had been tossing and turning and crying out. It hurt the young nurse to watch and listen to him. She had sat on the edge of the bed, tentatively at first, and then had leaned over and held the American, soothing him, speaking to him softly in her musical language. Somehow it had calmed him, and he had finally fallen asleep, but not before he spoke.

She had held him, listening, and she sang to him quietly and rubbed his brow with her fingers while she wondered who was the girl that he called for.

Who was Kathleen?

Silky watched in silence as Onyx Montilla and two other men sat around the small kitchen table, talking and drinking. She had seen the two men arrive together in a powder blue Cadillac. One looked to her like a Jewish businessman, in his early sixties, with a pale complexion and dark circles under his sad eyes. He dressed like one of the retirees that lives in a condo out in West Lauderdale, with knit golfing trousers and a pastel short-sleeved shirt, buttoned at the throat. When he had entered the house he took off his small-brimmed golf hat.

Silky had asked herself why a Jewish businessman would have anything in common with Onyx. He had smiled at her politely when introduced, and she had seen the intelligence in his eyes as he had appraised her. Silky decided she liked the man.

The other one was younger, in his twenties, with dark hair and pale skin, a mouth that seemed permanently cut into a sneer, and restless eyes. His clothes were flashy and expensive but they gave him a street look somehow. He looked like a young, tough hood.

When the two men had pulled into the drive in the Caddy, the young one driving and the old one perched on the right seat, golf hat centered on his bald head, Silky had heard Montilla mutter under his breath, "It's about time, you assholes." But when he met them at the door he was all smiles. The three men had talked business for a few minutes, conferring in low tones, the young one not saying much. Then, the business apparently settled, they got louder and more relaxed and into their drinks. Silky noticed that the young one laughed most, loudest, and longest.

"So, Onyx," said the Jewish businessman, "we heard where you had a little bad luck lately . . . twice even."

Montilla colored, took a drink, and said, "*Sí*, I guess I did, but I don't see any more of those problems in the future."

The old man settled back a little and mused, "To tell you the truth, Onyx, some of us were a mite surprised. I mean, some of the guys remember you telling us that you had an inside thing and that you would always know when the door was closed."

The young guy was openly watching Silky as she moved through the living room, his eyes showing appreciation for her body and the way it moved.

Montilla glanced at her angrily and hissed at her, his voice tight, "I thought I told you to stay out of the way!" She didn't say anything, but went into the bedroom. Then Montilla turned back to the old man and said evenly, "That's right, that's what I said. And so far it's been working out fine. Things just got a little screwed up last week, that's all. This guy I've got is right where he needs to be and he likes money just like every other cop I ever heard of."

The old man sipped his drink and said, "Onyx, you know I think of you like a son. You know I'm behind you in this. It's just that when the guys have money invested in the goods you're supposed to move they like to know you can do what you say. If you say you've got an inside thing, that's good enough for me. Nothing like another cop out there working for the cause, I always say."

Montilla just grunted, but the young guy laughed out loud and looked at the old man admiringly.

The old man got up and went over to the sink and tore a paper towel off the roll and blew his nose. Then he turned and said, "Oh, I heard something else the other day, Onyx. Heard that alligator-shoe lawyer you had has gone and disappeared. You weren't having problems or anything, were you?"

Onyx took a drink, swallowed, and said casually, "Naw. I don't know what the problem was with that guy. I hear he was tappin' some sweet young thing and they might have split after he grabbed everybody's retainer. I understand there's a lot of guys lookin' for him."

"Are any of the guys looking for him cops, Onyx?" asked the old man quietly.

"Not that I know of," said Montilla, "just clients and stuff. I think he just took off with his young pussy. Had some of my money too."

The young guy coughed slightly, turned in his chair toward the old man, and said, "Mr. Kolin, don't you want to ask about the other guy? Didn't you say there was some local dude missing along with the lawyer?"

The old man walked over to him and put his hand on his shoulder, squeezing hard, and said in a soft voice, "Well, yeah, Joe, as a matter of fact I was mentioning something like that to one of my friends, but don't you think it would be better if I was the one to ask Onyx here about that?"

The young guy looked down at his hands and said, "Yessir."

Montilla waited until the old man looked at him and said, "Turns out there's something odd about the local that was missing with the lawyer . . . something more to him than just a local cocaine hustler." He cocked his head and watched Montilla as he went on. "Some of us have heard that he might have been some kind of narc, although we're very puzzled about the fact that he would ride off in a boat with you without being wired, watched, or covered, if you know what I mean." He took the balled-up paper towel he still held and wiped his nose, then he shrugged his shoulders and looked at Montilla, waiting.

"Shit," said Montilla, "just another Fort Lauderdale player, that's all. Like a cocaine groupie, know what I mean? I know that lawyer had a little group of locals who thought he might be the big-time coke dealer around here. Maybe he and the lawyer had something going. Who knows?" He paused, then went on, his face turned to the window, his eyes avoiding Kolin's stare. "I can't remember any local clowns taking a boat ride with me, the lawyer either. More like the lawyer grabbed what money he could, the groupie scored a little coke somewhere, they ran off with the lawyer's young pussy, and they're down in some cheap hotel in Key West, doing a three-way."

The young guy grinned and Kolin grinned and Montilla grinned.

Then the old man sat down and said, "Well, maybe. But you know, Onyx, no one would be shocked to find out maybe he had an accident. I mean, we have a business to run, and if there's a potential problem out there we could understand that it would have to be dealt with. The thing is, Onyx, since what you do affects our little group, then *we* would have to decide if some action was gonna be taken. *Capish?* If, all of a sudden, someone in the group started making these decisions all by himself, why, some of my friends would start to get nervous and the next thing you know they'd be asking me if I had things under control or not. Know what I mean?"

Montilla didn't respond, he just sat there staring at a bottle of Scotch on the table until the old man said softly, "Of course, you're probably right about that Key West three-way wrestling match anyway, Onyx."

As he said this, Silky came out of the bedroom and walked slowly over to the kitchen table. She was wearing jeans and a pullover and tennis shoes, and her long hair was brushed back, shiny and lovely. She did not speak until Montilla slowly turned his head, gave her a hard look, and growled, "Now what do you want?"

Silky looked at her hands and said, "I'm going to go for a walk, Onyx. I'd kind of like to get out of the house for a while and get some fresh air. I won't be long, I promise."

Montilla looked at her as if she were a child, and said, "Oh, you would like to get out of the house for a while, huh? Every time you go out it costs me money, for Chrissakes. You must be the most expensive piece of ass in this town. Besides, you can see I have guests. Suppose I need you to hostess or something?"

The girl just looked down at her hands and rocked from one foot to the other slowly.

Kolin looked at her, hesitated, and says. "You were the

pretty thing that used to make ol' Sam Golden smile, right?"

Silky nodded, wary.

"Sure, I knew it," said Kolin. He grinned. "Golden must have had more than just a good money nose, huh?" His face hardened. "Too bad about him gettin' chewed up in the middle of somebody else's hit like that. They say he knew a lot of things, old Sam did. Things like names and dates and places, and things like numbers and accounts and corporation names. They say that a lot of that info sort of evaporated after Sam was killed. They say the cops would love to know what happened to it—they'd like to find someone who knew about Golden's work but wouldn't tell. And they say that some of Sam's old partners would get real excited if they thought Sam had passed on some of that info to, say, a close friend."

The room became very quiet. Silky realized she had stopped breathing. Montilla was very tense.

Kolin stretched and cracked his knuckles. He rotated his bald head on his skinny neck, cleared his throat, and smiled. "Silky, right? I always wondered if that had to do with the way you felt to the touch, or the fact that you are such a rare and expensive commodity. Guess my friend Onyx here must be a pretty lucky man. But listen, girl, I'll bet he's not the only one in this town who would be pleased to care for you."

He had said it with a smile, but Montilla was burning. Small beads of sweat formed on his brow, and his hands were bunched into tight fists. Kolin stared into his eyes now, testing him, and said through his smile, "I'm just kidding with Silky, Onyx, you know that. I'm very aware of what you Hispanic cowboys call honor and machismo and all of that. And I'm too old to fight you over a sweet young thing." He made a face and shrugged.

Joe laughed, tentatively. Montilla managed a contrived chuckle himself.

Kolin nodded. "That's better. And what the hell, let the girl go for a walk, Montilla. It won't hurt nothin'. Besides, I'm sure you can get whatever we need."

Montilla looked at him, then back at the girl. Finally he

said to her, "Okay, but don't be gone too long. After my guests have gone home I'm gonna want you back in *my* bed, on your back—with those legs spread—where you belong."

Silky kept silent, her head down. She walked to the door and quietly let herself out. Joe watched her all the way and pursed his lips as the door closed. Montilla saw him and gave him a hard look, but the young guy just smiled at him. Motherfucker, thought Montilla.

After pulling the door shut, Silky paused and listened. She heard Kolin say, "You know what else we need to discuss, Onyx? We need to discuss all the bad effects of the heavy use of cocaine, and how stupid it would be to let cocaine start to erode our decision-making abilities while we're involved in such a tricky business as ours is . . . right?" She didn't want to hear more, so she left and soon was strolling down the sidewalk. The cool breeze felt good against her face and neck and the quiet of the night, illuminated by an almost full moon, was like soft music on her mind. She walked the length of the isle, and when she got to Las Olas Boulevard she stayed on the south side and turned west, toward the section of the boulevard that had all the small, expensive shops. She knew they would all be closed now, but she liked to look in the windows. She reached the little bridge over Pirate's Canal and stopped in the middle to stare down into the dark water. The light of the moon and the pattern of small puffy clouds scattered here and there among the stars made a surreal reflection on the surface of the water.

Montilla's words were like fire in her mind.

She didn't even hear the carload of young guys as they raced over the bridge and yelled and whistled at her. She just stood there, with her fists on the cold concrete railing, staring, hearing it. "On your back with your legs spread— where you belong." She looked down at the water and she wondered, *Maybe, maybe it's true . . . maybe that's where I belong*. She looked down at her body. She knew it was a good body; long tight legs, firm round breasts, a smooth flat tummy. She was young and healthy and good looking, good enough to make men turn and look at her anywhere she went. In fact, men watched her with an intensity that sometimes made her uncomfortable. She had been young when she realized she could use her body to survive, and she had quickly learned the price. Thank God for Sam Golden, she thought. She frowned then, thinking of what Kolin had said. Was it a warning . . . or an offer? Or both?

She shook her head and then looked up at the soft gray clouds blowing by, and thought of Montilla.

Montilla's life was exciting, he took her places she wanted to go, with flash, and money, and style. The fast lane. Nice clothes, gold around her neck, diamonds in her ears, and that lovely little car. She bit her lip. But there was more, he wanted more from her. He wanted to dominate her. She wondered if that was part of the reason she had been attracted to him in the first place, even while Sam was still alive. There had been that brazen maleness, that aura of danger. It was real. Now, she knew, she had never been so completely and physically dominated. She sighed. It was not necessarily in bed, she thought. No, up until recently, she had been comfortable in bed with him, he excited her, and pleased her sexually. She shook her head, knowing she could experience more. Now he was dominating her with his very presence. He was volatile, violent, and arrogant. He was becoming more abusive every week.

Why did she stay?

Were all the material benefits really worth it? Was Montilla her only safe haven? Were her female wiles and Sam Golden's strongbox of secrets enough for her to barter for a safe and comfortable existence? And if so, who would it be? Another man like Kolin?

She felt her past was Montilla, and her future was Montilla, in one form or another. She felt trapped: she lived in luxury, but in a bartered cocoon. She thought about being a receptacle for Montilla's ejaculations.

Was that all she could ever be? Just a body? Just something for men to show off and then push themselves into?

An instrument of friction, lubrication, and hydraulics . . . ornamented with precious stones and motivated by the promise of comfort and safety?

"No," she said softly. "No, no . . . no."

She pounded her fist on the cold concrete railing, and again said, "No!"

Montilla's next morning began no better than the previous night had ended.

He stood naked in the kitchen, his hair tousled and his eyes red, sipping a cup of coffee. He looked out the kitchen window and there, standing on the dock with his back to the house, was the tough Latin who had taken him to Maximiliano. Montilla slammed the coffee cup down on the counter, spilling the hot liquid onto his wrist. He muttered to himself as he hurried into the bedroom, climbed into a pair of jeans, tucked a small automatic into one of the rear pockets, and went out the backdoor, headed for the dock.

The man turned as he approached and smiled.

"*Jesus Christe*, mi amigo," said Montilla. "In broad daylight?"

The other man opened his hands, and said, "*Sí . . .* in the daylight. But now I am dressed as the casual visitor, no? Standing on your dock admiring your wonderful boat."

Montilla looked at the man, who was wearing casual slacks and a Hawaiian shirt. He said, "Okay." He looked around, and seeing nothing unusual in the other backyards or across the canal, he went on. "So. Am I to go to another meeting? Will we talk some more?"

The tough Latin took another step toward Montilla, who tensed. The man had an amused look on his face as he said, "No, no meeting this time as my patrón is not in this country right now. Instead I am to give to you a message, and you are to look at me but pretend you are hearing the thoughts and the words of my patrón, not me. *Comprende?*"

"*Sí.*"

"My patrón asks this: "Why is it that some local, small-time *policía* in his little boat can cause so much trouble for you?" The man watched Montilla's face, as he had been instructed to do. Then he went on. "My patrón also asks: Are you capable of working for us? Can we have confidence in knowing you can do the job—or are you more a man of words and appearances than of deeds." The man turned slightly to the side then, his feet spread, his arms hanging easily at his sides. "Lastly, my patrón says this: God has decided to give us a surprise, a two-edged sword. My patrón will not tell you in detail about it until he meets with you face-to-face. But he says for you to think of it the same way one would remember a phoenix."

Montilla was stung, and not a little confused. He took a deep breath, grunted, and said stiffly, "You can tell your patrón that the recent troubles can be compared to some cosmic accidents. There will be no more problems of that sort. I have told him I can and will do what he wishes, and that will be it." Somehow feeling dramatic in the first light of day, he said with his chin out, "Also tell him that I am the son of Felix Ortiz. There is no cause to doubt me."

The other man smiled, and then nodded his head curtly. He turned and walked off the dock, across the yard, and out of sight without looking back.

Montilla stood on the dock, the boards cold and smooth against the skin of his bare feet. He looked at *Stiletto* laying there in the perfectly still water, and thought about what had been said, and what had been implied.

"Dammit," he said out loud. "The *policía* problem had better be solved this time because if it isn't I'll take care of it myself."

He walked back toward the house, angry and unsettled.

What the hell did a phoenix have to do with any of this?

TWELVE

"So what did Zaden and Maguire have to say, J.B.?" asked Bedlam as he eased the Plymouth into downtown traffic. They had been in the courthouse because Skids was to testify at a trial, but the case had been continued. While

Bedlam was learning of the delay, Richards had met the two Customs officers in the lobby and they had talked for a few minutes.

"Well, first of all, Skids, when they heard I was riding with you Zaden wanted to know how many strings of rosary beads I'd worn out, and Maguire wanted me to name him as beneficiary of my insurance."

Bedlam looked at Richards and grunted, changing lanes twice, apparently without even looking at the other traffic.

"They also told me that my man Montilla has insulated himself pretty well so far. They told me a federal task force turned over a lot of info and made some medium-sized busts, but they didn't get anywhere near Montilla, or any corporation he's supposed to be part of. Apparently they had their eye on a good potential witness, and the guy disappeared—that attorney."

Bedlam nodded, his eyes on the road. "You mean the one that Ted Novak was messin' with?"

"Yeah, that's the one. I guess without him they couldn't get anything solid on Montilla, so they decided to concentrate on other problems."

Bedlam, using the center lane to pass a large, slow-moving dump truck, said quietly, "How convenient."

"Uh-huh," said J.B., "but even so, things can't be all roses for that little bastard. Zaden said he and Maguire have an informant who's an islander. He told them that the natives are unhappy about Montilla pulling a stunt in their waters, with one of their people involved, which could eventually bring some heat down on them over there. Not that I've ever heard of any Bahamian worrying about heat that *we* could generate." He paused. "Word is that Montilla may not be mister popularity around Bimini right now. Not only that, you know that the coast guard has a female captain on one of their ninety-five footers?"

"Yeah," said Bedlam. "I saw an article about her in the paper, that reporter you know, Dave . . . he did it. Anyway, she's not a bad-looking lady, and they say she's squared away too."

J.B. turned in his seat, not wanting to watch as Bedlam leaned the police car into a fast left turn on a yellow light in a crowded intersection. "Everything I've heard about her says she can run that boat as good as anybody, and she's aggressive as hell. Maguire says last week she took down a small freighter that was loaded with primo grass, pressure packed into those small bundles like they do. They don't know for sure but they think that part of the load may have been earmarked for Montilla, or his money group. At least one of his boats was out on the banks at the time."

J.B. rubbed his face with one hand, and shrugged. "I don't know, seems like some of this stuff should be hurting him at least a little bit."

Bedlam said nothing, so Richards continued. "Zaden says Montilla must be busy trying to tighten things up again. He has to straighten out the situation on Bimini, and he's going to have to make some serious money to cover his losses, even if you only figure the equipment. By the way, Hank also mentioned that he's seen that yellow Scarab that I seized. The city got it out of confiscation so the narcs in OCB could use it for an undercover boat. He says so far he's seen it once with Erricks tooling around in it—with a couple of chicks from a waterfront bar—and once when it was full of narcs, sunglasses gleaming in the sun, hair blowing back rakishly as they whizzed right through a couple of No Wake areas."

Bedlam just shook his head, and said, "Well, think about it, J.B., what fun would it be if you were a narc and went around doing things without *flair*, without . . . piss-ass . . . or is that pizzazz?"

J.B. was quiet for a moment, then said, "About Montilla. I don't care what troubles he's having from enforcement interference, ours or the Feds. I'd just like to put my fist in his macho face—up to my elbow." He looked out the window at a wino leaning against the back wall of a convenience store. "Maybe it would make me feel better, for a little while anyway."

Bedlam looked at him, scratched his belly, and said, "Just stay cool, J.B. Everything happens for a reason, right?"

As they headed south on U.S. One in heavy traffic, the alert tone came over their radio and the dispatcher came on with: "Attention all units. Signal thirty, grand larceny, just occurred at Byron's department store, southeast Seventeenth Street Causeway. Suspects are two black males, one black female. Last seen westbound on the Causeway in a brown four-door Buick. Suspects took armloads of men's suits off the rack near the front doors and ran out. Store manager was injured trying to stop them. Any unit in the area that can respond, come to channel three."

"Rats!" said J.B. "Broad daylight, and would you look at the traffic!"

Bedlam didn't say anything but moved the unit into the center lane and accelerated toward the Causeway. As they approached the intersection they could see dust in the air and then a vehicle sitting at a crazy angle in the lot of the Wags restaurant on the corner. All the other traffic was stopped, and a man was standing beside the car waving wildly and pointing down the road, toward State Road 84. As they flew past, Richards heard the man yell ". . . me off the goddamned road!"

Bedlam said quietly, "There you are . . . and here we go."

Richards's head snapped back against the seat as Bedlam punched it. The brake lights on the brown Buick were visible as the driver slowed to make the turn west on 84. As the big car disappeared around the corner, headed toward Andrews Avenue, Richards knew they were too far behind to catch up. He hoped there were other units west that could intercept.

"Bravo five-six, we are in pursuit! The Buick just headed west on State Road 84, toward Andrews. Get some units west!"

"Ten-four . . . Bravo five-six in pursuit. Be advised we have no units west at this time. We will contact Florida Highway Patrol in case they go for I-95."

"Crap!"

Bedlam didn't say anything, he just pushed himself back into the seat a little farther, squinted his red eyes, and threw the police car into a screaming four-wheeled skid onto 84. As they came out of the turn they could see the Buick busting through the intersection of 84 and Andrews, still westbound. Richards gripped the dash with one hand while he braced himself with his arm. He yelled, "Still westbound past Andrews!" into the radio as Bedlam squeezed the unit between several cars that were trying to get through the intersection in the normal manner. The police car left the ground as they crossed the railroad tracks and approached Fourth Avenue. Richards could see, incredibly, that they were gaining on the Buick. A dark round face turned and looked out the rear window of the car ahead. Then the face turned back and he could see many excited gestures and arm waving going on.

The driver of the Buick panicked. Instead of pouring it on and going for I-95 as he should have, he slammed on the brakes, turned to the right, and made a wild cut north onto Fourth Avenue after tearing right through the gas station on the corner, sending people diving for cover.

Bedlam grunted, "Oh yeah?" Without touching the brakes, he put the Plymouth into another sliding turn, from the left lane to the right and north on Fourth Avenue behind the Buick.

"Oh, man!" said Richards as he fumbled for the mike. Then he yelled into it, "Now we're north on Fourth Avenue! Florida tag delta-hotel-yankee nine-seven-zero!"

"Ten-four, bravo five-six, copy on the tag. Be advised the med units say minor injuries to the store manager. Also be advised the air unit is out of service."

"Damn!" said J.B. Then he looked over at Bedlam and said, "Looks like we gotta go this one alone for now, Skids." Bedlam, one hand on the wheel, accelerator pedal on the floor, looked unconcerned and said, "Shit, J.B., these assholes ain't showed me nothin' yet."

As he said this, the driver of the Buick crashed over the concrete median strip and turned left on a side street, alongside the cemetery. A hubcap broke away from the bouncing car, rolled across the street, and crashed into the front window of a house on the corner. The glass was still falling as the police car went roaring by and an old man stuck his head out the front door and stared at them wide-eyed.

"You know we're responsible for that broken window

because we're chasing these guys, don't you?" yelled
Richards. Bedlam just grinned and shrugged. J.B. yelled
into the mike, "West on Twentieth Street, toward Ninth
Avenue!"

"Ten-four, bravo five-six."

When the Buick got to Ninth Avenue it turned right and
headed north again. Ninth Avenue is a narrow two-lane
road, and it is always busy. The driver of the Buick, now
driving crazily in his effort to lose the tenacious police car
behind him, hurled his heavy car in a suicidal charge up
the busy street, sending other drivers across the cracked
sidewalks and onto lawns in their hasty attempts to get out
of his way. Right through the middle of the chaos came the
police car, lights and siren blaring. Bedlam was pushed
back in his seat, with one hand on the wheel, red eyes
apparently unconcerned, but not missing anything going on
around him.

On the other side of the car sat Richards. He had his legs
flexed, and was gripping the dash stiffly with one hand
while the other alternated from clinging to the front seat for
support to grabbing the mike so that he could yell into the
radio. As they proceeded up Ninth Avenue, Richards was
heard to yell several times, "Oh my God!" and "Jesus H.
Kee*rist!*" and an occasional *"Holy shit!"*

By now other units were starting to converge on the area
from other sectors of the city and Richards knew the chase
would end soon. This did not lessen his anxiety, however,
for he knew that rarely did a high speed chase end without
someone getting hurt, or even killed. All that heavy metal,
hurtling down the streets at high speeds, had to result in
disaster when it all came to a grinding halt in a compressed
space of time.

As they stared out of the windshield of the police car at
the wildly careening Buick, their vision was suddenly cut
off by a blob of dark green. Then they could see again.
Then their world was burgundy, and Bedlam sat up so he
could glance out the side window. As the windshield
cleared again, Bedlam yelled at Richards, "Those idiots are
throwing all those men's suits out the window! They're

either trying to get rid of the evidence, or they're trying to screw us up so they can lose us!"

J.B. didn't say anything, he just stared out of the side window at a pair of checked trousers hanging from the side mirror. The legs of the trousers kept whipping in his open window and popping him smartly on his right ear, making it sting. As he looked up the street in front of him he could see that the air was filled with suit coats, trousers, and vests of all colors. They filled the air like autumn leaves, swirling and blowing in the wind. He could see that the person in the backseat of the car ahead of them was frantically heaving the clothes out of the right rear window, and looking back and staring at him.

"Now! Now, Kareem Knieval! Now you're all mine!" yelled Bedlam as both cars flew up the street toward the light at Davie Boulevard. Cars were backed up in both lanes waiting for the light, and a loaded yellow school bus had come out of a small side street and was sitting across the northbound lane, waiting for a chance to pull out and go south. The only thing the Buick could do was to pull into the oncoming lane and cut through the intersection that way. Just as the driver of the Buick swerved over into the oncoming lane a huge lumbering beer truck came heavily around the corner to go south on Ninth. The truck shut off the lane completely and left the Buick driver with nowhere to go, especially considering the car's high speed as it approached the intersection.

Both Skids and J.B. tensed, watching the blue smoke come out from the tires of the swaying car in front of them as the driver slammed the brakes and the Buick slid, and then began to turn sideways . . . the whole time moving with a deadly certainty toward the stopped school bus.

"If he hurts even *one* of those kids on that bus I'll kill that bastard!" yelled Richards as Bedlam threw the police car into a duplicate slide. He held his breath and watched as the Buick slid sideways toward the bus, with the Plymouth sliding parallel to it, at the same speed. Finally, in a swirl of blue smoke, dust, and several pairs of trousers, both cars screeched to a stop, the right side of the Buick flush up against the side of the bus. There was little if any impact. Richards could see the horrified expression on the face of the bus driver, a husky black woman, and he could see several startled faces of the kids as they peered down at the Buick and the police car stuck beside them.

The Plymouth had jammed to a stop right alongside the other car, and the three people inside the Buick were trapped. There was less than an inch of room on either side of the car. They couldn't crawl out the right side against the bus. When the driver of the Buick slowly lifted his head, eyes big, he found himself staring right into the sinister, evil black hole at the end of J.B.'s revolver. He rolled his eyes and licked his lips. J.B. leaned closer, waiting for the silence that came when Bedlam turned off the siren. He stuck the gun still closer to the driver's bulging eyes and said, "Halt . . . police."

Bedlam shut down the motor and jumped out and ran over to the beer truck. He climbed up onto the running board and shook the big red-faced driver on the shoulder. He waited until the man's eyes focused on his, and said gently, "It's all right! It's all right now!" until the big man finally lifted both meaty hands off the steering wheel, which he had been squeezing white-knuckled.

The driver looked at Skids and croaked, "I thought . . . I thought . . . I, he was either going to hit me head-on or drive right through that bus full of kids." Bedlam patted him on the arm, jumped down, and walked back to the unit.

Richards had slid behind the wheel, and now he backed the unit away while Skids kept the people inside covered. Richards joined Skids in the street and they dragged the three out of the Buick and lined them up beside the left front fender. The driver, a tall, thin black man in his thirties, wearing a blue pullover and jeans, had recovered his composure and was scowling at the police officers. The other man was smaller and younger. He had urinated in his pants, and he stood there staring down at the stain. The girl, who had been in the backseat, looked as if she were about fifteen years old. She had frizzy hair, and there was a big wad of gum in her mouth. She was still shaken by the wild ride and quietly hiccuped and snuffled.

Richards had searched the shorter man and the female, and was just handcuffing them together, right hand to right hand, when a deep melodious female voice made both police officers turn.

"Excuse me, Officers. Would you be kind enough to indicate to me which one of these individuals was operating this vehicle just now?"

Behind them stood the bus driver, a large, handsome black woman wearing a lemon-colored pantsuit and large hoop earrings. She wore her hair in a huge shiny natural, and her good-looking face needed little makeup. She had one strong arm extended and one finger pointing toward the hood of the Buick, which was starting to steam. Bedlam, preoccupied, jerked one thumb over his shoulder and said, "This cool dude in the blue shirt was the ace drivin' that car, ma'am . . ."

That's all he got to say before he and Richards were brushed aside as the big woman let out a huff and lunged for the tall thin black man. The man saw it coming but moved too slowly. He managed to hop backward onto the hot hood of the Buick, but that's as far as he got before one strong hand grabbed his shirtfront in a bunch and dragged him back toward the glaring face of the bus driver. Her nostrils flared as she put her face against his and yelled, "You . . . you, *idiot!* You *imbecile!* You sorry *excuse* for a man! You could have hurt one of my kids! Did you hear me, sucker? You could have hurt one of those kids on that bus—*my kids!*"

With that, while holding him firmly with one hand, she began slapping the man again and again with the other. Each time she brought her palm across his sweaty face there was a loud sharp *smack*, and each time, all the kids on the bus, who were all crowding to the windows on the left side, would cheer and holler.

J.B. and Skids looked at each other and smiled, and just stood there with their arms folded across their chests. They looked like spectators at a tennis match, their heads turning back and forth as they followed the grimacing black face of the Buick driver as the bus driver smacked him one way, and then the other. Once the man tried to squirm out of her grasp, but the big woman just said, "Oh *no*, sucker, I'm not finished with you *yet!*" She let go of his shirtfront and began using both hands, cupped, to box his ears.

Pow! Pow! Smack! Smack! went the big hands against the man's head until he couldn't stand it anymore. Covering his ears with his hands, he started screaming, "Officers! Stop her! Oh, *please* stop her! Help me, Officers!"

Bedlam and Richards just looked on as the man began to cry and slowly slid down beside the front wheel of the Buick and cowered on the hot pavement. With all the kids laughing and cheering now, the big woman stood with her legs spread, staring down at her victim. She gave a contemptuous sneer, tossed her fine head of hair, and walked back to the bus. No one moved. As she climbed triumphantly back into the bus and slid into the driver's seat, the kids stood up and gave her a wild and delighted ovation. She turned and said something quietly to them and they all jumbled around until they were seated again. Then she put the bus in gear, waited until the beer truck driver had moved his rig out of the way, and carefully eased away from the steaming Buick. She had to pull slightly onto the sidewalk to negotiate the turn, but there was no danger that anyone was going to mention it to her. As she got back onto the pavement and straightened out, Bedlam stood in the middle of Ninth Avenue. Waving all other traffic to a complete standstill, he gestured her south on Ninth, using both hands with a flourish. He and J.B. then stood in the middle of the road, grinning, as she drove away.

No one was surprised to see the beer truck driver, standing stiffly beside his rig, snap out a crisp salute to the bus driver as she passed him with her load of precious cargo.

J.B. and Bedlam were turning back to the job at hand when Lieutenant Whitney roared up, siren blaring, slid to a stop, and jumped out. Jumping out required several slow, distinct movements, but he finally exited his unit, jammed his gold-embellished hat on his round head, bustled over, and watched as Richards handcuffed the sniffling Buick driver.

"Why is this man crying, Richards?" he demanded. "You and Bedlam here haven't been roughing up a prisoner, have you?" He stood there with his hands on his hips, his chubby legs spread, in a pose he thought looked macho. No one said anything, so he puffed up his red face and tried again. "Well, why is this man crying? Can't someone tell me why this man is crying?"

Richards looked at Bedlam and shrugged, and Bedlam looked at the lieutenant and said evenly, "The way we understand it, sir, this poor hapless individual has just learned that his subscription to American Dirt Bag magazine has been canceled. And he was so looking forward to the Ted Bundy centerfold in this month's issue."

The fat lieutenant stared at him hard for a few seconds, saw Richards's even stare, grunted, and turned away. He busied himself stalking around officiously, looking at the Buick and the suspects and watching as they were read their Miranda warnings and stuffed into the backseat of the police car. Finally, he approached Skids and J.B. again and said, "The way I see it, here are the charges."

He took another spread-legged stance and began counting on his pudgy fingers. "Grand larceny . . . assault and battery against the store manager, resisting arrest by fleeing, and reckless driving. I think that should just about do it."

"There's one more, Lieutenant," said Bedlam.

"Oh, there is? Well, what is it?"

Bedlam stood beside Richards, looked at the bright green trousers caught in the grill of the police unit, looked at the slacks still hanging on the side mirror, looked all the way down Ninth Avenue at all the multicolored vests hanging in hedges and jackets draped over street signs. He looked at the slacks in the gutters and the suit coats on the lawns, and he said, "Littering."

Later that day, after Bedlam and Richards finished the paperwork related to the chase, they went back out onto the road. They were parked in the shade of a pine tree behind the ball fields next to Croissant Park Elementary School, having a cold drink, when a new rental car pulled up next to them.

Scott Kelly pulled off his sunglasses, grinned, and said,

"Hey, Skids, why don't you put those eyes out before somebody calls the fire department?"

Bedlam made a face, pointed at Kelly, and said, "Look who's talkin', you're supposed to be undercover—invisible—and you're walkin' around with a face that looks like seventeen miles of bad road."

Richards leaned forward in his seat and waved hello to the narc. Kelly's expression changed, and he said, "Uh, J.B. . . ."

J.B. looked at Skids, then back at Kelly and said easily, "He's in on whatever you want to say, Scott. Hell, Skids is my road partner now. Can't have any secrets from him."

Scott Kelly nodded, and said, "Finally got a call from that federal guy. Ready for this? CIA . . . guy's name is Buchanan." He watched J.B.'s face closely as he said it.

J.B. was immediately assailed with a torrent of emotions and mental images, and questions. He felt a cold pull in the center of his chest, and his breath became shallow. He found he was gripping the dash very hard with his right hand, and that he was staring at Kelly, but not seeing him.

Skids said quietly, "Hey, J.B., you all right, man?"

"What? Oh, yes," said J.B. He turned away from Bedlam and Kelly and stared out the window of the car. William Buchanan, CIA, he thought. *The last time I even heard of you was twenty years ago—and it was because of that killing*. He rubbed his hand across his face, hard, and grunted. He felt the approach of an inevitable dread, as if for all of these years he had known there was some terrible unfinished work to be done, and that someday it would present itself to him. The shock was too much for him to assimilate immediately. He would have to go off someplace by himself and try to sort it out.

Kelly cleared his throat, and waited. J.B. turned back toward him and Kelly went on. "Buchanan says I'm to tell you that the case is still open, and something about fate stepping in to fuck with everybody's karma. I don't know, he's apparently pretty high up in their command structure, and I'm sure he's professional and all that. But he sounded strained somehow, like there's a personal thing for him here."

J.B. nodded. He took a deep breath, hesitated, and then told Kelly and Bedlam about the killing so long ago, about the CIA, and about his leaving the department up north in anger and disappointment.

He did not tell them about the face of the small boy.

When the initial whirlwind of thoughts hit him after he heard Buchanan's name, the face of the small boy was there, floating around the edges of his mind. He had deliberately pushed it away because he wasn't ready to confront the possible consequences.

Bedlam and Kelly were very quiet for a few moments. A train pulled out of the coupling area and moved north on the Florida East Coast tracks just east of where the police car and the rental car were parked. It picked up speed as it cleared the first crossing at Seventeenth Street. Two small boys climbed the outfield fence at the edge of the ball field nearby, calling out to some other boys who were grouped around home plate. A pinecone fell from the branches of one of the trees, bounced off the hood of the rental car with a dry clatter, and hit the ground.

Kelly cleared his throat again, and said, "Buchanan was playing it close to the chest but wanted me to know that you were a great guy and that we're all on the same team." Bedlam rolled his eyes and J.B. looked down at the floorboards. "Here's the killer, J.B.," Kelly said evenly. "Buchanan said he would tell us more on a face-to-face, but that he wanted you to know his sources . . . CIA, I guess . . . have info that a foreigner was picked up in the waters of the Bahamas recently . . . seriously injured . . . and is now being held in Cuba someplace."

The stillness that descended on the three cops was in sharp contrast to the life going on around them. It was as if they had become instantly frozen in a Lucite bubble, silent, immobile.

J.B. was afraid to breathe, afraid to move, afraid to do anything that would snap him out of this unreal conversation and propel him back to normal life. He felt the hope starting to grow in his heart, like a small flower breaking its way out of a layer of spring snow, and he sensed the fear that came with the knowledge of just how fragile that flower, and that hope, could be. He turned his head away from his partners again, and stared, unseeing, out the window.

"Well," said Bedlam, his voice gruff, "is he sayin' it's Novak, or what? Our department's gonna be notified? State Department or one of those federal gangs gonna get him outta Cuba?"

"He's not sayin' any of that, Skids," said Kelly, both of them aware that they were having the conversation for J.B. "He's just baiting us right now. He's got some interest in it, and we figure into an angle for him, or he wouldn't have called me. For now you and me and J.B. are the only ones that know this, and needless to say we really have to keep a lid on it." He paused, and looked across Skids to J.B. "I really debated even telling you, J.B., false hopes and all. But I figure we're just gonna have to take this case as it comes, even if it does seem to be taking on extraordinary proportions."

Skids coughed out a short laugh. "Yeah, we're just three little Fort Lauderdale cops, right? What are we doin' messin' with the CIA, Cuba, drug smugglers all over the place, and God knows what else?"

"Two things," said J.B. quietly. "We're doing two things here. We're gonna put Montilla away." He turned and looked at Skids, then at Kelly. "And we're gonna get Ted back home. And if we have to go up against Castro, the CIA, the State Department, and the KGB, then *they're* the ones who'll have to watch their ass."

Scott Kelly nodded. Skids Bedlam grunted, and said, "That's my boy!"

Ten minutes after he first spotted Great Isaacs Light poking up over the horizon, and after altering his course slightly, Onyx Montilla idled the big black and gray racing boat carefully through the narrow channel that headed directly for South Bimini Island. Within a hundred yards of the beach he cut back to the left and followed the channel into the small bay between North and South Bimini. The clear green water sparkled in the hot sunshine, and waving sea fans and sponges and coral structures could be seen thirty and forty feet below the surface. The islands looked beautiful, as they always did. Swaying palms and sandy beaches could be seen, as well as quaint homes and other buildings, small wharfs and docks, marinas full of boats, and the inevitable piles of old white and pink conch shells. From a distance, the island colors are light pastels, faded and dusty. Other than a small catboat operated by an ancient islander, there were no other boats moving around in the bay. Montilla could see one big sloop anchored on the far side, near where the seaplanes took off, but other than that there was no activity. The sun was too hot and the fishing was too slow in the middle of the day.

As he eased the pointed bow of *Stiletto* toward the old wooden docks at Blackie's Marina, he saw that there were the usual number of island dockhands, fishermen, sleepers, bonefish guides, and kids hanging around. He watched as "Bo," the head dock master, slowly got up from his position against the icehouse wall and ambled out onto the dock in anticipation of catching a thrown line. One of the kids started to move toward the edge of the dock also, and Montilla knew that as soon as the lines were secured the kid would ask, "Hey, mon, you want your boat washed, mon? You want me to watch him for you, mon? Can I come on him, mon? I know all about these boats like him, mon." And he would tell the kid to beat it as he always did.

But now, as he eased the starboard clutches into reverse and the port clutches forward to turn the boat sideways against the dock, he saw the easy grin on Bo's face suddenly disappear. The lanky islander stopped in his tracks and stared hard at the boat. Then he looked at Montilla as if in confirmation, and muttered something to the kid, who stopped also and then turned and walked back into the shade beside the icehouse wall. Bo just stood there as the racing boat bumped against the dock. He wasn't just ignoring Montilla's boat, he was standing there letting Montilla and everyone else there know that he was not going to lift a finger to assist in securing the boat. Montilla knew that most Bahamian islanders gave slow and surly service anywhere, at any time, but he also knew that Bo was purposely giving him a message.

With some difficulty, Montilla managed to get his stern line wrapped around a small bent cleat nailed crookedly to the splintery boards of the dock. Then he just wrapped a spring line around a post and let Silky hold it while he jumped out with the long bowline in his hand. He secured that to another cleat and then jumped back into the boat, took the line from Silky and secured it, and then shut the engines down. Even though this took only a few seconds to accomplish, Montilla was covered with sweat by the time he was finished. There was very little breeze, and the hot sun beat heavily upon the docks without relief. Silky, who felt uncomfortable under the hungry stares of the men on the dock, was wearing just a small bikini and sunglasses. Now, as Onyx secured the boat, she pulled on a light halter top and a pair of weathered shorts. She slid her feet into her old boat shoes and waited for Montilla to climb out onto the dock and then reach down and pull her up. She wiped the perspiration off her forearms and started to follow Montilla off the dock toward the main street.

Montilla was angry, but he knew he dared not show it now. He passed within inches of Bo, who still just stood there without saying anything. Bo's eyes never left Montilla's face, but Onyx saw that all the other islanders were staring hard at the girl. He reflected that the islanders always stared at the white girls that came off the boats. He knew it was their common belief that the "rich white pussy" only came there to jump into bed with some "strong black island boy." As he walked toward the main street of the small town of Bimini, he also reflected that probably Bo and Cuda were somehow related. He knew that just about everybody was somebody else's cousin or nephew or uncle in the islands, and he knew there was a strong underground grapevine that made it hard to keep secrets.

Just as Montilla and Silky reached the main street they heard a strong voice yell, "Hold on there, mon!" and they turned to see one of the three Bahamian Customs officials on the island approaching. The man was in full uniform, epaulettes and all, and he carried a big clipboard against his hip. He slowed as he reached Montilla, then eased into the only nearby shade, leaving Montilla and Silky standing in the sun. He looked hard at the girl, up and down slowly, and then said, "You just entered a foreign country, mon. What you gonna do? Just stroll right in here without observing the laws of our islands?"

"What are you talkin' about?" asked Onyx. "You know I come in here all the time, and you know that boat and you know I never stop to see you because I'm on my way to visit Mister Cornelius Black." He stood there with his legs spread and his hands on his hips, looking up into the watery brown eyes of the Customs man.

The Bahamian just picked his teeth slowly with a red plastic toothpick, looked at him for a few seconds, and said, "Mon, there ain't nobody comin' to this island today don't fill out the proper forms and pay the entry fee—and nobody is you." With that he handed the clipboard to Montilla. Then slowly, making a production of it, he drew one of four shiny Cross pens out of his shirt pocket and lay it on top of the clipboard. Montilla looked at the clipboard, shrugged, and started to fill out the forms in a ragged, scrawled, inaccurate smear. He watched as Silky walked over across the street under an overhanging awning and stood there in the shade with her arms folded across her stomach.

As he angrily filled out the forms, Montilla told himself to be cool, not to get ruffled until he had a chance to see the big man. Then he knew he could get things straightened out. He knew he was being hassled here because they wanted to get him off balance, to frighten him a little. He knew the Customs officers had been on the take here since the first one was sent over from Nassau ages ago. It was common knowledge among the smugglers, and they took the cost into account when doing business here. He knew these guys and others like them, not to mention the commissioners, cabinet ministers, and the others, who had been actively involved in narcotics smuggling for years. They would not hesitate to leave a certain boat alone for the right amount of cash. Hell, he remembered one deal a couple of years ago where he had purchased almost a ton of grass from this same Customs man's boss. The grass had been seized from another group of smugglers who hadn't paid off the right people, and then with zero overhead to worry about, the grass was sold cheaply to Montilla's group—and everybody was happy.

But this treatment today pissed him off because they were just busting his chops. He also knew he had to see the big man and get things straightened out right away. He finished the forms, pulled a ten out of his pocket and stuck it onto the clipboard to cover the entry fee, and handed the board back to the islander without looking at him. He waved at Silky and headed down the street toward Blackie's Marina, Lounge, and Supper Club. The girl came up beside him and they walked easily along the side of the road, looking at the baseball-helmeted Honda riders, the two taxis, and the tourists jamming the two-lane road. No one waved at them or said hello as they passed. When they were less than half a block from Blackie's they came to the small gate that was the entrance to the Compleat Angler, a scenic old establishment that had been there for years. It had a flowered courtyard and patio, and inside it was cooled by hanging paddle fans. All the walls were covered with photographs of boats, fish, fishermen, and girls. Tournament after tournament was remembered on those walls, and many a famous face grinned out from under a peaked cap.

Silky had been to the Angler many times before, and she liked the sitting room on the east side of the bar. The room was furnished like an old-fashioned men's club drawing room, with a big fireplace, polished wooden floors, a huge slow-turning ceiling fan, and big deep furniture. These walls, too, were covered with pictures, but in this room almost everything was Hemingway memorabilia. There were photos of "Papa" on his boat, or with a favorite guide, or standing beside some huge blue marlin. There were also framed letters written by Hemingway, and news clippings and magazine articles about him. It was a peaceful, comfortable room, and Silky liked to spend time there while Montilla went off to do whatever he had to do.

Montilla turned to Silky and said tersely, "You wait here

for me. I don't know how long I'll be. Have some lunch or a Coke or something and relax for a while. I'll come and get you on the way back to the boat." Then he turned and stalked off.

Mister Cornelius Black wiped the already polished bar with a towel and then leaned on it with his small, bony hands. In the old days he had been called Blackie, not only because of his name. He was naturally a very dark black man, and years in the island sun had only deepened the color of his skin to the point where other islanders seemed almost pale by comparison. Now no one called him Blackie. Now it was Mister Cornelius Black. His family had been part of Bimini as far back as anyone could remember, and through the generations they had become more and more a part of the entire island chain. Cornelius's father, Archibald, had made a killing during prohibition days, and ever since then the Black family had become stronger and stronger. The common summation of the Black family of Bimini was that "They own that island." In a literal sense this may not have been accurate, but it was fact that very little went on there concerning business, tourism, fishing, island law, and smuggling of all kinds that the Black family didn't figure into heavily. With the already established Marina and Supper Club in his possession, Cornelius Black was set for life as an influential member of the island. That, combined with his enthusiastic participation in all aspects of the smuggling trade, made him one of the most powerful men in the Bahamas, not just Bimini. He had at least some control over anything taking place on Bimini or the nearby waters, whether smuggler-sponsored or government sponsored. Government employees, such as police officers or Customs officials, knew that he was the real boss there, no matter what Nassau said.

Physically he was a small man, wiry and hard. His tight kinky hair was worn very short, and there were patches of gray over the ears. He had small, sharp features, with a bladelike nose and a small black cut for a mouth. When he wanted to, for business reasons, he could show a wide grin full of big even teeth, but normally he wore a dour expression, his busy eyes rarely missing anything going on around him. Today he wore a sparkling white *guyabera* shirt. The shirt was Cuban-style, with large pockets. He also wore tan slacks and sandals. When seen standing there at his long, polished bar, under the slowly turning ceiling fan, he didn't look like a man to be reckoned with, but he was.

Mister Cornelius Black already knew that Montilla had arrived in his boat and that he was on his way to the lounge. He had anticipated the meeting for several weeks, and he was eager to hear what Montilla said, and how he said it. But now, as Montilla swung open the heavy doors and walked into the cool interior of the lounge and saw him and smiled and waved, Black looked at him as if he wasn't even there, turned slowly, and walked through a set of swinging doors into a back room without saying a thing.

Montilla watched him walk out of the room and said quietly, "Shit." He went over to the bar and sat on a stool. He put his elbows on the bar and rested his chin in his hands. He waited.

After several minutes, a large black woman came out of the back room wearing a stained apron and looked at Montilla and said, "You want somethin'?"

Montilla sat up a little and said, "Yeah . . . why, hello, Dorothy, how've you been?" The big woman didn't smile and laugh at him as she usually did. She just stood there looking at him. He looked down at the bar and said evenly, "Dorothy, I'd like a beer. And would you please ask Mister Black if I could speak with him for a few minutes?" The woman still didn't say anything. She walked slowly over to the cooler, pulled out a beer without looking at it, walked over in front of Montilla, and slapped it down on the bar, unopened. "Two dollars," she said. Montilla put the money down on the bar and asked, "Dorothy, can I have a glass please?" but she had already turned her back on him and walked into the other room. Montilla opened the beer and took a sip, swiveling around on the stool until he faced the door, and waited.

Ten minutes later the front door opened and in walked

Horace Princeton Ellis. Known locally as "H.P.," or "Hushpuppie," Ellis was another well-known and respected islander. Hushpuppie Ellis was not known for his money deals or his family background, which would have been hard to trace anyway. He was not well known for his prowess as a fishing guide or storyteller either. He was well known because he was probably the biggest, nastiest, roughest-looking islander anyone ever saw. It wasn't that he was tall; in fact, he was just under five nine. He qualified as big because he had about three hundred pounds welded onto that five-nine frame. At first glance he looked like a black sumo wrestler. Closer examination showed that, although he was round, he was not fat. Everything on him, including his round belly, was rock hard. His biceps were over twenty inches and his forearms were huge to match them. His hands were like two big paddles, with long, incredibly strong fingers. He could rip apart a coconut with his hands, shredding the husk with a grunt and a pull. Though none of the locals would ever seriously think of fighting him, he had been seen on occasion standing on his powerful thick legs in the middle of a wild bar fight, watching men bounce off him with contempt, or casually picking up one of the unfortunates and hurling him out into the street. When Mister Cornelius Black walked the main street of any island, or walked the streets of Fort Lauderdale, which he sometimes did, he was always relaxed because behind him always lumbered quiet, steady, Hushpuppie Ellis.

Montilla stared at Ellis as the big islander ambled into the gloom. As usual, Ellis had the orange plastic baseball helmet stuck onto his shaved, bowling ball head. As usual, the helmet looked ridiculous sitting on top of that shiny dome, and as usual Montilla did not make fun of it. Montilla nodded and smiled at Ellis, but the big man just stared at him, pulled out a chair, swung it around backward, and eased his huge buttocks onto it. Then he slowly folded his massive arms across the back and sat there.

Montilla turned his back on him and looked down at the now warm beer. He had made the trip today to talk business, figuring enough time had elapsed since he and Cuda had done their dirty deed in the waters just south of there. He knew that Black liked money more than anything else in the world, and he figured that Black would never hurt him as long as he was good for making those big smuggling dollars. Montilla sat there and hoped he had figured right.

One half hour later Montilla heard the chair scrape behind him, and when he turned he found Hushpuppie standing at his shoulder. His eyes followed the islander's hand as it reached out and picked up the small leather bag that Montilla had been carrying since he climbed out of *Stiletto*. Montilla held his breath as Hushpuppie squeezed the bag and turned it in his hand, apparently trying to feel if there was a weapon in it. Satisfied, he dropped the bag onto the bar and motioned for Montilla to follow. Montilla took a breath, picked up the bag, slid off the stool, and walked behind the big islander through the dining area toward the kitchen door. As they passed through the kitchen and out into the small courtyard separating the restaurant from the living quarters, Montilla relaxed a little. He knew they were heading for the private office that Black used for his meetings. When they got to the heavy wooden door, Hushpuppie knocked three times and opened it and stood aside. As Montilla squeezed past him into the small room, Black said quietly, "Thank you, Hushpuppie. Now if you'd be kind enough to wait there in case Mister Montilla here needs an escort back to his boat, I'd surely appreciate it." Ellis nodded and stepped out of the room, closing the door with a thud.

Mister Cornelius Black was sitting in his big padded office chair studying Montilla through a cloud of blue smoke generated from a nasty-looking little cheroot. He didn't say anything for a moment but sat back and made himself more comfortable by crossing one leg over the other, straightening his shirt as he did so. Montilla stood there in front of the desk, like a schoolboy in the principal's office. He could feel a trickle of sweat running down from the small of his back into his shorts. Finally Black said quietly, "Why, Onyx, how are you? Sit down, please, you look so dangerous standing over me like that."

The fact that the usual handshake was missing was noticed by Montilla as he pulled up the only other chair in the room, a small, straight, hard little thing that looked as if it were at least one hundred years old. He sat precariously on the edge with his hands on his knees, and said, "Thank you for seeing me, Mister Black. I know how busy you are, and I'm sure my business with you won't take long."

Black looked at the ceiling. "You know, Onyx, I hate to tell you this, but I'm not sure you and I are doing business anymore."

He still didn't look at Montilla, so Montilla cleared his throat and said, "But Mister Black, have I done something to anger you? Wasn't the money right on our last deal? Was it late?"

"You know it's not the money, Onyx . . . though you and I both know I've been giving your group some fine deals over the last few months. Actually, even if there *was* to be more business between us we'd have to discuss a whole new rate structure."

Crap, thought Montilla, but he said evenly, "Well, could you tell me what the problem is, Mister Black? I mean, things haven't been right here all day. No one will even speak to me and I feel like a stranger here."

Black swung his feet back to the floor and looked at Montilla for the first time. He took another pull on the cheroot, let out a thin stream of smoke, and said, "You came over here awhile back and picked up a cousin of mine, a man named Cuda. You had some other men with you. Then you and Cuda ran on down the chain a ways, and you killed those other men that were with you."

Montilla sat rigid, listening.

"I was not pleased, Onyx. Not pleased that you had to come over here, to our islands, to take care of some of your own dirty business. It bothered me that you didn't consult me about it first." Black looked at the small cigar in his hands, and Montilla was struck at that moment with the many similarities between Black and Kolin. Black went on. "You didn't consult me, and then you used Cuda to help you. Now I know you and Cuda have worked together for a long time, and that you liked him and trusted him.

But Cuda worked for *me*, understand? If he was going to do a job like he did with you, it would have to be authorized by *me*."

Montilla remained silent, not sure of where the conversation was leading.

"The other problem with what you did, Onyx, is the fact that that type of action, no matter how carefully planned and executed, has a way of coming back to haunt you sometimes. When you make people disappear it has a tendency to bring snooping policemen out of the bushes. And in this case it won't even be our *own* snooping policemen. It will be those from the states . . . and believe me, they can be very tenacious and thorough."

The room was quiet except for the muted humming of the small wall air conditioner to Montilla's right.

Black leaned forward to clean the end of the cigar in a glass ashtray on the desk, and this allowed him to watch Montilla's face closely as he said, "And now Cuda is dead."

Montilla's face showed surprise and alarm as he stiffened in his chair and whispered, "Dead? By who? How?"

Black leaned back and studied the other man for a moment, then began in a husky voice. "You know he had that little ol' whaler he used to zip around between here and South Bimini, and out to wherever his fishing boat was. Well, a couple of bonefish guides saw it drifting on the flats the other day, the engine not running. When they went over to it they found Cuda lying in it—or what was left of him. He was, in fact, very dead, and by the looks of his body he probably wished he had died long before he finally did. Understand?"

Montilla nodded, his eyes brittle.

"Cuda had spoken to me just before he went off the last time," said Black. "He told me he wanted to go down to South Bimini and have a hard talk with those Latins— Cubans and Colombians—that have moved in. Couple of the local men have been threatened when they went ashore down there, or were even just close to the beach. I had reports that men were seen carrying automatic weapons, and that there was a lot of nighttime boat traffic in and out.

So they had set up a forward staging area to facilitate their smuggling cocaine into Miami and Lauderdale. No big thing, right? Problem is they did it without even attempting to cut us in, or get our approval, or anything." Black sat there, glowering. "They come in to our islands with a lot of cash, buy a couple of run-down hotels with some rickety docks, and stomp around like they own the place. Brash about it, really. So, Cuda knew I was very unhappy about his getting involved with you in *your* business, and I guess he thought he could make it up to me by going over there and trying to find out something about those Latinos—or setting up a basis for communication with them or something." He pinched the bridge of his nose. "And then we find him in his little boat, savaged. What is it, Onyx? A warning to us? *They* come here and warn *us*? Did they have to torture him before he died to learn about me, and my operations? Hell, it's no secret what I do, what businesses I support. And it's also no secret that I'll work something out with people trying to make a living out here."

Black seemed to diminish in size now that he had had his say. He studied Montilla with a little less intensity, knowing that Onyx had already passed part of this test. Judging from Montilla's reaction, Black was sure he had no knowledge of Cuda's death.

Montilla chewed his lower lip, understanding the chill in the air now. Black knew, so of course everyone else knew, that he was of Cuban descent. They had even joked about it in the past. He knew the islanders would have trouble telling the difference between a Cuban and a Colombian, and would lump them all into a "Latin" bag anyway. And now there were Latins on South Bimini, a local man had been killed in some terrible way, and here was Montilla, dealing with Mister Cornelius Black to be sure, but still one of the last people to do work with Cuda, and still a Latin. For a brief instant, Montilla felt he knew what was going on down on South Bimini, and who was behind it, but he quickly pushed it out of his mind before Black saw the knowledge in his eyes.

He took a deep breath, and said, "Look, Mister Black.

I'm very saddened by what happened to Cuda. I liked him, and we worked well together. I can understand your concern. I was wrong and I apologize to you for involving Cuda in that work I had to do. And now I know I should not have done it over here anyway. I selfishly did not consider the potential threat it could be to you and your operations. But hear me, I did not have anything to do with what happened to Cuda. And just because my father was a Cuban does not mean I'm part of those Cubans moving in on South Bimini. They would consider me an American, and would not trust me or work with me." He paused to see if his words were having any effect. Black sat there immobile, silent.

"Also," Montilla plunged on, "if there is some way you can believe me and trust me, I'm sure we can go on with our previous arrangement, even if you must charge us more per pound—and we can both go on making money. My backers are pleased to be working with you and want to continue. They would be just as concerned with this situation as you are, but I'm sure they would want to move forward if it was at all possible." He licked his lips, a small lump in his gut as he went on. "One other reason I hope we can continue our business dealings. Up until now I have represented my backers who are content to buy from you the confiscated marijuana that you or your people occasionally come across. They like the profit, and they don't mind the hassles involved because they feel there is not much heat on grass these days. I've been working for them and watching how things go, and I feel it's time I took advantage of my relationship with you and my experience and equipment and branched out a little. It's time for me to take a bold step, with your help, that will make me a more important player out here." He squared his shoulders, and looked at Black dead-on. "I want to buy cocaine from you, Mister Black. I know you come across it once in a while. I can run it in with my group's grass and no one will be the wiser, except you and me. I've even figured a way to use the money they send you, if you agree, to mix my coke buys in with their grass buys, and run kind of a 'duel mule.' All of this, of course, if *you* agree."

Montilla sat back, his mind racing, the blood pounding at his temples. Now the plan he had been thinking about for weeks, the crazy plan that both excited and frightened him, was out on the table. Sure, he could keep on making money with the grass as part of Kolin's deal, and yeah, that Castro *patrón*, Maximiliano, was offering him a pretty heady mixture of money and intrigue—but all of that was somebody *else's* adventure. It was time for Onyx Montilla to start running some kind of gig on his own, even if for now he had to wrap it up inside one of the others. He almost grinned as he thought, *That's right, I'll fill the wallets of Kolin and his old cronies, and I'll strike some kind of blow for the revolution and the memories of my father with Maximiliano. And I'll do it all while I'm smuggling my cocaine for my profit. I am Onyx Montilla, and I can do it.*

He pulled himself back to the business at hand, aware that he had to win this battle first, and said, "I know when I start talking about cocaine you think about all the bullshit you've heard from other guys, mostly Americans, who come here and sing their songs about all the money you'll make if you just front them some coke. I know you've heard a lot of lies, and seen guys promise you things that they could never deliver. I want you to understand that I am different. I am real." He slowly unzipped the small leather bag that he held in front of him, reached in, and brought out a thick wad of money, held tightly together with rubber bands. "This is fifteen thousand dollars, in hundreds. I brought it for you, sort of like a security bond, so you'd know that I mean business. I hope we'll be talkin' kilos of coke, so this is just a drop in the bucket right now. But it's for you, if you think we can still work together."

Montilla watched as one small bony black hand slid across the desktop, grabbed the money, and scurried back toward the smiling black face. He took a sweet deep breath and let it out slowly.

Black cocked his head, almost laughed out loud, and thought, *Oh yes, Onyx, we'll work together, and I'll even consider letting you pull a fast one on Kolin with his own money. And yes, I'll sell you cocaine, if that's what you*

*want. But now I know it will be only a matter of time
before you take a fall. You're too greedy, Onyx, and not
just for money.*

Black smiled a small smile at Montilla, and said, "Onyx,
listen, no one here has accused you of anything. You know
how close all of us on these islands are. The people here
look to me when they're troubled, and they just weren't
sure whether you had anything to do with what happened
to Cuda or not, you bein' like a Cuban and all. So I had to
ask. Of course I never had any doubts about you, Onyx.
You and I have done a lot of business together and I hope
we'll do a lot more. Of course, now that this has happened
I'm probably going to have to spread the profits around a
little more than I used to until people get their confidence
back in you."

Montilla knew that meant everything was going to cost
him more, but he also knew he was all right now. Even if
Black still thought he had anything to do with Cuda's de-
mise, he had shelved it for the advantage of more business
profits and, of course, the "security bond."

Black stood up now, as did Montilla, and they shook
hands. He smiled at Black as he thought of something a
government police officer had told him once off one of the
out islands. The man had just "searched" Montilla's boat
without going below decks. With a neat little wad of cash
jammed into his front uniform pocket, the official had
eased himself back onto the dock, laughed, and said, "In
the Bahamas, mon, the dollar is everything."

Montilla felt a lot better as he stood at the gate in front
of the Compleat Angler, waiting for Silky. He watched her
hungrily as she jiggled slightly coming down the brick
steps. As she came through the gate she asked quietly, "Is
everything all right, Onyx? Is it okay?"

Montilla reached behind her, rubbed his hand smoothly
down the back of her shorts, suddenly squeezed hard, and
said, "Of course everything's all right. These island niggers need me a lot more than I need them. Shit, they're just
like everybody else. They love my money."

She looked at his grinning face, felt the hard digging of

his fingers, and asked, "Are we going back home now, Onyx?" Montilla let her go, turned, and began walking up the street, toward the dock. He looked over his shoulder at her and said, "Nah. It's late afternoon now. I don't feel like beatin' myself to death goin' back across the Stream in the chop, so we're gonna spend the night at the Big Game Club. We'll head back in the morning, *sí?*"

Montilla stopped and waited for her to catch up with him, then he put his face close to hers and said, "Besides, my good friend Mister Cornelius Black just gave me, as a gift, one ounce of very fine coke. I figure we can lay around in the sun, have a few drinks, some dinner at Blackie's—I can do a couple of lines of this toot." He kept talking and stared into her eyes and slid his hand slowly up the inside of her thigh until it could go no farther.

Silky said, "Onyx . . ." and tried to squirm away, hoping nobody in the street saw his hand.

He tightened his grip on her and grinned and went on. "And then I'm gonna get you on that bed and give it to you until you bark like *el perro* . . . if you're nice." He laughed, turned away from her, and headed for the docks. She watched him for a few seconds, sighed, and followed along behind.

When they got back onto the dock, Montilla was pleased to see that the word was already out on his popularity re-evaluation. He saw that *Stiletto* had been pulled around to one of the protected slips, and he saw that she had been washed down. Bo was on the bow deck, wiping off the windshield. He looked up and smiled as Montilla approached.

"Hey, there, Mister Onyx, we've got her all squared away. We went ahead and topped off the tanks and I checked the oil levels and all. It's on the house so don't you worry about it. You know she's tight if I checked her out, Mister Onyx."

Montilla looked at the islander smiling up from the boat. There was no trace of the earlier animosity. Stupid islanders, he thought, just can't figure 'em out. He smiled and said, "Thank you, Bo. I do appreciate it. And I for sure know you're one of the best people around here. If you say she's tight, she's tight."

As the lanky black dock master scrambled back up onto the dock boards and stood up, Montilla slipped a fifty into the man's left trouser pocket and said, "We're gonna see if we can't find something to do with each other here tonight, Bo." He saw the man look at Silky and grin. "And we'll be leaving in the morning. We won't be in a big hurry, but I'd appreciate it if you could have her ready to go for me."

"Oh, don't you worry about that, Mister Onyx," said Bo quickly. "She'll be ready to go in the mornin'. I'll see to it myself." Montilla patted him lightly on the shoulder, winked, and turned back toward the street with the girl.

Silky was silent and he was deep in thought as they walked in the afternoon sun. He knew he still had some problems. Over the last couple of months he had lost too many loads, and during that time he still had to keep laying out those heavy operating costs. He shook his head. Damn people would never believe how much it cost to run a full-blown grass-smuggling operation. All the boats, marine equipment, damn crews all wanting their money right now. Shit. When a couple of loads went through the money was real good, but it still cost a lot to keep things going. Then lose a load—his face darkened—lose a *couple* of loads, and hell, things started getting tight real fast. Crap, just paying the leases on all those waterfront houses was a pain in the ass. And—he shook his head—once you got used to living the good life and spending all that easy money it just seemed hard to go back on a budget. He let out a sigh. Maybe when this coke deal goes through things will be better. *Who knows,* he thought, *maybe I'll go into coke exclusively.*

As they turned off the sand path onto the pavement of the main street, they almost bumped into the Customs man who had made them fill out the forms earlier. Montilla stopped in front of the man and stared at him, but the man wouldn't look at him. Slowly Montilla reached into his shirt pocket, pulled out the shiny silver Cross pen, and said evenly, "Oh. I seem to have kept your quaint little pen, Mister Customs Inspector. I know how you just hate to keep having to replace them when some inconsiderate foreigner like me keeps one after filling out your oh-so-important little forms." He stood with his legs spread, throwing the pen into the air, letting it spin and then catching it again. The Customs man's eyes stayed riveted to the ground. Montilla looked at Silky and grinned, but she looked away. He went on. "I don't need your pen now since I've finished my business with Mister Black. So here, boy." With that he flipped the pen into the air again, watched the sun shine off it as it spun, and stepped back slightly so the pen then spun down into the sand at the Customs man's feet. Then he turned away.

The black man stood there watching Montilla's back as he and the girl walked slowly toward the Big Game Club. He clenched his fists and let out a hiss, closed his eyes, sighed, and shook his head. Some day, white boy, he thought. He bent down and picked up the pen and brushed it off. He slid it into his shirt pocket and said quietly to himself, "Some day."

THIRTEEN

Fidel Castro also wondered who Kathleen was.

He had returned from his brief revolutionary back-slapping tour to be greeted with the extraordinary news of the injured American who had been found in the Bahamian waters and was now slowly recovering from his wounds in a prison hospital.

He rewound the tape on the small cassette player and listened to Ted's voice again. When Ted's voice stopped because he had finally fallen asleep, the only sound was that of the young nurse, comforting him. Castro let it play until the tape ran out.

He sat back in his chair. He was in his office on the third floor of the Palace of the Revolution. It was very late at night, and the building was quiet.

The head of the secret police and the head of the prisons had virtually done a small dance in front of him when he had stepped from his limousine earlier in the afternoon, almost elbowing each other out of the way in their attempt to be the first to tell him about the American. Not only did they both want credit, but also they both wanted their organizations to take charge of whatever it was that he, Fidel, decided to do about the problem.

Was it a problem, Castro asked himself. Or was this injured young American a gift—something he could use to hurt or embarrass the government of the *Estados Unidos*. He pulled on his graying beard absently and let another thought come to the surface, one that had been nagging him more and more in recent years. Could this American, who had been thrown up from the sea, have some value in his plans to ease tensions between his government and that monstrous giant to the north?

He sighed. In his heart did he really want to ease tensions? No, not while he, Fidel Castro, was in power. But what about the future, what will happen when there is no Fidel, only a Raul and a Fidelito—and that huge, powerful bear in Moscow?

He pushed the cassette recorder around on his desk with one big hand while he thought about it. He was aware of the international reaction to the fact that his government was becoming more and more repressive instead of moderate. His was a totalitarian state, but then it had to be that way. The revolution had been, and still was, a success, and the pressure had to be kept on or it would weaken. He was sure of that.

But he was not blind, or stupid.

When he rode about the city in one of his limousines, or trundled about the countryside in a *Gazik*, he could see it. His people, the Cuban people, lived in a drab world—no color, no life—their faces tight with fear and their bellies sometimes growling for more food. Cuba had weapons, and schools, and paved roads, and helicopters. Cuba had wonderful rallies and speeches. Cuba had somber diplomatic ties with other revolutionary countries that wanted only aid, not ideology. Cuba was even building a couple of Russian-designed and engineered nuclear power plants. Yes, he sighed again, yes, Cuba had all of these things. But did Cuba smile? Did Cuba dance and laugh? Were her people filled with the vibrant fun and energy and love of color and music that was in their hearts when they were born?

Or had Cuba become a grim, gray machine?

He stood up suddenly, angry. Enough. Enough weak thoughts and worries about the future. He was Fidel Castro, and his Cuba was magnificent, and the Cuban people loved him and were happy. He rubbed his fingers through his hair and thought of the American again.

His secret police said the American was probably a policeman, a narcotics officer who had been found out by some smuggler and taken out to be killed. The man was obviously a fool, but a fool with some enormous luck, *sí?* The secret police said one of their senior operatives was very interested in the young American, and thought he could be useful to the cause. How? Is there some way the American narc can be given back to his own as a quiet but sure sign that he, Fidel, is a man of compassion, a man who is still open to maintaining some level of cordial relations with the American government?

Or should the inept and blundering narc be used as a gesture of contempt, a sign of superior intelligence services and capabilities? He could be used to create an international scandal and embarrassment. He might die of his injuries. Maybe he would die while resisting Cuba's valiant secret police, a cause of outrage among the Cuban people, an obvious attempt at interference by an outside government.

Fidel Castro stretched, and left his office. It was very late now, and he felt the need to go to the small apartment on Eleventh Street, in the Vedado District, to sleep.

This situation with the young *Americano* policeman had so many possibilities.

* * *

Richards left the station in the late afternoon after another busy and tiring day. The paperwork was finally finished, and he drove to the supermarket. He had to pick up a gallon of milk and a head of lettuce for Jane, and he knew he could always find plenty of other items they needed as he wandered up and down the aisles. He thought about the day, and about what had been pounding in his skull since Kelly had said it. It looked as if Kathleen was right; Ted might very well be alive—but alive in *Cuba*. Hell, he might as well be alive on the moon. He chewed his lips as he moved down the bread aisle, pushing a cart with one wobbly wheel. Should he tell her? Should he build up her hopes any further, knowing that even if Ted were alive in Cuba it would take a miracle to get him home?

The more he thought about it, the more he knew he would wait, wait until he had the face-to-face with Buchanan, to see what more info there really was. At the thought of Buchanan, the face of the small boy started to come into focus in his mind; it was the same face, but with an undefined new clarity about it. J.B. quickly and deliberately pushed the image from his mind.

He finished his shopping, surprised that he had come out of the market with so many full bags. A long string of yellow stamps fluttered from the top of one of the bags as he made his way across the lot to his truck. He drove home.

He let himself into the cool interior of the house, made his way through and around the four yapping dogs at his feet, put the groceries down on a kitchen counter, and looked around in vain for any of the kids. He started putting things away, deciding Kathleen was probably at one of her club meetings, and Erin was probably at her girlfriend's house down the street. And Ricky? God only knew where Ricky was, or what he was doing.

He changed into his favorite khaki work pants and shirt, made a cup of coffee, and eased himself into a lounge chair on the patio, near the small swimming pool. He sat comfortably in the shade of the awning, a few feet from the clear green water, and stared at the sparkling sunlight reflected off the surface. He saw that all around the edge of the pool the deck was wet, but he didn't think about it as he sat there and tried to let the events of the day settle down into whatever nooks and crannies there were left in his tired mind. What happens when there are no more nooks and crannies? He thought of all the things he had seen as a cop. Maybe it was time to get out and do something else. But what? Oh, he and Jane had talked of a small flower shop for years. Was that the answer? Would that clean out all the nooks and crannies? He shook his head and thought, Well, who knows?

He was sitting there thinking, just starting to come down a little, when suddenly the afternoon stillness was shattered by a high-pitched, bloodcurdling scream. He saw a flash of movement from overhead, and then there was an enormous splash in the middle of the pool, and he was immediately covered by a huge splash of cold water. He stood up shaken, dripping wet and sputtering, and stared into the foam rising like a spring from the bottom of the pool. As he watched he saw his son Ricky pop his head up out of the water, turn his face fast to get his hair out of the way, and rub his eyes. He stood there as his son yelled, "Woooeeeee!" and pushed himself toward the edge of the pool. It was then that Ricky looked up and saw his father standing there, soaked, staring down at him. He swam easily to the edge of the pool, crossed his arms over the tiles, and said, "Gee, Dad, you're all wet."

J.B. stared down at his son and asked, "Ricky, did you just jump off the roof . . . into the pool?" Ricky looked at him like any kid studying an old person who had just asked the totally obvious and said, "Well, yeah, Dad, I did."

Richards wiped his hand across his face, slowly put his coffee cup down on the deck, and said, "Oh. I see." Then he walked over to the edge of the pool, stood towering over his son for a few seconds, raised his hands into the air, yelled, "Of *course* he did!" and threw himself full-length into the clear water with a great splash.

Silky leaned back against the bolster seat in *Stiletto*, moored securely in the slip near their house, and let the warm sun penetrate her skin. It was early afternoon, clear and hot with just a slight breeze. It was a beautiful day for a boat ride. She relaxed in the sun waiting for Montilla to come out of the house.

He had told her to get ready because he wanted to go up to Runners, a popular waterfront lounge near the Oakland Park Boulevard Bridge on the Intracoastal Waterway. On weekends when the weather was nice it was hard to find dock space to tie up one's boat because of the clutter of craft, all powerful racers, all streamlined macho machines. Sometimes there would be as many as a dozen boats rafted off to each other from the dock. The boats were expensive, so the men who drove them had money. A few were legitimate businessmen, a couple were wealthy by inheritance, and many were from the higher levels of the criminal community, including smugglers. Of course, several of the more flashy boats were owned by local attorneys who just happened to represent those drug smugglers. Still, smeared with coconut suntan oil, bemedaled with gold chains and bracelets, and accompanied by at least one stunning young thing in a tiny bikini—who could tell the difference?

Silky had walked with Montilla to the boat and then had heard him curse and turn back to the house. He had forgotten the ignition keys. She turned her head now as he came out of the house, slamming the door almost hard enough to break the glass jalousies, and stalked toward her with his head down, muttering under his breath. As he jumped down into the boat and began raising the engine cover before starting the engines, she watched him and thought of the way he had been acting lately.

Since that last trip to Bimini, when he had successfully completed some kind of deal with that little Mister Black, he had been really hard to live with. His moods changed so suddenly she was always off balance. One minute he was so happy he was almost delirious, promising her the world and buying her gifts. The next he would be sulking, brooding, accusing her of petty indiscretions. And worst of all, he would lose his temper for no reason and fly into a rage, screaming at her and throwing things around. She was constantly on edge now, trying to anticipate his moods but usually being caught off guard. As she watched him run the blowers for a minute before firing up the engines, she thought to herself that she wasn't trying to anticipate his moods to make *his* life easier. It was to make *her* life easier. She knew she would have to break away from him soon; she just didn't know how to do it. She was alone in the world, she had no job, no training, and no money. And she was afraid of his temper and the latent violence that lurked within him.

Montilla jumped out, untied the lines, coiled them quickly, and jumped back into the boat. He didn't look at Silky or say anything to her as he idled the boat out of the canal toward the Intracoastal. Silky tried to relax and enjoy the day, looking at all the beautiful houses and boats along the way. It was a very fine day, and she knew if people saw her go by, she and her man, tanned and healthy, in their hundred thousand dollar racing boat, they would think she had the world by a string. She thought to herself wryly that those observing her should thank their lucky stars that they were not living with Montilla. Since the Bimini trip, he had been using more and more cocaine. It was odd because from the time she had first known him he had always been disdainful of those who used too much coke, and always said how stupid it was and how he had been, and always would be, very careful. The few times Montilla offered her a line of coke and she politely refused it he was a little puzzled, but being a basically greedy person he soon accepted it as one of her stupidities, which left more of the powdery drug for him. She would have some wine instead of grass or coke. When Montilla and his buddies got high together she found herself laughing less and spending more time by herself. The more she thought about the whole thing—grass, coke, parties, dopers, Montilla—the more of a waste it all seemed. Stupid. It was all so stupid. And it was all a waste of her life. As the boat idled past the Bahia Mar Yacht Basin she felt the sun on her shoulders and the wind in her hair, and she looked up into the clear blue sky and smiled. She was getting out. She didn't know how yet, but she was through with it, through with Montilla and through with living a life that didn't belong to her and meant nothing. She thought about leaving and discovered that in her heart and mind she was already gone, and only her body remained. She closed her eyes and smiled again.

Montilla, looking over, misread the smile, puffed himself up and pushed the throttles hard forward, making the engines roar and the bow of *Stiletto* lift up and then settle down into a plane. He pulled hard on the rubber-padded steering wheel to pump up his biceps as he pointed the bow under the Las Olas Bridge and up the Intracoastal toward Runners.

The girl hung on and enjoyed the ride.

There was a possibility that a few of the people jammed in and around the establishment called "Runners" were actually having a good time, but it was highly doubtful. What breeze there was had died to nothing, and the sun had doubled in its intensity. Under this sun, crowded into the meager shade provided by the thatched roof around the bar, were three times as many people as the place was designed for. Up by the pool, in an area just big enough to hold their equipment, under a brightly colored canvas fly, were four black men listlessly beating out steel drum music. The talk and yells and laughter of the crowd prevented all but the beat from carrying very far. There was a rather disconcerting clash of rhythms in the common area where the beat from the steel drummers collided with the pop-rock beat coming from the speakers over the bar. Those standing under the speakers experienced a kind of musical jet lag. Because of the sun and the beach locale the people there wore only shorts or bathing suits. Girls who had good bodies and knew it pranced around in the tiniest of string bikinis.

Of course, good body or not, male or female, what there was most of was skin: soft, hard, tight, loose, fat, flat, round, and browned. Pink skin, red skin, white skin, purple skin and, naturally, all the various brown and gold and butterscotch-tanned skin ever dreamed of in a suntan ad.

The drinks precariously balanced in oiled palms were, of course, the sun-drenched tropical fun-and-very-with-it drinks: margaritas, rum sours, daiquiries, planters punches and, of course, that little sleeper, the piña colada. All of these drinks were consumed with great élan and enthusiasm, the amount depending upon the determination of the drinker to have a good time and the ability to get served by a harried cocktail waitress or bartender. Those not caring about that tropical look hung grimly on to the American standard: beer. Those combining Continental flair with gastronomic health brandished their Perrier or Montclair like sparkling badges of self-discipline and style. Sprinkled here and there, there were even people who were drinking drinks they liked just because they liked them.

On the water side of the establishment, on the docks, close to all those fiberglass macho machines tied rail-to-rail against each other, could be found The Uniform. For men, it consisted of one pair of either brand new or totally destroyed boat shoes, name brand only. Next a pair of tan, khaki, navy blue, or white shorts with military pockets. If a belt was worn it had little nautical flags or sailfish all around it, or it was plain webbed with a military metal buckle. Other buckle options were ones that said *Porsche*, *BMW*, or *Ferrari—Sonic*, *Magnum*, or *Signature* on the front.

Next comes the shirt, which can present a problem because, besides having to display its expense by having some designer's name on it, it also has a tendency to cover the next part of the uniform, unless of course the wearer decides to wear the next part of the uniform on the *outside* of the shirt. Most of the men don't wear shirts because of the sun and the chance to show off those tight bellies and square pectorals developed with so much hard work at the spa. Besides, nothing looks better hanging on brown oily-sweaty skin than gold.

Gold. Ah yes, gold.

The last part of the uniform is always gold. Gold chains, gold pendants, gold charms, gold earrings (yes, still talking about the men). A half dozen chains is not too many. Stylishly tangled gold chains can do so much to add to the attractiveness of a distended belly covered with curly gray hairs. For the young healthy guys, the gold is worn in addition to their muscles and tight skin. For the older players the gold is worn instead-of. Of course, no one considers the gold hanging all over the place anything special. It's just part of the uniform.

An addendum to the gold, but with a subtle difference, is the Rolex watch. Wrists must have Rolexes, that's all there is to it. Naturally there are many types, styles, and values of Rolexes. The real heavies like to show some diamonds around the edge, and that special eighteen-carat band is always an index of success. The final part of the uniform for the man is having at least one very fine lady hanging on him at all times.

Her uniform is optional.

If she is wearing clothes they will conform to the style and quality of the man's; however, she is usually expected to show more skin than taste. The many variations of the bikini are all wonderful, and here a high-gloss tan is a must. Gold in this case is strategically placed, starting with the anklet (a diamond chip here for effect), then a gold tummy chain (on a nice tight tanned tummy, with a little line of golden hairs running from the navel downward), just the right amount of gold chains with charms hanging between the breasts. Here we have variations again—either completely tanned breasts, indicating she goes topless when possible, or with that distinct line between tanned and cool white. And, of course, the earrings and bracelets. Again, Rolexes for the lady are fine, but a Piaget or something similar is also permissible. What the girl does in real life is not important. It is important to know that she did not buy all of that gold for herself, that it was given to her, and that she always tries to stand or sit with at least one of the man's hands on her body somewhere. Out on the dock of Runners, there were many of these couples and triples, posturing in the sun and sipping their drinks and smiling at one another.

Silky had been at Runners with Montilla for over an hour and she was hot, bored, and had a headache from the drinks. She had left him standing with a group of dopers and lawyers and had climbed across two other racing boats to get back to *Stiletto*. She thought Montilla acted like a pompous ass when he was around his cronies, and the other girls there pointedly ignored her while the men eyed her constantly, fondled her when possible, and shared lewd comments with Montilla about her. She thought they were all a bunch of jerks. Sure, she had seen a couple of good-looking young guys with bodies that turned her on a little, but she was fed up with the whole scene and just wanted to sit quietly in the sun until Montilla was ready to leave. He was so engrossed in a conversation with an attorney about the banking system in Grand Cayman that he only nodded his head when she told him she would be on the boat. She could tell the drinks and the sun were starting to get to him, and hoped he wouldn't get rowdy before they left. She spread a towel out on the padded engine cover, shaded her face with a big straw hat, lay back with her eyes closed, and dreamed of being free.

Near the dock of the reputable, expensive waterway restaurant just south of Runners sat a small white center-console fishing boat. In it were the two U.S. Customs officers, Hank Zaden and Reggie Maguire. Sometimes on weekends, instead of taking out the Magnum with the Customs markings, they went out on the waterways in the small, unmarked runabout. If there was no brass around they would just wear jeans and T-shirts instead of their blue uniforms. It allowed them to relax a bit, and they could ease around and see things without being so conspicuous. They had drifted to a stop less than a hundred feet from the sleek red racer as a naked girl had started dancing, and then had sat there and watched the whole show. Instead of starting up the engine to pull away, Zaden appeared to be in a daze. He sat back against his seat with a small grin on his face, his eyes far away. His partner, Maguire, wore an expression that was a mixture of rapture and awe. He shook himself, took a deep breath, looked at his partner, and said, "For a minute there I thought I had died and gone to heaven."

Directly across the waterway from them, but six stories up, face pressed against the window, stood another watcher. She was in her late sixties, had never been married, and lived with her three cats. From the east windows of her condominium she looked down almost on top of Runners, the Intracoastal, and the bridge. She thought weekends were terrible. The rest of the week was not so bad, with the view of the water and the sailboats and the bridge going up and down. But the weekend was the time when all those idiots came out in those racing boats and made all that noise and all of those people packed into the bar with the dock and got drunk and carried on and she thought it was just terrible the way they acted. She too had seen the girl dancing on the racer, and when the crowd on the dock got loud and rowdy she gave a huff and called the police department and reported a riot at Runners. Now, as she saw a little toy police car pull up in front of the place, she looked at her watch and huffed again. It was twelve minutes after she had called.

Twelve minutes.

Why, suppose she was being raped or something?

Twelve minutes indeed.

Richards was still grumbling as he and Skids Bedlam climbed out of the police unit parked in front of Runners.

"Rats, Skids, I can't believe we're still out here on the beach. They oughta get the wagon out here again instead of makin' the beach units transport all their own damn drunk arrests, then they wouldn't always be havin' to get downtown units to come over here. Crap. Riot at Runners. Hell, everybody knows there's a continuous riot at Runners every damn weekend. What are we supposed to do about it—arrest everybody for having a good time?"

As Bedlam headed toward the crowd in the parking lot he said, "My, but aren't we cranky today? C'mon, J.B., let's go in and walk around for a minute so we can say we were here, then we can just write it off on a card."

Richards walked around the front of the Plymouth, joined his partner, and said, "Rats."

Silky now sat on top of the bolster seat with her feet dangling in the cockpit of *Stiletto*. She was ready to go home, and searched the crowd on the dock, looking for

Montilla but not seeing him. She did see the two Fort Lauderdale cops ambling among the crowd.

Montilla, who was by now fairly drunk, saw the two cops moving through the crowd and nudged the attorney he was talking to. He grinned and said, "Hey, look at those two assholes." The attorney said nothing.

Richards and Bedlam walked around slowly, looking at the men and smiling at a girl here and there when they smiled first—just moving through, checking the atmosphere. Soon, the manager, a big, friendly, robust man in deck shoes and golf clothes, bustled over and asked what the problem was. As Richards quietly explained what they were doing, and assured him that it was no big deal, Bedlam walked over and stood on the dock, at the edge of the water. He enjoyed looking at all the fancy boats and women. He noticed Zaden and Maguire in their little boat and he grinned and waved. They waved back. He noticed the girl sitting on the black and gray racer, and then he remembered that it was the boat that J.B. was always talking about.

As Richards finished with the manager and joined him to tell him they could leave, Bedlam pointed at the Customs guys and Richards grinned and waved. As Zaden waved and Maguire thumbed his nose at them, Bedlam said, "Look over there, J.B. There's that *Stiletto* you're always talking about. I wonder if that dude that goes with it is around."

As Skids said this, J.B. looked at the boat and the girl sitting on it, and grunted. He felt a tightening in his chest and clenched his jaw. Behind him he heard a slightly slurred voice say, "Yeah, cop. The dude who owns that boat is standin' right behind your fat ass . . . all you gotta do is turn around and you'll see him."

Onyx Montilla was surprised at the words that came out of his mouth, but not sorry. Something about seeing the big cop standing so close triggered an irrational and immediate anger. There was just something about this cop that put him over the edge.

Richards and Bedlam looked at each other. They slowly turned to see Onyx Montilla, with his boat shoes, shorts, gold chains, Rolex, and sunglasses, standing there on the deck, drink in hand and feet spread wide. The attorney who had been chatting with him had quietly but quickly moved away, so now he stood there alone.

"Could this be the notorious and powerful man who owns that beautiful racing boat and the woman perched on same?" Bedlam said this with his arms crossed, his red eyes glaring, rocking back and forth on his feet.

J.B. felt his spine turning to ice as he stared at Montilla. A wave of anger washed over him, and he fought the urge either to lunge for Montilla's throat or turn and walk away. There was just something about the guy that impacted J.B. with a frightening intensity. He stared at Montilla and said through dry lips, "Yeah, this is the little puke himself."

The blood was rising in Montilla's neck as Bedlam spoke, and by the time Richards finished he was set to explode. He glared at the name tag on the uniform shirts and sputtered, "You can't talk like that to me."

Bedlam leaned over and put his face close to Montilla's, red eyes bulging, and said, "We just did . . . sport."

By now, the crowd on the docks, always curious about any confrontation between cops and a hapless citizen, had formed a circle around them, watching and listening. J.B., ignoring the crowd, looked out over the water and caught Zaden's eye. He pointed at the black and gray racer and immediately the Customs boat began to move toward it slowly.

Montilla, seeing this, shifted to the edge of the dock and said loudly, "Hey, who are those guys? Why did you point at my boat? You fuckin' cops give me a pain in the ass. Why don't you clowns just get the fuck outta here anyway?" He heard his own words, and felt himself losing control, but he was like a man observing a train wreck and powerless to prevent it. "Nobody needs you here. Why don't you go write some parking tickets or something?"

Some of the people in the crowd laughed, and some just shook their heads. Those who had been around a little knew Montilla had probably just ruined his whole day for himself.

Bedlam put an amazed look on his round face and said,

"My, you certainly are a hostile little dirt ball, aren't you?" He sensed J.B.'s mood, felt the danger, and wanted to divert the heat.

"Dirt ball? Dirt ball?" shouted Montilla. "Who are you calling a dirt ball, *policía?* You can't call me that, *puta!*"

Some of the people in the crowd started to back away now, knowing what was surely coming, and Richards looked at Montilla and said in a voice like ice, "I think you'd better ease up a little, Montilla, or you're gonna get yourself busted for disorderly conduct." Then he turned and watched as Zaden moved the Customs boat alongside *Stiletto*, his mind in tumult, his stomach churning. He could see Maguire saying something to the girl, and he could see her take a line from him and wrap it around one of the cleats on the racer.

Montilla started to say something to Richards, but then he too saw the Customs boat alongside *Stiletto* and he completely lost control.

"Hey!" he shouted. "Get away from there! Get away from my boat! You can't tie that little piece of shit up to my boat! Get away from my boat!" He jumped off the dock onto the nearest boat and ran across the engine covers onto the next one, heading for *Stiletto*. Richards and Bedlam eased themselves down onto the nearest boat also, and the owner of the boat, an attorney, cringed when he looked at the big street shoes on the cops, but he saw they were being careful and he definitely didn't want any part of this hassle.

Montilla jumped onto the *Stiletto* and shouting at Zaden and Maguire, he began untying the line holding the two boats together. As he did so, Zaden, who was holding the boats together with one hand, stuck his gold badge in Montilla's red face and said evenly, "U.S. Customs, sir, and we're going to board your boat."

"Board my boat? Like shit you're boarding my boat! You've got no right to board at all, and I'm not going to let you do it!"

Maguire leaned over the rail, smiled, and said, "Hi. I'm Maguire here, from Customs too, and guess what, sir? I'm boarding your boat also, and if you'll look behind you,

you'll see two Fort Lauderdale police officers who are just praying you'll try to stop us."

Montilla turned and looked over his shoulder at the grim faces of Richards and Bedlam, and Zaden and Maguire smoothly climbed into the cockpit of the racer. Montilla leaned back against the cabin hatchway and said, "Listen, what are you? Federal cops . . . and these are local cops? Don't you know I can buy and sell you, you mother-fuckers? You better get out of my boat right now, or I'll make you wish you'd never been born." He just stood there glaring at them, breathing hard. He knew he wasn't handling the situation well at all, but there was just something about that big cop that twisted him.

Silky, who had climbed onto the engine cover when the Customs men came aboard, was silent. She was a little frightened, but it pleased her to see Montilla squirming. She looked up at the big, dark blond older officer with the ice blue eyes and saw him smile at her. He pursed his lips and made a gesture with his hand as if to say "relax," so she did.

Zaden looked at Maguire and said, "You know, Reg, I'm sure this is the same boat we saw earlier today coming in from the ocean, and since we think it came from outside that means we can legally board it, right? And not only that, I think I remember seeing a description of this boat on a 'watch list' somewhere. Don't you?"

"Absolutely correct as usual, Hank. I think we would be remiss in our duties if we didn't go over this vessel completely. This guy could be one of those smugglers we've heard so much about. Why, he could stuff as many as thirty Haitians into the forward cabin." He smiled at Montilla. "And now, sir, could we see the papers for the boat, please?"

Montilla, who had begun to sober up, said quietly, "Listen, why don't you guys just get off my boat, okay? I didn't do anything to you guys. Maybe I mouthed off a little to these *policía* here. But you've got no reason to search my boat. Why don't you just get off, okay?"

Richards stood on the padded engine cover of the boat beside *Stiletto* under the hot sun and thought about what he knew about Montilla. He thought about Ted Novak, and he made his decision.

"Montilla." He said it quietly, but it had a clarity that made the girl sit up and Montilla look down. "You're under arrest for disorderly intoxication, interfering with a police officer, and possibly corruption by threat because I heard you threaten these U.S. Customs officers as they legally boarded your boat. You are under arrest. Once I have said those words, that's it. I can't un-arrest you. If you like, you can walk with my partner and me across these boats and across the dock and the parking lot to our car. Or if you want to be difficult about it, I will very gladly jump down into your boat, truss you up, and carry you to my car. Now, what's it going to be, sir?"

Montilla stood with his hands on his hips, staring down at the deck. He wanted to hurl himself at the big cop, but he told himself, be cool, don't do anything stupid, just get an attorney and beat these clowns in court. He looked up into the ice blue eyes of Richards, with Bedlam standing beside him. He looked at Zaden and Maguire standing in the cockpit, and he knew he had done it to himself. His big mouth had done it again. These guys were just waiting to get him, and if he screwed it up any further they would do a number on him. He looked at Silky, but she had her back to him as she stared out over the stern of the boat. Bitch, he thought. He straightened his back, lifted his chin, and, mustering that sad dignity that sometimes comes with inebriation said, "Okay, cop. You want to be *estúpido* about this, you leave me no choice. You're fuckin' up here, and you'll hear from my lawyer about your trumped-up charges. I'll go quietly now—only because I would hate to see one of you fine *policías* get injured on the job, *sí*? When we get to the dock I'll ask one of my friends, and witnesses, I might add, to drive my boat home for me."

He climbed nimbly over the bolster seat and onto the engine hatch cover, but before he jumped onto the other boat he turned to the two Customs men and said, "You can search the boat all day if you want. It's clean. Just try not to break anything. Most of the equipment on this boat costs more than your yearly salary."

Zaden and Maguire just watched him as he climbed onto the other boat beside Richards and Bedlam. Montilla looked down at them and said, "Give me my pouch wallet. It has my ID and everything."

Maguire picked up the dark leather bag laying on the console and said, "Sure thing, Montilla. But first, since it's part of the boat's gear, I'll have to search it."

Montilla waved his hand in contempt and spat, "Help yoursel . . ." but then stopped and turned red and started tightening up. Bedlam and Richards, sensing a change, moved closer to him, and Silky, who had been unconsciously shaking her head, stared at the leather bag wide-eyed.

Maguire, with that certainty that experienced cops have, slid open the zipper, reached in without looking, and pulled out a plastic baggie containing at least one ounce of fine white powder. He held it in his hand and smiled. Zaden smiled, and Bedlam smiled. Silky put her hand in front of her mouth, and Richards looked at Montilla grimly and said, "Looks like I forgot to mention possession of cocaine when I listed the charges."

Montilla brought his fists up in front of his chest and hissed, "Wait a minute. This is . . . you can't. That shit belongs to *her!*" Silky said nothing, but straightened her back and lifted her chin and stared at Montilla evenly.

As Bedlam pulled out his handcuffs, Richards reached over and carefully pulled Montilla's arms down to his sides, feeling a strange sensation as he actually touched the man. As Bedlam handcuffed Montilla's wrists behind his back, Richards said, "Sure, Montilla, sure. I hate to tell you this, but that is your boat, your purse, and your coke. And I think the less you say at this point the better."

Zaden looked at the girl and said, "Miss, if you have any clothes or anything on board, you'd better get it together. We're taking this boat with us."

Silky nodded and climbed down into the cockpit.

Montilla shouted, "Taking the boat? What do you mean you're taking the boat?"

"This boat is now under seizure for transporting contraband material. We're seizing it, and the only way you can get it back is to get your attorney to petition the court. Hell, you know how it's done, Montilla." Zaden was tired of playing games. "We're seizing this boat, it's ours, and it will be ours for at least ninety days."

Maguire, knowing his partner, grabbed him lightly on the arm. "Okay, Hank, okay, man . . . c'mon, we've got a bunch of paperwork to do." Then he looked up at Richards and said, "Why don't you guys get the shit bird outta here? We'll take the boat back to the office, then we can meet with you there and do the evidence and arrest forms and stuff." He turned his back on Montilla and began to do the rest of the search. He knew it would be negative, but he wanted to do it anyway.

Montilla blustered and protested as he was virtually carried by the two police officers across the boats and onto the dock. He kept his head up and launched a loud harangue at the officers as they moved through the crowd, which was now quiet. He hoped to get some support, but there was none. His arrest was all just more entertainment. Besides, the others had their own grass and coke and 'ludes to worry about.

After Montilla was searched and put into the back of the unit, Richards told Bedlam to wait a minute and went back through the crowd to the dock. He wanted to have a final word with Zaden and Maguire, and he wanted to know more about the girl.

When he returned to the dock he called the dispatcher on the radio, and advised her they had made an arrest and would be coming into the station; he asked her to call for a taxi to meet him in front of the lounge. He looked at the boats and saw that Zaden was back in the Customs boat and that the engines were idling on the black and gray racer. He watched as Maguire assisted the girl across the rafted-off boats to the dock. Maguire was being extremely solicitous toward the girl, holding her hand and telling her to watch her step. Richards caught Zaden's eye and saw the big Customs officer smile and shake his head while he watched his partner work with the girl. Richards saw that she had put on a pair of shorts and a halter top and was carrying a pair of old beat-up boat shoes and a small straw purse. As she got to the boat nearest the dock, J.B. reached his hand out to pull her up, and he thought to himself that she really wasn't much older than his own daughters, Kathleen and Erin. But they were worlds apart, he thought grimly. He smiled at the girl as she stood beside him on the dock and shook out her hair.

"Okay, J.B.," said Maguire as he smiled at the girl, "Hank's gonna follow me back to the office in our boat while I drive Montilla's. We'll start on the paperwork. As soon as you finish booking our friend, meet us at the office and you can help us secure her."

"Right, Reggie ... and try not to hurt yourself in that thing on the way back."

J.B. stood with the girl while Maguire went back to *Stiletto*, untied the lines, and eased out into the waterway, southbound alongside Zaden in the small boat. The air was filled with the roar of the powerful engines of the racer as Maguire pushed the throttles all the way forward and the racer jumped out of the water and sped off toward Birch State Park, leaving the small Customs boat with Zaden far behind. Richards heard a couple of the men in the crowd let out some boos, and he heard someone else say quietly, "That'll be the only way one of those guys could ever afford to drive a boat like that," and someone else snickered, but he had heard it all before so he just turned with the girl and headed for the parking lot.

The girl was quiet and walked with her head down. When they reached the edge of the lot, she could see the police unit parked across the street with Montilla sitting in the backseat. He was leaning forward talking to Bedlam, who was sitting in the driver's seat writing on a pad. Richards gently touched the girl's arm and guided her to the cool shade under the front awning of Runners. "We might as well be comfortable," he said, "while we wait for your taxi."

Silky, not knowing a cab had already been called, was pleasantly surprised. She had dreaded the thought of walking through the crowd after the police left because she was sure several of Montilla's pals would offer to take her home. They would be as helpful as could be, but she knew their help would have a price. They would have to stare, to lean against, to touch, to suggest that maybe she was tired after all of the excitement, and wouldn't it be nice just to go to their place and relax in the Jacuzzi for a while?

She felt the big cop beside her looking at her. She turned and looked up into his blue eyes. She felt comfortable under his gaze. She somehow sensed he was actually trying to see who she was, trying to get inside her a little. She was so used to men just looking at the pleasant lines of her face, the clean fullness of her hair, and then moving hungrily over her body, with that intense, transparent look of desire that she was taken aback by the frank, open, concerned look on the face of the cop.

During the seconds that passed while they stood in the shade and looked at each other, she saw that he was powerfully built, maybe a little overweight, and that he was in his early forties, with some gray at the temple, which wasn't very obvious because of his full, dark blond hair. The sure, inquisitive, ice blue eyes were set in a good face, weather-beaten and lined with work, worry, and laughter. She looked at him and realized immediately that he could be trusted, that he would not hurt her, that she could probably talk to him as she had never talked with any man.

Richards turned and looked up and down the street, rubbed one hand across his face, and said, "Well, sorry the cab is taking so long. I guess the beach traffic has him slowed down."

Silky just shrugged her shoulders and smiled.

He turned again so that his back was to the police unit across the street, looked down into her eyes, and said quietly, "You know, he's going to take a fall pretty soon. Either some police agency is going to finally put a good one together on him and take everything he's got and send him up for a while, or one of the other players is going to see an opportunity and make a move on him. Either way he's going to lose. And depending on which way it goes down, those people closest to him will probably go down with him."

She was silent. He went on, "A guy like that—he's not happy just playing the game and making some money. He gets greedy and people get hurt and he makes mistakes and takes a fall." She just watched him as he looked at her with those ice blue eyes and said, "If you're actively involved in what he's doing—by that I mean if you're part of the decision-making process, and you're part of the profit split— well, then you are probably in too deep anyhow. Maybe you should think about using some of that cash to get a good attorney, or move to Wyoming or something. But, and this is how I see it, if you are just sharing your time with him, for whatever reason—I don't know, maybe you love the guy or something like that..." He stopped, scuffed his shoe on the sidewalk, looked up and smiled and went on. "Hell, I've got a couple of daughters just a few years younger than yourself, and to tell you the truth I really don't have a handle on what they think about boys and relationships and all that anyway. What I'm getting at is maybe you're into something here—maybe it's convenient, maybe you like the life-style, whatever—but you'd better start thinking of getting out."

The girl looked down at her feet and smiled.

"Oh, hell, anyway," he went on, "you don't even know me and here I've probably just ruined your whole day, and now here I am telling you how to run your life. Should mind my own business, I guess." With that he straightened up a little, folded his arms across his chest, and stood staring out across the lot.

Silky stood with her head down, staring at the sidewalk with a small smile. Then she reached out and touched him lightly on the arm, and said quietly, "Would you believe me if I told you I really didn't even know myself what I was doing with him—other than admitting that I thought it was better than sleeping in the street? Would you believe me if I told you that I want to break away from him very badly, but that I don't know if I can, that maybe I'm not even sure if I can make it out there in the world without being kept by somebody?" She looked at him with clear steady eyes and said evenly, "Would you believe I'm afraid?"

He looked at the police car, at the form leaning forward

in the backseat, his eyes squinting in the glare of the sun, then back into her face. He took a long, slow, deep breath, nodded, and said quietly, "Yes. Yes I would believe you . . . and I do."

She saw his eyes go far away for a few seconds, and then come back, and he said, "Here, I'm going to do something I've never done as a police officer before now." She watched as he pulled out his wallet, took out a card, and pulled a pen from his shirt pocket. She saw that he kept his back to the police car so that even if Montilla turned to look at them he wouldn't be able to see what he was doing. He quickly wrote something on one side of the card and handed it to her. She looked at the printed number on the back and then at him as he said, "That's my home number. It's unlisted. I'm not saying I have all of the answers, and I'm not saying I'm the all-American hero or anything, but if you decide to make a move, and you need help, or you're afraid, or whatever, then call me. If you call the station and I'm not working, or it's real late or something, then call my home. Someone is always there. If one of my daughters isn't yacking away with one of her friends, you should be able to leave a message. Just leave a time and place to meet if you can, and I'll meet you there. Tell you what, call yourself 'Chica' when you leave the message, and I'll know it's you, okay? Oh, and you'll have to excuse the card. It's the only one I have that's not an FLPD card."

She turned the card over and smiled. In very tiny print were the words: "Ooooooh Shiiiit." She looked at the number again, put the card in her straw purse, and said, "This is all very unreal, you know. I mean, I don't know you, but I feel I would be making a mistake if I didn't take this card . . . and I think I would actually call you if I need help." She shrugged her shoulders and smiled. "Thank you very much, sir."

As a cop he was very aware of her potential value as a source, but smiled back at her and turned as the cab pulled up at the curb. She almost bumped into him but then stepped back quickly as he opened the door for her. She slid into the backseat of the cab.

He just stood there watching as the cab pulled away, the girl staring straight ahead.

Richards walked across the street, slid into the seat beside Bedlam, and said, "Okay, Skids, let's go book this dirt bag."

He felt Montilla staring at him, and he knew it was obvious that he had been talking with the girl for more than a few minutes while they waited for the cab. Before he could say anything, Bedlam looked over and asked, "So how was Mister Montilla's lady . . . very helpful?"

Richards looked at his partner and saw by the expression on his face that he knew exactly what he was doing, so he responded by saying, "Shit. Our man Montilla here has found himself one first-class grade 'A' bitch. She says she don't know nothin'. Says the Customs guys planted that coke in Montilla's purse. Says Montilla's just a fine upstanding fucking citizen and we had no right to mess with him at all. Hell, I asked her for a name and she just laughed and said she didn't have any ID anyway so what was the difference. I'll tell ya Skids, just a five-speed, gold-plated bitch."

Montilla sat in the back listening as the police car sped out onto Atlantic Boulevard. He listened, and he smiled, but he wasn't quite convinced.

As the cab moved slowly through the evening traffic, Silky sat in the back and thought about what had taken place. Her mind was a jumble of conflicting thoughts, pulling her this way and that. She was filled with resolve one minute, and doubt the next. Finally one thought pushed its way to the top and stayed there: The cop was a good man and he would help her. She went over the whole thing again and considered the one thing that had convinced her more than anything else. He hadn't asked her for anything.

There was no trade. He gave himself to her just because he knew she needed help. He had offered to help, and he had asked her for nothing.

He hadn't even asked her for her name.

FOURTEEN

J.B. and Skids Bedlam walked out of the marine patrol office and headed across the small parking lot to their personal vehicles. They had left the police unit at the station after booking Montilla so that they could go straight home after finishing up with Zaden and Maguire.

"Better go home and get some rest, J.B.," said Bedlam. "I know an old guy like you can't go too long without recharging his batteries."

"You got it," said Richards with a laugh. "And you keep your head down, right?"

"Hey, J.B., you know me."

"That's right, I *do* know you . . . that's why I'm telling you to keep that pumpkin head of yours down."

Bedlam waved and walked off. As J.B. threw his gym bag onto the seat of his old pickup truck a voice behind him made him turn.

"Hey there, J.B., got a minute to talk with a snoopy reporter for the local rag?"

Standing there with a smile was the reporter for the Fort Lauderdale *Herald* whom J.B. knew as Dave Kuhler. They shook hands, and J.B. said, "So what are you snoopin' about today?"

"There's a narcotics cop missing, and the police department either just doesn't care, or for some reason is keeping a tight lid on it."

J.B. studied the man for a moment, trying to gauge how much he knew. He waited.

"We're talking over a week now, J.B.," continued Dave, concern on his face. "I know FLPD put out a quiet search request to all Florida agencies, local, county, state, and federal. But it doesn't say much, just asks for any info if the cop, uh, Ted Novak, is seen." He rubbed the bridge of his nose. "Just doesn't seem right somehow, like FLPD is not sure itself what's goin' on. Is the guy missing, or not?"

J.B. crossed his arms over his chest, looked up into the early evening sky, and said, "He's missing, and for now he's considered just AWOL. The official stance at this time is that he is missing but not due to any job-related situation."

"What's that supposed to mean?"

"That means that the administration claims it knows of no police matter that Ted would have been involved in. It means that the brass would rather think that Ted is having personal problems—girlfriend or something—and he ran off to deal with it."

"Okay, but what do *you* think?"

J.B. stood silent, still looking into the sky.

Dave tried again. "But J.B., a cop is missing for this length of time and we all just sort of go along, holding our breath and waiting for him to show up after settling his problems with a girlfriend? C'mon, this is a cop we're talkin' about, a new narc. You mean to tell me he wasn't working *anything* that could be considered a possible cause for his disappearance?"

J.B. sighed and looked at Kuhler. He said quietly, "I'm giving you the official view, Dave. Between you and me many scenarios are being considered. And to be perfectly honest and up-front and all that, nobody really knows what happened."

Dave nodded, his face grim. "Well, listen. I'm doing a story on this for tomorrow's edition. I'm not going to point fingers, I'm just going to present it to the readers, and ask some questions. I'm a reporter, and this is a story, sure. But there's more to it than that, J.B." He looked down at his feet and went on. "I'm one of those rare reporters, I guess, that thinks you guys are the good guys. I'm on your side, and if your own administration is gonna sit there on its hands, I'm not. Maybe an article that asks a bunch of questions will light a fire under somebody's butt, I don't know."

J.B. nodded.

"And look, J.B., you've got to tell me, flat out, if a story at this point would do anything to hurt Ted Novak, or hinder his return."

J.B. bit his lip, thinking, then he said carefully, "At this time I think a story would help more than hurt. I say go for it, I'd like to see what our brass has to say about it. And, I'll even make you a deal."

Dave nodded his head and waited.

"If you'll tell me what you dig up, and what you're going to say in future stories, then at the end of this deal— if and when it ends—I'll give you an exclusive on what *really* happened here." He watched Dave's eyes carefully as he said, "At this point you can't hurt the situation. In the future maybe you could. All I'm asking is that you check with me before you put somethin' out, and I'll square with you, and only you, at the end."

Kuhler hesitated for a moment, then he smiled and said, "There's a story here, J.B., I *know* it. It's a lot bigger than it appears at first glance." He stuck out one hand, and they shook. "Deal, J.B., I just want the story; I don't want to do anything that will hurt Novak."

They parted, and J.B. went home.

J.B. climbed out of his pickup, parked in front of his house, just as it was getting dark. A few stars could already be seen, and he could smell the sweet jasmine coming from a neighbor's yard. He picked up the evening paper from the driveway and went in the front door.

He found the inside of the house almost dark, but he could see the glow of light coming from Kathleen's room. He whispered hushed hellos to the furry bundles of energy jumping around his legs, dumped the paper and his gym bag on the kitchen table, and went looking for his family.

He found Erin and Ricky in Ricky's room, which in itself was odd, as Erin considered Ricky's room a no-man's land of sloppiness and bad taste. Erin was doing her nails, and Ricky was thumbing through a surfing magazine. They both looked up when he stuck his head in the door and waved. He could see they were subdued, and he heard worry in Erin's voice as she said quietly, "Mom is in Kathleen's room, Dad . . . with Kathleen."

J.B. nodded and went down the hallway and stepped into Kathleen's room. In the glow of the small bedside lamp he could see his wife, Jane, as she sat on the edge of the bed, holding his oldest daughter. His daughter was crying quietly, and his wife looked up at him, her expression a mixture of sadness, concern, and anger. As he took in the scene in front of him he allowed himself to examine his years as a father, his years spent raising his first child.

Kathleen was twenty-one years old and lived at home. She had gone to all of the dances and the prom, but she had never really had a steady boyfriend during her school years. She had always been a "nice girl," participating in clubs and school activities, shunning the wild parties and the groups of kids known to experiment with drugs. J.B. knew he was guilty of trying to shield her from much of the negative input of the real world. He asked himself, as he had many times before, Did he encourage Kathleen to attend a local college because she could get the courses she needed there, or was it because he knew he could keep her at home? Certainly, most girls, nowadays, had their own apartments with friends by the time they were twenty-one. Certainly, they were out on their own by then. Did he want her to be daddy's little girl forever? Was that it?

Kathleen rubbed her eyes and looked up at him, and he felt his heart melt. *Maybe,* he thought, *yeah, maybe I am guilty of wanting her to be my little girl forever.* He shook his head imperceptibly. Was it a mistake to be so protective all these years? Had he raised children who would be vulnerable, children who were not prepared for the harsh realities of "out there"?

Jane smoothed her hand over her daughter's lovely hair and said, "I knew she was taking all of this just a little too easily. Ted is missing, and Kathleen has just been a powerhouse of activities—classes, clubs, friends, the church—going along, apparently content in the knowledge that Ted was alive, somewhere, and that those in power would bring him home." She hugged Kathleen tightly, and kissed the top of her head. "But I could see it in her eyes, see the pain." She looked up. "The pain is very similar to what I've been seeing in your eyes, J.B."

Richards took a step forward and reached out one hand. Jane took it in hers, and continued. "I got a call from the college, from one of the teachers, not official or anything. He was worried because Kath has been missing from class, and that's not like her. Got another call from the mother of one of her girlfriends. She told me that on the nights Kathleen and her daughter are supposedly going out to the movies, or whatever, they just lock themselves in the daughter's room and talk all night. Her daughter is very worried about Kathleen."

Kathleen sat up, and leaned back on the bed, her eyes red and puffy.

Jane squeezed J.B.'s hand. "Honey, she's not eating, she's not sleeping, she's just waiting. And it's killing her."

J.B. sat down on the other side of the bed, reached out, and brushed the hair off Kathleen's face. He said gently, "So what happened this evening? Your mother tried to talk with you about it, and you lost your temper? You yelled at her and tried to hurt her by saying that she and I don't care about Ted, and that we're doing nothing to get him back home because we don't believe he is alive like you do."

Kathleen picked up a pillow, squeezed it across her chest, and nodded, huge tears forming at the corners of her eyes, and then running down her face.

J.B. shrugged. "Hey, Kath, it's okay to yell at us. It's okay to take out your anger and your frustration. Your mother loves you, and so do I, so it's all right to blame us for things that hurt you." He smiled. "But listen. Your mom and I have known Ted even longer than you have. We knew him when he was just a little boy, and you know he's like family to us. Don't you think it hurts us to think that he's in trouble somewhere? Of course you do. And don't you think we'd be doing everything we could to get him back if we had that power?" He stood up and began pacing back and forth across the room. "There's more information that coincides with your feelings that Ted is alive." He heard the catch in his daughter's throat, and saw his wife's eyes widen. "But it's information that is very tenuous, not verified. I'm very much afraid of coming home and telling you things that might turn out to hurt you more in the long run. You know how I am about work-related stuff. I'm careful and cautious, and I try to collect all the information I can before I make a move. This case has an eerie feel to it. It's . . . abstract somehow . . . and it's a case that started out small and is growing before our eyes in some crazy, mysterious way."

He stopped pacing, and looked at Kathleen. "Tell me what you were planning to do, Kath."

His daughter lifted her chin, sniffled, then said haltingly, "I . . . I got the phone numbers and the addresses of your chief of police, and of the State Department, and the FBI. I wrote a letter to '60 Minutes' that I didn't send, and I found out how I could contact a local newspaper guy." She sat up straight, leaned forward, and said, "I was just going to raise *hell!* I was going to call everyone, demand answers, challenge them, push them . . . threaten them with exposure of police incompetence and possible corruption. I was going to just make their lives miserable until they promised they would *do* something. No one is doing anything, Dad . . . no one is doing any*thing!*"

He said gently, "Maybe nothing is being done because no one really knows at this point what *can* be done." He sat on the edge of the bed again, and took one of Kathleen's hands in his. Jane reached over and took the other. He looked at them both, sighed, and said, "You remember Scott Kelly? Probably the best narc we've ever had? He's back, and he's working with me on this. You know Mister Tommasen—Fat Harry? He's in. So are two really good guys that work for Customs. There's a news reporter I think can be trusted, and he'll help us when he can. Skids Bedlam is in, of course. And now there's a CIA guy named Buchanan sniffing around, trying to set up a meeting with me." He saw his wife's eyes widen. He hesitated, then went on. "Word has filtered down, through secret channels, of course, that someone was found in the waters off the Bahama Islands and taken to Cuba."

Jane gasped, "Oh my God!" Kathleen stiffened.

J.B. continued. "And it *may* be Ted. If it *is* Ted, then we can be thankful that he's alive. But we also must be aware of all the difficulties involved in getting him back." He paused for a moment, his face grim. "Here I am telling you, my family, all of this ... but you must realize how sensitive it all is. Can you imagine how dangerous it must be for someone in Cuba to sneak out this kind of info to the CIA? Someone there is fighting against Castro, living right there under all of that repression, and cares enough about what he, or she, is doing to smuggle out info to our guys. And then our guys get the info ... then what? Can we go pound on the State Department's door, demanding that they do something? Or the CIA? What if we did that, and Castro, or whoever is in charge of Ted—if it's him—got spooked, killed Ted, got rid of the evidence, and then just denied Ted was ever there? See what I mean, Kath? Each of us wants to do *something*, but we have to be *so* careful."

The room was quiet, all three wrapped in their own thoughts. J.B. watched as his daughter came to grips with what he had told her.

"I'll make you a deal," he said, then laughed slightly. "The second deal I've made today. From now on, I'll share every piece of info that comes along ... if you'll promise to trust me and not do anything like you were going to."

He saw the determination on her face, and nodded.

Kathleen then turned to her mother, reached out for her hand, and began crying softly. "Oh, Mom, I'm so sorry, I didn't mean to say..." Jane took her in her arms and held her, rocking her gently on the bed.

J.B. heard movement behind him and turned to see Erin come into the room, then, more slowly, Ricky. They had been standing outside the door, listening. Erin was crying, too, and as she and Ricky grouped around J.B. and Jane and Kathleen, Ricky said in true concern, "Boy, Ted really got himself into the jalapeño sauce this time."

Ted Novak sipped the cold juice, moved his right leg slightly and winced, and waited.

He was sitting up in the bed, the ceiling fan above him

barely pushing the warm air around the room. In the morning he had been examined by the unpleasant doctor, and then bathed by two orderlies while the pretty young nurse stood by, smiling encouragment. He was over his fever and was starting to feel much better, his strength coming back hour by hour. So far, all of his feeble attempts at communication had been shunned, coldly by the doctor, patiently by the nurse.

She had surprised him a few minutes ago by bustling into the room, helping him sit up, giving him juice, then smiling, saying one word: "Visitors."

Ted heard footsteps, and then two men entered the room, followed by the nurse. They were the same two men he had seen before, the chubby one in the opera uniform and the lean one in the dark suit. They stood at the end of his bed, examining him, then the chubby one said in a thick voice, "Señor Max, your English is much better than mine, so I will listen as you speak . . . *sí?*"

The lean one nodded without turning his head, studied Ted for a moment, and said in a quiet voice, "The doctor tells us you are getting better. How do you feel? Do you think you will recover from your injuries?"

Ted swallowed, nodded, and said in a husky voice, "Yes, I think I will recover. Please tell me where I am."

The lean one looked at him with sad, patient eyes, and said, "For now, señor, I will ask you the questions, *sí?* Your position here is . . . not good. I suggest you be careful, and patient, yes?"

Ted nodded.

"Good. Please tell us your name now."

"Ted, uh, Theodore Novak."

"Where are you from? How did you get here?"

"I'm from Lauderdale—Florida. And I don't know how I got here. Wait . . . I was on a boat! They brought me here. I'm in Cuba, right?"

The chubby one in uniform grunted, and started to speak, but the lean one cut him off with a gesture.

"So, you are Señor Ted Novak, from Florida, and you came here by boat. And what is your purpose here, Señor Novak?"

"My purpose? What purpose? I was brought here, obviously hurt. I just want to get back to my home." He sat up straight, beads of sweat forming on his forehead. "Listen, I'm an American citizen, and I want to speak to someone from the American consulate or the embassy or something. Maybe there's someone on Guantanamo I can see."

The short fat one rattled off a string in harsh Spanish, and the lean one nodded. Ted could sense the animosity between the two, and racked his brain in an attempt to figure out a way to use it to his advantage.

The lean one pulled on his hawk nose, and said evenly, "So you came here by boat. What were you doing before you got on the boat? Working?"

Ted licked his lips, and said, "I, uh, I was on another boat, near Bimini. I fell off."

There was a pause, the room was quiet except for a muted click that came from the ceiling fan as it spun.

"You fell off a boat, and then another picked you up and brought you here? How could that be?"

"I . . . um . . . we were fishing, and drinking beer, and I fell off and my friends turned to find me and accidentally ran over me with the boat and that's how my leg got hurt. And then they left because they thought I was dead, and then another boat picked me up and brought me here. I'm an American citizen and you have to send me home." Ted's head lay back on the pillow, the sweat running down his face.

The pretty nurse walked to the side of the bed, and gently patted his face with a small towel.

Ted raised his head again, and said weakly, "I was fishing, and was hurt, and was brought here against my will."

"Lo es un mentir," muttered the uniform. Again he was stilled by a gesture from the suit.

"So," said the lean man in his quiet voice, "you have a fantastic story about how you came to be here. And you tell us you are an American, but you have nothing to show us, no proof of that. Are we to believe you are an American just because that is what you say? And if so, are we to believe your wonderful and innocent story of why you are here?" Maximiliano wanted to keep the young American frightened and intimidated, and he wanted to keep the director of prisons at his side off balance. His voice hardened, and he went on. "Listen to me, Señor Novak. You are in a place where a man who claims to be American, and who tries to come here secretly, is considered a threat. Do you understand? *You* make demands on *us?* You demand to see someone from your government? I think, señor, that you are more than just a simple fisherman."

Ted could feel the man's intensity as he leaned forward at the foot of the bed, his eyes bright.

"I think you are some kind of spy, Ted Novak. You had better think about that, and be ready with some answers the next time we speak."

The lean one then turned and headed for the door, the chubby one hesitated, looking from Ted to the lean one, then he too walked out. When they were both gone the nurse leaned forward, looked into Ted's eyes and smiled. She soothed his brow with the towel again, and as his leg throbbed and his mind raced she said softly, *"Confianza."*

Faith?

Why faith? thought Fidel Castro. He punched the button on the cassette player to stop it and again thought about what he had heard. So, Maximiliano of the secret police wanted to meet with him now, before the director of prisons had a chance to claim the prize. Being a jailer must make some men obtuse, he thought. Maximiliano is so obviously right. Not the part about this Novak being a spy, but about the value of this prisoner. He will be much more valuable as an item of barter or intelligence than as a guinea pig for another experiment in "reeducation."

Castro had purposely delayed the meeting with the intelligence man so that he would have time to get the tapes from the prison and listen to them before he went any further. He leaned back in his chair, took a deep breath, and called out, *"Entrar!"*

Maximiliano came into the room, walked across the carpeted floor, and stood in front of the desk. He waited until the gesture was made, then took the only chair. He straightened a crease in his trousers, and took note of his leader's simple fatigues. *So,* he thought, *Fidel dresses for his game . . . I dress for mine.*

"My friend, how are you? You are looking fit and trim, as always," began Castro. Maximiliano nodded. "And I hear you are still able to move in and out of the United States without much difficulty, and that you have several delightful schemes going to advance our cause?"

Again Maximiliano nodded, knowing the less he said the better. His leader would do most of the talking for both of them.

"This young gringo that has been brought to us in such an extraordinary manner. He could be a source of fun, no? An embarrassment to the Yankee government? A trading tool? A source of intelligence about anti-Castro activities?"

Maximiliano was surprised to hear his leader openly say there *were* anti-Castro activities. He remained silent.

Castro cut a slice of melon, offered some to Maximiliano, who took a small piece, and went on, scratching himself across his large chest vigorously. "We could trade the gringo to the stupid and always bothersome CIA, could we not? They have their ways of finding out about what goes on in our Havana. They will learn of the gringo."

He stretched and cut another piece of melon. "I don't like the CIA very much, but sometimes I feel I know the nature of the beast. You know I've dealt successfully with them in the past made deals with them, played games with them, and then laughed in their faces. But you have to admit, blundering as they are, treacherous as they are, they still manage to mess up our plans and hurt us occasionally."

Maximiliano knew his leader was off on one of his favorite subjects now.

"They're still out there," said Castro, his voice grave, "gathering spies and informants against my government, spreading false information among my people, and heading off revolutionary plans among the Latin-speaking peoples of South and Central America."

He shook his head, and ran his long fingers through his beard. "You know, it's funny . . . sometimes the CIA even works with me. Well, not exactly, but sometimes they know what I'm doing, and why, and they don't try to stop me. Why? Sometimes, to be truthful, it bothers me. Why do they sit there on their hands as I play a little here and there in the international narcotics games? They must see our fingerprints in several of the operations in the south where cocaine turns into money and money turns into weapons for local revolutionary causes, no?"

Maximiliano shifted in his chair, uncomfortable with a conversation like this out in the open.

Castro laughed, a short, sharp laugh. "Hah! Cocaine, what a great source of revenue. Isn't it ironic that the very consumer . . . the rich idiots who throw the money at the cocaine importers, are the very ones the money will be used to destroy?" He smiled. "Even I, Fidel, participate in the cocaine importation into Miami. And I *know* they know! Sure, it's old news. Even local policemen have bumped into the operations, or pieces of them, occasion-ally."

Suddenly his face grew stern, and he leaned forward across the desk, his eyes boring into Maximiliano's. "So tell me, Maximiliano of my secret police. What am I to do with this young American? Is he a spy, as you said to him? Is he just some local narcotics cop that bit off more than he could chew? Is he just an unfortunate fisherman? And so what, what if he is any of these things . . . then what? Is there some way we can use him to further our case? I want to hurt the CIA if I can, but at the same time I see this as a time to keep things on the status quo with the American government. There have been more outcries lately because of what goes on in our jails. The way we handle political dissenters is being questioned in the free world. It's all bullshit, but it brings heat with it, yes? Maybe we can use the young gringo for a gesture of our brotherly feelings, show them what good guys we really are by sending him home. Or maybe we should just let him die and disappear as have so many behind our prison walls. Maybe he should be killed and sent back as a message to the DEA. Maybe he should be made to help run a load of cocaine, and then get caught—or killed and *then* caught. See what I mean? The possibilities are endless."

He reached into a drawer and pulled out some papers, studying them. Maximiliano knew it was time to go. He knew he had received the answer he desired, and it was confirmed as he stood. Castro said, without looking up, "Tell the director of prisons to release the prisoner to you . . . I want him to get back into health . . . and I *don't* want someone to write another book about our jails, *sí?* Assign that young nurse that is with him now to work with you temporarily, and please advise me as to what safe house you take him, all right?"

Maximiliano straightened, nodded, and said simply, "*Sí.*"

As he walked out of the room Castro called behind him, "And think about the possibilities, about how we can use him for the cause!"

FIFTEEN

The two cars were parked in the evening darkness under the giant tree in the schoolyard. The red T-bird had California tags this time, and it was parked side by side with the black BMW with the gold pinstriping. Lieutenant Billy Erricks, in the T-bird, sat fidgeting as Montilla, in the BMW, went on and on in a rabid tirade against all cops, everywhere.

Finally, after venting most of his frustration and anger on a fidgeting Erricks, Montilla brought the conversation back to the original problem. "Anyway, after I got my fucking attorney down there to bond me out I asked him about the boat seizure. And he said that even though your boys made an illegal grab, it could take well over a month for him to get the court to give it back to me. That really sucks. What I need you to do is use your inside influence to get your legal adviser—or whatever he's called—to release that boat to my lawyer without us having to hassle with the court. Understand?"

"I can try, Onyx," said a subdued Erricks. "But I don't know how much pull I'll have on this one. Once the paperwork has been submitted it's real hard to reverse the process, even if we all know it's wrong. Believe me, that street cop, Richards, knew exactly what he was doing, and he lined up everything he needed to seize your boat, book you, and get the cases accepted by the state attorney's office. He did it just right, knowing the whole time he didn't have a prayer of beating you in court. He did it to take your boat away from you for a while . . . he knew . . ."

"I *know* what he did, asshole!" said Montilla through clenched teeth. "Now I want to see you earn some of that goddamned money I'm paying you, and get my fucking boat back. I'm saying this to you . . . that cop, Richards, has pissed me off for real this time. If you can't bring pressure to bear on him from the inside, then I'll do it from the street. I'm telling you right now, Erricks, I'll take Richards out of the picture for good unless you can control him from inside."

Erricks looked down at his hands in his lap for a moment, then straightened up and looked Montilla in the eyes. "I told you when we first talked that I was just a source of info. I told you that I didn't want to become involved in your business. And I told you I would have nothing to do with anything that meant people would get hurt or killed. Now here you are telling me you want to do something tough about Richards. I don't think I can sit here and let you threaten the life of another police officer."

Montilla stared at Erricks, smiled, and said quietly, "So what are you gonna do, drive away? Hit me? Shoot me? Turn me in to the police? Huh? Who the fuck do you think you're kidding, Erricks? First of all, you seem to have forgotten that even though Richards is a cop, if I need your help in getting him outta the way, that's it. You work for *me*. This is not the time to get your loyalties mixed up. If I want to threaten Richards's life in front of you, I will. It's just business, and I'm your boss. What, all of a sudden you got morals or somethin'?"

Erricks stared at Montilla balefully as Montilla turned slightly in his seat and looked at him and went on. "Don't you see that I own you, man? You're mine. If you make one move against me I'll dump so much crap on your chief's head about how helpful you've been to me that he won't know whether to shit or go blind. I'll give the grand jury so much hard info on you, they'll indict you so fast it will make your head spin. You and I both know that an ex-cop like you, especially a lieutenant of the narcs, would be real popular with all of the other prisoners, *sí?* There'd be a line of niggers a block long waitin' to shove it in your ass. The only way you're gonna survive this thing now is to stay with me all the way, no matter *what* I do." He paused, gauging the narc lieutenant, then went on. "So just relax, go with the flow, because I'm gonna do what I have to do. If it means killing a cop, then he'll be dead—that's all there is to it. If you can bring some shit down on that cop's head from the inside, then maybe I can stay out of it for now. If you can't, it will be my turn."

Erricks was just watching him, his face pale. Montilla, knowing he had to keep the narc lieutenant off balance, played one more card. He started his car, put it in gear, and said quietly, "Just so you'll know I'm playing for keeps, Erricks, here's something else to think about." He reached out and handed a Polaroid photo to Erricks, grinned, and drove off slowly.

Erricks looked at the photo, filled with dread. The photo showed the front of his home, or what used to be his home before he divorced his first wife. His wife was leaning into the car, getting something out, and his youngest daughter was standing at the end of the drive, looking into the camera with an expression of curiosity. He took long, deep breaths, and let the photo slip out of his fingers and fall into his lap. Even though the evening was cool there were beads of sweat on his forehead.

The red T-bird did not move out from under the tree for a long, long time.

Silky saw Montilla's BMW in the driveway as she pulled in and parked her small Mercedes. She hadn't seem him since yesterday, when he had been arrested. He had come home late and left early, and she had either stayed in her room or had been out driving around aimlessly. She knew he was inside now, waiting for her, and for a few seconds she hesitated, asking herself why she had even driven back there in the first place. Why hadn't she just driven away, never to return? She looked at her pale reflection in the smoked windows of the BMW, and the face that looked back was filled with fear—fear that he would find her. She unconsciously brushed he hair back off her forehead with her fingers and walked slowly into the house.

"So, the mystery slut returns. Where the hell have you been?"

Montilla stood unsteadily in the middle of the living room, a drink in one hand. His eyes were red. He hadn't changed since yesterday, and his beard looked frizzy and unkempt. She could see that the hair on his chin was matted from the drink he kept spilling on it. On the coffee table beside him she could see a couple of joints and a small gold box half filled with cocaine. She looked at him standing there glaring at her and knew he was totally wrecked. She didn't think talking to him would do any good, but she said, "Onyx," and before she could go any further he started.

"What the fuck you think? Think you can just do whatever the hell you want? *Puta!* I saw you talkin' to that fuckin' cop. He told me later that you were very . . . uncooperative . . . and you wouldn't tell him anything." He rubbed his face. "You little bitch, if you told him *anything* at all, I'll kill you. You'll be *dead!*" He waved his arms around, lost his balance, and almost fell, sitting down heavily on the arm of the couch. He stared at her silently for a few seconds, his eyes drilling into her. Then he said, quietly, "No, no, I think you're too smart. You wouldn't tell him anything because you know I can give you away with what you did with Sam Golden. And because you know I could kill you."

She watched him, silent.

"Well, little smart bitch, you'll be happy to know that I've bonded out. Here I am. My new lawyer is gonna take care of everything. And that squirrel cop I own is gonna take care of that big cop that's been fuckin' with me because if he doesn't, then I'm gonna do it myself! Then we won't have to worry about it anymore."

Silky's eyes widened at this, but Montilla didn't notice. She just stood there, head down, as he went on. "So, you'll be happy to know that I have everything under control, I am still in charge, and anyone who fucks with me will pay a hard price, *sí?* Even you, little girl . . . even you."

He stood up awkwardly, looked around the room, smiled at her, and said, "And now you'll be pleased to know that I want to fuck. Get into the bedroom and get yourself ready for me. I'm going to fix myself another drink, and then I'll be right in to make you very happy." He leered at her, turned, and headed for the kitchen.

She stood there for a moment, looked at the front door, hung her head, and walked slowly toward the bedroom.

She lay on her back in the darkness waiting for him. She was naked, and while she waited she ran her hands over her smooth body. Her skin felt cold. She tried to force herself to relax, to relax enough to let him enter her and pound himself against her, as he had begun to do recently, until finally he would shudder and fall heavily onto her. She waited in the darkness thinking about what he had said about the cop, and thinking about being scared, and thinking of how to leave and never be found.

She heard him enter the bedroom. She heard him unzip his pants, and she felt the bed move as he fell back onto it. She heard him say, "I'm gonna fuck your brains out, you little . . ." And then she heard his deep, ragged, uneven snores.

She smiled at the ceiling.

The brave little macho man had Scotched, grassed, and coked himself into never-never land.

She reached over and turned on the light. He was lying on his back, naked except for his pants, which were bunched up at his ankles. His head was turned to the side and his mouth was open with the tongue just visible as he snored. With one hand he gripped a portion of the sheet, with the other he held his flaccid penis. She looked at him and shook her head.

It would be so easy.

Easy to kill him now, or easy to leave. She looked at him and thought about the weapons he kept around the house. She knew there was a small pistol in the drawer of the night table, not three feet away. She could get it and shoot him. Simply point it at him and shoot him again and again until there were no more bullets. Then call the police. Tell them he was drunk and had attacked her. She was in fear of her life. She could get an attorney and go for it.

But first she had to kill him.

She looked down at him on the bed and she knew she could not. And would not. Damn. Okay then, what about leaving? Get some clothes together, find whatever money was laying around the house, get in the car, and drive away. Just leave.

He belched loudly and she caught her breath and watched as he played with himself and muttered something she couldn't understand. She watched him and knew she couldn't leave. Not now. Not yet. Not when she would have to spend the rest of her life looking over her shoulder, always waiting for the time when he would find her and kill her. She closed her eyes and thought about that. Yes, he *would* come looking. Her walking out on him would be something he could not let happen. He would keep looking until he found her.

She sighed. She would have to bide her time until it was right, until she could get away from him forever.

She put on the extra large T-shirt she usually slept in, left the bedroom, and stretched out on the living room couch, where she watched the late show, trying to relax.

As she began to fall asleep, she realized that while she stayed with Montilla she might find some way of helping that big cop, Richards. She might help him stay alive and help him take Montilla down.

That thought pleased her very much.

Early the next morning Montilla had awakened to find himself alone in the bed, and he had hurried out of the bedroom to look for Silky. His head was pounding and he felt unsteady. He found her sitting quietly in the screened-in porch at the back of the house, sipping a cup of tea and looking out into the backyard. She had made a pot of coffee for him, and he was just pouring a cup with a shaky hand when the phone rang.

"My patrón will be pleased to speak with you this morning. I will pick you up in fifteen minutes, *sí?*" Montilla had no time to reply before the line went dead. He carried his coffee to the back porch and spoke to Silky's back. "I have to go out for a while. It's important." He hesitated. "I want you to stay here and wait for me to come back." He remembered fighting with her, yelling at her, and then taking her to bed, but he could not remember how the night had ended.

She turned slowly in her seat, ran her fingers through her hair, back from her forehead, and smiled at him. "I'm not going anywhere, Onyx. It's a pretty morning, and I'm a little tired after last night." Her eyes looked into his, and he held her stare. "You go ahead. I'm going to read a little and relax." She smiled again. "I'm fine, really."

He turned to go take a fast shower and get dressed, almost reassured.

Maximiliano's agent pulled into the drive in a small beige rental car, left the engine running as Montilla came out and climbed in, and then drove quickly off the isle and onto Las Olas Boulevard. He was silent as they went east, and then over the bridge. As they crossed over the Intracoastal, Montilla could see a lovely panorama of docks and anchorages on the waterway, filled with sailboats and yachts, and beyond, farther east past the intersection of AIA and Las Olas, the sparkling green of the Atlantic Ocean. It was a good day to be on the sea, with just a slight breeze and only one- to two-foot waves. Montilla could see one heavily laden tanker moving south on the horizon and a couple of fishing boats closer in.

The silent driver of the rental car turned south on Seabreeze Boulevard, past the small docks where rental boats were kept and a couple of drift fishing boats tied up, past the Hall of Fame swimming pool, and kept going. Montilla sat stiffly, glad of the driver's silence, his head still fuzzy.

They pulled into the entrance to Bahia Mar, took a ticket from the automatic gate, and drove around the right side of the complex. The driver found a parking space close to the west end of the lot, next to the long face dock on the Intracoastal Waterway, got out and began walking easily toward several of the large private yachts tied up there. Montilla followed along, taking deep breaths, trying to will his mind into sharp focus.

Maximiliano's agent stopped before a shiny gangway leading up to the starboard side of a beautifully kept luxury yacht. Montilla guessed her to be at least one hundred feet long, and a quick glance at the wheelhouse, with the many antennae and radar, told him she would be carrying state-of-the-art electronics. He did not see her name carved intricately into wooden name boards, but he did see a Canadian flag hanging from her stern. He stepped aboard.

Maximiliano was waiting for him in the main salon. He was seated comfortably in a deep chair beside a glass coffee table, and he held a small cup of coffee in his hand. He watched as Montilla sat in the matching chair and took coffee from his agent. He noticed that Montilla's hand shook slightly as he held the cup.

As Maximiliano studied Montilla, he thought about his last meeting with his leader, Castro, and about the plans for the young American being held in Cuba, and the plans for Montilla. After being briefed on what Maximiliano had learned about the links between Montilla's father and the Fort Lauderdale policeman, and then Novak and Montilla —fantastic and incredible as it was—Castro had laughed out loud, excited about the "possibilities." Castro still wanted Montilla to be used to smuggle cocaine into the U.S., but now he thought there might be a way to bait Montilla with Novak.

Maximiliano had nodded in agreement, but privately he had his doubts. He was beginning to question the wisdom of using Montilla for any job.

"So, Onyx, you look slightly ill on this pretty morning. Are you all right?"

Montilla just nodded, sipping his coffee.

"Good. Things are beginning to come together now, Onyx, and I must know that you are feeling up to it. I must say, we are slightly worried about these most recent events taking place between you and the local police. All of this time you have been clever at avoiding the heat from the task forces and the big investigations, and yet, suddenly, you have allowed yourself to get hit, repeatedly, by a regular policeman—not even a narcotics policeman." He waited, watching.

Montilla very carefully set the coffee cup down on the glass table, sat back, and looked at Maximiliano with a steady gaze. He bit back his first response, then said quietly, "Luck. They've had some luck and stumbled into a couple of things, that's all."

"It is the kind of luck your father would have already done something about, Onyx," said Maximiliano, his voice soft, one hand held up to halt Montilla's coming protestations. "We have been watching you because you are important to us in our plans. We need someone with not only your father's courage, which we know you have, but also your father's brains, which, frankly, we're beginning to question."

Montilla felt the blood rushing to his temples, but he remained silent.

Maximiliano took a sip of coffee, rubbed his fingers over his chin, and went on. "This latest episode, at the lounge. This local policeman comes there and arrests you in front of everyone and then has his federal friends drive away in your racing boat. This takes place in the broad daylight, everyone is watching. You are drunk and loud and you have with you some cocaine. And you get arrested." He shook his head slowly from side to side. "You acted like some small-time street hood. Not smart—brash, crude, unprofessional." He leaned forward, and his voice took on a cold edge. "We cannot have this kind of person working for us! Do you think we are some cheap smuggling group who needs your services because you can drive a boat and shoot a gun? From the time of your father we have fought the best, and won! The men that work with us do not make the mistakes you do because those kinds of mistakes compromise the mission . . . and get people killed. One of the reasons you were approached is because we were told you were one of those that could smuggle the cocaine without being seduced by her, *sí?* Do you understand? I ask you now, here. Is it because you are sticking the cocaine up your nose that you are acting so foolishly, or is it because you are a fool to begin with?"

Montilla gripped the sides of the chair, his back stiff, and felt himself ready to lunge forward toward Maximiliano. No one spoke to him like this, and he felt the need to release his mounting temper. Out of the corner of his eye he saw the other Cuban agent moving closer, and watched as Maximiliano waved the man away with a small gesture. Their eyes locked, and Montilla tried to steady himself, his breathing very deep. He swallowed hard, twice, and then said thickly, "I am Onyx Montilla, and I do what I want, when I want. Yes, I take the cocaine occasionally, just as I take a little Scotch now and then, but it does not mean I have been 'seduced' by it—or that it controls me." He sat back in the chair, trying to arrange his thoughts. "That was an accident . . . what happened at the lounge. Yes, I had the cocaine with me . . . but no more than what I always carry for my friends to share with me. It's mostly for the girl, *she* needs it. But that one cop was there, the same one who has stumbled onto a couple of my boats. I think he has decided he has found a big criminal, and he finds a way to undermine me. He is nothing!"

Maximiliano gazed at Montilla steadily.

"Besides," said Montilla, "I've got another cop, a narc,

on my payroll now. He is making sure that the other cop will no longer be a problem. And if he doesn't, I will."

Maximiliano studied his nails for a moment, then said in a relaxed tone, "Listen, my young friend. I had to ask these hard questions, to clear the air, *sí?* I knew your father, and I know you, Onyx Montilla. And I know you can do this job for us." He watched Montilla very closely. It was time.

"Let me tell you a story that you might find interesting, Onyx. It is a story about you and your father that you do not know. But before I do, I must be unpleasant again for a moment, *sí?*" He leaned forward. "What I will tell you now will upset you. It will be like igniting rocket fuel in your heart. In a way it will be a test for you because if you can control yourself and do what we say, we will know you are capable of doing this assignment for us. I have already told you that our plans are very important to us. If I feel that you cannot be trusted, and that you may act prematurely, I will have to take steps to neutralize you. Do you understand me, Onyx? I am about to tell you a great secret, and then I must gauge how you are handling it. If I think you will jeopardize what we are doing, I will have you killed."

The room froze in chilled silence. Montilla could feel a great weight on his chest, and his mind was a turmoil of anticipation, curiosity, anger, and fear. Finally, he nodded slowly.

"You watched as your father, a hero to our people, was gunned down in the street by a policeman." Maximiliano paused, watching Montilla; then he went on. "That policeman is named J.B. Richards. He has moved from the north and now works for this local police group. The man who has been seizing your loads of marijuana, and the man who took your boat from you and arrested you for the cocaine, is the same man who killed your father twenty years ago."

Montilla sat rigid, his mind swirling, images crashing into one another in a confused frenzy. The big policeman who had stood there pointing his gun as his father fell to the pavement had a lean, stretched face, his mouth and eyes open wide. And the big policeman who had arrested him for cocaine had eyes that stared at him in a disconcerting, knowing way. He took a deep breath and felt for a moment that he would vomit. Could it be? Could it really be? And if it was, it would be like a chance from God . . . a chance to avenge his father's death. His eyes shined brittle-bright as he stared at Maximiliano and nodded.

Maximiliano made a fist with one hand and cupped it with the other. "It is indeed a bizarre coincidence . . . but there is more, Onyx. The story becomes even more unreal as we go further. Just before I met you for the first time you took two men in your boat to the near islands. One was a lawyer. You had help from an islander, and you killed the two men, leaving their bodies in the sea."

Montilla waited, and a clear understanding of what had happened to Cuda jumped into his mind.

"You will be pleased to know, Onyx, that the other man with the lawyer was a cop, a narcotics policeman from this same local police group. His name is Novak. I see by your expression that you are not surprised; perhaps you had already guessed that. So, you would like to hurt this cop, Richards, very much. What would you say if I told you that you have already hurt him, in much the same way he has hurt you?"

Montilla said softly, "I would be pleased." Then he waited.

"The policeman, Richards, he had a very close friend who died before he moved his family to this city. The friend had a son who is very close to this policeman, Richards. Like a son, I'm told. The son of Richards's friend who died moved here also and became a policeman, a narcotics cop. He is Novak, the one you killed off Bimini."

Montilla's face was covered with sweat, and his eyes bulged out. His lips curled back from his teeth, and he hissed, "So! Richards killed my father . . . and now I have killed his son! Soon I will kill him too!"

Maximiliano sat back now, a small smile on his face. He was playing Montilla along now, bringing him in slowly to where he wanted him. He poured more coffee for himself, deliberately taking his time. Finally, he said, "The problem is, Onyx, you did not kill the narcotics policeman, Novak. He is still alive."

"No way!" said Montilla, alarm on his face. "That sucker was in the water, and I flat ate him up with my props. Then we sat and waited, to see if there was any sign of life. No way he's alive."

Maximiliano's agent, always silent, always watching, let out an almost imperceptible huff, and Maximiliano knew it was the man's way of saying what he thought of amateurs.

Maximiliano went back to the task at hand. "Listen to me, Onyx Montilla. Sometimes things happen in this world that are hard to explain. It is said that there is a reason for everything, *sí?* Believe me when I tell you that Novak is very much alive, and in our care."

Montilla sat quietly, rubbing his temples. Then he looked up and asked, "But how? How did you get him. And what are you going to do with him?"

"Those are questions that I will not give you answers to—at this time. You can see, Onyx, that this situation is bigger than it first seemed, *sí?* And you can see that my people have a much better grasp of the entire picture than you do. I must say this again to you, you are involved in a very large and important operation. You have been selected because we know you can do the job. If, however, we even think you will let your emotions—or the cocaine—get the better of your judgment, then we will have to take you out of the picture."

He saw Montilla's face harden again, knowing the man did not like to be threatened. He threw out the bait. "Work with us, Onyx, keep your feelings under control, stay as a professional, like your father, and you will have what you seek. We are the ones that have Novak, and we are the ones that know about Richards. We can give them both to you, to do with what you wish. But *only* after our goals are met. You must trust me, and cooperate fully with me, so I can have total confidence in you. Understand?"

Montilla's face relaxed, and his breathing came back to normal. Finally, he shook his head, grinned, and said easily, "I understand . . . and I'm with you. I'll work with you, and do as you say, as long as *you* understand that when this is over, Richards is mine."

Maximiliano bowed, letting him have his personal victory.

After his agent had taken Montilla off the yacht to drive him back home, Maximiliano thought about the conversation. His original doubts about this whole thing were now reinforced. Onyx Montilla was not Felix Ortiz, that was certain. Montilla had been raised without a father in the bosom of an affluent democracy, had enjoyed the given freedoms by growing up on the streets of Miami. Felix had grown up in the bosom of a dictatorship, and then the revolution. Maximiliano chided himself. Maybe they really don't make them like they used to. A scowl crossed his face as that thought led him to a nagging concern. What would happen when there is no Fidel? He, Maximiliano, had been a faithful soldier of the revolution for all of these years, fighting the dirty little fights in the back alleys and dark rooms, fights that never made headlines. He had never questioned his leader, or his direction—until now. Now he wasn't sure. In a relatively short time great changes would occur, and he wondered if anyone was making plans for that day.

The Russians would be waiting, he knew. Waiting to see what leader Cuba had who could stand up to them as Castro had for so many years. The Americans would be waiting too, but they would be different. He asked himself, already knowing the answer, if we needed to deal openly with one of the super powers to survive, which one would be better for the Cuban people, America . . . or Russia?

These thoughts stemmed from his feelings about this case. He was not comfortable with this case; there was a bad feeling about it. The American narcotics policeman was too lucky by far. Then there were all of the connecting links from the past to the present. He rubbed his nose, and thought, *if I was totally honest with Montilla I would have told him that it was Felix Ortiz who lost his head and started the shooting when he could have just run off and faded into the crowd as he had done so many times before.*

Well, maybe Felix was tired of running by then. No matter. What does matter is our attempt to smuggle cocaine into this country, to share some of the profit from our Colombian, and yes, our Canadian friends. And to do this I am using Onyx Montilla, and baiting him with the lives of two local policemen.

He stood up and walked out the aft salon doors. He leaned against the transom, shiny with fresh varnish, and watched a small sailboat putter past, a young girl at the helm. The girl smiled and waved at him and he waved back, liking her for waving. Then he sighed, and thought, *I have always followed the orders of my leader, but this time I may have to make some changes.*

Silky sat looking out a window at the last colors of a beautiful sunset. She had watched for almost an hour as the light of day ended and found it relaxed her in a gentle way. The colors and patterns had changed second by second, and she had been fascinated by the thought of her small part of the world rolling away from the sun, welcoming the approaching night and the first bold stars, letting the quiet and peace envelop it.

There had been no peace with Montilla in the house all day.

When he had come back from his morning meeting, Silky noticed a sheen of perspiration on his face and his eyes were bitter-bright. He would not tell her what had happened other than to say once, "You would not believe what I have learned today." He spent the rest of the day rambling around the house like a caged animal. He could not sit still, he could not watch television. Several times he laughed out loud, but the laugh sounded to Silky as frightening as the manic expression on his face. She was finally able to enjoy a couple of hours of quiet when he carried several of his guns—pistols, a shotgun, and two sinister automatic weapons—out onto the back porch and sat humming to himself as he broke them down and cleaned them.

She saw him now, sitting behind her in the living room, his foot tapping a ragged tattoo on the carpet while he bit his lip and idly played with a small pistol in his hands. They both heard the sound of an approaching car, and she saw him jump up, tuck the gun under his shirt, and walk quickly to the door.

Silky looked out the window as the baby blue Cadillac pulled slowly into the circular drive, the young hood named Joe behind the wheel. She could see the businessman, Kolin, look at Onyx grimly as he got out of the passenger side of the car. Montilla, rather than wait for them at the door, had walked out to the drive to greet them. Silky sighed, closed the blinds, and went back to reading *Passages*.

As Montilla held the door for the old man and his bodyguard he noticed that Kolin did not make any move to shake hands, and the smirk on the young guy's face only worried him more. He knew that Kolin liked to hold discussions at the kitchen table, but he usually waited until Montilla offered them a seat in the living room and then made a joke about being closer to the beer. This evening, however, Kolin marched right through the living room and into the kitchen where he took a seat at the small table without waiting for Montilla to say anything. Joe looked around the house a little, smiling at Silky, which only annoyed Montilla more, and then stood quietly behind and slightly to the left of Kolin. When Montilla offered him a seat as he took his own, Joe just shook his head and smiled.

"So, Mister Kolin, you look great," began Montilla, feeling very unsure of himself. Before he could continue, Kolin gave a small wave of his hand and said sharply, "Look, Onyx, today we don't need nice small talk. Today we need answers, okay? I'm gonna get right to it, Onyx, because we have some definite problems."

Montilla was already sitting on the edge of his chair, and he felt the knot in his stomach grow tighter as he said, "Okay, Mister Kolin, sure, you know I'm always ready to talk business, and I'm always ready to help out with any problems."

Kolin studied him for a few seconds and then went on. "Yeah, well listen, Onyx, the last time I talked with you I told you some of my business partners were a little concerned about your track record lately. You know, you lost some loads so we all lost money. And while we were losing money, you were losing people—your lawyer, and that boat guy that died because he panicked in the face of the law. It all looks pretty shitty, to tell you the truth, Onyx."

Montilla was going to reply, but Kolin held up his hand. "So I came over here as your business partner and friend the last time and I told you to put your affairs in order and keep a low profile. You know that I want to keep doing business with you, Onyx, even though you are just a very small part of our setup. Thank goodness we've got little groups like yours from here to North Carolina, all pulling their share, or we'd be pretty skinny businessmen, huh?"

Montilla's face was getting red but he managed a quick nod of his head. Behind Kolin, Joe was grinning openly.

Kolin sat back, pulled his watch off his wrist, and began massaging the skin there with his other hand. He looked at the ceiling and went on. "Of course you know that you are the only representative we have buying directly from the Bahamians. Most of our good stuff still comes out of Colombia on those shit-box freighters all the way up the coast. You know we have to pay the price when we deal with those people, and the stupid freighters still have to run that long gauntlet before they can safely off-load somewhere. You know we've liked working with you because we can save a little operating money by dealing directly with those islanders, with their zero overhead. It's worked out real nice for everybody, except of course, the competition. Yeah, things have been good. Until recently." Now he pulled his watch back on to his wrist, stood up, and put his hands into his pockets. Montilla stayed in his seat, watching carefully as Kolin walked back and forth in the kitchen, talking the whole time.

"Onyx, you know one of the rules we've always insisted on is *no* cocaine deals and no cocaine on any of the working equipment. You and I both know coke brings more heat faster than any grass ever did, and who needs that? Besides, people start stuffing that shit up their noses and all of a sudden they ain't worth a damn. They start to get unreliable, know what I mean? Stuff messes with their heads, and from a business point of view we just can't have that, can we?"

He had his back to Montilla now, and Montilla said nothing. Without turning around he went on. "So what happens? I come over here. I ask you, please, Onyx, get your act together. I tell you my partners are asking me if I'm in control here. I tell you to cool it and you go out and get yourself busted in broad daylight by a couple of street cops. You make an ass of yourself, and they drive away with your big macho racing boat already!" The old man was facing him now, his arms outstretched in front of him, his small hands like blades pointing at Montilla. "You lose your boat and get busted for coke in front of God and everybody, and before the ink is dry from your fingerprints I got my phone ringing off the hook with my partners asking me what am I doing—what kinda guys I got working for me? I'm on the phone all day telling them you're cool, and you can still do the job for us. You know I don't like telling you this, Onyx, but some of them were even worrying that now you got a bust hangin' over your head, all of a sudden you're gonna decide to tell all, hmmmm? See what I mean? I practically talk myself hoarse covering for you, and now I want you to tell me why I did that. Tell me why I can still use you, Onyx. Tell me why we still need you around."

Montilla sat motionless, his face a chalky white. He watched as Kolin came back and sat at the table, facing him with a waiting look. Over his shoulder the face of Joe hung there grinning. Montilla took a deep breath and forced himself to relax.

"Let me tell you this, Mister Kolin. I can still do the job for you . . . and I want to. I'm not gonna try to give excuses about what I did. It was stupid, it was wrong. I've been under pressure lately, what with losing those loads and all and having you jump on me the last time. I don't know, I guess I was using the coke to unwind a bit. It was stupid. Of course, that broad I got shacked up here loves that shit and I keep it around here mostly to keep her happy."

Kolin gave a little grunt and Montilla could see in his eyes that he didn't believe him.

"Anyway, Mister Kolin, let me tell you where I stand with all this shit. First of all, the coke bust, even though I was stupid enough to have that shit in the boat, it's really just a hand-job. Those particular cops," he said as he felt his chest tightening and his throat drying out, "have a hard-on for me and they made some remarks and got me hot and the next thing I knew they had some Customs pals of theirs on my boat and they had the toot and there I was. So what could I do? My attorney has already started proceedings to get my boat back, and has told me that the coke charge is never even gonna get to court. I've still got two really clean Striker sportfishermen with crews; they look good and they can do the job. Most important, I have been back to Bimini, and my contact over there is still hungry for my business and he wants to keep things going. What I'm saying is this. I've still got the connections, I've got the equipment, and I can do the job. In fact, when I do the next one for you I'm gonna ride along, just to be *sure* there are no problems. Honest to God, Mister Kolin, all I need is another chance and I'll show you that Onyx Montilla is a man of his word."

Montilla stared at Kolin now, and thought, *C'mon, you old fuck, one more time. I've got to make this run for you, it's important to* everything. *One more time and then I'll never have to look at your pinched face again.*

Kolin stared back, and thought, Oh you're gonna get another chance, Onyx, don't worry about that. While you do this last one for us we're gonna have our money courier whisper in the ear of your Mister Cornelius Black, and from then on we'll do this whole gig on *our* terms. And when that happens, you smart-assed greaser, you are going to find yourself extremely dead.

Kolin gave a long sigh, stood up slowly and stretched, and began walking around the kitchen again, rubbing his bony fingers across his chin and making little clicking noises with his tongue. His every move was followed by Montilla and Joe. Kolin appeared to be in deep thought. Finally he turned and said, "Look, Onyx, you know how I feel about you. I want to keep working with you. It's just that I'm going to have my neck stuck way out if I let you work again."

Montilla, sensing a chance, blurted out, "Listen, Mister Kolin, we can work this out any way you want. I'll work for less if I have to, I'll run it for just the operating costs if that's what you want."

Kolin still walked around, thinking to himself, *Oh, no, Onyx. I'd never tell you, or any other operator, that they worked for free. You put a man out on that Gulf Stream on a boat with a couple of tons of grass, knowing he's not getting paid what he should, and it's almost a sure bet he'll start thinking of ripping you off.* He shook his head slightly, and said, "Look, Onyx, that's not what I want to do. I appreciate your offer. No, what I need is some kind of handle on things as they progress. Tell you what, Onyx, I'll give you the go-ahead on another run, but you have to take Joe here with you and keep him with you all the time. What do you think of that?"

Montilla thought it sucked, and he almost blurted that out, but caught himself in time to swallow hard and say, "Well, sure, Mister Kolin, I'd be happy to have Joe come along. Actually it will be good having someone around who is close to you, so he can come back and tell you how good my setup is over there." Inside he was seething. This could screw up everything. That little hood would stick with him like glue, his eyes wide open the whole time. Shit, shit, shit. *Just when I had things set up for the big one,* he thought. Even though his mind was in turmoil, he said calmly, "Sounds good to me."

Joe, who at first appeared just as startled as Montilla, recovered his composure enough to say, "Yeah, no problem at all. I always wanted to see Bimini."

Kolin smiled broadly and said, "Great, great. I'll tell you, Onyx, I was really hoping we could work this out somehow."

Montilla was still seething, but he felt a little better. Having Joe on the trip would make things a little shaky, but he was sure he could still pull off his plan. At least now he had a chance.

Kolin asked for a beer, and the tension in the room relaxed. Onyx got cold beers for each of them, and they sat back and began to talk about the numbers. Prices for marijuana constantly fluctuated, depending on where it was being sold, what local weed had come on the market to compete and, of course, the quality. People had been smoking grass for a long time and had become demanding. Quality marijuana, with a high THC content, could be sold fast, anywhere. Good money could be made for a group like Kolin's, and the operatives, like Montilla. Out of Montilla's cut came expenses for the boats, load houses, crews, electronics, countersurveillance, and all the other things needed to bring the load safely into the country. Still, when the bills were paid, he came away with a good profit, cash money.

Kolin sipped his beer, watched Montilla, and thought, *Hard to believe you could be making that heavy money these last months and still be so hungry. You want too much, Onyx, too much with the houses and the cars and the boats and the women and all that expensive dust you pack your nostrils with. And what is that edge I feel about you tonight? That intensity in your eyes. You are carrying a barely concealed excitement. Are you high now, or do you have a secret?* Kolin gave an almost imperceptible shake of his head as he thought of the amount of money Montilla must have thrown away over the last couple of months, just getting high. Stupid bastard, he thought. Not this time, Onyx. This time you bring us the load while we take over your connection, and then you will get a visit from someone who does things for us for less money than the prices of one of your fancy cars out there, and then we'll *all* make more money in the future. Except you, of course.

While they talked of times and dates and places, Montilla looked at Kolin's head bobbing on his skinny neck and thought, *Yeah, you old fuck. I'm doin' this one with you, but you just can't imagine what is involved. I'll be working with people who wouldn't let you shine their shoes, Kolin, and I'll be running my coke and their coke right under your runny nose. I'm playing where the big boys play now.*

"Well, Onyx," said Kolin with a smile, "feels good to have you back on the team again. I'm glad we were able to work this out this evening. You let me know when you're ready to go, so we can get the money over there to your connection. And I'll have Joe come over too, okay?"

Montilla shook Kolin's small leathery hand as he stood by the front door, and said, "Yessir, Mister Kolin. I expect to go on this one in a couple of days. I'll contact you when it's time." As he stood at the door watching the baby blue Cadillac drive slowly away his mind was working furiously. He was charged up, and felt good. He had to get over to Bimini quick before the boats went over so he could set things up with Black. They were talking about ten thousand pounds of grass. He would split the load, and use the group's money to get maybe twenty kilos of fine cocaine. Then he could bring that in with the half load of grass, shoot it to his own buyer, make his bucks, and then turn around and haul ass back there and pick up the rest of Kolin's load, paying Black out of his coke money. And the whole time he was doing *that*, he'd be taking Maximiliano's cocaine too. He would deliver it wherever Maximiliano wanted it. And then they could talk about what would happen to that cop, Richards. He knew it was complicated, and for a fleeting moment wondered if he was trying to do too much, too soon. No, he was tired of doing shit for other guys. He would work this whole gig to his advantage . . . sure, it would take some tap dancing here and there, but it would work out in the end.

After Kolin left, the house became quiet. Silky still sat reading, having followed his orders and stayed away from the meeting. Montilla tried to relax. He tried to sit back and calm down, to let his mind think of other things. He had a drink. Then another. He smoked a joint, walking around the backyard and standing at his empty dock, staring down into the water. He was wired, and couldn't get himself to come down.

He told Silky to get dressed. They went to a restaurant near the tunnel on Las Olas. Their dinner was nice, but he was quiet, almost vibrating as he sat and listened to Silky's small talk. She was aware of his mood, slightly mystified, but very careful. They went home, and he fixed them both strong drinks. Finally he could stand it no more, and he opened up his ornate glass box full of cocaine. He knew it wouldn't help, but he had to do it anyway. The whole day of emotions ate at his mind and his heart, and he felt as if he would explode if he didn't do something. He did line after line, while Silky sat nervously and watched him. It took him most of the night, but he finally came crashing down, the molten bubble in his heart bursting out in a torrent of release. Before he fell asleep in Silky's arms, he told her everything.

SIXTEEN

DO WE HAVE A COP MISSING?
Narc Mysteriously Disappears

J.B. read the article in the Fort Lauderdale *Herald* a second time as he walked across the back parking lot of the station. He had been summoned again, along with Skids Bedlam this time, to a meeting in the major's office. He was to meet Tallert and Skids and then go up to the second floor.

The reporter, Dave, had done a nice job. Most of the article was about Ted Novak, how he had quit his work as a teacher and moved south, and how he had joined the Fort Lauderdale Police Department with great hopes of doing a job that he had dreamed of for so long. Two letters of commendation that Ted had received were mentioned, and a couple of quotes from sergeants taken off Ted's early rating forms were included.

The article told of Ted's recent transfer to the narcotics unit (giving that as the reason for not including a photograph), and mentioned some recent narcotics cases Ted had been involved in, without going into details. Dave then

asked the reader some questions: Did Ted follow up on one
of the earlier cases without his bosses knowing about it?
Was that standard procedure? And, if he did, had he been
killed by the bad guys? Was he being held hostage somewhere? Had the administration already received demands
from the hostage takers, and was that why it was all so
hush-hush?

The article gave the official line—that Ted Novak was
absent without leave, and that the administration suspected
he may be having personal problems. Dave had looked into
that too, giving quotes from Ted's landlady and others who
knew him as a neighbor. The general concensus was that
Ted was very much involved with his work, and that he
was "a nice man, who stayed pretty much to himself."

J.B. was pleased that the article did not mention the
family connection between himself and Ted.

He stopped near the backdoor, the sun warm on his
back, the breeze fluttering the edges of the paper as he read
Dave's last paragraph.

"Has the inevitable finally happened? Has our tropical
arena of drugs and money taken one of our own from us?
Can we proudly claim to be 'Pan-American' and still think
our only problem is small-time criminals? Isn't it time we
realized that all narcotics smuggling activities in our area
are really on an international level?

"When one of our local narcotics officers goes out on the
street tonight to fight the problem in our community, in all
actuality he will be fighting a criminal organization that
extends far beyond our small municipal and county
borders. He will be fighting a machine that works within
the entire Caribbean basin, Central America, and South
America. Did one of our local cops, armed with his badge
and a lot of courage and resolve, get swept away by the
tidal wave of drugs and money that has changed the very
shape of our world?"

J.B. folded the paper neatly, took a deep breath, and
went into the station to meet with Tallert and the major to
learn what they had planned for him now.

They were back in the major's office.

Tallert sat between Richards and Bedlam against one

wall, facing the legal adviser, Harper, Captain Fransetti, and Lieutenant Whitney. The major sat at his desk, smoking a cigar and shuffling through a small pile of papers in front of him. Finally he looked up at Tallert and said, "Jed, I'm beginning to get the feeling that neither you nor your people listen to a thing I say."

Tallert gazed back but said nothing.

"Here we are all sitting in the office again. And I'm going to have to caution your people again. And I've got another complaint from Erricks in OCB about your people again. And I've got the legal adviser here telling me your people made another questionable grab again. And this whole thing is beginning to give me a big pain in the ass."

Bedlam looked at his hands, Richards looked at the ceiling, and Tallert just kept looking into the major's eyes. Harper appeared to be bored, Fransetti mildly amused, and Whitney pleased beyond words. Even though Richards was temporarily assigned to Whitney, the fat lieutenant spent a lot of time and energy making sure all of the other brass knew that Richards was, ultimately, Tallert's problem.

The major picked up the pile of papers on his desk and let them fall. "Mister Harper advises me that the legality on the cocaine arrest is marginal because it followed a really marginal disorderly conduct arrest. He says the prosecutor's office will probably file the case because of the cocaine, but he also advises that it will never get to trial and that any defense attorney worth his salt will pick it apart without even trying. Needless to say, this makes the seizure of the go-fast boat a very iffy thing. I don't know for sure, but I'll bet those two Customs guys have already heard from their own legal department about it." He leaned forward suddenly and looked directly at Richards. "Look, J.B., I know this Montilla is an asshole, and I know you played it by the numbers, and I know just taking the boat from him for a while is enough to break his balls and it makes you feel better. But dammit, you're gonna have to leave it alone. Erricks called over here all pissed off because you and Bedlam went crashing right into the middle of somethin' him and his super-snoopers were working on. You have to admit you went in there with all the grace of a water buffalo. So he calls over here and wants to know if my orders can just be disobeyed by any patrolman who thinks he feels like it. He even went so far as to suggest that it could appear that you are purposely interfering with their case."

Richards started to say something but was silenced by a look from Tallert. Bedlam just snorted and shook his head. The major went on. "Okay, you know I think that's ridiculous too. I know in my heart, J.B., that you are just trying to do your job. I also know in my heart that this Montilla thing is becoming more than just another case to you." He sat back. "So, in order to have the legal adviser relax a little, and in order to convince Erricks that you're not trying to screw up his game plan, and in order for me to have a little peace and quiet around here, I'm ordering Lieutenant Whitney, with Lieutenant Tallert being aware of it, to assign you and Bedlam to the northwest. You are going to be assigned to a zone in blacktown and you're gonna stay there and just do your usual fine police work with our less fortunate brothers across the way there. You and I both know there is plenty of work to be done across the tracks, and I can't think of anyplace in this city farther removed from the waterways, the go-fast boats, the drug smugglers, Montilla, and all that other shit."

The major paused, then struck out in a completely different direction. "All of you people see that article in the paper about Novak?" Everyone nodded their heads. The major pushed the papers around on his desk for a moment, then said quietly, "That reporter asked some questions I'd like some answers for myself. Had a meeting with the chief this morning, and he has fired a rocket over to the narcotics unit, telling them to find out one way or the other if Ted is missing because of a case-related deal. Guess we all sort of sat on our hands long enough, hoping young Ted would just come walking in the front door, grinning, with a story about how he met some topless dancer who took him on a trip around the world . . . or somethin'. Hell, I've seen this department spend more time and energy looking for a missing dog." His face pulled into a tight grimace as he went on. "Maybe it's like that reporter said, you know, maybe none of us wants to admit that we send our guys out there without really considering the consequences all the time."

The room fell silent, everyone wrapped in his own thoughts. J.B. had the distinct impression that the major was giving him a quiet apology about the administration's slow reaction time to the situation. Then the major looked up, all business again, and said brusquely, "Listen, J.B., get in that squad car with your partner, go out and win the hearts and minds of the people, and forget about anything that happens in this city east of the FEC railroad tracks. Got it? Now will you all please get out of my office? Thank you."

"No hablar," said the pretty young nurse as she held one finger against her lips. She looked into his eyes for a moment, squeezed his arm, then turned, her hip brushing against him.

Ted was out of bed, out of the room he had come to hate, and he was walking in a small, wet courtyard with the nurse. The courtyard was surrounded by an old stone wall that was partially covered by a lush green vine and small red flowers. It was early morning. The open air Ted filled his lungs with was heavy with moisture, still cool, even though the sun had already risen above the flowers. It was very quiet, and somehow lovely, even though it was still a prison in a foreign land. Ted was wearing plain pajamas of a heavy cotton material, and the pain in his right leg caused him to limp badly. The nurse, dressed in some sort of military-type fatigues but still very feminine and comforting, tried to take most of his weight off him as he slowly walked around the perimeter of the small courtyard.

He had finished a simple breakfast of juice and fruit when the nurse had come into the room and helped him out of bed. He had started to ask her questions then, and she had just said, "No," and shook her head. He had walked with her, apprehensive at first, then more relaxed as he understood he was just being exercised, and it took him only a few minutes to realize that she had been ordered to keep him silent as they walked. It was surely easier to eavesdrop electronically on a small room than in a court-

yard. Still, moving his body again, and seeing the flowers
and the sunshine and the nurse's lovely black hair and soft
brown eyes had made Ted feel good. He was alive, and he
smiled. He had stopped, turned to her, and asked her to tell
him her name.

"No speaking, huh?" said Ted quietly, feeling too good
to stay quiet. "So what will they do, run me over with a
boat and then take me to a prison in some foreign country?" She squeezed his arm but did not look at him. But she
did not tell him to stop either. He tried again. "Look at me.
Walking wounded, wearing these pajamas, being helped
around this picturesque courtyard by a lovely nurse . . . I
feel like young Lieutenant Henry in *A Farewell to Arms*.
Of course, he was there because of a war."

The girl was still silent, her eyes on the wet stones at
their feet, a small smile on her face.

Ted took another long, deep breath, savoring the minutes
he was sharing. The girl was another living being, a person, warm and strong and alive. He spoke and his words
fell on her ears. She turned her head and her soft brown
eyes swept across his face and she saw him. He was struck
with the realization of just how much she meant to him.
Other than a few guards, the dour doctor, and the two men
who questioned him, he had seen no one else. It was not
just that the nurse was the only woman that he had seen, it
was her manner with him . . . gentle and caring, yes, but
also concerned and able to lend him her strength. What
was that one word she had said to him once? Faith. Yes,
and because of it he knew she was a friend. He had berated
himself then. Friend? Here? A young and pretty nurse who
is the only one kind to you, pats you on the head, smiles at
you. Of course you think she's a friend. But more probably
she works for them. Sure, and they know you'll relax
around her and spill your guts because you trust her.

Spill your guts? He had almost laughed out loud then.
Ted Novak, you superspy, what the hell do you know that
they would want to hear anyway? So she's a plant, to learn
what? What cases the narc unit of FLPD is gonna work
tonight?

He looked at her now, in the morning light of the courtyard, and shook his head slightly. No, he felt comfortable with her, and felt he had a friend because he could feel it in his heart. The girl really cared, and she was different from the rest. She seemed peaceful somehow, even in the oppressive atmosphere of that hospital room in a prison. She was like a person . . . committed. Like a person with a secret.

"So. Here we are, you and I," he said softly. "Two normal people out for a normal—well, kind of gimpy—morning walk to give us healthy minds and bodies. But are we really so normal? Isn't it true, dear nurse, that I am really some kind of spy, and you are really a person with a deep, dark secret?"

She stopped, and he felt her grip on his arm tighten. It was obvious that she understood English. Even though she still looked down at her feet, he could see that her face had paled. Then she turned her head and looked into his eyes, her eyes very wide as she looked at him. She seemed so young then, and beautiful, and for a fleeting second, frightened.

He turned away from her gaze, knowing they were being watched, and even though his leg was beginning to throb and his head hurt he began walking again. *"Lo siento, señorita . . . yo es estúpido."* *Yes, I am stupid,* he thought. He felt her beside him, still tense, so he made himself relax and said with a smile, "You know, I'll bet you're the same age as Kathleen, and you're certainly very pretty, like her, but different of course. I mean, you're very dark and Latin and all and she's . . . well, she's fair, golden-like." She turned toward him again and tilted her pretty head and looked at him with pursed lips that still allowed a tiny smile. Her dancing eyes and small frown gave her face an expression like that of a young girl chastising a naughty, teasing boyfriend.

They stood together like that for a moment, their bodies touching, her lovely I-don't-know-what-I'm-going-to-do-with-you look filling his whole world.

Suddenly a heavy wooden door at the far end of the courtyard was pushed open with a scrape and a thud, and a poker-faced guard stood there silently. The girl put her head down, squeezed his arm, and led him slowly back toward his room.

He was surprised how much the short walk had tired him. His leg ached and there was a sheen of sweat on his forehead. He leaned on the nurse heavily as they walked down the hallway, the guard striding along in front of them. Just before they got to the doorway into the small room, she slowed him, and while the guard's back was still to them, she leaned very close, so that for a moment her lips brushed against his ear. Her voice was hushed and warm.

"Carmelita," was all she said.

Maximiliano sat stiffly in the back of the small black car as it made its way through the early morning sunlight on wet curving roads. He felt the need to discuss the conversation he had had with Fidel Castro, but he had left his aide in the *Estados Unidos,* to watch over things while he was gone, and he was not personally familiar with the agent who was assigned as his driver on this day. Sure, the agent came from his own office, but still, one had to be very careful, even here in Cuba. He remained silent, watching the lush green hills and fields, broken here and there by small settlements, some very new with that prefabricated sameness, and some very old, with that drab sameness.

The car slowed as they passed a group of men pushing a very large old truck around a curve, and then sped up again once it was clear. Maximiliano felt drowsy in the backseat, the rocking motion of the car lulling him. It had been a long night. Castro hadn't summoned him until after midnight, and the meeting really didn't get going until much later. False dawn had been breaking as he left the Palace of the Revolution. He had stopped briefly at his office, used the bathroom there to wash his face, grabbed a cup of stale coffee, and headed out for the prison.

Our leader has changed his mind again, he thought. *I wonder what it was this time—some report from one of his political experts, some news from the U.S., or one of his "gut feelings" again?* Whatever it was, Castro was no longer interested in "possibilities" with the young American policeman. He felt nothing would be served by holding him as a spy, or as a hostage, and he did not want to make any friendly overture to the United States government by returning the injured policeman, even if they could explain how he came to be here anyway.

Maximiliano rubbed his eyes with his fists. No, Castro had decided to just get rid of the bothersome prisoner. Simply get rid of him.

Maximiliano sighed. *At least Fidel had listened to my suggestion,* he thought. Was it not possible that agents had already told the CIA that the policeman was here? Even if he just disappeared now, wasn't there the possibility that questions could be raised? Castro had drummed his fingers impatiently while the suggestion had been outlined. The subject, Montilla, though not the most stable or professional agent, could do the job of smuggling at least one good load of cocaine into the U.S., for a good profit, *sí?* The young policeman was still very good bait for Montilla, yes? Wouldn't it be better to use the young policeman for this purpose and kill him at the end of the run?

Castro had pursed his lips, and nodded then, and Maximiliano had gone further. It would quell any report that the policeman had been anywhere—the Bahamas, or certainly not all the way to Cuba. No, the policeman would be killed at home, on his own turf, so to speak.

The young policeman would be found dead, right in the Port of the Everglades, or maybe one of the many waterways in his own city. He would be killed apparently as a result of some local drug deal that went bad. And what of all those still-healing scars on his leg? That would be a mystery *their* police would have to solve. Either way, he would die at home, not in Cuba.

Castro had agreed. The case no longer amused him. The young American was a problem, and he didn't want any problems. Just get rid of him, and bring home more money from the cocaine so the revolution can continue.

Castro had been staring intently at the ceiling as Maximiliano quietly left, wrapped in his own thoughts.

Maximiliano watched as the driver slowed and went around another curve in the road. The prison came into view. He took a deep breath, cracked his knuckles, rubbed his eyes again, and said quietly, *"Buenos días, prisioneros de la revolución."*

Ted was just beginning to drift off to sleep, the pain medicine taking hold, when he heard a commotion in the hallway. He opened his eyes to see the young nurse hurry in, a knapsack of some kind thrown over one shoulder. In one hand she carried a small black bag, similar to the one in which the doctor carried his various medicines, and in the other a plain leather bag, like a purse. There was concern on her face, and she glanced at him quickly. A warning? Then she looked over her shoulder and stepped aside as the doctor came into the room, followed by the lean dark man in the suit, and the chubby one in the uniform. They were arguing.

Ted could not understand all the words, but heard *"camion,"* *"viaje,"* and *"secreto."* The lean one wanted something to happen right now. He wanted a truck for a secret trip, and the chubby one didn't agree. The doctor just shrugged his shoulders, and walked out. Ted was glad to see him go. The one in the ill-fitting uniform argued some more, waving his hands in front of his face and speaking very rapidly in a tight, almost pleading voice. Suddenly the lean one had had enough, and with one arm outstretched, one finger pointing toward some distant mediator, said brusquely one rapid-fire sentence that included the words, *"Palacio de la Revolución."*

The chubby one bit his lip then, waved his hand at Ted as if to say, "The hell with it," turned on his heel, and walked out, the back of his neck very red.

After he was gone, the lean one looked at the girl, smiled and shrugged, and made a gesture toward Ted. The girl nodded, opened a drawer, and pulled out some clothes —trousers and a shirt—like a work uniform. There was no underwear, and no socks. The girl helped Ted sit up on the edge of the bed and then checked his bandages. Satisfied that they were clean and tight, she helped him stand and then take off the pajamas and put on the work clothes. From another drawer she pulled out a pair of old but clean tennis shoes, and gently helped him into those. She reached behind the door and pulled out a new windbreaker, handed it to Ted, then reached past him, took the pillow from the bed, stuffed the pajamas into the case, stood back, and smiled.

Maximiliano pointed toward the door and nodded, and the nurse took a step, but they both stopped when Ted said, "No way. I'm not going anywhere until somebody tells me what's goin' on here. You taking me home . . . or you taking me to the wall?"

The young nurse looked at him wide-eyed but was silent. The lean man said with a small smile, "But must you be so dramatic, señor? Would we take you to the wall only to put bullet holes into that new jacket you wear? No, but it is time for you to leave this place now. We will take you to another, better place. A house, very nice." He paused. "I cannot tell you too much at this point, señor, except to say to you that you are alive, we have cared for you, and still provide for you a nurse, *sí*? We will travel now for approximately two hours by truck. The truck will be covered so you will not be able to see out. Neither will others be able to see in, understand? If that is not to your liking, I can very easily have our kind doctor here come back and give you a shot. Then you can sleep peacefully during the trip, *sí*?"

Ted hesitated, then nodded and moved toward the door, his leg numb. The lean man held up his hand. "Listen to me, señor. You are now in my custody and care. You will rest at this house we are going to, and then there will be more travel for you, possibly by boat, or by aircraft. You have no choice but to trust me and cooperate with me for now. You will be closely guarded, and sedated if necessary. I would rather not have to treat you improperly if I do not have to. As I told you during one of our earlier meetings, your position here is not good. Try to work with us without compromising yourself and things may work out for you."

The man turned to go. The nurse reached out and took Ted's arm and they moved into the hallway. Ted still didn't like it, but he didn't like the alternatives either. He said quietly, "All right . . . I hear you. But can't you at least get word to my family or someone at home that I'm alive, that I'm okay?"

The lean man ignored the question, walking ahead of him with his back straight.

The ride in the back of the canvas-covered truck was brutal—long, hot, and bumpy. After a short while Ted's leg was throbbing, his head was pounding, and he felt acute motion sickness. The young nurse rode beside him, holding his hand, and squeezing it when he would take a sharp intake of air each time the truck bounced on the road. He had tried to talk with her when they first started the ride, but she just shook her head violently, then was silent, occasionally looking at him and smiling encouragement. He could see that she too was uncomfortable, her face flushed and her hair hanging in disarray. Ted didn't know how much time had passed; the truck went up a steep incline, so steep that the girl started to slide toward the back of the truck on the seat, and Ted had to put his arm around her waist to hold her close to him. Then there was a pause while the truck stopped and men spoke back and forth, the sounds of a gate being opened, a short and twisting drive, and then the truck stopped completely.

Ted could hear still more voices in conversation, then the sound of a car stopping near the truck, then starting up again and pulling away. The voices went away, and it got quiet.

The gate at the back of the truck went down, the canvas was pushed aside, and the lean man in the dark suit beckoned to them. They climbed out stiffly, the girl helping Ted hop down on his good leg, then reaching in behind him and grabbing her bags and the pillow.

It was a small house, but nice, with awning windows, red barrel tile on the roof, and a well-kept lawn all around except where they stood, which was a paved drive. The house was done in some kind of off-white plaster with a heavy wooden front door. The lean man held this door open for them as they entered. The interior of the house was very clean and neat, with shiny tile floors, simple but comfortable-looking wood and leather furniture and muted watercolors on the walls. There was a small kitchen on one side of the main room and two bedrooms on the other. The main room opened onto a screened porch. Beyond that could be seen more lawn, some citrus trees, and in the distance the ocean.

Ted had seen the sun on his left when he climbed out of the truck and faced the house, so he knew now that the ocean was to the north. He had also seen the new-looking, very high chain-link fence to the east and west of the yard.

Almost as if he knew what he was thinking, the lean one said, "As you can see, this is a lovely little house, and you will be comfortable here . . . to rest, and to grow healthy, *sí?* It is also what we call a 'safe house.' It is surrounded by a good fence, and the grounds are patrolled by people who work for me. They are professionals, dedicated. They have dogs, and they have the property surveilled by state-of-the-art electronic gadgetry. They are only there to guard, not to hurt you."

He watched as the nurse took her bags and the pillow into the bedroom closest to the back of the house. He walked over and straightened one of the watercolors, and with his back to Ted, said evenly, "I suspect that you will think of an escape attempt. You will want to run away from us, and make your way back home. Please, when you are feeling stronger, take a long walk all around, look at the fence, at the dogs, at the men, and then come back here, to your safe house and relax."

"When will I be leaving?" asked Ted. "How long will I be here?"

The lean man smiled, his hands up. The nurse came out of the bedroom, her face washed and her hair piled on top of her head. The man spoke to her rapidly. She nodded, apparently pleased. Then he walked to the front door, opened it, and turned and said, "Señor, stay here, eat good fruit and fresh fish. Watch the sun come up, listen to the birds, drink a little wine. Spend some time with your nurse, exercise your leg, and live these moments of your life as if they were a gift, yes?" He closed the door and was gone.

Carmelita watched the floor for a moment, then smiled,

a full smile for the first time. She walked over to Ted, took his hand, and led him out of the main room through the porch and then onto the green grass of the backyard. She walked until they were several hundred feet from the house, then stopped and looked around. The hills surrounding the house were lush with trees and the ocean stretched out before them, green close to shore, then turning deep blue farther out. They were some height above the shoreline; it was below their line of sight, beyond the grass and trees that made up the perimeter of the house's property. The sky above them was very blue, with puffy white clouds.

The girl turned in a slow circle, taking it all in. Then she took one of Ted's hands in both of hers, squeezed it, and smiled . . . her eyes searching his.

Ted had taken in the simple beauty of the place too, and the nice vista his eyes were feasting on after the drab sameness of the hospital room. He looked into the lovely face of Carmelita now, saw the sunshine in her eyes, felt the warm strength in her hand, and thought, *I'm alive. I don't know why.*

I'm alive, I'm getting healthier, and I'm standing here feeling the sun and smelling the grass and seeing that beckoning ocean out there. Maybe that guy is right. Maybe I should just put my worries on hold, take it one day at a time, rest up and wait. For now. What was that about a moment of life? He's right about that.

He looked into the soft brown eyes of his nurse.

Yes, this is a moment of life, and all I can do is live it.

J.B. sat with his right foot propped against the doorpost on the passenger side of the squad car. Both doors were open. Even though it was early evening, it was still hot enough for both Richards and Skids Bedlam to silently thank the Lord every time a small breeze made its feeble way across the front seat. They were parked under a huge oak tree that spread its limbs across most of the dirt lot adjacent to the old Baptist church building in the heart of the northwest, or black, section of Fort Lauderdale.

They had been working the black section for several

days now and were already very much settled in. Most patrol officers start out their careers working in the poorer areas, and almost all become familiar with it in a short time. Younger officers find it exciting at first because there is usually more action than in other areas of the city. Any weekend shift can count on a couple of cuttings and at least one shooting, and vehicular chases can take place at any time. But after a while, the shine wears off and the younger officers get tired of the dirt, the poverty, the unhappiness, the hostility, and the general depressing aura that goes with knowing, day after day, that things are not going to get any better.

Older patrol officers who, for any number of reasons, find themselves again assigned to the streets of blacktown, learn to their surprise that the duty is not really that bad compared with other areas of town. There is dirt in any poor neighborhood, and violence, and hostility, but the dirt of black Fort Lauderdale is not the filth of tropical Fort Lauderdale beach. The violence that might flare up between two black bricklayers in Bradley's bar is not the same as the violence that happens between two fathers with ball bats at a "nice" neighborhood Little League game. The hostility that comes from the poor is more honest and direct than the hostility that comes from the rich. Sometimes a street cop who is tired of the deceit, the corruption, the double and triple standards of the law, can find it a refreshing change to get back on the street in the middle of blacktown. Things seem so much more clearly defined there.

Because Bedlam knew that Richards loved to listen to the choir rehearse in the church, they had driven over to the chicken place at Seventh Avenue and Sistrunk Boulevard, got their clearance from the dispatcher, and took their dinners under the huge oak tree, where they sat and listened as the choir tuned itself up for the coming Sunday services. Bedlam was a solid country and western music fan, and Richards was a frustrated jazz bassist, but the almost unbelievable purity of the rich voices, the strong and constant harmonies, and the driving strength of the gospels sung by the all-black choir never failed to bring them a certain peace. They would sit quietly for half an hour or more, just eating and listening, and when they had to be cops again they would drive away refreshed.

As Richards wiped his fingers on a paper towel and cleaned up the bags and cups laying all over the front seat he said, "You know, Skids, sometimes when I listen to those people sing I feel like I'm being gently lifted right off the seat. I swear the power that comes from the music is very real, like you could touch it. Know what I mean?"

Skids wiped his mouth with the back of his hand, and to Richards's surprise, instead of belching or making some crude reply, he was quiet for a few seconds, and then said, "The thing is, J.B., they *believe* it, you know? These people aren't just singing the words, man. As far as they're concerned, the music tells it like it *is*."

They both sat quietly then, with their own private thoughts. Finally Richards said, "Remember I was telling you about the discussion I had with Zaden and Maguire about there maybe bein' a leak somewhere?"

Bedlam nodded his head. Like all road partners, he and Richards discussed everything under the sun during the quiet periods of their shifts. Secrets that were not shared with the wife in bed were shared with the road partner in the squad car.

"Well, I talked with them again and they both feel strongly that we've got one somewhere, possibly over in OCB. Of course they're still keepin' it to themselves until they can get something solid. To tell you the truth, I kinda hope they don't . . . Oh, hell. I guess I can't say that either. I mean, whoever it is, is definitely putting the screws to effective law enforcement of guys like Montilla. But, you know, it would be bad for the department. The other thing is that they've got some good people over there in that narc unit. Sure, Scott Kelly is back, and he's the best, but there are others who are good, and care about what's goin' down too. Maybe they're fighting with one arm tied behind their back."

Bedlam turned the rearview mirror toward him, and using a thin comb, combed the hair he had left on the side of his head back behind his ears. "Yeah, I know what you mean, J.B. I been thinkin' about it too, and I ask myself,

'How does this guy do it?' You know, this cop. I mean, how can he sell out to the other side? Then I think about the pimp attorneys and the judges on the take and the puke-bag senators and congressmen who are *directly* involved. And I think about this cop out there bustin' his ass for less money than the average garbage man and I say to myself, 'Maybe.'"

"Yeah, you bust your butt on the smuggling cases, knowing you've got the suckers dead to rights every time, and then watch them walk out as smooth as you please. Last week I was sitting there in my used boat shoes in one of the courthouse hallways listening to the doper, the doper's lawyer, the prosecutor, and the judge, *all* standing there with their pimp-assed Rolexes talking about the slope conditions at Vail where they went last winter, and where they might go this year."

Bedlam started the car and advised the dispatcher they were back in service and they closed the doors. Richards sat up as Bedlam eased out of the lot onto the street. As he snapped on his seatbelt, J.B. said, "I guess I could understand it, sort of . . . I mean if the money was right and all. Shit, probably some poor bastard who's been divorced twice and is payin' alimony up the wazoo. Two of his kids from the first marriage need braces on their teeth, and his new bride wants a bigger house and he looks around and sees these twenty-year-old punks driving around in their BMWs and Porsches and he figures, 'Screw it, I'm gonna get me some of that.' So he does. Hell, I don't know, Skids. I could see how it could happen. Still, I think it would be hard to play it both ways . . . you know?"

As he said this, the dispatcher came on with an all-channel appeal for backups for an officer who had broken up an armed robbery in progress, so Bedlam threw the car into a wild U-turn and headed that way.

It turned out to be a crazy night, events and the dispatcher sending them this way and that all over the northwest part of town. They helped search, in vain, for the robbery suspects, they held battered bodies together at the scene of a serious auto accident until the medical units arrived, and they broke up a vicious domestic argument that had one antagonist waving a starter's pistol, the other a broken bottle. They spent some time trying to say something that would comfort an elderly woman who had come home to find her small house ransacked, the old black and white television set taken, and worse, her mother's cheap jewelry that had been left to her was gone. They drank hot coffee and ate pasty doughnuts and swapped tales with a couple of the other units during a short lull, and ended their shift by accidentally finding a stolen car sitting in an alley. That would have been bad enough, with the paperwork involved so late in the shift. To keep their luck consistent, though, slumped in the front seat, dead, was the apparent car thief. It appeared he had overdosed on the crack he carried in a small vial.

They had to call out the detectives, gather information on the scene, wait for the medical examiner, and finally drive into the station and do all the paper.

It was late, and they were worn out when they finally finished and walked out the backdoor of the station . . . and they thought the night was over.

SEVENTEEN

J.B. Richards and Skids Bedlam walked across the rear parking lot of the station, tired after their long and busy shift. They were headed for their own vehicles, parked under the trees in the fenced-in lot at the southeast corner of the compound. They were just moving into the shadows under the trees, Skids turning toward J.B. to say good night, when Scott Kelly stepped out of the darkness and intercepted them.

"Hey, you guys, do you work this late every night? What are you trying to do, save the world all by yourselves?"

They looked at the narc, standing there wearing a tight-fitting polo shirt and creased trousers, his muscular arms hanging at his sides. Skids smiled and nodded. "Hey," he said, "it's a dirty job but somebody has to do it, right? And what are you, some kind of off-duty mugger, waiting for us here in the shadows? Gonna take my wallet? Here, please, take it."

He reached for his back pocket, but Kelly held up his open hands and said with a grin, "Why the hell would I want your wallet, Skids? We all know there ain't nothin' in there but maybe two or three very tired dollars, some stamps from the grocery store, and that same rubber you been carryin' around in anticipation since you got out of high school back in the sixties."

The narc looked around the parking lot and said quietly, "I'd guess both you guys already called home and told them you're gonna be late because of what you ran into at the end of your shift, right?"

Both patrolmen nodded. Kelly went on. "Okay, J.B., I told him you'd probably want Skids in on the meeting. He was undecided at first, but then agreed."

William Buchanan hadn't changed much since the last time J.B. had seen him. He was heavier, of course, his short brown hair flecked with gray, but his broad face, even with the creases of time, was as intense as ever. He sat in the darkness of the backseat in Scott Kelly's rental car now, examining the face of J.B. Richards.

Richards sat in the back with the CIA man, and Bedlam and Kelly sat in front, turned to face the back. The car was parked in the shadows in Rodi park, south of Davie Boulevard, near the railroad tracks and the south fork of the New River. They were just a short distance north of where the yellow Scarab had plowed up onto the mud.

The short drive from the station had been made in silence, and J.B. was wondering if he was going to be the one to break it, when Buchanan spoke. "First things first. You don't know me, you don't know who I work for. I'm not here, and you've never sat in this car with me. Things I'm going to say are so classified that they don't even exist. I'm going to tell you things you never really heard. Are you with me so far?"

Kelly nodded. Bedlam thought to himself, Right, and this tape will self-destruct in ten seconds.

J.B. just waited, trying to control his emotions and his fears.

"Hear this, Richards," Buchanan went on. "You shot and killed one Felix Ortiz twenty years ago. We wanted him because he was a Cuban agent. We were hoping to take him alive and use him against his own people, but you came along and killed him before we could. All right, I didn't come here tonight to rehash whether or not you did the right thing on that day." He paused and turned in the seat to make himself more comfortable, exposing a large automatic under his suit jacket. The suit was still gray, J.B. observed.

Buchanan looked out the side window, then back at J.B. "Now, here's where we get to the interesting part—the crazy part. When you killed Ortiz, he was trying to get to a meeting with an old woman who had his young son. We're sure the kid was there where we confronted Ortiz, and he witnessed you wastin' him."

J.B. felt his chest tightening and heard a low rushing sound in his ears. He held his breath, entirely focused on Buchanan's words as a montage of images flitted through his mind.

"The kid and the old lady faded away in the excitement, and that's the end of the story—except that it's not. The kid grew up down here, and took the name of the old lady who raised him until she died. His name is Onyx Montilla."

No one spoke. J.B. sat frozen, seeing the face of the small boy, hearing him cry out. The face of the small boy faded then and was replaced by the hard image of Onyx Montilla, staring at him. J.B. felt icy fingers of fear probing him deep inside. He realized with razor sharpness that some kind of powerful inexplicable circle was being completed. He felt he was being swept along now by the events in his life, a participant but probably not in control. He looked at Bedlam and Kelly, and saw that they were both staring at the CIA man, apprehension on their faces.

Buchanan cleared his throat and said, "There's more, guys, which is one reason I'm telling you all of this." They waited. "So Richards kills Montilla's father, and then Montilla gets into the drug games down here in your fucking tropical fantasy land. He gets himself tied in with some local syndicate biggies and bingo, he's an up-and-coming drug success story. For some reason he does a couple of dumb things. His own lawyer gets busted for coke with *his* money, and he not only gets pissed he gets worried. He takes the lawyer and the lawyer's 'connection' and goes for a nice boat ride in that honker that you guys scammed away from him the other day. He kills the lawyer and the other guy." He looked at each of them then, one at a time, into their eyes. "You guys know what's next, right? Sure ... the other guy was one of your fuckin' new centurian, Miami mice narcs. A new guy. Ted Novak. Novak is run over by Montilla and left for dead ... shark bait, right? Oops, fate steps in again, and Novak, cut up, bleeding, and no doubt very waterlogged, gets rescued by some kind of boat. Is it a submarine? A charter boat? A Hobie-cat sailed by the Norwegian all-girl sailing club? We don't know. Probably a fishing boat of some kind. Whatever ..." He paused again, savoring their full attention. "And to keep things really going now, where does the boat take our wounded young narc? To Cuba, where else?"

Bedlam said softly, "Jesus, can this be real?"

"Sure it's real," said Buchanan with a grin. "As real as it gets in this world of ours. You guys certainly don't have to know the how's and why's, you only have to hear what I've got to say. Castro's revolution is such a big fuckin' success that we've got agents planted all over the damn island. He's got unhappy people living there, and some of them will help us with info when they come across it. You guys read *Against All Hope*, by that Valladares guy? It just came out awhile back. You can get an idea of what I'm saying here." He was surprised to see all three local cops nodding their heads as if they knew the book. "We've got an agent in place there, grew up there—a native Cuban, child of the revolution, and all that. Saw big brothers and dad beaten and carried away to the prisons, and it left its mark. This agent managed to assume a new identity there, which is *very* hard, and now covertly transmits info to a source that eventually gets it to us."

The men in the car remained quiet as they digested the story. The wet night air was pierced by the plaintive horn on the railroad trestle, warning that it would lower into a closed position in a few minutes. Buchanan turned his head to listen, then went on.

"Our source has told us that Ted Novak arrived in Cuba in bad shape, but was held in a prison hospital where he was treated and is apparently recovering from his injuries. He was just recently moved from there, and our info dried up for now. Their government has made no announcement of any kind that they are holding him, so if we raised a fuss all they'd have to do is deny everything and Novak would *really* disappear. We don't know what they plan for him, but I'm guessing that they may have put the same links together that we did . . . as far as Ted Novak being almost like a son to our man Richards here. Why would that mean anything to them?" His eyes went out of focus for a moment, then came back. "Tell you guys something. Even though I think Castro is a lying Commie bastard, I have to give a small bow here to some of his intelligence operatives. They're pretty good. Of course, that has to be balanced with the knowledge that they work against us in our nice open free country here, while we try to work against them in that fuckin' maniac-controlled green machine. So they would get the info that Novak equals Richards equals Montilla equals Ortiz."

He moved his shoulders and cracked his knuckles, staring at J.B. "So what about Montilla, right?" He hesitated, then plunged on. "Our idealistic revolutionary leader there, Castro, sees that his country is an economic disaster, right? So he gets into the cocaine business. The big money comes from supplying the fuckin' Americano consumer with the good toot, so he gets into it in a big way. Mostly into Miami."

Kelly was staring at him with an angry expression, but Bedlam put his thoughts into words for him.

"You mean you *know* Castro is running coke into our country? What the hell is going on? You're high-level, right? If you know somethin' like this is going on, then what the hell are guys like Kelly here, and poor Ted Novak, goin' out on these friggin' streets to fight the dope for? Shit, you guys could stop it at the source."

There was anger in the air, and tension. J.B. was the only one who seemed withdrawn, deep within himself.

Buchanan looked at the two cops in the front seat of the car, and shrugged. "Hey, like I told you guys. First, you didn't hear this shit from me, and second, you guys have to remember that you're fightin' your little battles right here on these tiny, unimportant Lauderdale streets. I'm out there fightin' the war, baby, the big battles, and the whole world is my arena. I can have a deal going down in the Mideast that can pop its secret head up in Central America if I want, see? Yeah, we know about Castro and cocaine, hell, it's actually old news, been goin' on for years. How's he gonna finance the next third-world revolution . . . mount a war bond drive?"

J.B.'s voice was quiet but held an icy edge as he said, "Get this, Buchanan. We've seen your big battles, and the way you guys have been going at it for years. I think you guys could fuck up a wet dream. So why don't you knock off the chest-pounding and tell us what you think is going to happen to Ted. Or how we can get him back. Or what you want us to do here."

Buchanan was not used to being spoken to like that, especially by some local hick cop. His eyes narrowed and his jaw clenched and he said in a tight voice, "Look, Richards, I could respond, but it would be counterproductive. You wanna get down to business, all right. Montilla is now somehow hooked into the Cuban intelligence players. There's one old veteran of theirs that's been in and out of the country, covertly of course, a couple of times recently. He's slick, knows his shit, and we've never had a real handle on him. We think now he's got Montilla on his payroll . . . gonna have Montilla run some cocaine for Castro. Hell, it would probably be a good deal for them. I mean, Montilla is already crossing the Gulf Stream all the time for his syndicate guys and their stupid loads of marijuana. You believe people still smoke that shit? Anyway, we've got Cuban agents, we've got Novak in Cuba, we've got Montilla, son of Ortiz who you blew away. I don't know why—I can't figure it either—but for some reason this is all coming back to you, in Fort Lauderdale, and I can see it coming."

He leaned forward then, one strong hand gripping J.B.'s left forearm tightly, his eyes intense, and his voice dry as he said, "I can just hang back and observe and gather info about all of this, Richards, or I can participate. You want to do battle with Montilla. So do I. You want to bring Novak home? You can't do it without me, even if you don't like the way my outfit gets things done. I say this, Richards, and this goes for you other guys too, since you're in on it, and those Customs guys too—this case is bigger than you and your buddies here. It's very big, and we've got a chance to break some Commie balls here and hurt fuckin' Fidel for once. And we might even be able to get your little narc back home for you." He sat back now, his face stern. "But here's the deal. I'm *in*. I work this thing with you guys. I'll mostly hang back and collect info, which I'll pass on to Kelly here, and you guys can pass stuff back to me through him. Right? When it starts to go down, we'll work together to reach our special goals. We'll be a team, so this time you and me will be going after the same guy in the same way."

J.B. looked at him, feeling his power, the weight of the entire government, his to call at an instant's notice. He nodded, and said, "Sure, Buchanan, as long as we both recognize the priorities. Ted home safe, first, then we squash Montilla."

Buchanan looked at each of them, smiled, and said, "Absolutely."

Onyx Montilla was feeling pretty good.

He stood braced against the swing-back seat of the Donzi racer with his left hand gripping the wheel and his right hand resting on the twin throttles. The boat belonged to his new attorney, and he had borrowed it for the day. It was a clean and neat rig, with small V-8s and Volvo outdrives. It didn't have as much power as *Stiletto*, but it was still nice and capable of running across the Gulf Stream with no problem. The bow of the boat was pointed west, toward Fort Lauderdale, and the color of the ocean at that point in the Stream was a pure, deep blue. Montilla could feel the power of the engines surging through the glass hull as they easily pushed the Donzi along in the low forties. He had idled out of the cut between North and South Bimini slightly over fifteen minutes ago and headed home, Silky standing silently beside him. It was a beautiful day and he leaned back, relaxed a little, and thought with a grin of what he had accomplished back on the island.

Things were taking longer than "just a couple of days," as he had told Kolin, but were still going as planned. He had called the night before and left a message at Blackie's Marina that he would be coming over in the morning. After arriving at the dock and tying up, he was met by a silent but relaxed Hushpuppie and escorted immediately to Mr. Cornelius Black's office, dropping Silky off at the Compleat Angler along the way. Black had been cordial to him and they had wasted very little time in getting down to business. Montilla couldn't be sure, but he could guess that the deal they had set up made Black very happy.

Over the last month or so the Bahamian authorities had made several seizures of yachts loaded with grass from Colombia and Jamaica. Things were busier in Bahamian waters again since Baby Doc Duvalier and his charming bride had been forced to run away from the half of Hispanola that his family had plundered for at least two generations. While Duvalier was there, Haiti had become a safe transshipment point for smugglers in boats and airplanes; they were able to avoid the Bahamas, which not only had a lot of DEA types running around, but also became just plain crowded what with all of the smuggling groups trying to work in those waters at the same time. Onyx laughed out loud, remembering one dark night early in his running days, when he had brought a "bank boat," recently loaded from a freighter, across the banks to the west side, near Cat Cay. Visibility had been bad and he couldn't find the two sailboats he was supposed to load. So he had transmitted on one of the regular marine channels, saying, "If you're out there waiting to meet me, give me a blink," hoping one of the sailboats would hear him and flash its masthead light. The darkness had been speckled with bright flashes, like the flashbulbs in a large crowd at a rock concert. Sailboats and other vessels all over the place flashing their lights on the banks, hoping *their* load boats would find them.

The Bahamian waters were getting more traffic again, and three of the yachts seized recently by the patrol boats had been escorted into Bimini; the marijuana was off-loaded and tagged by the Bahamian Customs offices as "evidence." It was then stored in two pink concrete block homes located behind chain-link fences just north of the community area. The crew members of the yachts, mostly young Americans, had been released along with the boats after they, or someone else who came flying in from Fort Lauderdale, paid a sizable cash bond. They motored or sailed off into the sunset, chagrined at the thought of all that grass lost but positively thrilled with the knowledge that they wouldn't be spending the next few years in Fox Hill Prison. The cash secured from the "bonds" was distributed to the local participating officials and citizens (including Black) who had contributed to the effort. The marijuana, a little over ten thousand pounds of it, all of fairly high quality, was ordered destroyed by the minister of the interior back in Nassau. Now it just sat there, safe and dry and properly tagged as evidence in the two pink houses. This almost free supply of marijuana (Black still had to grease the usual palms to keep things cool, and when he moved the stuff there would be those, in and out of uniform and political office, who would expect their little piece of the action) waited now for Montilla or some other buyer with cash to come along and snap it up.

Black was in a good mood during the negotiations with Montilla, joking and making sure they had enough drinks and snacks. Black did not tell Montilla the reason for his pleasure, but as the social and business machinations went on he had let his mind wander over a recent incident that he liked to think of as "manna from heaven."

Bartholomew Strong was married to Cornelius Black's youngest daughter, Serena. He, like all the Bimini islanders, was well aware of Black's power and he had been thrilled to marry into the family. He had not been disappointed. Black kept him busy taking care of minor business matters all over the out islands, which meant he didn't get to be home with his young wife much, but it had its compensations. He made a lot more money than most islanders and he carried with him Black's authority and at least a small slice of his prestige and power. More than anything else in this world, Bart Strong wanted to captain his own sportfishing charter boat out of Blackie's Marina. As a kid he had hung around the docks watching the boats and fishermen, the tournaments and the rich and famous guys from the States with their pretty girlfriends. He had seen how the captains and mates and guides were treated with respect, how they were paid and tipped. He had seen how the other islanders all envied those captains and mates and he had wanted it so bad he could taste it.

So, when Mr. Black sent him down to Andros Island to bring back a small fishing boat that had been on loan to one of Black's many acquaintances, Bart Strong kissed Serena on the forehead lightly and took off for Congo Town, South Andros Island, on the first boat headed that way.

He got into Congo Town late one afternoon and, after checking out the boat and seeing that it was ready to go, he made plans to leave early in the morning. He then begged a ride into town in a hand-painted black and red 1963 Chevrolet. The driver of the Chevy, a local Andros islander, had been surprisingly friendly and had even shared some of his rum with Bart. After learning that Bart was spending the night and was there on a mission for Mister Cornelius Black of Bimini, he arranged for him to meet his sister Lonnie. And that's how Bart happened to be lying on the beach in the middle of the night when the airplane came over, dropping things out of a side door.

The airplane, a small, private twin-engined job, had been reported stolen a week before in south Georgia. The day before Bart saw it, the plane had been flown up from Jamaica after staging out of somewhere farther south. There were over two hundred kilos of high-quality cocaine in the airplane, along with the two pilots. The trip north, which should have been pretty routine, had gone badly, with navigation problems, fuel problems, and finally a series of intermittent electrical problems that kept both pilots busy and worried. With things going from bad to worse, they had decided to slip into the airstrip at Congo Town to see if they could figure out what the problem was. They landed just as it was getting dark. After giving the Customs captain, who had arrived at the end of the runway in a jeep, a fat wad of twenty dollar bills, they had been left alone to check over the plane as best they could with flashlights. They had taped some frayed wires, tightened as many screws and bolts as they could see, and drained the fuel sumps one more time. Then they had decided to wait until about 2 A.M., so they could stay down low and slip under the radar as they approached the coast of Florida. They would be shooting for the radar gap between Fort Lauderdale and West Palm Beach, over Boca Raton, and if they timed it right they could be on final approach into the small dirt strip in central Florida just at sunrise.

Finally, when it was time, they strapped themselves in, cranked up the engines, did a quick run-up, and eased the throttles forward, heading her down the strip and into the black night.

They were both tired and they wanted to go home.

Just after they lifted off, the pilot raised the gear and as they passed through three hundred feet they felt the gear thump into position under the wings. At the same time the left engine quit, causing the plane to yaw to the left and start to roll that way. Both pilots instinctively stomped right rudder to the cabin floor and tried to level the wings as the chief pilot brought the throttle back on the right engine, reducing power. This kept the plane from rolling over on its back but just barely staggering through the air. The pilot, staring into the night, not knowing where the black sky ended and the black ocean began, decided to turn around and try for the runway. As he coaxed the wallowing plane along on its one engine and began a gradual turn into it, he yelled for his copilot to jettison the duffel bags of cocaine. Several hundred pounds could make all the difference. The pilot managed to get the plane turned and pointed back toward the coast of Andros as the copilot struggled to push the cabin door open with his back, far enough to wiggle one heavy green bag out onto the wing and down. The partially open cabin door affected the flight characteristics of the plane and both pilots cursed and struggled as the plane lost more and more altitude. The copilot managed to get the one bag out and was reaching for the second when the pilot yelled, "Shit! We're not gonna make it! We're gonna put it right into the fucking town!" He tried to parallel the beach and put the plane into the shallows. She was sluggish in the turn and then the remaining engine coughed and quit. There was nothing left and they flipped over in the turn, spun in, and violently impacted the water just outside the beach reef.

Bart Strong was lying on the beach with his hand up under Lonnie's dress, sucking noisily on her left breast as the airplane had flown over them and out toward the ocean. He looked up as it went over and thought it sounded funny, and then he and Lonnie just lay there and watched as the plane made a sloppy turn and headed back for them. They stared wide-eyed as the plane got lower and lower. They stayed there, frozen, he with his hand still under her dress, while a big green bag thumped loudly into the sand not fifty feet away from them. Then the airplane dove with an awful splash of spray and foam into the water. Neither of them moved for a few seconds until Lonnie pulled away from Bart, shakily stood up and pulled her dress down straight. She walked slowly over to the bag, followed by Bart. The top of the bag had come undone and scattered near it were a couple of blue lumps, the size of big coconuts. One of the lumps was broken and Bart could see that it was a ball of white powder, wrapped in plastic and covered in some kind of blue wax. He and Lonnie stared at the bag for a moment and then Lonnie said in a breathless voice, "I got to fetch my brother, mon. You stay here and don' let none of the other peoples mess with this bag." She turned and ran lightly up the beach.

Bart stood there looking out into the night where the plane had crashed. Then he picked up the bag, closed the top as best he could, looked around quickly, and ran down the beach toward the small marina where Mr. Black's boat was. He left two of the blue coconuts laying in the sand on the beach. Stumbling and sweating, he ran through the night, off the damp sand, through a small stand of waving palms, to the rough wooden planking of the dock. He threw the bag onto the deck as he jumped aboard, fired up the small diesel engine and untied the spring line. Then he jumped back out, cast off the stern, ran to the bow, un-cleated that line, climbed back into the cockpit, and reversed hard away from the dock. He was just clearing the channel, rolling into the waves from the ocean, when he heard a horn blaring and looked back to see the old Chevy with only one headlight shining toward him. He could see several figures jumping up and down beside the car, waving and shaking their fists at him. He turned his back on them and headed out into the dark night.

A few minutes after clearing the small harbor entrance and turning north, he could see figures with flashlights moving on the sandy beach. He passed over the spot just outside the reef where he was pretty sure the plane had gone in, but the night was dark and lonely, and he knew in his heart that the chugging of the diesel engine in his boat would not disturb whoever was trapped in that airplane resting somewhere beneath him. He shuddered and drove on.

Through that morning's sunrise and into daybreak he had navigated along the east coast of Andros Island and, later that afternoon, had spotted the Northwest Light and had made the turn for the banks and headed back toward North Bimini. While he drove across the green-on-green seas he thought about the bag of cocaine he had with him. He knew it was worth a fortune, but how could he sell it? How could he keep it a secret? He knew it would only be a short time before Mr. Black learned of what had happened that night. Then what? After he made his decision he relaxed and felt a lot better, although he kept looking over his shoulder. He would head right for Bimini, hand over the coke to Black, and act as humble as ever. He knew he would be rewarded, he knew he would make big points with his father-in-law, and he knew *that* was better than all the money he might be able to make if he tried to keep the coke and sell it himself. Mr. Black was a sure thing.

That had been a week before Black's meeting with Montilla and it had given Black great pleasure to be able to tell Montilla that he had all the cocaine that Montilla needed, and he had it right there on the island. They had made the deal for the full load of marijuana plus fifty kilos of cocaine, using the money Kolin's courier would bring to Black just before the run, ostensibly to cover just the cost of the grass.

From Montilla's point of view, both prices were very good, although he wasn't that concerned about the cost of the grass. He also knew, but of course he didn't say it, that even though Kolin and everybody else made a lot of noise about what a great deal they got from Black, both marijuana and cocaine could be purchased for much less, especially when you were dealing with tons and kilos. He knew the closer you got to the source—Jamaica, South and Central America—the less the cost of the product. Any big group should have been able to get tons and kilos at wholesale prices down there. Kolin wasn't dealing with Black just for the profits, he was dealing with him because he wanted the Bahamian connection. He wanted to do business with people in the government of the Bahamas, even if it was fronted by one of their island citizens. Life was so much easier when everything was official.

At any rate, Montilla felt good about the price of the cocaine because he normally purchased as a user, and it was outrageously expensive in small amounts. Besides, he was getting it with Kolin's money. Black gave no hint that he figured out what Montilla was doing when Montilla had explained that he would bring his two boats over on a Friday and pick up half the marijuana load and all fifty kilos of coke. Kolin's money, then in Black's possession, would equal that deal. Then, Montilla had explained, he would come back on Sunday to pick up the rest of Kolin's grass. At that time he would have the cash necessary to finish the deal based on the agreed-upon price.

They had shaken hands when it was time for Montilla to leave, and Black was in a good mood as he told Montilla to take a look at the new charter fishing boat his son-in-law Bart was running out of the marina now.

As Montilla had idled out from the dock in the Donzi, Silky beside him, he had looked over the clean-looking little Bertram tied up to the outside dock. He saw that the young captain was busily washing her down, and he saw the name on the stern and wondered idly what it meant.

The name was *Manna*.

Now, as the Donzi racer dashed across the Gulf Stream toward Fort Lauderdale, Montilla leaned back in the warm sun and mused about what he had set up. It would be tricky, especially with that grease ball Joe around, but he knew if he stayed tight and kept his head he could pull it off. He knew he might have to stop at South Bimini on the way in, maybe not, but he must get both his boats to Black's place eventually. There he would get half of Kolin's grass, his own coke, and hop right back to South Bimini to meet Maximiliano for *his* coke. Then, back across the Stream with both boats, unload the grass into a "stash" house in Lauderdale, deliver Maximiliano's cocaine to whoever his contact was—a Canadian? Then meet a guy named Pete. He would sell Pete the coke, all fifty kilos, then turned right around and make it back to Bimini with some of that cash to get the rest of Kolin's grass. Then back home.

He loved it.

Kolin would have his grass ready to ship up north in his vans, the Cuban, Maximiliano, would have successfully funneled another sweet load of nose candy into the American scene, his money channeled through a system that Montilla did not know about—or want to know about—

and he, Montilla, would not only be back in favor with everyone, but also he would be home free.

At that point, once the dust settled, he could continue to work for the Cubans or Kolin, or just take the nice pile of cash he would make for all of his complex machinations and proceed with great vigor into the coke business on his own.

Montilla looked over at Silky and saw that she had taken her top off to let the warm sun shine on her breasts. She had her head back and her eyes closed. Montilla could see that the motion of the boat and the wind across her bare breasts had made her nipples hard, and this aroused him. Without saying anything he reached over with his left hand and began gently playing with her breasts. She opened her eyes and looked at him with a small smile and then leaned her head back again. He let go of her long enough to undo his shorts and let them fall. He kicked them off. Then he grabbed her arm and pulled her to him; pushing himself further back against the seat so there would be more room between him and the wheel. He squeezed her breasts again, playing with the taut nipples with his fingers. He reached over her shoulder, put his hand on the base of her neck, under her hair, and pulled downward gently but firmly. She looked at him steadily for a few seconds, smiled her knowing and somehow secret little smile, and went down on her knees in front of him.

It was a beautiful day for Onyx Montilla.

EIGHTEEN

A few days later Montilla and Silky were in the black BMW with the gold pinstriping and smoked windows, heading back into the southeast section of Lauderdale after spending the day at a small marina at the western end of the south fork of the New River. It was one of those overcast days, with a sky that promises rain all day but gives you only a solid, sticky heat.

One of the Striker sportfishing boats Montilla would use in his next run was kept there. The Striker is a beautiful boat, with clean lines, strong hull, powerful twin twelve-cylinder engines, and all the gleaming paraphernalia that a boater could ever want on board. The two that Montilla owned were both painted a high-gloss gray, in Awlgrip, with black trim, highly polished brightwork, and blacked-out ports and windows. They were both fifty-four footers and were identical except for the names. One was *Spirit* and the other was *Ghost*.

It always gave Montilla a good feeling to be around one or the other of the boats. They were status symbols, for one thing. Whether or not he owned them outright, in his name, or had them buried in some bogus corporation, it had taken him a long time to get the money together to possess them, and people in the marine community, in and out of the drug business, were impressed with the yachts. He loved the constant tinkering and cleaning and adjusting required to keep them in top form.

He had started the day in a good mood, anticipating being happily busy on one Striker, and then going down to Dania to the other small marina where the twin was kept. Because the yachts were very beautiful, and because they were identical, keeping them together attracted too much attention. They were just too hard to miss. Anyone who had any appreciation at all for fine boats would have to stare at them and check them out, including cops. Each Striker had a full-time captain and part-time crew member. It was up to their discretion to bring another man along to help them hump bales when they went for a load. Both crews had been with the boats, and Montilla, for almost a year now, had been used sparingly and had been told in no uncertain terms never to keep the boats together.

Montilla's good mood ended when he arrived at the little marina in the morning. There, tied side by side, were the two sister Strikers, gleaming in the sun. As Silky silently sat in the car, Montilla had flown into a rage, jumping out and storming down the dock to begin a loud harangue with the two crews. He had finally waved them all into the main salon of *Spirit*. Even with the sliding glass door closed, Silky could still hear his loud and angry voice as he reprimanded the crews.

Silky had stayed in the car, reluctant to walk down on the dock during Montilla's tirade. He was still being so unpredictable, first brooding and then wanting to party, then going berserk over some little thing. She had been trying to keep her distance from him as much as possible, afraid of his moods and his violence, but since they had returned from that last trip to Bimini Montilla had been keeping her close to him. If anything, he seemed more possessive than ever, hardly letting her out of his sight. She knew he was excited about a big deal he had just put together. She knew, too, he was feeling considerable pressure because of its complexity. She watched him as he increased his already substantial use of cocaine, even during the day, and she watched as he crashed out almost every night after drinking, smoking grass, and snorting all the coke he could handle. His volatile moods were not helped by his inability on most nights to consummate the evening's sexual boasting when he was high. The few times he was still conscious when she took him to bed were failures and he would get up in the morning brooding about it. Silky would then spend the day walking on eggs, trying to make every effort to avoid the subject completely. As he became more and more irrational and unpredictable, it made her more afraid of him and more determined to find a way out.

They had spent the long hot day at the marina working on the two Strikers for a couple of hours before Montilla sent *Ghost* back to her slip in Dania. He stayed in his foul mood all day, and it got progressively worse as the day wore on. Finally, the captain of *Spirit*, a tanned muscular young man who knew his way around boats and kept an appreciative, if furtive, eye on Silky as much as he dared, suggested that they were finally ready for the upcoming weekend. He told Montilla that there was no need for him to stick around any longer in the heat.

Surprisingly, Montilla had agreed, and after setting up the time and location for a final operational meeting before the actual run, he had loaded Silky into the BMW and headed back to town.

As he turned the BMW onto the causeway leading to the beach Onyx said, "Crap. I'm hot, tired, and thirsty. I'm gonna pull into this Big Daddy's up the street here, and you run in and get us a couple of six packs of beer. Make sure they're cold."

Silky looked at him but said nothing.

The liquor store was located in a small shopping center area on Cordova Road, across the street from a larger center. The area, which was close to the beach and to several marinas and boat ramps, was always busy. The traffic in the lot was congested, with a nerve-tightening and chrome-bending combination of local people trying to get groceries, and tourists and boaters and beach-goers all trying to get ice, beer, suntan oil, and all the other usual items.

Before Montilla had even gotten close to a parking space, he was almost hit by a Cadillac with Ontario plates that backed away from a curb. Then, moments later, he had blown his horn and yelled obscenities at two old people who were strolling arm in arm slowly across the lot in front of him.

"Will you look at those assholes! Jesus."

He gripped the wheel hard with both hands, looking for a space. "Look," he said, "you jump out and run in there and get the beer, and don't take all fuckin' day while you're at it. I'll get a space while you're doin' that. Just look for me when you come out."

Silky didn't say anything as she opened the door and got out. As she closed the door and ran across the lot Montilla watched as three navy guys almost gave themselves whiplash watching her. This only angered him more. He saw a spot open up at the end of the lot and made for it. Just as he prepared to pull into it, a yellow sports car with three teen-age girls in it came quickly around the curb and slid neatly into the space, cutting him off perfectly. When he leaned on his horn and shook his fist at them, screaming and yelling behind his smoked windows, the girls all smiled sweetly and waved back at him. They climbed out of the open car and, giggling and bouncing and smiling at the navy guys, they ran off across the street.

Montilla sat there, fuming, blinded in his anger, until the passenger door suddenly opened and Silky sat down, placing a paper bag with the two six packs on the floor between her feet. She said, "All set, Onyx."

Montilla looked at Silky, then at the beer, then over at the open yellow sports car. He said in a hiss, "Gimme two of 'em... c'mon, c'mon, gimme two of the beers!" Silky tore two cans out of the plastic retainer and quickly handed them to Montilla. A horn blared behind them, as the BMW still sat in the middle of the lot, blocking the way.

Silky heard Montilla yell, "Fuck off!" as he climbed out. Then she watched as he walked over to the yellow sports car, ripped open the beers, and poured the contents of both cans in the front seat of the car. Then he bent one empty can and threw it into the small space behind the seats, where the third girl had been sitting, and set the other empty can carefully on the hood, right in front of the windshield.

He turned then, gave the finger to the entire area at large, ambled back to the BMW, climbed in, and drove away, squealing his tires and narrowly missing another car as he roared out onto the street.

* * *

J.B. looked at his daughter Kathleen again and asked himself for the hundredth time if he was making a big mistake. She sat on the right side of the pickup truck cab, left hand flat on the seat beside her hip, right hand gripping the vent window post. She had her long hair stuffed underneath a green canvas big-billed fishing cap, and was wearing aviator-type sunglasses. She had a set expression on her face, jaw closed tight, lips compressed, eyes scanning everything.

Richards was off duty, in his usual khaki pants and work shirt, and Kathleen was wearing jeans and a light cotton top. He had been working around the house on his day off, then decided to do a little following up on the Montilla deal on his own. He wanted a close look at Montilla's house from the street. He had seen only the back of it, briefly, from the canal. If there were any cars out front then he could snatch the tag numbers from them. He just couldn't sit around and do nothing about what was happening to Ted, no matter what his major or the CIA or anybody else said.

He had grabbed his keys off the counter near the door, turned, saw his daughter sitting at the kitchen table staring out the window, and made a snap decision.

"Hey, Kath," he had said, "I thought I'd drive around and take a look at this guy Montilla's house. He's the one I told you about, the one we think was with Ted." He had hesitated, watching her face closely. "I've been ordered to stay away from it. Oh, hell, there probably won't be anything to see anyway, but I just thought I'd drive by and take a look. Want to come along and be an extra pair of eyes for me?"

She had pushed the chair back, walked quickly to her room, and had come right back out wearing her hat and sunglasses, headed for the door with him.

Now they were on Las Olas Boulevard, heading east, toward the Isles.

J.B. was still filled with misgivings about having his daughter in the truck with him as he began to slow down, going over the small bridge over Pirates Canal. He would have to make a right turn on the first isle off the boulevard. He knew Montilla's house would be on the left, or the east side of the street, about halfway down. He was explaining this to Kathleen, who was sitting straight in her seat, when he spotted the black BMW coming toward them, west on the boulevard at a high rate of speed.

"Okay, Kath, see that black BMW heading toward us, coming this way? The driver is our boy, and that's his girlfriend with him. Look at his speed, will ya?" J.B. watched the BMW carefully. "All right, we're not gonna turn onto his isle right now, we'll go on by. As we go past them, look straight ahead or out to the right, not at them. Wait a minute!"

Montilla, who should have yielded to oncoming traffic, including the beat-up pickup truck in the curb lane, got to the break in the median strip, kept his foot on the gas, and turned the wheel sharply to the left. He was still hot from the parking lot scene. The tires on the BMW squealed slightly as the car made the corner, shot across the eastbound two lanes, and sped down the isle toward Montilla's house.

J.B had slowed, and then hit the brakes as the BMW made its turn off the boulevard and onto the isle. He and Kathleen both stared into the windows of the small car, but they saw that both people in the car were looking straight ahead. J.B. had the fleeting impression of the girl's stiff posture as she sat in her seat, hanging on through the radical turn. Then they were past the isle and moving east on the boulevard.

"Great driver, huh?" said J.B., but Kathleen was silent, her face grim. J.B. drove two blocks, made a careful U-turn, came back up to Montilla's isle, paused, looked, and then turned onto it. He drive slowly, and could sense Kathleen tensing up on the seat beside him.

"All right now, we have the tag on the beemer, so don't worry about memorizing or copying unless there's another car there. Easy . . . here we are. And what do we have?" He kept his eyes on the road, adjusted his sunglasses, and kept his left elbow on the door frame, his big hand covering the left side of his face.

Kathleen leaned forward slightly, making quick glances in the direction of the houses on the left side. He heard her catch her breath, and then say quietly, "Okay, Dad. They're out of the car. I just saw his back as he went into the house. He left the door open. The girl's getting out . . . she's beautiful. She's carrying a shopping bag."

They drove past the house and headed for the turnaround at the dead end of the isle. Kathleen went on, still quietly. "They seem very tense about just getting into the house quickly. She's in now, and the door is closed. There was only his car, but there's a large garage, with the door closed, so there could be another one."

J.B. nodded and drove to the end of the isle. He made the circle and then stopped, the engine idling. "Let's see if they forgot something." They sat quietly for a few minutes, and then he put the truck into gear and started moving back down the street, not hurrying. As they drove by the house this time, they could see no activity at all.

He stopped at the end of the isle, checked the traffic on Las Olas, then turned right and headed for the beach, wanting to drive awhile before heading home. Kathleen was silent, staring straight ahead.

As they approached the Las Olas Bridge, J.B. heard his daughter sigh, and then say, "Man. I think I was holding my breath the whole time! And look . . . my hands are sweaty. I didn't realize I was so nervous. I don't know how you and Mister Bedlam and Mister Tommasen do that kind of thing all the time."

J.B. smiled at her, wiped his palms on the legs of his trousers and said, "No matter how many times you do it, you still get the cottonmouth and the wet hands. You did good back there . . . good eyeball."

She nodded, her face set again. She looked out the window at the boats moving on the Intracoastal Waterway and was silent for a few minutes while he drove.

As they went past Bahia Mar and then into the "S" curves on Seabreeze Boulevard, he heard her fingernails tapping a rapid tattoo on the vent window. He thought about what he had done, about taking his daughter out with him to surveil a bad guy. He knew if the professionals he worked with, even his friends, heard about it, they would tell him he was absolutely crazy, exposing any member of his family to "the street." Well, phooey, he thought, my family is already involved in this damn case, and she had just as much right to feel like she's somehow helping to get Ted home as anybody.

Kathleen pulled the canvas cap off her head and ran her fingers through her long hair. She turned in her seat, looked at him, her hands balled into fists, and said, "We're gonna get him, Dad!"

The evening shadows softened the contours of the central room of the house. The hot clear day, with its spectacular sunset, was being chased away by the bolder stars already shining in the eastern sky. From where he stood, looking out through the back porch at the ocean beyond the grounds, Ted could just see the last flicker of distant fires from the western horizon and the blue black night sky reaching down to the gunmetal blue sea. The house was quiet now, inside and out, and he could hear Carmelita washing the dinner dishes.

They had dined on a light meal of *arroz con pollo* that she had prepared and some wine. He considered it a fairly full day. An odd thing about the house was that there was no radio, or even any books or magazines. He guessed it had something to do with the place being a "safe house." He had awakened early and done some stretching and bending. She had made him sit down then, and she pulled up the right leg of his pajamas and gently explored his wounds. He could see they were healing well—still very raw looking but clean and dry. She had nibbled her lip for a moment, made a decision, left the room, and had come back with her small black medical bag.

Quickly, efficiently, and with a concerned deftness, she pulled the stitches from the worst wounds inflicted by the propeller. Once done, she cleaned the leg with alcohol, looked up and smiled at him.

Afterward, they went into the yard and walked a bit, he stopping and stretching occasionally, working his leg as she watched with approval. This caused the biggest scar, however, to start weeping slightly. She pursed her lips as she examined it. She took him back inside then, and cleaned the wounds again.

Eventually, when the sun had risen high in the sky, it became time for their siesta. Ted was still not used to sleeping in the middle of the day but found that he was ready for a rest after his exercise. Since they had come to the safe house, Carmelita had been sleeping in his room, in the other bed on the side of the room closer to the door. She would go into the bathroom, wash up, and come out wearing a white full-length cotton nightdress, her black hair tied up in back with a ribbon. He thought she looked beautiful. He was not used to sleeping in pajamas but would have been uncomfortable being nude around her, nurse or not.

They took their siesta in their clothes, taking their shoes off first. They usually went barefoot in the house anyway, and Ted liked the feel of the cool tiles on his feet. Lying on the bed, with the ceiling fans moving the cool air around the rooms in the house, was pleasant, but on this day Ted had not slept. He had lain there staring up at the ceiling, his mind filled with thoughts of survival. At present his only contact with another human being was with Carmelita, a beautiful, dark, warm, and caring nurse and partner in a safe house. He was surrounded by her. She was with him almost every minute of his day, and she was so female, soft, fragrant, and warm.

He heard Carmelita behind him, and turned to find her standing there with a smile on her face and a glass of wine for each of them. He followed her out onto the darkened porch, where they sat and sipped their wine and looked out into the night, quiet together.

After the siesta he had put his shoes back on and, with her following behind, had walked the entire perimeter of the grounds around the house, examining the fence and the light sensors and the path that the guards walked. He had hoped to spot a guard or a dog team, but was disappointed. He knew, of course, that just because he didn't see them didn't mean that he and the girl weren't being watched. He could feel it.

He felt her touch him now, as she took his left hand in hers. He watched her as she took a sip of her wine, her eyes dancing over the rim of the glass. When she took the glass away from her wet lips he could see her patient smile. He smiled back, feeling his heart pounding, and his mouth going dry in spite of the wine.

Her fingers entwined with his, then broke away, then softly traced the outline of his hand. He did not take his hand away, and when she put her glass down and leaned forward on her seat, he held his breath. She looked into his eyes, then gently ran her fingers down his cheek, across his chin, and over his lips. She tilted her head then, closed her eyes tight, took his hand, and she stood up.

She led him into the bedroom.

She stopped beside his bed and in the darkness began undressing him. The sound of their breathing was the only sound in the room. As she pulled his shirt away from his shoulders she leaned forward and kissed him on the chest, nuzzling him, then looking up and kissing him full on the mouth. She stepped back, pulled his shirt all the way off and moved her fingers at the waist of his trousers, unsnapping them and pulling down the zipper. She knelt in front of him, pulling the trousers down, and he stepped out of them, naked now.

She still knelt before him, and looking up into his face she rubbed her hands smoothly up the back of his legs, stopping at his buttocks, which she squeezed tightly as she pulled him toward her. He was already very aroused, and as he felt the soft skin of her cheek brush against him he caught his breath. She touched him lightly with the fingers of one hand while she kissed him there, making a sound much like soft purring. Then she pushed on his hips until he sat on the bed, and she stood up.

He watched as she undressed in the soft shadows of the room.

Her skin was almost a uniform light brown, the areas never exposed to the sun a dusky caramel color. Her body was full, with heavy round breasts accented with full dark nipples, long legs, and smooth, full hips. Her pouting navel was at eye level as she stood before him then, the black hair just below it shiny and soft.

She was utterly lovely.

As she crawled into bed beside him, one hand on his chest, lightly pushing him down on his back, she said quietly, *"Por tanto mi espia . . . tu hay en la casa de usted un amante? Este es tu casa esta noche."*

Her words were musical and lovely in the dark room, and he felt her warm body against his and moved to her, running his hands gently down the length of her body. He slid his fingers down past her navel and found she was already very wet. Her breathing grew deep and strong. He held her like that for a moment, looking into her eyes, wanting her badly. Then he moved to her.

The first time was quick and fiery and sweet and strong.

He was swept up in it and could not wait, losing control very quickly. She arched her back and cried out sharply as he released his wet warmth into her, squeezing her tight against him, feeling her hard nipples against the skin of his chest. They lay like that for a time, she not letting him move, until their breathing eased up. He began kissing her, softly, sweetly . . . nibbling, tasting.

The next time they came together was after he had explored her completely with his lips and his tongue and his fingers, and it lasted longer and consumed them both. He heard her breathing change and felt her back arching again as he moved his hips against hers, and he knew she was close. Finally she shuddered and her eyes closed and he felt her fingers digging into his back as she cried out softly into the darkness, *"Sí . . . sí . . . sí!"*

They lay together for a long time after that, resting, she stretched out beside him, her head on his left shoulder, the scent of her hair so close to him. Her fingers rubbed him warmly, and for a time he felt he was in suspended animation, floating on a bed of downy clouds, her feathery touch his only link with any conscious awareness. She spoke to him in her language, quietly, dreamily, telling him of hopes and wishes and feelings, most of which he didn't understand but which pleased him anyway. She made contented sounds, words of gratification and of promise.

It was a night of sharing for them. They gave and they were given, and for those hours of gentle darkness before the dawn, which they shared with each other, nothing else existed.

They fell into peaceful sleep, their bodies still touching.

It was past midnight. Richards sat brooding in his big recliner in the living room. The house was quiet and he looked around slowly, finding himself actually aware of the quiet and liking it. He enjoyed the early mornings also, before all the radio alarms kicked in on their various stations. The quiet of the early morning was an expectant quiet. The quiet now, late at night, seemed to him as if the whole house was giving a comfortable sigh of relief after a noisy day.

He heard his wife's bare feet on the floor, and her soft voice calling, "John Brian." And then he felt her cool fingers on the back of his neck. "You're not going to fall sound asleep in this recliner are you?"

He looked at her as she sat down on the arm of the chair, rubbed his face with his hands, and said, "Sorry, Jane . . . didn't want to keep you up tossing and turning, that's all."

She took one of his big hands in hers and said, "You've been brooding around here like a big bear for too long now. I know you're upset about those new stitches in Ricky's hand from that crazy little dirt motorcycle *we* decided to buy him. But it's the thing with Ted that's really eating at you, right?" He looked at her, made a face, and nodded. "Remember what you always tell me about 'compartmentalizing,' J.B., how all of my problems together look huge but once they're broken down into units they become manageable? Much of what's going on is out of your control, in the hands of God, or whatever. You can only prepare yourself and stand by, right?" She leaned over and kissed him on the forehead. "That was very fine, what you did with Kathleen today, only—be careful. Anyway, you know you have some good people working on your side, and it's a miracle that Ted is still alive. So all you do here is just keep on keepin' *on*."

"Hey." He smiled at her. "That's my line."

She waited.

"You know me," he sighed. "I don't get into it personally. I try to get the bad guys when I can. I work pretty hard at it and I do a pretty good job, but hell, that's all it is, a job. The bad guy breaks the law and I try to catch him, bust him, and go on to the next one. You know that between here and the old department up north I've put away some heavy ones, some of them just filthy animals, but aside from the usual feelings of pity or disgust for them I never really carried anything personal, you now?"

She nodded her head yes and massaged his forehead with her free hand. She watched as he made a fist.

"But now here I am involved with this tough little bastard, this Montilla. I killed his *father*, and now he's caused Ted to be taken from us. It's just too much, like we're all caught up in some kind of unstoppable roller coaster ride."

The room grew very quiet.

"You know..." He pulled away from her gently and stood up. "I'll do anything to get Ted back home safe. I'm worried about him. I'm worried about the girl that Montilla has trapped with him. I'd like to help her get away from him if I can. I've even offered to help her—as if I had some magic that could make things right." He stood facing the door, punching one big fist into the other palm.

"I want this guy. I want him really bad."

She came softly up behind him and hugged him tightly, her face against the middle of his back. She held him like that until she heard him sigh again and felt him relax. Then she reached down and took his hand and pulled him silently to bed.

The light of the sun brought Ted out of his deep sleep.

He sat up, alone in the bed, and wondered if the night before had been a dream. He stretched and scratched his head. No, that was very real indeed.

He sat up on the edge of the bed and rubbed his face, wondering where Carmelita was. He went to the bathroom, washed up, put on his trousers, and as he started to walk out of the bedroom she was there, in the doorway.

She looked at him and he could see an urgency in her

eyes. And sadness? She put one finger against his lips, watched him for a moment, then moved forward and kissed him quickly, squeezing his arms tightly as she did. He started to speak but her eyes went wide and she shook her head. He looked deep into her eyes again and she turned away.

He walked out into the parlor to find the lean man in the dark suit standing there, waiting quietly. The girl kept her head down and walked past the man, over to the porch, where she stood looking out at the ocean.

"So, señor, you have rested well? And I see you are walking much better. Our little house has been good for you, no?"

Ted was silent, unsettled by the girl.

The lean one glanced at the girl, and then back at him. "Now it is necessary for you to travel again, señor, away from here. It will be in a covered truck again, I'm afraid, but it is not a long trip." He hesitated, then went on. "This time you will be accompanied by one of my men, all right? Your nurse now must return to her regular duties."

To Ted the man's words sounded like a sentence being passed. He turned and got his things. He came out of the bedroom and walked to the front door, where he and the lean man waited while the girl collected her few belongings. Ted could hear men talking outside, and a car door slammed. He felt his stomach tightening.

Carmelita came out of the bedroom, stopped in the middle of the parlor, and turned in a slow circle, looking at everything. Then she joined them, her eyes on the floor.

The lean one looked at the two of them, one at a time. He opened the door and said, "You have a moment." Then he stepped out, closing the door softly behind him but not latching it. They knew he was standing just outside.

Carmelita dropped her bags and came into his arms. He held her tightly, squeezing her and kissing the small tears out of the corner of her eyes. She pulled back from him, looked into his face, as if to record in her heart every line and curve, and then kissed him again, long and full.

She pulled away from him then, her eyes wet, and said in a whisper, *"Vaya con Dios, mi amante."*

She opened the door and walked out. The lean man
pointed to a black car and she walked past the truck,
opened the backdoor and climbed in, sat stiffly, and stared
straight ahead. She did not turn her head as the car drove
out of sight, down the winding road toward the trees and
hills beyond.

Ted stood beside the lean man watching the car until it
was ought of sight, a deep emptiness within him.

He was led to the back of the truck. Another man, muscular and tough looking, opened the gate, and he climbed
in. When the other man climbed in also, sitting across from
him, the gate closed and the canvas top was tied down.
Doors slammed and the truck's engine was started.

Here we go again, thought Ted.

Maximiliano sat in the truck as it made its winding way
down the road toward the small harbor a few miles away.
He hoped getting the gringo back to the islands would go
smoothly. He would feel better when they were there,
safely hidden in the old hotel on South Bimini.

He thought of the girl then, Carmelita. Sure, he knew it
wasn't an accident that a lovely young girl, with the English language, had been assigned by the prison director to
stay close to the injured gringo. And he knew he would
have access to the information she would report back with,
if anything. Too bad, he mused, too bad she works for the
prisons . . . and too bad about the looks I saw her exchange
with the young American. He sighed. *I think she's smart
and capable. I wonder if I can get her to work for me
somehow,* he thought.

NINETEEN

Silky sat in the still darkness on the dock behind Montilla's house and pulled the little business card softly against her lips as her mind explored possibilities. She looked once more at the phone number scrawled on the reverse side of "Ooooooh Shiiiiit" and then jammed the card into the back pocket of her jeans. She stared up at the myriad stars sparkling in the clear night sky and knew it was time. Time to make a move. Time to go . . . whether she was ready financially or otherwise. Even if she was scared to death, it was time.

She turned her head as raucous laughter tumbled out of the house. Montilla had surprised the boat captains by calling for a meeting tonight. He wanted to give them last instructions before the upcoming weekend. She heard more laughter and knew he just couldn't have the meeting without showing the other men what a great guy he was with all of that wonderful toot to stuff up their nautical noses.

She turned her back in disgust.

What about her? How much trouble was she in?

Her knowledge of Sam Golden's activities would still make her an interesting person in the eyes of a local organized crime prosecutor, she knew, but her earlier fears of one of Golden's old partners coming for her had started to ease with the passage of time. She knew that if Montilla had been approached by some of the seriously bad guys on the fringes of Golden's activities, he would have given her away. More recently, because she spent so much time with Onyx, she could certainly be included in any kind of narcotics conspiracy case made against him, or Kolin, for that matter.

So, if nothing else, she definitely had troubles with the law hanging over her head.

She thought of the big cop then: J.B. Richards. He was "the law," wasn't he? He would be part of the system that would view her as a criminal partner with Golden and with Montilla. Maybe. She looked up into the stars again, not seeing them. And now there was this constant talk of killing that big cop. The cop had offered to help her, had offered to help and never asked for a thing in return, and now Onyx was working himself up to kill him. She knew Montilla had met again with that lieutenant he owned and had learned that the big cop was still monitoring Montilla's movements through his friends, even though he had been transferred from waterfront duties.

Montilla had been tight as a drum when he returned from that meeting—cranky and miserable and dangerous. He had told her it was definitely time to do something about the big cop. She was aware of a curious frustration as he spoke, as if there was something that held him back in spite of his bluster. She didn't think there was time for Onyx to set up a hit on the cop before this big weekend of his but she wasn't sure. Besides, he might get all coked up and do it himself.

She held her bunched fists against her breasts and rocked slowly back and forth, feet dangling over the dark water below her. It's time. Time to do *something*.

She heard his voice angrily calling her name out into the darkness and she stood slowly and walked toward the house. She knew he had to leave in the morning to meet with somebody he said was important; she guessed it had to do with the cocaine he was sneaking in under the grass. He wouldn't leave her for long, but maybe long enough. If she could call the number tonight and meet with the big cop in the morning, maybe that would work.

"Hey, woman! Didn't you hear those guys leavin'? Didn't you think I might be ready for some of your sweet company now that my business is done for the night? Didn't you think?" Montilla looked at her, stoned, and leered, "Oh, yeah, what am I saying? I pay for your pussy —not your brain, huh?"

She just looked at him for a few seconds and then turned to walk away.

He grabbed her hand and said coarsely, "Listen, Silky, just get in that bedroom and get those jeans off 'cause I've got something hard here for you and I'll give it to you just the way you like it. And if you're nice, I might even give you a bracelet for your pretty little wrist."

She stared at him and said quietly, dangerously, "Not tonight, Onyx."

He stared back incredulously. "Not tonight? Not tonight? What the fuck are you talking about? It's *tonight*. Tonight or any other night I want it—or the morning, or *any* damn time!" His eyes became flint-hard and shiny black. "You seem to be forgetting something here, girl. I *own* you. Hear me?" He stepped away from her, and then turned. "Look at yourself and then at me. What do you see? I am the one with the money. I am all those little gold trinkets you like to hang on your body." His voice got quieter now, and she could see the spit falling into his beard as he moved toward her and she slowly backed away. "Not only that, Silky. I am the *man*, I am the power, the *erection*. You are only here to receive me into your not-so-unique body." He was very close to her now, and she could feel his sinister power washing over her. "I am everything you are, Silky. Because of *me*, you exist . . . I am every reason for you. I . . . am . . . *you*."

She had backed up until she felt the couch against the back of her legs and now she stood there staring into his wild eyes. As she looked deep into the twin vortexes his words pounded into her brain, and for a few seconds she thought she *could* see herself in his malevolent eyes. She shuddered and turned away. He reached for her and she twisted her hips to avoid his grasp. His clutching fingers missed her belt but grasped the top of her jeans pocket as she moved, and he pulled and the pocket ripped off in his hand. They both stood there breathing hard as the little white business card fluttered down to the carpet. She sucked in her breath as he moved like a cat and scooped up the card with one hand while he grabbed her hair with the other.

His voice was soft now. "Ooooooh Shiiiiit, is it? And what's this on the back? Oh, it's a little phone number. How nice." He looked at her, his face savage, as she said, "Oh, Onyx, I just forgot it was in there, that's all. It was just some guy at the bar the other night. You left me there when you went to the bathroom and this guy hit on me and told me to call him and he gave it to me and I thought the front was cute and I just stuffed it into that pocket and forgot about it. Really, Onyx, he was just some jerk. If you had been there with me he would never have even tried it." As she spoke she moved her leg softly against his thigh, leaving it there now, warm.

Onyx looked at the card again and then back at her.

Silky hung her head down and let her hair frame her face. She ran her fingers down his arm as she whispered, "I'm sorry, Onyx, about tonight I mean. You had those guys here all night and I felt like you were ignoring me and I guess I just got snotty, but I didn't mean to." Small tears formed at the corners of her eyes. "And that card, that card is nothing, really." She lifted her chin and looked into his eyes, pouting slightly. "He wouldn't have given it to me if you had been with me, Onyx. I hate it when we go out to those places and then you leave me alone. And besides, I know he could never get as hard as you do . . . he could never please me like you do."

She held his hand now, trying to pull him gently toward the bedroom, but he just stood there looking into her eyes.

Finally he sighed, looked down, and ripped the card into many small pieces. He dropped the pieces into a large glass ashtray on the coffee table, took one of his long-stemmed matches from beside the ashtray, and lit the pieces. As he stood there watching them curl and burn and blacken to ash, he thought, It is time. Time for this little bitch to go for a boat ride. He had planned to leave her at the house, closely watched, while he made this run, but not now. Not now. He looked at her watching him silently and in a soft voice, edged with malice, he said, "Okay. That's the end of the guy in the bar. And you're right, there's no way, who-ever he was, no way he could have fucked you like I can."

She kept telling herself it was the last time.

She kept telling herself it was nothing that a hot bath and a little soap couldn't make go away.

She allowed herself to be taken by him physically, and he used her completely. He wanted her tongue, her lips, her teeth. He filled his insistent hands with her breasts and squeezed until she hurt. He used his maleness as a probing weapon, entering her roughly, everywhere on her body. He knelt behind her, holding her face down against the bed-ding, violently pounding against her as she bent before him. He turned her, pulling her by the hair, pulling her face between his thighs. He made her lick and nibble and suck and touch. He made her whisper dirty things in his ears while he manipulated himself, and her. She called out to him, "Onyx, oh, Onyx!" as she feigned shuddering cli-maxes.

And finally, finally, he climbed onto her, pushed himself into her, and a short time later, after a ragged series of gasps and grunts, lay spent and drifting to sleep on top of her.

She lay holding him, breathing easily, until she knew he was out. Then she slowly eased away from him and forced herself to lie beside him for another fifteen minutes. He moved slightly as she slipped out of bed and stood there holding her breath, but he continued sleeping as she turned and padded out of the bedroom and into the kitchen. Did she remember the number she had practiced committing to memory? She would tell him to come for her now. She would put on her jeans and slip out the door and wait for him at the end of the street. He would pick her up; he would make sure she was protected. She would do some-thing, move, get a job . . . something.

She dialed the number quickly, not thinking about it, just punching the buttons. As she did, she opened the refrigera-tor door. With the phone against her ear she listened to the ringing, again and again. Oh God, she thought, it's late, too late. He's asleep. But no, the phone was answered. A woman's voice, heavy with sleep was saying, "Yes? Hello? Hello?"

She leaned against the refrigerator door. His wife. Of course, of course he has a wife. She thought she heard something, a noise coming from the bedroom. She spoke softly, but urgently.

"Tell Mister, I mean Officer . . . um . . . Richards, that Chica needs to meet with him in the morning. Ten o'clock. Chica at ten in the morning at the small park on the river with the churches, not far from Chica's house. Please, please tell him."

She hung up. She stared at the phone for a few seconds, reached into the refrigerator and grabbed a can of grapefruit juice, closed the door, and walked silently back into the bedroom.

Montilla was leaning on one elbow, staring at her.

Silky felt a chill similar to the one she felt standing in front of the open refrigerator as he reached for her, and knew she should turn and run, naked, out onto the street, screaming.

But she couldn't.

She just stood there in front of him as he reached up, grabbed the can of juice from her hand, and said groggily, "What the fuck time is it, anyway?"

She heard her own voice say, "I don't know . . . it's late, honey." He greedily sucked down the cold juice from the can and threw it onto the floor. He looked at her again, shook his head, and lay back against the pillows. As she watched, he fell immediately back into a deep sleep.

She turned slowly, went into the bathroom, and began running hot water and bubble bath into the tub.

At first, Richards thought he was dreaming about his wife shaking him and asking him a lot of insistent questions in a slightly demanding tone. As he woke up he realized he wasn't dreaming but was still confused by the questions for a few seconds. When it hit him, *his* tone became slightly demanding and he made her repeat it again and again, and then once more. He was silent for a few moments, then explained gently what, and who, it was. He held his wife and talked to her softly for a long time until she finally went to sleep.

Then he just lay there holding her, thinking about the morning.

It was one of those Florida mornings that make you stand by your open door and just stare in wonder all around. Everything was impossibly clear and bright and clean, the clarity so definite you almost wished for a few clouds or shadows to soften things a little. It was warm, but because it was mid-morning it wasn't unpleasantly so. Where the sun hit it was peacefully warm; where there was shade it was peacefully cool.

The sun's light made everything it touched sparkle: the red tiles on the roof of the old church, the cracked sidewalks lined and filled with soft green moss, the branches of the gnarled old trees, the lush carpet of grass, the steady flow of dark water of the New River, weaving through Tarpon Bend, and the chrome on the police unit parked behind the stucco walls of the church.

Skids Bedlam leaned against one of the dark wooden pews, the leather of his heavy gun belt creaking softly. His arms were folded across his belly as his red eyes roamed the interior of the church.

"You know what, J.B.?" he said quietly, "I'll bet this is one of the oldest churches in Fort Lauderdale, if not the whole area. It's beautiful, just absolutely beautiful."

Richards, somewhat surprised by his partner's aesthetic appreciation, buttoned his beige *guyabera* shirt and looked around the interior of the church. "Yeah," he said.

His uniform, including the gun belt and radio, was folded across the back of the pews, and he was dressed in what he considered semiformal attire for his meeting with the girl. He was wearing one of the new shirts he had found hanging in his closet. He felt the Cuban-style shirt, which hung smoothly on the outside of his belt line, hid what he saw recently as just slightly too much girth around the middle. Of course, he would never admit that to his wife, or to Bedlam for that matter.

Bedlam, eyeing him now, said, "Nice shirt there, J.B.

Now all you need is a greasy bag of *bollos* and a piña colada."

Richards started to respond but stopped when a distinguished-looking gray-haired priest walked quietly up the center isle of the church. He stopped beside the two officers, looked at the uniform and gun belt with its empty holster on the pew, looked at Richards's clothes, and then looked out the slightly open large wooden doors, over the front steps and out into the park across the street.

Richards saw the question in the old man's eyes and said evenly, "It's just a short meeting, Father. No rough stuff, no arrests or guns or anything like that. My partner will wait in the church and watch while I'm in the park. It won't take long."

The old priest looked at them both again, and then back out into the sunlit park. He patted Richards lightly on the arm, looked at the Saint Jude medal hanging under the Cuban-style shirt, and walked between them, back toward the dark interior of the church. As he left them he said only, "Be careful, my son."

Richards sat in the cool shade on an old wooden bench under a huge banyan tree in the middle of the park. He always felt at peace here, next to the river, almost surrounded by the four old churches clustered together at the end of the street. When he used to work alone in a downtown unit he would come to this spot for lunch, no matter how the day was going, and if he spent a few moments there he always felt better when he left. He looked slowly around the park again as if to savor it once more before getting his mind ready for the job ahead. He looked across the tree-covered street to the front of the nearest church. One of the huge wooden doors was slightly open. Though he couldn't see him he knew Skids was just inside the shadows, waiting.

He looked down at his shirt and wondered again if he should have worn a "wire" and recorded this meeting with the girl, and again he rejected it. As of now, no one on the department knew about the meeting except Scott Kelly. If he had requested a wire he would have had to give a reason; and worse, the wire would have come from OCB, home of Lieutenant Billy Erricks. Richards wasn't sure why, but he continued to have a bad feeling about Erricks and his efforts to curtail Richards's anti-drug-smuggling activities. It was probably just interoffice rivalry—or was it? No, he had decided to meet with the girl alone, with none of the brass or anyone else from the police groups knowing about it. Then, if what she told him could lead to more action, he would go from there.

He sighed and looked up into the reaching branches of the old banyan tree. He was taking charge, and he knew it. This case was going to be his no matter what the major or anyone else thought. He knew it should properly be done with much planning, lots of equipment, and many good policemen on the local, state, and federal levels. He knew all of the resources of the police and judicial community could work this case with a lot of decisions, and orders, and administrative activity. And he acknowledged that was probably the way it should be handled.

But no, the feeling was there, way down inside him, that the system had somehow been stymied so far. Montilla had been able to function all this time. The system had had its chance. Now maybe Montilla could be taken by surprise by a police officer working within the system, but one who worked without letting the system know what he was doing. One tired cop, with a little help from his friends, could do it.

And J.B. knew he was that one tired cop.

From his position inside the church, Bedlam could see the girl approaching the park before J.B. could. He glanced at her hurrying along, almost running, and then scanned the tree-lined street behind her for a vehicle moving slowly, or another person on foot in the shadows. Satisfied that there was nothing, he again observed the girl. She was wearing a pair of faded jeans, a T-shirt, and jogging shoes, and as her athletic body moved easily along he thought to himself, Why the hell do all the really good-looking ones hang around with such assholes?

J.B. smiled and stood up from the bench as the girl

walked up to him. As she stopped and smiled back tentatively he saw that she was terribly nervous, looking back over her shoulder, and then all around the park. There were small beads of sweat across the bridge of her nose. They stood awkwardly for a few seconds, and then Richards said, "Well, good morning. Glad you could make it. Let's sit down, it's nice here under the tree."

They picked opposite ends of the bench and sat facing each other. She looked at him and then quickly looked away again and he said softly, "It's okay, really. It's quiet. I used to come here when I worked this area because it's so peaceful and out of the way. The squirrels and pigeons will see soon enough that we have no food, and they'll leave us alone. And we're too early for that tour train that will show up later with the tourists and their cameras." He pulled on his nose, watching her. "My partner is with me. He's in the church across the street there." He saw her face turn that way, then come back to him, a question in her eyes. "I ride in the police car with him. I trust him. He does not have a camera, and I am not wearing a tape-recorded mike. He's there to cover your back, to make sure you weren't followed, and that we can be safe here."

She looked at him and nodded. She felt his strength and his confidence, and it calmed her. She felt safe with him.

"I . . . I like your shirt," she said quietly. Then she saw his look and added, "No, I really do. It looks nice on you."

He smoothed the front of the shirt, liking it even more now, and said, "I'm very glad you called me last night. I'm sorry I didn't answer the phone myself, but I'm glad to be here and I want to help if I can."

She looked away and he watched as she played with the hem of her jeans until she faced him again, and said, "I was afraid to call you, and I didn't want to bother you so late. But last night was bad. The last couple of weeks have been really bad. I've just not been sure of what to do. I wish I could tell you how good it made me feel to see you sitting on this bench this morning. I was afraid after I called you that something would happen and I wouldn't be able to make it, but he left like he said he would and I waited a few minutes and ran here and the whole way over

I kept telling myself not to get my hopes up. That maybe you wouldn't get the message, or maybe you couldn't do anything for me . . . and oh, I don't now. But here you are, and here I am and I've never asked anyone for help in my whole life and I don't know what to do anymore. I always thought I was tough and I always thought I could land on my feet, and now I don't know and he's really getting crazy and scaring me and I don't know what to do or where to go, and . . . and . . ." She was crying softly, looking down into her lap while her fingers played with the stitching on her jeans.

Richards hesitated, cleared his throat, then said, "I want you to understand that I am working with you in an unofficial capacity. You remind me very much of my daughters, but you're trapped in a world that you can't seem to get out of, and if one of my daughters was in that position I'd do anything I could to help her break free, Silky."

Silky looked at J.B., wonder on her face, and said quietly, "You know my name."

J.B. nodded. "I learned your name through another policeman who is working with me on this case. And that brings me to another piece of news. I hope you don't think I was trespassing by checking up on you, but it really had to happen if we were going to move forward on the case."

Silky understood, and found that she was grateful that the big cop had clearly defined the rules of the meeting and the relationship. She felt a warm and good feeling about this man who was trying so hard to work with her, and at the same time show her that he intended to keep it on a professional level. After a lifetime of dealing with men who, no matter what, always were working toward that bedroom goal, she now found herself slightly taken aback by a man who was going to treat her as a person. She smiled.

"Yes, I know your name," said J.B. "And I know all about Sam Golden and your involvement with him. My friend has access to the organized crime intelligence files, and even though he's a narc he's very well versed on many criminal activities in the area."

Silky looked down into her lap, biting her lip.

"Look, Silky, you'll have to trust me here. As far as we can see, you would have never been in trouble with the state attorney's office anyway, except that they would have used you as a witness, and if you had refused they could have brought some heat on you." He reached out and took her hand again. "I would guess that our man Montilla has used the Golden thing to hang over your head like a dagger—that he would give you to the cops if you didn't do what he told you. You've probably already figured out that if any of Golden's old partners had wanted you to work for them, or wanted to make you disappear, it would have already happened."

Silky cocked her head. "So what you're saying then, Officer Richards, is that 'the dagger' that Onyx has been threatening me with is meaningless and that I'm not in trouble with the law."

"That's how I see it."

She frowned. "Well, that's one thing out of the way. Now all I have to deal with is my terrible fear of him. I'm sure that if I try to break away from him now, he'll never let me go. If I run, he'll come looking for me and he'll hurt me."

Silky rubbed her face with both hands, looked at the cop, and said, "First of all, Officer Richards, Onyx wants you killed. He's either going to pay someone to do it, or he will try it himself somehow. He's getting so crazy lately I know he means it. Also, that narc that he thought he killed is alive somewhere, and he's being brought back here as some kind of prize for Onyx. Onyx is doing his grass thing with that slippery Kolin character, and he's set some kind of cocaine thing up with that little Mister Black, over on Bimini. And he's somehow involved with a spy." She saw how J.B. was reacting. "No," she said, "he really is. I don't know all of the details, but he keeps bragging about how he's now working for a group that makes all of the other groups look like nothing, and this spy keeps meeting him and that's where that narc fits in. And it's all very spooky and mysterious—and complicated." She watched as a squirrel made a cautious approach toward them, stopping and looking around with quick movements as it did so. "I think it's just another cocaine scam of some kind. Most of those guys live in freaky fantasy worlds anyway, always claiming to be hooked in with the government or some bullshit."

There was a stillness then, almost as if the park itself had stopped to take a deep breath, the birds quiet, the squirrels frozen in various postures, waiting.

J.B. pinched his nose, and sighed. It seemed a sign that released the park from its hold. Pigeons flapped noisily up into the branches of the banyan tree, and the ones on the ground walked around examining things, their heads moving back and forth like Egyptian dancers. The squirrels resumed their endless hunt for goodies among the leaves, discarding pieces of paper and other worthless finds with disdain. Even though J.B. felt his pulse pounding, he kept his voice calm as he said, "Why don't you start from the beginning and tell me about it? I need to know his plans, not just the part about him trying to kill me. If I can work into what he's planning, then I can hurt him, and maybe get Ted back. And maybe I can take him away so he's out of your life. Tell me what you can, and then we'll know what we can do."

She looked at him, took a deep breath, and relaxed. She knew she couldn't ask the big cop to take her away now and protect her, not yet. She knew now that she wouldn't leave until she helped this man do what he had to do. Rather than run, she would stay with Onyx, and as she thought about it she was surprised to feel a surge of self-value come to her, and a warm calm. She looked into the steady ice blue eyes and said, "I'll tell you what I can. I won't run away from Onyx Montilla now, not until this is over. I'll work with you, Officer Richards, because what you do is *real* . . . and important."

He looked at her, understanding the risks she would be taking, nodded, and said, "We'll all work together, and we'll do it."

Bedlam, in the cool shadows inside the church, watched the girl with J.B. for a little over an hour. After many years of stakeouts under all kinds of conditions, he did not find it difficult to relax and at the same time pay attention to the two on the bench. As he watched his partner with the girl, he saw her become animated, gesturing strongly, and once she stood up suddenly and walked around in front of the bench. He saw her put her face in her hands and sit down again and watched as her shoulders heaved as she sobbed.

Finally, they stood, the girl took both of J.B.'s hands in hers, stood on her toes, and quickly kissed him on the cheek. Then she turned and walked away. He watched as Richards stood there with his arms folded across his chest, until the girl was out of sight.

J.B. watched her go, stood for a moment looking around the area, then slowly walked across the street, up the steps, and into the cool interior of the church.

They didn't speak as J.B. changed back into his uniform and folded his civvies into a paper bag. They were quiet as they eased out a side door, across a small courtyard with a fountain, and through an old wooden door in a stucco wall. The police unit was in the alley, invisible from the street. As they drove off, Richards looked back and saw the priest standing by the old wooden door with his hands clasped behind his back, staring into the sky.

They drove in silence for a few minutes. J.B. stared out the side window, not seeing the traffic. Finally he took a deep breath, sighed, and said, "Well, Skids, for starters, Montilla wants to blow me away. Doesn't know whether to do it himself or pay someone to do it for him."

Bedlam, slouched nonchalantly against the driver's door while he weaved the unit through the downtown traffic, gave a little belch, and said, "Decisions, decisions."

"Tell you the truth, Skids," said J.B. quietly, looking at his partner, "I can understand his motivations." He paused. "I *did* kill his father." Skids was silent. Richards went on. "Looks like Montilla has got himself a big one coming up this weekend, and this may be the one that somehow will involve Ted. It's a grass run to and from Bimini, but there's cocaine underneath, coming from two separate sources. Whatever we have to say about the guy, he gets credit for dreaming up some pretty complicated deals."

Bedlam turned into a side street and parked against the

curb. A heavily made-up and formally dressed old woman walked by on high heels, being led by a tiny and extremely nervous white poodle with pink ribbons. The little dog sniffed the front tire of the police car, but decided against it, and they moved on.

"Are you gonna call in the cavalry on this thing?" asked Skids. "Advise the major and get the narcs and the staties and the Feds and the Boy Scouts together for a combined attack here?" His face got serious. "What about the home scene, J.B.? Since this is turning into quite the personal situation between you and this asshole, don't you think you're vulnerable? Shouldn't you have some guys watching your house, your family? And you're gonna let this Silky chick go *back* to the asshole so she can get info for us? Are you gonna play this by the book . . . or what?"

Richards looked over at his friend, his face tight, and said grimly, "I'm afraid it's going to have to be 'or what,' okay? You think this is easy for me? Crap." He looked away, and they were both silent until he went on. "Look . . . operationally I've got to have Silky next to Montilla until it goes down. I don't like it, but if I pull her now it will spook him for sure . . . also . . . she insisted, she *wants* to do it, and I'm not even sure I could persuade her to run anyway." He pinched the bridge of his nose, and Skids saw how tired he looked. "Skids, you know how I am about my family . . . hell, I still haven't really opened up to all of the kids about this whole thing with Ted. I've *always* tried to shield them from this sewer we work in . . . and yes, I know how vulnerable I am because of them in this case. *But* . . . my feelings are that at this point it would be too soon to call for the cavalry to come in and surround my home. We'd have to call in the brass, everyone would get involved, and I just can't have that yet. For now, with Silky in place, I think I can safely monitor Montilla's direction . . . hell, as it is now, when I'm not working *him*, I'm at home, and I'd be there if something went down." He looked down into his lap. "I hope." The few seconds of strained silence were broken when he sighed and went on. "Remember the leak? Remember our suspicions? The whole time you and I and every other cop around here had anything going against Montilla, guess where he got the word from?" He was angry now, punching his right fist into his left palm. Bedlam just sat back and waited. "Good ol' Lieutenant Billy Erricks, OCB, FLPD. That son of a bitch."

Bedlam studied his nails for a moment. "Just fits his personality, if you ask me. Well, I guess that negates any ideas we might have of working this case with the brass. I think we should take care of it ourselves anyhow."

"Hey, what's this 'we' stuff? Hell, your career is already looking as bleak as mine."

Skids turned in his seat, placed both of his hands on his stomach, looked at J.B. with his glaring red eyes, and said, "Do you actually think for one minute I would let you go off after this asshole and not get involved? You dumb shit. From what we already know about this deal it's gonna be big, and spread out, and there's gonna be stuff happening all over the place. One guy just ain't gonna be able to do it. You are crazy if you don't think Zaden and Maguire and Fat Harry—and even that Buchanan guy—have some right to be a part of this. And me. I am *in*. Got it?"

J.B. nodded, his eyes far away. "Yep . . . you're just as stupid as I am." He grinned. "Somebody will have to eyeball Montilla's place, and help Silky get out after he goes for the run. He might leave someone there with her to watch her while he's gone. Then again, he might be ready to waste her too. He's got to be getting paranoid by now, with all the shit he's got goin'. She says the skunk's got it set up for the weekend. Maybe he'll leave on Friday. Lots of recreational boating going on during the weekend, as usual, so his boats will blend in with the crowds." He began lightly punching the dash of the unit with one big fist. "I'd like to work it so I could be out there, on the water, when he comes in with the load." He became very still. "Maybe he'll have Ted with him then. If not, I'll speak with him privately for a few minutes. And then I'll *know* where Ted is."

Skids was quiet for a few seconds, and then said, "'Course, you don't have a boat anymore since you and the fattest of Harrys were so unceremoniously kicked out of the harbor unit. But then, knowing you, you'll probably steal one."

They looked at each other, and smiles broke their faces.

"Ah yes," said J.B. "Great minds *do* think alike."

TWENTY

Ted woke up very groggy and with a severe headache. His mouth felt dry and his tongue felt as if it were wrapped in cotton.

He lay on his back on a bed, looking up at a plaster ceiling, cracked and water-stained here and there. He carefully moved his head, letting his eyes wander over the room. It was small, with one doorway that he guessed would be a bathroom. There were windows behind him, shaded, and an old clattering wall air conditioner across from him. On the wall to his left was a large framed print of a mountain and a lake and a hunting dog. It was dull and lifeless, as was the room. The bed he lay on was covered with a dingy, threadbare spread, and to his right, beside the bathroom door, was a small glass and iron table and chair set. The carpet was dark beige, tough and cheap, with stains and cigarette burns spotting it.

Charming, he thought.

He sat up slowly, thought he might vomit, then swung his legs over the edge of the bed. He looked at his right leg. It didn't hurt but still looked bad, scarred and discolored. Oh, well, he thought, at least it's still there.

He stood up, using his hands to help push him off the bed. The room swayed and he closed his eyes, felt sick, and quickly opened them. He moved awkwardly to the windows, feeling pain in his leg now, and moved the shade aside to look out. Nothing. The windows were apparently covered with something on the outside, light paper or some other material. Great. He went into the bathroom, saw two or three stringy towels, a bar of soap, and some throwaway toilet articles. He unzipped his pants, and standing at the bowl, relieved himself as he stared at the small, opaque bathroom window. All he could see through it was some sort of metal security screen. He washed his face, toweled off, and began to feel better. He went back into the main room and tried the door. It was locked.

He sat down in one of the straight-backed chairs to the table and tried to put together what had happened.

He had been in the back of the covered truck for over an hour. The ride was hot and bumpy again, but this time only the stern-faced and silent guard shared it. When the truck had finally stopped, the gate was let down, the canvas was lifted, and as two more men climbed in he had seen a glimpse of the ocean, close by. Outside the canvas he could hear the sounds of work going on, engines running, men talking, gulls shrieking. Gulls? He remembered trying to see more, then being grabbed by the guard who had ridden with him and one of the others. He saw the needle coming and had tried to struggle away, but the third man jabbed it into his upper arm, and he felt the burn as the drug was forced into his bloodstream.

The last clear image he had was that of the lean man in the dark suit, watching him patiently.

He turned in the chair now, stretching his arms overhead and twisting his torso back and forth. It felt good to move. He remembered fighting the drug, and losing, and then the rest was just fragmented images of being moved, carried, covered, strapped down. Again movement, again strange smells and feelings and sounds. Again the sickening and continuous motion. He rubbed his temples with his fingertips, feeling the headache easing. He would bet money that he had gone for another boat ride.

Where to this time . . . oh Lord, where to this time? He thought of the girl, Carmelita. What had happened to her? Had that last night been real? Was there more to her than just nurse and caretaker? Of course. Nothing that was hap-

So, my friend, he thought. Now you are so close to home. You have to enjoy one more boat ride, awake this time but still a prisoner. And then you will once again see your Fort Lauderdale.

He sighed.

I hope your last view of that lovely city is a good one, mi amigo.

In the organized crime unit office Lieutenant Billy Erricks sat alone, thinking.

The confused, intense, terrifying thought that had been running around in his head for the last several days, keeping him awake at night, making him irritable during the day, had finally solidified into a decision. It was a decision he was curiously proud of, although it scared him a little.

He shook his head, remembering how easy it had been at first.

Hell, he was one of the first people to have any good info on Onyx Montilla. He could have nailed him easily. He tried to remember what had been on his mind the first day he had approached Montilla and suggested they talk. Was it the divorce? Probably part of it. He sighed, thinking of trying to make it on his salary, which the average citizen might not think was too bad, considering he was "brass" and all. But the alimony and child support and two house payments and all the rest of it added up fast.

He had been on the verge of running away, close to just walking away from the whole mess and forgetting he was ever anything or anybody. But then that crazy idea formed in his mind. Like all cops, he had seen too many bad guys walk when it came to court time, especially the drug smugglers. They could afford the best attorneys, and those attorneys could get information on the state's case against their client through "rights of discovery," information that might show weaknesses in the case that could be worked to get the client off. He knew that the dopers spent huge sums trying to discover what the cops knew. They had to have that information to keep on playing the game. And then Montilla was standing there right in front of him, and he had enough to burn Montilla. But he knew Montilla's attorney would probably get him off anyway. And if Montilla had to pay a lawyer, why not pay him instead?

He remembered how Montilla had jumped at the chance, and how funny he felt the first time he took the money. It hadn't taken him or Montilla long to realize that after the first time he, Erricks, was trapped. Montilla had him, and the money had him.

He had tried to relax and enjoy it, and for a while it worked. He admitted to himself that he liked being able to call up his first wife and offer to help if there were any financial problems. It made him feel good to be able to buy things for his daughters, including her orthodontia. He smiled as he thought the money hadn't hurt his social life either, though of course he had to be careful. Sure, he bought a Corvette, but it wasn't a new one, and he had made a lot of noise about how hard it had been to finance it through the credit union. He was able to date more often and go to better places and buy little gifts for no reason, and it was great. Of course, there was no way he could join any of the more exclusive clubs or invest the money openly or really wield the money power he would have liked, but it wasn't too bad.

At first.

Then, slowly, things began to change. Either he imagined it or people started taking more of an interest in his life. It seemed to him that he was always answering questions about where he went to dinner, or wasn't he seen at the so-and-so with some totally unreal lady. Or, "What did you do, rob a bank?" every time he went anywhere in the Corvette. He started to get more and more paranoid about the people he worked with, listening to every tone and inflection in their voices, watching their eyes, searching for some hidden accusation or suspicion.

Then there was Montilla himself

The guy was definitely losing it. He was getting absolutely crazy and he was going to fall, and when he fell it was going to be a big tumble. Erricks looked down and saw that this knuckles were white where he gripped the arms of his chair. This stuff lately with the Polaroid shots of his ex-wife and one of his daughters in front of the house . . .

no question what Montilla was saying there. Then there was the mounting evidence that Ted Novak was working something connected to Montilla when he disappeared. Was he, Erricks, working for a cop killer? And now this noise about Richards, about actually killing Richards if the waterway cop couldn't be made to get off Montilla's case some other way. Could he sit there and do nothing while Montilla killed another cop?

Erricks looked around the room at the walls of his office. The plaques, the citations, the photos of him on the Harley-Davidson, of him with some guys in patrol, him getting his sergeant's badge a couple of years ago. What had happened? He had been a street cop, had been out there with partners, had been liked. He remembered hearing that he had "changed" after he was promoted to lieutenant, but so what? They said that about a lot of the good guys. He looked around the room and reflected on it. He had been a cop, he was still a cop, and there was no way he could be any part of a cop killing.

He sighed and looked down at his hands.

He thought of what would happen if we went in and told the whole story. He would be fired, certainly. He would go to jail, almost positively. And he would definitely be humiliated and scorned in front of everybody, including his daughters. There was no way he could, or would, sacrifice himself. He would resign, he would leave, take the money he had left from all the fun and games and go off somewhere and start all over again. Hell, Montilla was probably mostly talk anyway. He was too busy worrying about smuggling dope to worry about Richards, who should be out of the picture now because of the transfer.

Erricks sat back in his chair and tapped a pencil on the desk blotter. He'd stay around through this weekend so as not to spook Montilla, and then he'd resign and disappear. After that it would be every man for himself.

Onyx Montilla sat alone in the Florida room of his house, looking out across the backyard to the canal. There was no boat tied up to the dock and he scowled when he thought of it sitting high and dry somewhere in police custody. Stupid lawyer was taking too long in getting it back for him. He heard the dishes rattle in the sink and thought of Silky in the kitchen. She had been quiet today, and compliant. He sensed a change in her but couldn't quite define it. He had taken her to bed in the afternoon. He had returned from his meeting with "Pete," the guy who was going to buy the cocaine from him. The meeting had gone well. Pete was anxious and seemed flexible. He was already asking if there would be more in the future.

Montilla smiled grimly. Yeah, my friend, there sure as hell would be more. He wasn't totally satisfied with the arrangements he and Pete had made for the exchange at the hotel, but he could work on that later.

He thought again of this afternoon, when he had taken Silky to bed. It had been good for him, but he had felt a difference this time, almost as if she were waiting patiently. Waiting for what? He took a sip of Scotch from the glass at his side and put it down. Well, whatever it was, he wouldn't have to worry about it much longer. Silky had to go, permanently. He'd take her with him on this run and no one would ever see her again. No problem.

His face darkened and he took another drink. There was a problem, though, with that cop. That cop had to die, too, and it had to be soon. He thought of what Maximiliano had told him about that Ted guy. All right, first Ted gets killed —*for sure* this time—in your face, Richards. I hope it twists your fucking guts. Then, after this crazy weekend is finished, *you* go, big guy. He rubbed his chin, his fingers cutting through his beard. Hell, he could afford to make a contact in Miami, one of the old street players he used to run with maybe, a real pro by now. Get one of those guys to take care of it, nice and clean. Spend a few bucks and another cop gets blown away. Hell, be doing the community a favor. He thought of that T-shirt he had seen once in St. Croix: "There is a sleeping policeman in each of us."

He must be found, and killed.

He smiled, dreaming of seeing the evening news about how some veteran local cop got himself blown away coming out of a restaurant after having another free meal.

But the more he thought about it, the less intense it

seemed. He should do it himself. He should spend a few bucks, get the right equipment, maybe a high-powered rifle with a good scope. Nah, maybe it would be better up close, so Richards could see him, could know who did it, and he, Montilla, could watch the big man's eyes as he died. Maybe a nice solid twelve-gauge pump shotgun, up close and personal, blow a hole as big as his fist in that shiny tin badge. Yeah. That would show some class. No way they'd ever make *him* on it, but the street would know. The street would know it was Onyx Montilla's hit.

He took another drink and sat back grinning. First we do that Ted guy . . . one more time. That stupid Erricks probably thinks I'm bullshitting him about killing a cop.

Madre de Dios, is he ever wrong.

Having made the decision to stay with it through the weekend, Lieutenant Billy Erricks was ready to go through the motions during another routine workday. He was still nervous, but at least he had gone over it in his mind and felt he knew where he stood.

The organized crime offices were almost empty, except for a couple of secretaries and the equipment aide. The day shift was usually pretty quiet. It was the later shifts, when the sun went down, that saw the action. Narcs, like other nocturnal animals, felt uncomfortable in the glare of the sun.

As Erricks looked out of his office door he saw Scott Kelly standing at a desk he shared with another narc. Erricks wondered what the veteran narc was doing there at this time of day. As far as the lieutenant knew, Kelly was working up a case against a small group of Davie-area businessmen who were trying to set up a deal with the Seminole Indians. The Davie businessmen wanted to bring an airplane carrying cocaine into a small strip somewhere on the Seminole reservation, where local, state, and federal law enforcement efforts could sometimes be avoided. The town of Davie was still very Western—ranchers and feed barns, saddle shops and boot stores. It was not uncommon to see horses being ridden right downtown, and every year there was a big Western parade and at least one rodeo.

Erricks thought about the deal that Kelly was working with the Davie businessmen and the Seminoles . . . cowboys and Indians and cocaine.

He decided to get a cold drink from the lounge, and on the way by check with Kelly to see how things were going. As he left his office he saw Kelly turning over some papers in a file on his desk.

Kelly, absorbed in his reading, did not see the lieutenant walking his way, but he did hear a little squeal of dismay coming from the front door to the offices, and looked up to see one of the young secretaries coming in the door. The girl had managed to turn the doorknob with one burdened hand and then push the door open with her foot. She had then side-slipped through, carrying a huge pile of files, and now that huge pile was leaning forward, slipping faster and faster away from her grasp, preparing to scatter all over the office floor. Scott Kelly took it all in with a glance and quickly moved toward the girl, just getting there and reaching out in time to stop the slide. Then he and the secretary, laughing, tried to keep the mess balanced while they made their way to the nearest desk.

Erricks had seen the situation too, observed that he was too far away to help, and kept moving toward the lounge. As he passed the desk where Kelly had been standing, he glanced down at the file, expecting to see papers pertaining to the cowboys or the Indians.

Instead his eyes were seared by the handwritten names inked onto the page.

Montilla . . . dead attorney.

Dead attorney . . . Novak.

Novak . . . Montilla?

Sam Golden . . . Silky . . . Montilla (Golden-Montilla?)

Sam Golden . . . Kolin . . . Montilla.

Yellow Scarab . . . *Sausea Girl* . . . Arnold Brukker.

Montilla . . . Novak?

Montilla . . .

Scott Kelly's hand cut across the lieutenant's vision and slowly closed the file.

Erricks looked up into the veteran narc's eyes, hesitant, reluctant to see what would be there, waiting for him. Erricks knew that Scott Kelly did not think much of him as an organized crime cop, and he knew Kelly was aware that he, Erricks, had been one of the loudest voices keeping Kelly out of his old job when he had recovered from the wounds that had taken him out. Kelly had been reassigned to OCB over Erricks's protestations, somehow knowing that Erricks fought him simply as a result of the deep-seated resentment and envy that administrators sometimes develop against street cops who are respected because they are real.

Now Scott Kelly stood there staring at him, and Erricks was very still. He could feel the intensity of the narc's stare. His hard eyes held the lieutenant's, and in a very soft voice he said, "You don't have to read this file, do you, Erricks?"

Lieutenant Billy Erricks backed away from Kelly, his eyes wide, his lips dry. He suddenly felt stripped naked, exposed for all the world to see. He knew it was irrational, he knew his own paranoia was intensifying Kelly's implied accusation, but all of his fears overtook him and he was overwhelmed by them.

He said nothing as he backed away from the desk and slowly turned his back on the narc. He could feel the narc's stare as he walked toward his office. He moved on numb feet, stepped inside the office, and closed the door. Still, he could feel the stare. He leaned against the door, and took several deep breaths. Think . . . think now.

How much did they know? How far along was the investigation? Did they have him yet? His name wasn't on that list.

He sat down at his desk and made a phone call. When he left his office twenty minutes later, Kelly was gone.

It was a short meeting.

The major, incredulous, mystified, accepted Bill Erricks's typed resignation from the Fort Lauderdale Police Department. The three-line letter said "personal reasons." What personal reason? The major did not ask, and Erricks did not offer to tell. Erricks was brisk and businesslike, but strangely subdued, brushing aside the major's offer of "any

kind of assistance" with a shake of his head. Erricks told
the major he would be clearing out his office that day and
would begin two weeks vacation immediately. He would
take care of the administrative matters with personnel and
the city during that time. When he was done, there was a
strained and painful silence, Erricks sitting in front of the
major's desk, his face flushed, his eyes on the floor. The
major sat looking at him in confused amazement.

The room was filled with many unanswered questions.

Erricks suddenly stood, as did the major, and reached
out to take the major's hand. They shook strongly, the
major willing Erricks to look at him, but the lieutenant
avoided his eyes. Without another word Erricks turned and
walked out the door.

The major watched him go, then looked down and read
the letter of immediate resignation again. He sat down
slowly, staring at the letter until he noticed his secretary
standing in the doorway with a puzzled look on her face.
He looked at her and saw the tears forming in the corners
of her eyes.

He rubbed his forehead with one hand, reached for a
cigar, and said quietly, "Well, Christ Almighty."

As Richards drove home through the evening traffic he
was uneasy. There were too many things hanging. This
whole case was about to turn into a monster and he didn't
feel as if he had control. He was worried about the girl. He
berated himself for ever letting her go back to Montilla's
place, even though she had insisted, but then reminded
himself that if she hadn't gone back Montilla would have
called off the deal for this weekend for sure. He had to let
her go back, but he would feel a lot better when Montilla
sailed away and left her at the house so Skids could get her
out of there. She said she thought they would leave on
Friday. She would call and tell him if she could get to a
phone unobserved. If not, Bedlam had been able to wran-
gle a day off from Witless Whitney in exchange for some
of the "comp" time he had built up. That would be Friday,
and Skids would watch the house all day. He'd know when
Montilla split. Then, because they were both senior men,

they both had the weekend off so they could spend some time with their families. Not this weekend, thought J.B.

He and Skids would be ready for the weekend.

He still had to get in touch with Fat Harry and Zaden and Maguire. Then they could put it together. He should be hearing from Scott Kelly soon too—and Buchanan. His face darkened when he thought of the CIA agent. Will Buchanan play it our way? Does he have some other plans for all of us? Are we stupidly playing what we think is our game, while he uses all of us for one of *his?*

He thought about his family, about Kathleen. He thought about Ted, alive somewhere, and he thought about Silky in that house with Onyx Montilla. As he pulled into his driveway and shut off the engine he said quietly, "God, I hope I did the right thing."

It was Thursday evening, and Silky and Onyx had finished their dinner and were having coffee in the living room. Montilla waited until Silky was seated beside him on the couch before he reached over, picked up the phone, and called the young captain on the *Spirit*. Silky, feigning indifference, listened closely to the conversation.

"Hey, my man, how's it hangin'? Yeah, yeah . . . I just wanted to give you the word on when we're leaving. Did you catch the weather report on tonight's news? Yeah, I know, it looks like it could get a little sloppy out there. Anyway, listen . . . how about we make it for eight o'clock Saturday morning? Eight o'clock Saturday. That should be real fine, give us plenty of time to do the whole gig, with lots of weekend traffic to mingle with. Okay, I'll be talking to you then."

Silky, scanning the *TV Guide*, looked up at Onyx and smiled. He made a silent toast to her with his coffee, stood up, and said, "I'm gonna grab a shower and change clothes. Maybe after a bit we can go out and have a couple of drinks or somethin' if you feel like it, okay?" He knew he would have a visitor standing quietly on his dock, out back, later, but for now he wanted the girl to feel relaxed and happy.

Silky smiled and nodded and watched him as he walked

off into the bedroom area. She waited patiently until she
heard the shower running, made sure he was in it, and then
ran to the phone in the kitchen.

Erin Richards was sitting at the kitchen table staring
balefully at the pile of homework in front of her. It galled
her to be wasting precious time on this stupid homework
when she could be using it to do her nails, wash her hair,
and deciding what she would wear to school the next day.
She sighed and looked at the clock. Her parents had gone
out for a quick dinner, which she thought was neat—her
mom and dad dressed up and going out together. Kathleen
was in her room reading, and Ricky was out in the garage,
trying to reassemble the pieces of his dirt bike. Before she
could begin to concentrate on the homework the phone
rang and her arm flew out as if spring-loaded and snatched
the receiver off the wall.

"Hello?"

"Hello . . . is Officer Richards there?"

"No, he isn't, he's out for the evening. Who's calling,
please?"

"Could you take a message for me? It's very important,
J.B. *must* get it."

"Sure, go ahead."

"Okay. Would you tell J.B. that Chica called, and to
make it on Saturday morning instead of Friday. That's Saturday morning around eight instead of Friday . . . all right?"

"Uh-huh. And your name is Chica? And this is for my
dad?"

"Yes, that's right. It's very important to him and to me,
so please make sure you pass it on. Thanks. Bye-bye."

Erin hung up the phone and stared at it. The voice had
been that of a young girl, well, younger than Mom anyway. She sounded nice and she spoke of Dad as if she
knew him.

Who was it?

It certainly wasn't anyone from Dad's work. Even when
one of the women from there called they sounded like
policemen. No, this was just a girl, and she even *sounded*
pretty. Chica indeed, and the message was important.

Hmmmm, Erin did not like what she was thinking. *Wonder if Mom knows about this? Wonder if I should tell her?* What about Kath . . . nah. *Wonder if I should confront Dad —to get his reaction?* She did not like the sound of this at all.

She got up from the kitchen table and began pacing back and forth, a frown on her face. Ricky walked into the room, covered with grease. As he gingerly tried to open the refrigerator door without smudging it he looked at Erin and asked, "Who was that on the phone?"

Erin just looked at him and snapped, "Nobody."

Ricky reached into the refrigerator and pulled out a can of juice using only his thumb and the side of his index finger. "Well, did they leave a message, or what?"

Erin put her hands on her hips, shook out her hair, and said briskly, "Just mind your own business, okay? Some things go around this house that you don't need to know about." Then she turned and walked out of the kitchen, through the living room, and into her bedroom, slamming the door behind her.

Ricky ripped the pull-tab off the top of the juice can, made a face, and said, "Well. Excuuuuuuse *me!*"

The captain on the *Spirit*, located in the small marina off State Road 84, pulled on his shoes and got ready to notify the men on the other Striker so they would be ready for the switch. Montilla had previously told him that when he got the call with the departure time he should move the boats, exchanging their dock space. For some reason Montilla wanted *Spirit* at the marina in Dania, and *Ghost* out of 84. The captain thought that moving the boats back and forth made no sense at all, but hell, he just did what he was told and collected his pay.

He thought about the call now. Montilla had said eight o'clock Saturday morning. Based on the code they always used when talking times and dates on the telephone, he mentally subtracted twelve to fourteen hours from the time Montilla had said. That would be the real time. Montilla had said Saturday at eight, which meant he and the other crew had to be ready to go between six and eight in the evening on Friday.

J.B. left his house early Friday morning feeling edgy. The first thing he noticed was that the wind had picked up out of the southeast, and it was one of those cloudy gray days that are somehow hot, windy, and rain-threatening all at the same time. Being a boat person, he knew that the ocean inshore would be getting a little dirty, probably three to five feet, with chop, and out in the Gulf Stream it would get bigger. As he started his truck and headed east toward the water, he reminded himself that nature can still make or break your whole day.

He didn't even have to pull off the highway to check on the fifty-four Striker called *Spirit*. As he reached the top of the old bridge over the south fork of the New River he could look down and to his left and see her there, looking somehow just as gray and sinister as the weather. He gave her another glance on his way down the bridge, noticed no one moving about on her, and thought, Man, is she lovely.

When he got down to Dania he drove past the big jai alai building, turned left on a small paved road, and bumped slowly down into a dirt parking lot fronting another old, tiny marina. He scanned the dozen or so yachts tied to the docks and saw *Ghost* sitting nicely in the middle of the pack. Again he saw no movement aboard so he just swung the truck in a circle and drove off toward Las Olas Boulevard.

He drove slowly by the palm-lined isle twice before he saw the figure of Skids Bedlam walking easily up the street toward Las Olas. He swung the truck around, pulled alongside, waited as Skids hopped in, then drove off toward the beach.

"Good morning, partner. How's it look so far?"

"Well, J.B., you were right about that house with the big trees in the yard. The owners are out of town, and I've got my car under the largest tree in the shade. I can keep a good line of sight on Montilla's place without sticking out like a nun at the Crazy Horse Saloon. In fact, I can even see part of the canal behind the place, so I should be able to pick up any boats coming or going. You gonna be listening for me on our regular channel? I'll just ask the dispatcher to have you go over to records channel if I have to talk. If you don't hear from me, then there's nothin' goin' on, okay?"

Richards had turned back toward Montilla's isle, and as he slowed to let Skids out again, he said, "I'll be listening, and I'll come by again if I get a chance."

Bedlam jumped out and made his careful way back to the stakeout. J.B. hurried to the station so that he could change into his uniform in time for early briefing. He still had a lot to do today and he wanted it to go right. A gust of wind blew some leaves across the road in front of him and he looked up into the gray clouds again and shook his head.

After the briefing, Richards went immediately to the write-up room to phone Fat Harry over in the court liaison office. In order to insure having a couple of hours away from the public, the brass, and the dispatcher, J.B. called his former partner, Harry, who would call the dispatcher with the news that Officer Richards would be required in court on this Friday morning and that the case might go to trial, so Office Richards would be unavailable for any radio calls until he advised he was again ten-eight.

A few minutes later, when J.B. did advise he was ready for duty, the dispatcher directed him to report to the court liaison office, and to advise her when he was clear from there.

He was then free to take care of the business at hand.

He had told Harry to meet him at the U.S. Customs office as soon as possible, knowing that once the morning rush of business was over it was possible for Harry to slip away for a while. He knew Harry usually spent this free time in a little restaurant down the street from the courthouse, flirting with the waitresses, harassing young lawyers, and enjoying his second large breakfast of the day. As J.B. headed for the habor patrol office, he smiled, thinking it probably wouldn't hurt ol' Harry to miss one breakfast once in a while.

Richards parked his unit in the lot on the east side of the

Customs office and climbed out. Mike Kendall grinned and waved one greasy arm at him from the engine compartment on one of the police boats, which was up on blocks at the end of the lot. The front door to the building opened and Liz Fox stepped out, opened the mailbox on the wall, and saw J.B. walking toward the Customs stairs. She smiled and waved, and called out, "Come over for a cup of coffee later if you have a few minutes, J.B. Love to visit with you." He waved and she went back inside.

He had decided not to tell Liz or Mike about the upcoming weekend until after it went down. He would need their help then, and he knew they would give it, but he wanted to shield them from the flack that would surely come if things fell apart. It was better that they did not know what he had planned.

He sighed and began walking up the wooden steps alongside the building leading to the side door. Suddenly he was attacked by an orange blur that reached out with small, quick paws from behind a railing post. A couple of clawless swipes at his pant leg and she was gone. Then she was back, between his legs and down the steps, then back again, rubbing herself against him and purring softly. He bent down and gently lifted her up, saying, "Well, if it isn't that wonderful Salty-girl, still the prettiest girl around here, huh?" She looked at him with an expression that said, "Of course," and when he put her down again she proceeded him up the steps and waited for him to open the door.

He knocked twice, didn't wait for a reply, and walked in.

Hank Zaden was sitting at his desk, working on a report. Reggie Maguire was leaning back in his chair holding a cup of coffee in one hand and a bagel in the other. Maguire looked at J.B. standing there with Salty rubbing between his legs, turned to his partner, and said around a mouthful of bagel, "See? I told you J.B. wasn't above getting a little strange pussy when he could."

The big Customs man just looked at his curly-haired partner and grunted. "Hey, J.B., good to see you, man.

Grab some coffee and ignore my partner; he's still all screwed up."

Richards headed for the coffeepot and Salty jumped onto Maguire's lap. He began feeding her small pieces of bagel and said to the cat's face, "Let me tell you something, lady. I had another red-haired girl who used to eat out of my hand too, but her legs were more hairy than yours."

They sat and shot the breeze for a few moments, catching up on the latest gossip and stories and dirt that always floated around the police community.

"Did you guys hear about who they finally nailed down in Monroe County last week?" Or, "Yeah, I hear he's gettin' divorced again. Saw him the other night with some chick that was a fox but looked like she was all of sixteen." Or, "Man, a couple of those heroes from brand-X almost got themselves wasted by some Dade Public Safety guys the other night. Everybody trying to make a bust on a big coke deal and they're all cops. Twelve cops all pointing their nine millimeters at each other and screaming 'Halt, motherfucker!' Damn DEA never tells anybody what it's doin'."

Finally they all turned and looked at Fat Harry as he walked into the side door carrying two paper bags. They all knew immediately that one had the coffee, the other the doughnuts.

J.B. briefed them on what he had learned from the girl and what he planned to do about it. They were quiet as he spoke, nodding their heads. When he told them about Lieutenant Billy Erricks, Zaden just grunted and shook his head. Maguire said, "Shit."

Harry chewed his doughnut and said, "So that explains what I heard this morning." Everybody looked at him, so he went on. "Yeah, the major's secretary is bosom buddies with our girl over in the liaison office. She told our girl this morning that Erricks suddenly resigned yesterday. They haven't been able to reach him at his place. Nobody knows where he is."

Richards, who had been leaning against a desk, began pacing back and forth in the center of the room. "Dammit," he said, "I hope he hasn't told Montilla. From what the girl said Montilla is paranoid as hell about this weekend already. Maybe just the fact that he can't reach Erricks will spook him."

Zaden stretched his arms over his head, fingers splayed, and said easily, "Hell, J.B., maybe they had a deal where Montilla wouldn't hear from Erricks unless there was a problem concerning the operation. Besides, you've got that red-eyed wild man on Montilla's place. We'll know soon enough if he starts acting hinky."

Maguire nodded and added, "Yeah, J.B. Don't give yourself an ulcer worrying about maybes. You've got good info here and it looks like we've got a real chance to nail this asshole. Hank and I will stay on standby today, and we'll be ready for the weekend. You just keep us posted and we'll work with you any way you want."

Richards looked at the two of them, so different, yet so much the same. This was why he liked working with them —no bullshit.

"Okay," he said, "you guys still have that source on Bimini who might be able to tell us when those two Strikers arrive there, right?"

Zaden and Maguire both nodded, and J.B. went on. "And you have the Magnum up and running for this weekend?" Again the nods.

Richards looked at Fat Harry and said, "Okay, Harry, here it is. Once we know the Strikers are over there, we'll get ready to borrow a boat from the city. Then we have two boats out there, either outside or in the port when they come home—Hank and Reggie in their Customs Magnum with twin three-fifties . . ." he gave his partner a wry look ". . . and you and me in our twenty-two-foot police rollerskate, with its one tired three-fifty and chewed-up prop, courtesy of the city of Fort Lauderdale."

Harry smiled and Zaden asked, "Hey, J.B., I know they're shorthanded in the harbor unit, and I know guys are on vacation and stuff so there probably won't be anyone around over the weekend, especially in the evening. And I know that the police boat keys just hang in a cabinet over there, but the place will be locked tight. How are you guys gonna get one of those police boats for your very own?"

Harry and J.B. both smiled as they picked one key from their key rings and held them up with their fingers. Harry said around a mouthful of cream-filled doughnut, "Oops . . . looks like we forgot to turn in our keys when we were transferred out."

They talked for a few more minutes, solidified arrangements, and then broke it up. Harry grabbed the remaining doughnuts and headed back to his office. J.B. carried Salty down the steps, petted her a moment, then got into his unit and headed for the station.

He still needed to meet with Scott Kelly and talk with one more person before it went down.

The first thing Richards saw when he walked into the office was a pair of shiny black cowboy boots up on the desk. Lieutenant Jed Tallert was leaning back in his chair, reading a report. He smiled at Richards, pulled off his reading glasses, and rubbed his nose.

"Hey there, J.B., how the hell are ya doin'? Haven't heard nothin' bad about you in days." He grinned. "You all right?"

Richards grinned back, comfortable with the lieutenant who still acted like a cop. He turned and closed the lieutenant's door.

"Need to talk with you for a minute, sir. Okay?"

Tallert put his glasses back on, pulled his feet down, sat up, and said, "Shoot."

J.B., hesitant at first, began slowly. "This is gonna sound really stupid, Lieutenant, but I'm here to ask you— kind of alert you actually—that before this weekend is over I will probably need some backing from a friend in a high place. I'm hoping it will be you. Actually there's no one else, and you know it."

He held up his hand as the lieutenant's eyes widened. "Wait, please. Let me go on. I'm not going to break the law or anything like that, I'm just going to have to get involved in something that I've been told to leave alone. It's heavy, and it's very important to me. I've done a lot of thinking about it and I know I'm doing the right thing. The problem is, no matter how it turns out, good or bad, I'm gonna have my tit in the wringer again." He crossed his big arms across his chest and smiled at the lieutenant. "Besides, sir, you've got more experience defending my butt than anyone around here."

Tallert turned his chair so he was facing the wall. He made a steeple of his fingers, looked up at the ceiling, and said quietly, "Two weird pieces of news. First, a deniable feeler came squiggling through the chief's office, a federal one. Just a whisper that an FLPD narc, Novak, might be alive, might be held by a government not sleeping with ours, and might be part of something that could go down on our streets, or in our canals. Scott Kelly's been keeping some absolutely strange gray-suited company lately, and my poor old cowboy's nose smells some strong federal manure being scattered about." He paused, pleased with the sound of all that. "Second. I guess by now you've heard of the resignation of ex-Lieutenant Erricks. He suddenly decided to pull the plug after all these years here and run off to raise chickens somewhere." He turned in his chair and looked at J.B. hard. "Seems kinda strange, don't it, the way everything seems to be coming together—or falling apart—all at once?" He made a fist, and hit it on the desktop. "Look, J.B., do what you think you have to do. Make it good, and try not to get hurt. I don't want to know nothin' about it now." He picked up the report he had been reading when Richards walked in. "Now get outta here."

Richards stood up, opened the door, and sighed. As he started out he heard the slow drawl behind him. "Oh . . . and good luck. Kick his ass if you get the chance. And boy, you better hope that this friend in a high place has got enough brass to keep you from swinging from the nearest flagpole."

Richards smiled and stepped into the hallway. As he turned to walk away he heard the lieutenant mutter, "Crazy Yankee cops come down here and just don't know when to quit."

TWENTY-ONE

When J.B. left the station he advised the dispatcher he was finished with court and back on the road. After being chewed out on the records channel by Lieutenant Whitney for not keeping him informed of his court requirements, J.B. went back to his regular road patrol duties, riding solo because his partner, Bedlam, was off "taking a comp day."

He spent a fairly routine day, answering calls and handling a couple of minor fender benders because of the rain. He kept one ear to the radio, hoping to hear from Skids, and he developed a gnawing worry because he had not heard from the girl since the other day in the park.

She should have called by now.

Even if he wasn't home when she called he knew there should have been somebody around the phone to take a message. By the end of his shift he was more than a little concerned, thinking of a hundred different ways of handling it and hoping that Montilla wouldn't get spooked and call it off.

The weather just got worse, and that only worried him more. What if Montilla postponed until the seas calmed down? What if another week went by?

No way.

He just had a gut feeling that Montilla would go for it now, this weekend. Montilla wanted it bad, the girl had said. Damn. The girl. He wished now he had not let her go back. He wished Skids had her and she was safe. He wished he could just think of her as any other informant, out there in the land of the bad guys, taking her chances like the rest of them.

Dammit . . . why didn't she call?

When he finished the shift he changed quickly and drove his truck out onto Las Olas Boulevard again. After one pass he picked up Bedlam and they drove a little way down the street.

Bedlam ran his hands across his thinning hair and said, "Well J.B., it's been pretty quiet all day. I watched Montilla go out once. He was alone and wearing street clothes. He was gone about an hour, came back, and that's the last I've seen of him. Nothin' else . . . no boats, no cars, until about ten minutes ago when a cab dropped a guy off in front of the place. A real grease ball. He went right inside. Carried a small bag, like an overnight bag, with him, and I'll tell ya, you could take one look at this guy from one hundred yards away and know he was a player, just absolutely dirty. Walked like he might have been carrying a gun under his shirt too. Thing is, he didn't really look . . . boatish, if you know what I mean. Looked like he would be a lot more comfortable working the street than cruisin' the islands on some yacht. Don't think he's the money either—too young and a bit lightweight. The only thing I can figure is maybe he's somebody Montilla uses to watch the girl while he's out on the high seas."

Richards made a U-turn and headed back to Montilla's isle.

"Silky told me that the money guy had a young hood with him all the time, like a bodyguard or something. I think you're probably right about him being there to watch her. Anyway, at least we'll know where she is when Montilla leaves. Think you can hang in there for another hour or so? Let me run back to my place and make sure the brood gets fed and my wife hasn't left me for some attorney or somethin'. Soon as I can I'll get back here and we can decide whether to spend the night. The girl said they'd be leaving either today or tomorrow morning, and since there hasn't been any activity here, and we haven't heard anything different from her, that's the way it'll probably be. We can get out here at 'O-dark-thirty' and watch them head out. Then we'll figure out a way to get her out of the house, sit back, and nail the little bastard when he comes home with the load."

Bedlam said, "Sure, sounds good to me, J.B. See you in awhile then." He jumped out of the truck and headed for his position down the street, under the tree.

J.B. drove home, his mind filled with visions of two big beautiful Striker yachts, loaded with bales of grass, cocaine, and the key to recovering Ted.

He wished he would hear from Silky.

He was home a half hour before his wife Jane trudged in from her day at work. By that time both of the girls were busy in the kitchen with the dinner that was almost ready. When J.B. handed his wife a cold glass of white wine she smiled, brushed a lock of hair off her forehead, and sat down in his big recliner. She looked at her husband, saw the creases in his brow and the way he stalked around the kitchen, checking the progress and quality of the girls' work, and asked, "Got something going on, John Brian? You look like a man waiting for a train. Look at the dogs scattered all over the place. Even they're tired of trying to keep up with your pacing."

"Yeah," he said, "I'm just waiting for the word. I might have to go out again this evening."

Kathleen was listening closely but said nothing. Jane made a face and said, "And where's Ricky, or shouldn't I ask?"

Kathleen put the salad on the table and said quietly, "He's been out in the garage ever since he came home from school. I think he's still working on that funny 'atomic bomb' project of his."

Erin, pouring iced tea, said coolly, "I'm sure."

J.B. looked at his younger daughter and said, "Erin, go tell Project Manhattan to finish up and get in here for dinner, okay?"

His daughter just looked at him and sighed, turned away, and walked toward the garage door as if the weight of the world was on her shoulders. Richards gave his wife a questioning look and she just shrugged. He looked at Kathleen, who said, "Don't look at me, Dad. She's been acting freaky since yesterday."

They were all sitting at the table, the meal just starting, when J.B. took a shot in the dark and asked, "Anybody here take any messages for me from a girl who calls herself Chica?" Kathleen looked at him sharply, but no one said anything until Erin dropped her fork on her plate loudly. She was staring at her father wide-eyed.

"Well, what's the matter with you, Erin? Did you hear from her?"

Erin stared at him and pushed her chair back. "Yes. Yes, Dad, I did hear from her. And I can't believe you would bring it up at the table—right in front of your wife and children."

As she stood up he looked at her, confused, and said, "What? I mean . . . ?"

He saw that Jane had covered her mouth with her hand and was laughing softly. Kathleen shook her head, looked at her mother, and said, "We should have told her."

Richards sat there staring as Erin marched into her room until Jane, still laughing softly, said, "You'd better go explain to her who Chica is. And while you're at it you can tell her for me that you're getting too old for that kind of stuff anyway."

He looked at his wife, slowly comprehending, and left the table. He knocked softly on his daughter's bedroom door and let himself in. He came out ten minutes later and went right to the phone. As he dialed, he said to Jane and Kathleen, "I'll only have to go to a quick meeting with Scott Kelly. Other than that things are on hold for tonight." He grinned. "Damn, just when things were getting interesting."

Erin followed behind hesitantly, obviously embarrassed. As she sat down at the table her mother leaned over, patted her on the shoulder, and said, "Don't feel bad, honey. When she called your dad last week at two in the morning he had to do a whole *lot* of talking before I was convinced." She grinned at her daughter, and laughed. "We'll keep him straight. The man hasn't got a chance."

Ricky asked, "Is Dad gonna eat that other piece of chicken?"

J.B. called Fat Harry, Zaden and Maguire at their homes and told them all: "Saturday. They leave here Saturday." Then he got his police radio, raised Skids through the dispatcher, and had him go to the records channel. When they were cleared to talk, he advised him of the same thing, using double talk, covering as if they were speaking about an extra duty detail. They made arrangements to contact each other in the morning and he went back to finish his dinner.

He felt better knowing that everything was stable and secure for the night. Skids could go home and get some rest, and they could all be ready for the weekend. The girl would be all right, too. She was with Montilla, true, but she was in Lauderdale, and she was all right.

Silky was in fact still in Lauderdale, but not for long.

Two hours after Joe's arrival at Montilla's place, and just fifteen minutes after Bedlam had received word from J.B. and had abandoned the stakeout, Montilla told Silky to put her shoes on. They were going out for dinner.

"But Onyx, I've got these old jeans and this T-shirt on. I need to change if we're going out."

As Joe walked out toward the car, carrying his bag, Montilla took her by the arm and said, "Nah, c'mon. We'll go to Dirty Ernie's place on South Federal Highway. You don't have to dress up for conch chowder and corn on the cob."

Silky didn't really feel like going out for dinner but realized what he said about Ernie's was true. Besides, maybe she could learn something else about the weekend if Onyx and Joe talked during the meal. The two seemed to be getting along easily enough so far.

As they headed south through the city in a slow drizzling rain, Montilla thought about his last orders from Maximiliano's Cuban agent. Here he was beginning the biggest cocaine run of his life, but before he could go he had to stop and pick up a stomach-bomb take-out order for the

Cuban secret police. Whatever you say, Maximiliano, he thought.

He looked over at Joe and said, "Tell you what, mi amigo. Since this weather is kicking up a little, why don't we swing down into Dania and take a look at my Striker there to see how she's riding."

Joe shrugged his shoulders. "Okay with me, Montilla."

Onyx slowed the BMW on Federal Highway and turned left before he got to the Seventeenth Street Causeway. He drove past the sign of the golden arches and pulled into the drive-through.

Silky knew that there would be a captain or crew member on the yacht all the time to check the lines, so she thought perhaps Montilla just wanted to show off his pretty boat to Joe. Now here they were placing a take-out order at a burger place. She leaned forward from the backseat and said, "A dozen cheeseburgers and large fries to go with them, Onyx? What are we doing?"

He was counting out money from his wallet and didn't look up as he said, "Boat crews will have to eat, and I don't want them leaving to go get food."

Silky still had her doubts but remained silent.

They drove past Ernie's restaurant, and past the airport, some of the renovation still going on, and made their way down into the small town of Dania. The Federal Highway was flanked by many antique shops, their windows full of odd assortments of treasures. Eventually they pulled into the small marina, got out of the car, and walked over to the dock beside the big yacht, Montilla carrying the two bags of food.

Silky got right to the dock before she saw that the boat was the *Spirit*, which had been at State Road 84. She saw the young captain but no other crew members.

"Go ahead, Joe, climb aboard," said Montilla as he waved at the captain up on the fly bridge.

Joe, liking the sound of the powerful engines, and marveling at all the shiny gear and equipment, said, "Whew, what a neat boat! Sounds like those diesels are healthy, too."

Montilla put down the bags he held, took Joe's bag, and

helped him and Silky aboard. He grinned and said, "You'd better believe it."

Silky looked at the captain on the fly bridge, waved up at him, and asked, "Onyx, why is he running the engines?"

Montilla, untying the stern line, turned his back on her and said, "He's got the engines running because we're leavin' Lauderdale tonight . . . right now."

A dozen thoughts flashed through her head as she watched him move quickly to the other lines. The boat was already easing out of the slip when she grabbed his arm, thinking, *the phone . . . I've got to get to a phone*. She said nervously, "But Onyx, I didn't know . . ."

The way he looked at her frightened her, and he said quietly, "That's right, baby, you didn't know. But here you are and we're on our way, so why don't you make yourself useful and take your tight ass down into the galley and fix us all something to eat? And I don't mean those burgers either. Just leave them alone."

She put her hand slowly to her throat and stepped back from him. "All right, Onyx."

He turned from her, jumped onto the fly bridge ladder, and called out to Joe, "Hey man, c'mon up here and take a look around."

Silky just stood there on the aft deck, watching the canal slide by as they pulled out from the marina and headed east on the Dania cutoff canal. She was still standing there when they made the turn into the Intracoastal Waterway and headed north, toward Port Everglades.

Jump . . . I should jump into the water, she thought as she looked at the last of the sunset through the clouds. But she knew if she did, and got away, that Montilla might abort the run that would leave the policeman, J.B., and his daughter standing on the dock forever waiting for the young narc, Ted. She just had to see it through.

"Hey, you stupid split-tail, get below like I said! Quit sulking. I'll take you to dinner when we get back."

She went down into the beautifully appointed main cabin, and as she worked in the galley she watched out the window and observed the turning basin of the port coming into view. As the yacht started its first lifting and rolling from the swells coming past the cut, she saw the sleek but sinister shape of their sister ship, *Ghost*, come into the basin from the north and turn east, following behind them.

An hour later they were already well out into the Gulf Stream, on a heading of 122 degrees, going for the Bimini light. Once they were beyond the inside chop, and actually into the Stream, the ride was much better. The movement of the ocean was indeed bigger, but the waves had round shoulders and they were spaced better, so both of the big sportfishermen moved steadily through the water, taking on a moderate pounding. Both captains were running the engines in the mid-range, not wanting to beat themselves to death against the large seas.

Silky had moved out onto the aft well-deck after their quick meal. She was wearing a dark windbreaker that was much too big for her, but it felt good wrapped around her body. Joe was already slightly seasick, and Montilla was up on the fly bridge with the captain, smoking a joint and shooting the breeze.

When both boats were in a trough between the waves she lost sight of the mast light at the top of the other boat's tuna tower. The black of the night and the powerful surges of the huge waves frightened her. She shuddered, but at the same time she saw an awesome beauty there. She felt surrounded by an immense force, forbidding, yet lovely. She shuddered again, and crossed her arms against her breasts, feeling like a tiny windswept speck of dust, alone in the universe.

The young captain, up on the fly bridge with Montilla, checked to see how his sister yacht was running, checked his course on the big red-lighted binnacle again, and looked down at the small figure standing against the rail in the well-deck. He then covertly glanced at Montilla beside him and felt an inexplicable fear. There was something about the guy tonight, something about the way he had been treating the girl, as if he had already dismissed her from his mind.

The young captain knew how violent Montilla could get. He had sat around the island bars and heard the rumor about Montilla taking two guys out in *Stiletto* and running them down and killing them. He had seen for himself Montilla's complete lack of concern when they learned about the young crew man on that *Sausea Girl*. He had died and Montilla had been worried only about the heat it might bring him.

He checked his course again, looked out over the bow for any unseen dangers in the waves, and felt alone in the dark and the salt spray. He promised himself that when this run was finished he would leave Lauderdale, *Spirit*, and Montilla forever.

The two Striker sportfishing yachts arrived off the Bimini islands before midnight. Once inside the drop-off, and into the shallows, the large seas subsided and they were in calmer waters, in the lee of the wind. The night was still dark, with heavy cloud cover and some blowing rain. The lights on North Bimini cast a glow into the somber sky, those on South Bimini visible but not as prominent. The red lights of the radio tower, however, could clearly be seen.

Silky stood on the fly bridge of *Spirit* now, holding the windbreaker tight around her body. During the ride across the Gulf Stream she had found strength in the night sky and blowing salt wind and spray, and she had found quiet peace in the hypnotic growling of the boat's engines and the constant powerful surges of the rolling seas. She had stared for long moments into the unbelievably pure blue water, awed by the majesty of it, her mind taking her beyond what her eyes could see down into the embracing depths of the ocean. Once or twice during the trip she had glanced up as the clouds were torn by the wind, and in between their shredded edges she glimpsed the stars beyond, embedded in an almost silver-clear universe. She had wanted to stand at the rail then and stretch her arms out over her head, her fingers spread wide, her long hair blowing behind her. She had wanted to stand and call out, "I *am* . . . I am someone, and I am alive! Do you hear me, Gulf Stream?"

But she did not call out. She did not speak. Instead she watched and listened and felt. And waited.

As the Strikers neared the cut between the two islands they drew close together, riding almost side by side for a

few moments, the rumbling of their engines the only
sound. Other than a couple of large tankers heading north
out in the Stream, they had seen no other traffic. The
waters around Bimini were empty of boats on this windy
night, and the only lights to be seen on the water were
those of the channel markers.

Joe, who had been lying on the couch in the main salon,
was feeling better now that the rolling motion of the boat
had eased a bit. He had washed his face, gulped down a
cold drink, and was standing in the aft well-deck. He
watched the companion sportfisherman turn away from
them and start heading for the other nearby island with all
the bright lights. He turned and called up to Montilla on
the fly bridge, "Yo, Montilla! Where are they going? Why
aren't we going that way too?"

Montilla, absorbed with picking out the channel markers
for the south island, looked down over his shoulder, and
called out, "I told them to go on ahead of us into North
Bimini. They'll tie up at the dock and wait for us."

Silky also wondered why they were heading for the
south island but had remained silent. The last hour or so on
the fly bridge had been quiet, with her and Montilla and
the captain all keeping their own company.

"Silky, go on down to the deck and get ready to help me
with the lines," said Onyx. "We have to stop for a little
while over here before we go see Blackie. Tell the greaser
to come on up here."

Silky climbed easily down the fly bridge ladder, sent Joe
on up, and started gathering the lines.

Joe stood unsteadily beside the captain, watching the
huge white-painted bow slowly swing from one slight
course change to the other. He thought the yacht was gigantic and had no idea what all the red and green lights
flashing out there in the water meant. He knew he was out
of his depth, but he still had a job to do.

"You never said nothin' to Mister Kolin and me about
havin' to go into some other island while the other boat
goes somewhere else."

Montilla sighed, and rubbed his face with his hands. His skin felt salty, his beard wet. "Listen, Joe," he said as he worked at making his voice sound patient and friendly, "I know a lot of what goes on out here is going to seem strange to you, and I can only say trust me. These people know me over here, and I've got the connection, but I still have to play their silly games . . . that's why I'm still welcome. *Ghost* will wait at Black's Marina for us, and she won't be boarded or inspected by the Bahamian Customs people because *we* are going to formally enter the country over here on the south island. I don't know why they have it set up this way, but there it is."

The captain remained silent, but he was as mystified as Joe.

"When we get in here, somethin' else is gonna happen that you won't like," Montilla continued, "but there's nothing I can do to change it."

"What's that?"

"Once we get tied up here I've got to go ashore for just a couple of minutes. I lay out some cash, I scribble on a couple of forms that they present to me, and we all smile. The problem is, while we're there no one can get off the boat but me." He saw that Joe clearly did not like the sound of that. "Look, Joe, I know you're supposed to stick with me and watch me get the load and all that. But for one thing we don't even pick up the load here, we get it over on the north side, where *Ghost* is now."

Joe nodded, not really wanting to upset things. He was supposed to just observe and report back.

Montilla, feeling Joe relax, grinned and said, "We go in, we tie up, and I go ashore. Then their stupid formalities are taken care of, and we can get on with it."

They were in the channel now and could already see the outline of the old docks in front of the small motel complex, palm trees, their fronds blowing back and forth with the wind and a strip of beach, pale in the diffused light.

Montilla reached down, opened a cabinet under the

steering station, and turned on a radio. He held the trans-
mitter to his lips and said softly, *"Hola, hola!"*

Immediately a sharp guttural voice said, *"Entrar!"*

He turned to Joe and said easily, "We've seen all kinds
of characters runing around over here—Cubans, Colombians, Haitians, Jamaicans, the locals of course—like a
Caribbean melting pot. Some of them carry guns, and I've
found it the best policy to just mind my own business when
I'm here."

Joe nodded his head, understanding the ways of the
world, if not the ways of the water.

"One more thing, Joe, so there won't be anymore surprises for you," said Montilla, watching as the captain gingerly put her port side against the dock, the bow facing the
shore. He watched as Silky wrapped the port stern line
around a piling and ran forward lightly to pass the bowline
across to a dark figure on the dock. When he saw that the
Striker was secure, and that Silky had moved to tie in a
spring line, he went on, "Silky will get off here with me,
and she will probably stay for now. We'll pick her up on
the way out because we have to stop again to clear anyway." He saw the question in Joe's eyes and said, "Two
reasons, Joe. I don't like her over on the north island with
me because I don't want her to see and know too much,
right? And the other reason is that those niggers over there
think she's some sweet piece of sugar, and one of these
trips one of them will make me an offer I won't be able to
refuse."

Again Joe nodded, understanding. The young captain
busied himself shutting down the engines and the lights.
He had heard Montilla, knew the lie, but remained silent,
knowing there was some kind of game going on that he
was not a part of.

The dark figure on the dock had walked away from the
boat and was now waiting near the patio that would lead to
the pool deck and the rooms beyond. Montilla climbed
down from the fly bridge, went into the main salon and
came right back out with the bags of hamburgers and
french fries. The captain and Joe just watched as he took

Silky by the arm and led her off the boat and up the dock, walking quickly.

Silky, feeling Onyx's firm pressure on her arm, said quietly to him, "Onyx? Why are you taking me off here? What's going on?"

Montilla kept walking until he was off the dock and onto the pool deck. He went over to where there was a tired-looking metal umbrella and some webbed chairs. He pulled one out for her and said, "Silky, be patient with me, okay? This whole gig is different from what I've done before. I'm only trying to follow Black's instructions. I took you off the boat because I don't want you sitting there with that crud ball Joe while I'm over here conducting business. Please . . . just wait here for a few minutes. I'll be back and we can get out of here and over to North Bimini and I'll put you in your own room at the Big Game Club. Then you can get some sleep."

She was aware of how nice he had been to her since they left, and she heard the polite insistence in his voice now, almost a pleading, and she had found a peace out on the Gulf Stream that she was reluctant to disturb. She did not hear any warning bells in her mind as she looked at him and said, "All right, Onyx. I'll wait here for you."

Montilla patted her hand, turned, and walked away.

Maximiliano embraced Montilla warmly, taking the bags from him and handing them to a silent and serious man beside him, the same man who had taken the lines at the dock. They were in the small dusty office of the complex with its old calendars, bright yellow dial phone, and wrought-iron furniture. They stood.

Maximiliano watched Montilla for a moment, and said, "I can see something is bothering you, but first let me tell you this news. I have for you here, in one of these rooms, the policeman Ted Novak that you tried to kill once." He saw Montilla's eyes widen, and heard his sharp intake of breath. "When you come back from getting your load over there on North Bimini, he will be here. I will give him to you. I want you to take him back to his own city for me—and kill him there."

Montilla's eyes glittered like shiny coal, his face glowed with sweat, and his lips compressed. He smoothed his beard, and nodded. "Can I see him? Can I let him know that I will now have my way with him?"

"Not yet, Onyx... not until you come back from the other island and you are on your way home." Maximiliano put his hands behind his back, rocked on his feet for a moment, and asked, "And what is troubling you? Is it the girl? Is that why she waits there in the dark?"

Montilla, again feeling like an errant child in front of the Cuban agent, looked at the silent man standing beside Maximiliano and hesitated. Without turning, Maximiliano gestured and the other man left the office, closing the glass door silently behind him, and standing just outside.

Montilla sighed. "Yeah... it's the girl. She's been with me for some time now and I party with her a lot, and I don't know... sometimes I need someone to talk to."

Maximiliano was motionless, his eyes never leaving Montilla's face and his lips barely moving as he said, "So you have talked to her about what you are doing. How much does she know?"

Montilla paused, then said quietly, "Almost everything."

Maximiliano was not surprised. So, the girl's fate was sealed, but was there more damage?

"That is not good, Onyx... not good at all. All right, she knows, but who has she told?"

Montilla, more sure of himself now, back on firm footing, said, "Nobody. She hasn't had a chance to tell anything, to meet with anyone, nothing like that. I've kept her close to me, and I know there's no one she could tell even if she wanted to."

Maximiliano was quiet, thinking about it. His agents here could get the girl to tell him if she was an informant in very little time, of that he was sure. She had to die anyway, and it wouldn't hurt to do a damage assessment before she did. Then he could reevaluate Montilla's too.

He nodded.

Montilla grinned, almost reached out and patted him on

the arm, caught himself, and said, "I brought your guys all those burgers like you told me. Guess they like some Americano food once in a while, huh? And now you have Silky. You cán kill her when you want, but first why don't you give her to your men? Like a toy? *Comprende?*"

Silky saw Montilla coming back across the pool deck. Another man walked beside him, a lean, dark man, with a hawklike face and a black mustache. The man wore a tan linen suit and carried himself easily. She stood to meet them.

Montilla stood beside the other man, looked at her queerly, and said with a grin, "Silky, I'd like you to meet Señor Maximiliano."

Silky put out her hand and felt the firm dry grip of the other man. She saw sadness in his deep brown eyes and he said, *"Tanto gusto, señorita."*

Suddenly she felt the air being crushed out of her by two terribly strong arms that encircled her, pinning her arms to her sides and lifting her off her feet. Before she could cry out another hand came from behind and a towel was pressed against her mouth and nose. She felt herself being carried backward, tried vainly to strike behind her with her elbows, brought her heels back sharply and kicked only air, and then realized she was blacking out. The last thing she saw before she lost consciousness was the grinning face of Onyx Montilla.

Maximiliano stood in the darkness, feeling the wind against his cheek as he watched the beautiful gray and black sportfisherman ease away from the dock, turn, and head back out into the tricky channel. He watched it until it faded from sight, the night enveloping it with an eerie suddenness. He turned and walked back to the hotel rooms.

He stood outside the end door on the south side of the complex, knocked twice, and waited. The door was opened slightly, a swarthy face inspected his, and the door was pulled open the rest of the way. He walked in, seeing Ted Novak sitting morosely at the glass and iron table. He nodded the guard out.

"So, Señor Ted, now I have a surprise for you which will cheer you up."

Ted looked at him skeptically, and said, "The last time you said something like that I wound up getting drugged and transported from one unknown place to this unknown place."

Maximiliano shrugged, as if to say all of that was just the way life goes. He smiled, and said, "But this, I think, you will find more to your liking. Yes, we have here in this place, dismal as it may be, a special kind of stove. A microwave, I think. One of those splendid boxes that cooks things in a flash, sí? And we have had something brought here for you, a surprise."

He turned and clapped his hands, and the guard came back in, carrying a tray. On the tray were the two paper bags, napkins, and a cold can of Coca-Cola. Ted saw the logo on the bags, smelled the aroma of the just reheated burgers, and said, "No . . . it can't be."

Maximiliano, pleased with his reaction, nodded again and said, "Yes, a dinner for you that is more like what you eat at home. The guard will not be in your room now, so you can eat in peace. He was only asked to stay with you for a short time while we had others guests around, sí?" He flourished his last surprise. "And so you'll have something to keep your mind occupied—these."

Ted eagerly took the four magazines, all back copies of *Florida Sportsmen.* On the cover of each was a photo of a pretty girl and some great Florida sport fish. Ted loved the magazine and was genuinely pleased.

"Thank you, señor. I appreciate these very much." He hesitated, then asked, "It is nice, what you've done, but now can you tell me when I'll be going home?"

Maximiliano looked into Ted's eyes, sensed the man's pain and longing, and said, "It is not good for me to get your hopes up, señor, but let me say this to you. You are close to your home now, and if we do not have a problem with you, or any unforeseen misstep, then you may be home as soon as tomorrow evening. All right?"

Ted, afraid to break the fragile hope that those words

created, simply nodded, and Maximiliano left the room, locking the door as he went out.

Ted sat down to his meal and his magazines, elated. The excitement of the news had his stomach churning, but he hadn't been fed in almost more than a day and was ravenous. He dove into the burgers, trying not to think of home.

Maximiliano walked back out onto the docks to feel the wind and the rain and to stare out across the tumbled water and night sky.

His mind was carefully examining the situation and his own feelings. Did old secret agents get sentimental? And if they did, was it a sign of weakness? He guessed that it was, and was mildly surprised to find that he wasn't unduly bothered by it.

He thought of the young nurse back in Cuba. Carmelita.

Yes, the prison directorate had hired her, ordered her to work for them, actually over a year ago. They had hired her as Carmelita, but he now knew that was a false name, not her real name. He had discovered the lie when he had his interior agents, the secret police, do a thorough background check on her before she was approached to work for him. The girl had lost a father and two brothers to the revolution. To the revolution, not to Batista. His agents had followed her and watched her and listened to her conversations, and it was clear that she was connected to a group that was working against Fidel in many ways. The most common way, and sometimes the most damaging way, was in the passage of information out of the rigidly controlled country.

He rubbed his eyes. The girl was smart and tough. She could have made her way to Miami easily, to begin a new life in the "free world." Maximiliano sniffed, disdainful of those Cuban "freedom fighters" who blustered noisily in the streets of Miami. How much courage did you need to protest against anything in the *Estados Unidos?* How much courage did you need to "fight for freedom" on the free streets of a free country? He knew nothing would ever be changed in Cuba by "patriots" who marched with puffed-up pride in Little Havana. Why not come to the *real* Havana and try to change Cuba?

But the girl, she was different. She could flee, but she stayed. Apparently she *had* been fighting Castro, right there within the revolution.

So. What to do about her? Whisk her away to La Cabana, or to the Isla de Piños, or even to Boniato? She could be tortured, questioned, her contacts and underground cells revealed, then put against the wall and shot, like so many others. Or she could be turned around, broken down, re-educated, and made to work against her former allies. He thought about that. No, she would be too strong, she would resist. Better just to squeeze from her what she knew, then bury her.

Well, she was being watched for now, so she wouldn't be going anywhere.

He thought he heard a fish splash the water nearby, and watched the waves surge and roll past the dock for a few minutes. His mind would not let him rest yet.

There was young Ted Novak, in that small room, waiting to go home. Yes, you will be going home, mi amigo, and there you will meet your fate one last time. He thought of the American policeman sitting in the room, eating his last supper like some kind of sacrificial lamb. Will you figure out why I had Montilla bring you those hamburgers all the way from your town? Don't you understand that if there has been a leak of information, from Carmelita or somewhere else, about your being in our country we must try to negate that? Yes, they will find your body, freshly killed. There will be mysterious partially healed wounds on your right leg. They will do an autopsy. And what will they find in your digestive track? *Arroz con pollo?* Fruits or grains or meats from Cuba? No, they will find that you dined on local fast food within one or two days of your second death.

Ah, what a tangled web we weave, he thought.

And now there is this Silky. Silky . . . a lovely name for a rare and fine and beautiful woman. He asked himself why it seemed so often that the loveliest and most challenging women spend time with such low-caliber men. Yes, she would have to be questioned, and yes, she would have to be killed.

Maximiliano turned into the wind and walked back up the dock to the old hotel. The night was not over yet. As he walked he thought about what Montilla had said about leaving Silky as a toy for the Cuban agents stationed on the island.

Maximiliano snorted. He, Maximiliano, was an old spy. He had been fighting small and bitter battles for many years. He could work with torture, though he never did it himself, and he could work with killing, which he had occasionally done himself. But he, Maximiliano, was from the old school.

Silky would be tortured for information, *sí*. She would be killed because she could be dangerous, *sí*. But to give her to coarse men as a toy?

Never.

TWENTY-TWO

In the windy darkness, *Spirit* idled through the channel separating north and south Bimini islands. She was covered with salt spray, and manned by a tired crew—Montilla, the captain, and Joe. The channel between the two islands can fool a captain who is not paying attention, especially at night. This captain, however, had been there many times before, so the shiny gray and black sportfisherman moved easily into the protected waters of the harborage.

Montilla directed the captain to back the yacht, stern to her sister ship, which was already lying against the dock, port side to, bow facing the marina. The crew of *Ghost* stood by with fenders and caught the lines, and *Spirit* was made fast and shut down. With the two Strikers stern to stern, identical bows facing east and west, it looked as if someone was doing a trick with mirrors.

Bo, the dock master, appeared out of the darkness, moving silently on the wooden planks of the dock to assist with the lines. Montilla looked around and saw that the marina was almost full. He saw a couple of Black's fishing boats and some pleasure yachts from the States. He looked out into the protected waters of the nearby anchorage and saw a couple of masthead lights. It was quiet here, and calm. He turned and looked toward the town. There was still some activity on the King's Road, actually one of the main streets of town; there were only two that ran north and south. Friday night and the joint is jumpin', he thought, and then reminded himself that it was always the weekend on Bimini.

Montilla stepped off the stern of the sportfisherman onto the dock and made out the hulking form of Hushpuppie Ellis standing in the shadows. He waved at him and the big islander moved toward him in that easy flowing way of his. Montilla thought he could see a gleam in the man's dark eyes as Hushpuppie approached, but then the big man tensed as Joe climbed awkwardly up onto the dock.

"Hey, Hushpuppie, it's all right," Montilla said quickly. He grabbed Joe by the arm and breathed into his ear, "Listen, Joe, I know you're supposed to watch me for Kolin, but I thought we agreed that you're only concerned that the boats get loaded, right? If you go barging in with me now and spook my contact here it could screw up the whole deal. You'll just have to be patient."

Joe, tired of being jerked around, pulled his arm away and said, his face very close to Montilla's, "Yeah, and you hear this, Montilla. I'm supposed to watch your every move for my boss, and I've already done too much standin' around with my hands in my pockets while you play your little games."

Montilla, feeling the anger starting to boil up inside him, tried to control it as he said in a tight voice, "Get this, Joe. My job is to get that load of grass for Kolin. You want to go charging around here and fuck things up? Great, we'll just all climb back aboard and go home, and *you* can explain to your boss why we don't have the load. While we're here you do it my way or not at all."

He waited.

Joe looked at him, glanced over at Hushpuppie watching him impassively, thought about the ride over, and whispered, "Okay, it's your turf, Montilla. I'll wait . . . but I don't want to wait too long."

He climbed back aboard the Striker as Montilla and the big islander walked off toward the main street.

Montilla was gone less than fifteen minutes. When he returned his face was broken by a crooked grin. He clapped his hands together and said to Joe, "All right, my man, things are cool. Things are good. All we have to do is leave the crews and the boats alone and by sunup they'll be loaded and ready to go."

Joe looked over at the two Strikers. *Ghost* had a captain and only one crew man, and *Spirit* had only the captain. He rubbed his face and asked, "Are these guys gonna be able to load the shit by themselves? Are we supposed to stay and help? Are they gonna do it right here, at this crappy little marina, surrounded by all these boats? And what about when we get home? How are we gonna unload all that shit by ourselves?"

Montilla made a face and a quieting gesture with his hand.

"Jesus, keep it down, will you? Just be cool. Each boat will be moved, one at a time, up the harborage a little ways to a private dock near a waterfront house on the inside here. Then the other. My man here will provide a load crew, and our guys will just supervise. When we get back to Lauderdale we'll tie up at a couple of leased waterfront homes where there will be off-load crews to help. My man has reserved a couple of rooms for us over at the Big Game Club. Why don't you and I slide over there and relax. Maybe we can rustle up a little action. All that's gonna happen tonight is humping bales, and we can leave that to the islands. In the morning you can come down and inspect the load bale by bale if you want."

Joe looked at the other men, who all appeared relaxed.

He looked back into the cabin of the boat on which he had just spent what felt like ten years of his life, and said, "Sure, let's check this place out."

As they walked down the street toward the Big Game Club, Joe was amazed at the things he saw. Definitely a party night. He noticed that the islanders seemed to ignore them, but were friendly to one another, smiling and nodding their heads as they passed a fellow islander. The only time they were noticed was when a black guy would lean out of the shadows and say, "Hey there, brother—you lookin' for some reefer, mon? I got some good bales. How about some of that nose candy or crack for my mon?"

Joe saw that Montilla just ignored them until he noticed that they weren't being asked anymore. He looked over his shoulder and saw Hushpuppie walking behind them, quiet, powerful, and dangerous. They passed by the Compleat Angler Hotel, which seemed to have a good crowd of guys and girls, both black and white, pushed up against the bar and around the outside patio. Watching them, Joe got the impression that the blacks in the crowd were somehow predatory, but he couldn't define it. He looked at Montilla inquiringly, but Montilla just made a face and shrugged. He looked behind him and Hushpuppie looked up into his face and gave what could have been mistaken for a smile. A little farther down the road they passed the Famous Door Lounge. It was a small, dirty place, with the allegedly famous door hanging completely off its hinges, and a concrete floor. A jukebox in the corner blared out reggae tunes and sweaty black bodies jerked and turned in the smoky center of the room. Joe saw only one white face there, that of a heavy middle-aged woman, her face thick with makeup, one pudgy hand wrapped around a beer bottle.

This is goombay? thought Joe. This is a magical night on a fun-filled tropical island?

As they made their way down the street they had to twice make way for cars. Joe found this strange as there was only this one narrow and poorly paved road. One of the cars was a new Mercedes four-door sedan, the other a big black shiny Cadillac with tinted windows. Both of these vehicles seemed to be traveling back and forth, up and down the road constantly, their horns sounding briefly as they passed the pedestrians. The only other motor traffic on the road was the profusion of mopeds and little scooters. These usually had at least two people on them, and the drivers were all wearing plastic baseball batting helmets. He turned around again and observed that the helmet sitting on Hushpuppie's bullet head carried the logo of the Pittsburgh Pirates.

He saw a lot of gold.

Women wore flowing print dresses, no shoes, and gold —gold chains, gold earrings, gold rings, gold pins. The men wore designer jeans, gold earrings, gold chains, gold spoons, and gold watches. Joe noted more than one island blade wearing at least six pounds of gold around his neck, a Cardin or Members Only shirt, Halston slacks, and red, green, or yellow high-topped sneakers. He looked over at Montilla and said softly, "This place is crazy."

Montilla made a dismissing gesture and said, "Well, I've heard it referred to as a wild adult theme park—like Dope World, or Six Banners Over Smugglerville, or something like that. But I'll tell you, Joe, what you really have here is just a bunch of simple, good, island folk, trying to make a living . . . just simple island folk."

Just then, the Mercedes went slowly by, and as the driver said "All right" and waved at Hushpuppie, Joe saw that the man was wearing a gold Rolex with the El Presidente band, diamonds and all.

Just simple island folk.

When they got to the pink and white two-story building Montilla and Joe waited while Hushpuppie went into the office. Ten seconds later he emerged and led them up the stairs and down the outside hallway to their room. The inside was air-conditioned, and Joe felt better immediately. He looked at the two double beds, checked the view out into the anchorage, smiled, and said, "Hey, classy . . . not bad at all."

Montilla said something to Hushpuppie, who turned and left, and then said to Joe, "Listen, my man, why don't you grab a shower? I'm going to see if I can score some toot.

And who knows? Maybe I'll even find a couple of chicks that look reasonably clean. Ever had any black pussy, man? Brown sugar and all that."

Joe just grinned and Montilla walked out, closing the door as he left.

Ten minutes later Joe stepped out of the shower. As he dried himself with the dingy hotel towel he thought he heard the sound of giggling coming from the bedroom. He dried himself quickly and stepped out into the room with the towel around his waist.

He looked at one of the beds and stopped.

On the bed were two girls.

One was black. The other was white.

Joe looked at the trail of clothes that led from the door to the bed. Both girls were nude, and God, the black one had nice tits. The white one had dynamite legs and she was a blonde, all the way . . . unless she bleached it there too.

They both smiled at him and the blonde said, with a classy, British-sounding accent, "Well, the stud arrives. Looking just as good as Onyx said he would . . . and not a moment too soon."

They both laughed, and then the black girl, whose voice sounded singsong, Jamaican maybe, said, "Yes, he's looking good, and maybe he'll help us with this bit of cocaine that Onyx left for us." She held up a small plastic bag of the white powder, twirling it in her fingers.

Joe moved toward the bed as if in a trance.

As he stood there, the blonde giggled again and said, "Now then, luv, where was I?" She knelt on the bed, pulled the black girl's long legs apart, and began licking her noisily, humming and laughing at the same time.

The black girl said, "Ummmmm," and began arching her back and grinding her hips against the blonde's face while she put her right hand against the back of the other girl's head and pushed her harder against her. Joe looked down at them, licked his lips, and stepped closer. The black girl turned her head, and through half-closed eyes looked at the towel around his waist and said, "Say, there, white boy, what's that trying to poke itself out from under that towel, hmmmm?" She reached out with her left hand, pulled him to her, ran her pink tongue over her lips, and took him, hard, into her mouth.

Joe felt his knees go weak and he braced himself against the side of the bed and thought, Oh yeah, the loading can take care of itself.

While Joe was thus occupied at the Big Game Club, both *Spirit* and *Ghost* were loaded. Each one slowly eased away from the dock, moved down the anchorage to the private mooring, and took on twenty-five hundred pounds of marijuana. The bales were burlap and plastic wrapped and weighed eighty to one hundred pounds. Either yacht could have easily carried the entire load, but Montilla wanted it evenly distributed between the two. None of Montilla's or Black's people thought it odd that the loading took place within a stone's throw of the main road on the island, with all of the clubs and people. It was just business as usual. Finally, when all the grass was aboard, Hushpuppie came padding down the dock with a canvas duffel bag over his shoulder.

Montilla's palms were sweaty as he brought the bag aboard. He had already checked the quality of the stuff with Black, and made sure they still had an understanding of how the money was to be divided. In the bag were fifty kilos of good cocaine. He quickly stashed the bag under a bench cabinet in the main salon, moved some bales in front of it, locked up the cabin, and sprawled out in one of the fighting chairs on the aft deck.

Hushpuppie left, and Montilla's crews were trying to get some sleep. Daylight would come soon, and then they had to waste the day away until it was time to leave. Maximiliano had told him to come back to the south island when it was getting dark. It meant sitting on the north side all day, and it meant getting into Lauderdale around ten or eleven Saturday night, but it would still work out all right. Bimini would be busy because of the weekend, and the two Strikers would just be part of the crowd. The boat traffic during the day would keep the cops busy at home too. There shouldn't be snoopers out in the port on a Saturday night or he would have heard from Erricks before he left.

Besides, Erricks knew the radio channel he would be monitoring when he came in and could give him a "bonfire" if there was a problem. Making the deal with Pete that same night would require some hustle, but he still felt he could pull it off. If not, he'd make it in the morning. It still gave him all day and night Sunday to finish the deal for old man Kolin.

Montilla lay there thinking about the cocaine in the bag, about the narc he would carry home and kill, about the Cuban government's cocaine, about the money—and about the other cop he would kill to put the icing on the cake.

He felt light-headed, and thought, Jesus, this is going to be a long, wonderful weekend.

J.B. Richards awoke before his alarm went off and lay there listening to the rain.

He felt uneasy and anxious about the day. He washed up quickly, gulped down a cup of coffee, kissed Jane lightly on the forehead, and was out the door and into his truck before any of his kids' alarms went off. Once outside he found that the rain fell in a desultory drizzle, pushed around a bit by occasional gusty winds from no steady direction. He shook his head as he headed east. The weather man on the radio advised any listening boaters that they could expect "confused seas." Along with everything else about this deal, he thought, now I must have confused seas.

This time, when he drove over the top of the New River Bridge and looked down to his left, he saw no gray and black Striker in the small marina. He felt a thrill as he drove by, but was still uneasy. He reminded himself that the action couldn't start until the boats were on the way to Bimini. It was as it should be, as Silky had told him it would be. It was Saturday morning, and the boats had probably just cleared the port and were on their way across the Gulf Stream now. With a sense of foreboding, he thought of his conversation with Scott Kelly of the night before.

The CIA man, Buchanan, had been there too.

Buchanan had chided him about the way a little group of local cops was going up against the big time, but J.B. got the feeling that the chiding was some kind of bait, as if Buchanan was feeling him out. The CIA man had said that he thought sitting around on the word of the girl, waiting for the boats to come in with Montilla and the cocaine, was a pretty slim way to run things. This time, he said, when they took Onyx Montilla, he, Buchanan, would decide what happened to him. J.B., however, could be in on the interrogation about the whereabouts of Ted Novak.

Buchanan wanted to know why there were no electronic bird-dogs or homing devices covertly planted on the Strikers. He wanted to know why no air units were on standby—even if just for a Bimini fly-over—to confirm the presence of the Strikers there. Kelly had looked at J.B., and J.B. had told the agent that it was his decision to keep it simple, to keep it tight and controlled. Airplanes and electronics meant more people, more units, more administrators. He didn't want that, and he didn't feel he needed it. He reminded Buchanan that he had been close to putting Montilla away weeks ago, before he was ordered to back off.

Before the meeting ended, Buchanan threw another small kernel of hope at J.B. He said that their source on Cuba was experiencing some trouble but had refused to be extracted. The source had indicated that the American policeman, Novak, had been taken from Cuba, drugged, and put on a boat, destination unknown, but thought to be possibly one of the Bahama islands. Wouldn't it be ironic, said Buchanan, if they had somehow made Ted a part of this cocaine deal with Montilla?

Now J.B. found himself driving faster toward Dania to check the other Striker. Dammit, maybe they should have put an electronic device on at least one of them.

When he pulled into the lot in front of the marina in Dania, J.B. immediately noticed the gap in the line of yachts tied to the dock. Both Strikers had pulled out, both were on their way, so now Silky would be sitting in Montilla's place waiting to be contacted by Bedlam. The worst that could happen to her now had only to do with whomever had been left behind to watch her.

He sat in his truck, listening to the drizzle, still uneasy. Something felt wrong.

He got out of the truck and walked over to the empty space on the dock. He stood on the edge, staring down into the brown water and feeling the rain drip down the back of his neck. He looked over his shoulder at the motley collection of cars along the edge of the lot and saw Montilla's BMW pushed up onto the wet grass. He turned and looked down into the water again and realized he wouldn't be able to concentrate until he knew Bedlam had the girl and she was safe.

He spun around quickly as a rough voice said, "Hey, mister, you lookin' for a charter? Hell, it's a miserable day, but we could still get out and drag some bait around if that's what you want."

Richards looked at the grizzled old boat captain standing on the aft deck of the clean-looking old Norseman sportfisherman tied stern-to against the dock beside the empty slip. The boat was old, the gear was old, and the slim captain was old, but all appeared to be well maintained and in good working order. The old man wore a pair of khaki pants and a clean white T-shirt. He crooked his head at J.B. and said, "No . . . no, I don't think you want to go fishin'. You lookin' for somebody?"

J.B. gestured toward the empty slip and asked, "Do you know what time the Striker left the marina this morning?"

The old man looked at him, hard, and picked up a rag and began to wipe off the brightwork around the transom of his boat.

"You a cop?"

Richards looked into the clear steady eyes, hesitated for a few seconds, and nodded.

The old man looked away and said quietly, "Hell, son. They didn't leave this morning. They left last night, or last evening actually. It was just before dark. Captain had the engines running before the others showed up. Then they all jumped aboard and they moved out. Didn't waste any time about it, I'll tell ya."

Richards got a sinking feeling in his guts, looked away from the old clear eyes, and said, "Yeah. I guess it would have been a couple of guys and a girl."

The old man bent over and picked up a piece of mop string that was lying on the deck and shook his head. "Yep. She's a looker too, I'll tell ya. I've seen her here before with that fella with all the gold around his neck. Yep, three of 'em came in that little car there, the guy with the gold chains, a slick-lookin' guy who wasn't a boater, and that girl. She didn't look too happy when they pulled out of here either."

Richards turned away and began walking back to his truck. Then he stopped, looked back at the old man, and said, "Thanks, Captain."

The old captain watched him as he hurried to the pickup, got in, and drove out of the lot, the rear wheels spraying mud before bumping up onto the paved road.

Richards drove headlong down the road toward Federal Highway, pounding his fist against the steering wheel and cursing quietly through his clenched teeth.

Stupid, stupid . . . how could I have been so stupid? Dammit, it was the only thing Montilla could do at this stage of the game. He hated himself for not thinking of the possibility.

He picked up his radio and got the dispatcher to notify Bedlam and have him go over to the records channel. J.B. knew his red-eyed partner had probably been sitting on Montilla's house since before dawn.

"Off duty four-forty-four to off duty five-one-five."

"Yeah, five-one-five here. Listen, J.B., I've been here since before the sun was and there hasn't been any movement at all. The BMW is gone, though it might be in the garage. No sign of the girl."

"This is four-forty-four. Listen, Skids, the girl is gone. She's gone and so is everybody else. They left yesterday evening after I told you to split. They took her . . . and they're gone."

Zaden and Maguire were quiet as Richards told them what he had learned. They were sitting in the Customs

office, waiting for Bedlam to arrive. Richards drank three
cups of government coffee, but the knot in his stomach just
stayed there. He had stopped castigating himself for now.
All he wanted to do was to get the job done.

"Well, J.B.," said Zaden, "I don't think it will make
much difference if the girl is aboard one of the yachts as
they come in. We're gonna nail 'em both anyway, and
we'll just scoop her up along with the dirt bags. In fact, it
might work out better. Once they're all in custody, under
arrest and Miranda'd and all that, we'll separate them anyhow, right? So this way all Montilla will know is that she
got popped when it went down. Then you can get her secured with the prosecutor's office, and they can take care
of her. I think it might work out."

Richards fooled with his coffee cup and nodded his
head, but he thought to himself that there was still a problem; he knew in his heart that Montilla would not passively
submit to arrest this time. Montilla had too much riding on
the deal, and Silky had told him Montilla's state of mind.
He looked down into the cup and admitted to himself that
he had been readying himself for a long time for this. He
was going to take Montilla down, and if Montilla wanted
to play rough, so be it. But if Silky was on the boat he
would be handicapped. She could be caught in the middle
and get hurt.

Maguire, making notes in a folder, looked up and said,
"You know, Hank and I have that Confidential Informant
over there on Bimini. We'd planned to call him on the
phone later today to see if the Strikers had arrived. We can
call and confirm that, and maybe we can get our guy to
detain the girl or somethin'."

Bedlam walked in the side door, gave the Customs men
a wave, patted J.B. on the back, and slumped heavily into
a chair. Richards looked at Maguire and said, "I thought it
was difficult calling that stupid island. Don't the calls have
to be routed through Nassau? It could take all day trying to
get through to your source."

Zaden shook his head and started punching numbers on
the phone. He tucked it under his ear and said, "You're
right. The calls are beamed out of Nassau, but they hold

some circuits for us. Our source is official and so are we
. . . so we can call him direct. Sort of."

The Bahamian Customs captain sat in his office at the
south end of Bimini and stared out the window at the
yachts tied up at Blackie's Marina and Supper Club. He
doodled with one of his shiny pens and smiled. *So, Mister
Onyx Montilla, done got your pretty Strikers all loaded up
courtesy of Mister Black and jus' feelin' pretty good about
it, I'll bet. Well, we'll see.* He leaned back in his wooden
chair and tapped the pen on the desk.

Like everyone else on the island, he had some part of his
life controlled by Mister Cornelius Black. There was an
understanding that went back generations between the
Black family and the Bahamian Customs officials. He let a
lot of things slide by, and he was paid for it. He knew there
was no way to fight it. Those who did were immediately
transferred, fired, or worse. Normally the islanders didn't
care at all what happened to a boat or planeload of dope
once it left there. In fact, there had been times when a boat
was loaded on Bimini with full knowledge of the Customs
man, and then when the locals had their money and the
boat left, the Customs man would wait until the boat
cleared local waters and either board it himself or radio for
one of the government gunboats to do it. Once the load
was seized again it just meant more money for everybody,
except, of course, the people who had purchased it in the
first place.

Sometimes it was different, though. There were smugglers who dealt with Black and who paid slightly more per
kilo because they were guaranteed safe passage out of Bahamian waters. This was really best for everyone because it
kept the flow going and those people who did business
comfortably, with no restriction from the island government, always came back for more.

The Customs man sighed as he thought of some of the
deals he had seen go down. He had gotten tired of getting
only a small slice, so he had figured a way to make it at
both ends. He always got his cut from Black, or any other
islander who dealt from there. But he had recently made

contact with two U.S. Customs men when he was over in Lauderdale.

The U.S. government would pay up to ten percent of the street value of a load seized to any informant whose information led to the load. Sure, there had been talk of putting a ceiling on the amount an informant would be paid, but it could still be worth it. Of course he was an official of another government, supposedly involved in the same war against drug smuggling as the U.S. guys, so there was some question as to his eligibility for the reward money. The U.S. Customs guys had figured out a way to identify him only as a citizen for their records; thus he could collect any monies they allotted him when he gave direct info toward a seizure.

It had worked nicely on a couple of small ones, but this one with Montilla would be the big test. He felt his palms get sweaty as he thought about it.

He wasn't sure whether Black really cared what happened to Montilla or not. He was sure, though, that Black would not appreciate his making money behind his back on any of Black's deals. He thought of Hushpuppie and wiped his palms on the sides of his uniform trousers.

From where he sat, he could look out across the anchorage at a little scrub-covered island called "haunted island" by the locals. All the people on Bimini knew there were thirteen bodies buried on that island, and no one ever went there. No one except Hushpuppie, who was known to take a guest from Black's place for a short boat ride now and then, and come back alone. The Customs man didn't fool himself for one minute thinking that if he angered or cheated Black he wouldn't find himself being boated over to the little island. He just had to be careful, that's all.

He looked again at the two sleek black and gray yachts at the marina. He'd be careful, but he was going to hurt that Montilla—today. He had received the call from the U.S. Customs office on the official line a few minutes ago. He had put them off, had told them he would call back when he had the info they requested.

He looked again at the gray yachts and picked up the phone.

                              *   *   *

Zaden hung up the phone and looked around at the faces
in the silent room.

"No girl, J.B. Our guy says they did get in late last night
and as far as he knows they'll be leaving there later today,
which should bring them to Port Everglades sometime
tonight . . . *if* they come here. But there's no girl, J.B. You
heard me ask him three times. He says he even knows who
we mean; he's seen her before, but she isn't there now.
And she wasn't on either Striker when they pulled in."

No one said anything.

Bedlam looked at his partner, and Maguire looked down
at the floor, then broke the uncomfortable quiet by saying,
"Hell, J.B., maybe she got off at another marina just down
the way from where they boarded. Maybe he dropped her
off someplace here in Fort Lauderdale before they cleared
the port. Hell, she could be anyplace."

J.B. looked at him for a moment, stood up, said,
"Yeah." He walked out of the office, and from there out
onto the docks. Bedlam, Maguire, and Zaden watched him
go, saying nothing.

Richards sat on the concrete dock with his feet hanging
over the water. One of the police boats was tied a few feet
away. He felt Salty rubbing against his hip and he petted
her absently while he stared into the calm water of the
canal. His heart felt heavy. He felt himself sliding into a
deep depression, but at the same time he realized that he
was burning with an anger that he had not known before.
This was the capper. The girl left Lauderdale on the yacht,
and when the yacht gets to Bimini there's no girl.

He bunched his fist and began hitting the edge of his leg.
He examined all of the terrible possibilities that Montilla
could have initiated, and they all spelled out one thing
for Silky. She couldn't be allowed to live. Was this the
way Montilla solved all of his problems? Take people for
a ride on his boat and make them disappear? He had done
it with Ted, and now the girl. As he thought of Ted he
was consumed with sadness and an intense feeling of impotence.

God, would any of this—these wild plans they had made—bring about the return of Ted? Now he was after Montilla for the dope, for the girl, and for Ted . . . but even if he destroyed Montilla, would it help them?

He looked down and saw Salty staring at him. He asked her out loud, "Will it help them, or am I just looking forward to some form of violent, revenging masturbation? No matter how hard I hit Montilla, will it bring Silky and Ted home?"

Salty just stared at him with unblinking but seemingly curious eyes.

He stood up, glaring down into the water, his mind full of hopes and maybes and what ifs.

"Dammit, will anything I do make a difference?"

Montilla stood on the aft deck of *Ghost* with Joe.

The captain had the engines running and the mate was working with the lines. The fighting chair had two big roller-guide rods with gleaming Penn 50s stuck in the rod holders, and trolling tackle had been laid out in preparation. *Spirit* lay tied to the dock, still and quiet.

"I think you'll enjoy this, Joe," said Montilla with a smile. "Some of the best big-game fishing in the world takes place right offshore here. Like I said, we've sat around all morning, everyone is rested and fed, and now we're getting into the afternoon and I think we can start thinking about moving out."

Joe, who was really getting into the trip, the boats, and the island, said, "You *know* I had a good time last night, Onyx. And yes, I've checked the loads on both boats and you did just like you said you would. But I just don't know about this . . . goin' off on the other boat, fishing, while you take your boat back over to that other island. You sure I don't have to go along?"

Montilla hit him lightly on the arm. "Spend a couple of hours offshore, drag some baits, catch some big ones, and relax. For one thing, it will *look* natural as hell, *sí?* For another, it will separate these twin Strikers for a while. As the sun starts to go down we'll take *Spirit* back over to the south island, go through the motions of their stupid paper-

work and pick up Silky and come on out. We'll give you a
shout on Channel sixty-eight then, and we can meet outside
there. You can come back aboard *Spirit* then, if you want
to ride back with me, and we'll go home. *Sí?*"

Joe, smoothing his new "It's better in the Bahamas"
T-shirt that he had bought to go along with his new fishing cap and sunglasses, nodded, and said, "Yeah, all
right." He hesitated, then said, "You know, Onyx, I guess
I had the wrong idea about you before. You're a stand-
up guy . . . and I kind of like this boating stuff."

Montilla grinned.

"Good. Go fishing. We'll go over to the south island,
then meet you just as it's getting dark." He jumped off the
boat, helped with the lines, waved, and said, "Catch some
big ones."

Fat Harry looked at J.B. and said, "We've got a problem."

J.B. just waited.

Bedlam had gone off to round up some food for everybody, and Zaden and Maguire were down on the dock
checking out the Magnum in preparation for the evening.

Harry looked at Richards sitting on the dock and said,
"Would you believe I've gone through every key in the
cabinet, read all the maintenance reports and everything,
and can't find one stupid Fort Lauderdale Police boat that's
running? Two of 'em were down for major overhauls, one
has that same old steering system that falls apart occasionally, one has a bad fuel leak they can't find, and number
five—your old boat—was run across an oyster bar at
high speed . . . flat ate the outdrive right off it. So we got
nothin', old buddy."

J.B. looked at his big partner and said, "Rats. What are
we gonna do, ride around in the port tonight in rubber
rafts? When is this city going to understand the importance
of the police boats and get some kind of decent budget out
here?" He pinched his nose, calming down. "Well, we
could all ride in the Magnum. It would be a little tight with
four of us in there." He looked at Harry and grinned.
"Especially with your lard ass squeezed in around us."

Harry grinned back and nodded, glad to see J.B. relax. He had been worried about J.B. since Bedlam had told him about the girl. Richards went on. "There's two Strikers coming in, Harry, so we've got to have two boats, the Magnum and somethin' else."

Fat Harry looked down the dock to the sleek shape of the Customs boat for a moment and said, "I'm going back into the office. Meet me there in a couple of minutes. We'll make a phone call." J.B. walked back into the office. Harry grinned at him, looked up a phone number, dialed, and sat heavily into the sergeant's chair.

"Hello? Intrawaterway Marine? Yeah . . . is this Herb? Hey, you skinny shit, how's it goin'? Yeah . . . yeah, no shit? Well, listen, I'm calling on official business here. Gotta have you get a boat out of storage for me and make sure she's ready to go in a couple of hours. Can you do that? You can? Good." He lifted his head and winked at J.B. "Yeah. You know that black and gray macho machine, *Stiletto?* Yeah, that's the one. You guys didn't pickle the engines yet, did you? No? Good, because we gotta have it, ol' buddy. Somethin' to do with the city attorney or some bullshit. Yeah. We're supposed to get it out of there today and get it down here to the police docks. I know it's a pain in the ass for you guys, but if you need us to sign anything . . . what, we don't have to? You *trust* us? Holy shit, guy . . . let me talk to you later about some precious metals paper I'm willing to sell cheap. You're glad to get rid of it? Great, we'll pick it up this afternoon. Thanks a lot, my man. Don't get any on ya . . . bye."

He hung up the phone, leaned back in the chair, crossed his arms across his ample belly, smiled at J.B., and said, "Oh well. In for a penny, in for a pound."

TWENTY-THREE

Onyx Montilla looked to his right and watched the beginning of a spectacular sunset on the Gulf Stream's horizon. It was still windy and rainy, but it was breaking up slightly, the clouds tearing here and there, letting the day's final rays of the sun shine through in shifting corridors. He was on the fly bridge of *Spirit* and they were between north and south Bimini islands, closing on the channel that would take them back to the dock and old motel complex.

As he watched their progress, Montilla thought of the night ahead. To this point, Joe did not realize that each Striker carried only part of Kolin's load of grass, and he did not know about the cocaine. This was all to the good, but Montilla knew that somewhere along the way he would have to tell Joe that they had only half the load and would have to come back tomorrow. Maybe it wouldn't be that much of a problem. He could blame it on the temperamental islanders, wanting more control of the load, and fill in with some story about the local Customs guy not letting them slip out with all of the grass at once. He believed that Kolin wouldn't care anyway—one trip, two trips, as long as he got all of his grass this weekend. Hell, Joe might even want to get off and report to Kolin, tell Kolin how cool everything is, and then let the Strikers go back for the second half without him.

His other concern was twofold. Once the boats were tied up in Lauderdale and being off-loaded, he would have to make immediate contact with Pete so he could haul ass up to Pompano and make the deal with his coke. And he still had to hear what Maximiliano wanted done with *his* cocaine. He would probably just have to drop it off someplace.

He saw the docks, with the run-down motel buildings behind them, coming into view. His face was grim, thinking of the narc that he would also be carrying. Easiest thing to do would be to just kill him right there on the aft deck and dump him over the side. This time there would be no mistake—a bullet behind the ear and maybe another in the teeth. The body could be dumped into Port Everglades, or maybe they could wait and carry him a little way up the New River. That would add to the mystery of where he had been.

Again there was one dark figure waiting to take their lines.

As the last of the sun's light fought its way through the low-lying clouds at their backs, the Striker was secured to the dock and her engines were shut down. A couple of lights were already on inside the office of the hotel and some stars could be faintly seen in the darkness of the eastern sky.

Montilla left the young captain on the boat and walked toward the office, his stomach tightening in anticipation. He was aware of the guards lounging here and there around the pool deck area watching him. Probably the most activity these guys have seen around here in awhile, he thought. He got to the office, pulled open the glass door, and stepped inside.

Maximiliano, wearing a linen suit, was waiting for him. Beside him was a large leather suitcase, old, with heavy straps and buckles helping to secure it.

"It is a sizable amount of very fine cocaine, Onyx. Please see that nothing happens to it along the way."

"No problem, mi patrón. Just tell me where you want it delivered, and it will be there before midnight."

Maximiliano smiled at the title and said, "You remember the lovely yacht on which you visited me at Bahia Mar? The one with the maple leaf on the flag? Good. She still sits there, waiting. You can get to her by your car, or naturally, by one of the boats. It is up to you. The marina people will have no knowledge of this, of course, and my friends on the boat know your face, and your car, and your boats. They will expect to see only you. They will know this leather *maleta*, and they will see immediately if it has been tampered with in any way."

Montilla frowned, hurt, and said, "Hey, I may be crazy, but I'm not stupid."

Maximiliano smiled. "Yes."

"All right. Now can I see him?" asked Montilla. "Now can I see the narc?" He bent down and lifted the heavy leather suitcase, waiting.

Maximiliano held the door open for him and they stepped outside. "We need to discuss that too now," he said. "Listen carefully to me, Onyx ... so you will understand." They stopped, standing in the shadows near the pool deck, and he began speaking in low, serious tones, Montilla beside him, listening, but impatient to be gone.

Silky paced back and forth in the dingy room, angry and scared. There had been some kind of drug in the towel that had been pushed against her face, and she knew she had slept for a long time. How long she wasn't sure. She had regained consciousness stretched out on her back in this motel room with its cheap prints on the walls, stingy towels, shades over the front windows, and some kind of grill over the bathroom window. She had seen enough of the place from the outside while she sat waiting for Montilla ... was it yesterday? She could form a mental picture of the layout, the buildings, the pool deck area, the docks, and the ocean beyond.

Montilla had given her away.

That lean dark man had to be the "secret connection" to another government that Montilla had bragged about. And she knew that Onyx suspected she had informed on him, or *would* inform on him. So he had given her to the secret guy.

She wondered if they were the people who were holding Ted, and if he was here too, and if Onyx had already loaded up all his grass and cocaine and God knew what else. She was trapped, being held prisoner, and she knew she would be killed eventually.

I wonder why he didn't just kill me in the middle of the Gulf Stream, she thought, *then for* sure *no one would have ever seen me again*. With that thought she suddenly realized that she was more angry than scared. *Screw it*, she thought. *He* didn't *kill me on the way across, so these spies or whatever they are probably will kill me here, and this sucks*. She was pleased with her anger, it gave her strength. She was tired of being pushed and pulled around, a pawn for men. She had been an unwilling participant in all of this for far too long now. Swept along with Montilla's ugly scams and deals, forced to be window dressing in a game that she wanted no part of.

That bastard had just stood there smiling while they grabbed her and carried her away.

And that big cop back in Lauderdale, J.B. He was counting on her, and so was his daughter. And here she was held like a condemned prisoner waiting to be blown away.

But that wouldn't happen. She would break out of this crappy room, run off, and get to a phone or a radio somewhere on the island, and call out the marines.

Then she looked at the new addition to her problems.

Just a few minutes ago the door had opened, there had been a flurry of guttural Spanish, and a squat, darkly tanned man had stepped into the room. The man was not much taller than she was, he might have been five seven, but he was heavy . . . solid heavy. He wore khaki work clothes that looked like a uniform, no hat on his short black hair, and a watchful, wary expression. The man had a cheap watch on his left wrist, and some kind of automatic pistol on his hip, in a covered holster. Somehow he did not look at all out of place in the weary motel room, staring at her.

She could not know that the man had been ordered to guard her for a time inside the room. The man had been just outside her door, but the man's leader had wanted him inside for now, in case she started to call out or make any noise that might alert the other prisoner being held at the other end of the row of rooms.

The man stood now, with his back to the door, and watched her in silence.

She sat down on the edge of the bed, frustrated. She knew the longer she was held, the less likely she could get out. She rubbed her face, hard, then ran her fingers through her long hair. She remembered the bathroom, and began to develop an idea.

She looked down at what she was wearing: a peach-colored polo shirt, no bra, soft jeans, underpants, and boat shoes with no socks. She had left the windbreaker on the boat. She stood up beside the bed, stretched, and silently thanking Onyx for the few words of Spanish she had picked up, said, *"Yo quiero la ducha."* She knew it was correct, but didn't like the sound of it, so she added, *"El baño . . . sí?"*

She thought she saw a flash of surprise cross the guard's face, but he said nothing, and did not move, except for his eyes, which followed her across the room. She could feel his eyes on her back as she stepped into the bathroom and closed the door.

She slowly counted to ten and reached in and turned on the shower, brushing aside the cheap plastic curtain as she did so. When the water was running strongly she took one of the towels, wrapped her fist in it, leaned over the sink, and began punching at the bottom half of the window. She knew the grill was still there to contend with, but first she had to get the glass out of the way. Each time she hit the glass the muted sound bounced around the room like a pistol shot. She leaned on the sink with her left hand, and hit the glass again and again with her right fist. Suddenly it cracked, right across the bottom, and she was elated. She began hitting it along the top edge now.

The pain burst across her eyes, and she thought she heard something in her nose crack.

It wasn't her nose, it was the glass breaking farther as her forehead was pushed into it.

She felt strong arms pinning her, her hips crushed against the sink, warm breath against her neck and ear.

"Estúpido!" the guard hissed. *"Estúpido!"*

He turned her roughly, still holding her. She did not

struggle, bright flashes still going off behind her eyes. Slowly he let her go and stepped back. He brought his hand up fast, as if to slap her, and she flinched, but he stopped the blow inches from her cheek, and said again, more quietly, *"Estúpido."*

She felt her nose running, and slowly reached up and wiped it with her right hand; she was surprised to see bright red blood on her fingers as she brought her hand away.

He saw the blood too, and shook his head.

"Es nada," she said. She found the towel in the sink and held it against her nose.

He was using his left hand to open the door behind him, and his right was tucked into the front of her jeans, at the belt line, pulling her out of the bathroom. She saw the muscles bunching in his arm and the determined look on his face, but she dug her feet against the tiled floor and shook her head.

"La ducha," she said quietly. *"Es verdad."*

He hesitated, and in one motion she dropped the towel, grabbed the tails of her polo shirt, and pulled it quickly over her head. As she dropped it onto the floor she saw his eyes widen at the sight of her firm breasts, with their perfect pink nipples bouncing slightly only inches from his sweating face.

She stepped back, feeling her buttocks hit the sink. Without taking her eyes away from his, used first one foot, and then the other to step out of her boat shoes. She wiped her nose again, saw there was very little blood now, and reached her right hand into the still-running shower, rinsing her fingers. Then she brought her hand back out, dripping, and began rubbing it over her breasts, cupping them, and teasing her nipples. Her skin shone with the film of water and the pink gleam of blood.

He glanced quickly over his shoulder, turned back, looked into her eyes, and said, *"Alto!"* but he did not grab her again.

She heard the lack of conviction in his voice, reached down, unbuttoned her jeans, and pulled them down off her hips. She heard him catch his breath as she bent slightly, still looking at him, and stepped out of them. She turned away from him then, reached in, adjusted the water, amazed to find it was hot, and unwrapped a bar of soap that was in a nook beside the sink.

She watched as he leaned back against the door, which was now closed at his back. She chanced a smile, saw his face remain expressionless even though his eyes were burning into her, and pulled off her underpants. She kicked them onto the pile of clothes and ran one hand down between her legs, the fingers spread. His eyes did not follow the hand down but stayed on hers. She did see him lick his lips, though.

She stepped into the shower, letting the water run through her hair, over her shoulders, and down across her breasts.

God, it felt good.

She left the curtain open, pushed against the wall near the guard, picked up the soap, and began washing herself.

The guard stood there, his arms at his sides, his eyes never leaving her body. He knew he was just supposed to watch her. He knew that he was much too close to her, and he understood what she was trying to do. She was tempting him . . . but for what? What could she do against him, alone and unarmed? She was just a girl. A beautiful girl, *sí*. A beautiful, ripe, honey-colored woman, wet and soapy and hot. *Sí*, hot. Look at the way she looked back. He had heard from some of the others that she would be killed but that she would be passed among them first. He sighed. He was a veteran, *sí*, and a professional, *sí*, but in this group he held very little seniority. If they gave her to them his turn would not come soon, if it came at all.

Silky soaped herself completely, generating as much lather as she could with the motel soap. As she did she played with herself teasingly, watching the guard. She could see that his face was sweaty, and he was licking his lips more frequently. When she reached down between her legs again and moaned, she saw him shift uncomfortably, the bulge in the front of his pants becoming prominent.

She laughed, looked at his groin, then back into his eyes. While she caressed one breast with her fingers she pointed between his legs with one finger on the other hand, and said, *"Yo quiero."* Then she laughed again, and licked her lips, running her tongue around slowly.

He couldn't take it. He looked over his shoulder again as if to see through the closed door, and moved toward her, his arms reaching out. His eyes had narrowed to slits, and his voice was hoarse as he said, *"Tu diabla . . ."*

She waited until he wrapped his arms around her, pulling him toward her chest, his fingers digging hungrily into her bottom. She was slippery, the water was still running, and he had soap and water on his face. As she lifted her arms over her head her breasts were pushed against him and she felt his mouth and his tongue on her. She grabbed the unpainted iron curtain rod running the length of the tub, screwed into the plaster walls at both ends, and pulled down as hard as she could.

The screws on the end near the door pulled first, and as the end of the bar broke loose she jerked down with all of her might and the bar crashed onto the top of the guard's head with a thick sound. He bit into her nipple as it did and she felt the quick stab of pain. With both hands she brought the bar down again and again, hitting him solidly on top of the head. He cursed, punched her hard in the kidneys, and as she gasped and started to collapse he pulled back and the bar came down across his nose and mouth.

He gasped then, and blew blood out from his nose and torn lip. She was reeling from his single blow but managed to lift one foot, and as she slipped back against the wall, she kicked him very hard in the groin. Her wet back hit the cold wall, and she bounced forward again, groaning. His teeth were clenched, his breath hissing as he bent forward, his hands between his legs. He glared at her and she knew he would lunge at her. She grabbed the iron bar again and slammed it forward at him as he came at her. The bar caught him full in the throat, and she saw his head snap back before he fell in a heap on the bathroom floor.

She was sobbing now, and her hands were shaking. She watched him for a few seconds and saw that he was taking deep, ragged breaths. She thought she might have crushed something in his throat.

She grabbed the bar again, held it near his head, closed her eyes, and then brought it down solidly—once, twice, three times. The bar made a sickening hollow sound as it hit his head. She turned, shut the water off, and then stepped out of the tub, trembling and sobbing. Taking deep breaths, she held herself tightly for a moment, staring down at the still body on the floor.

Then she ran her fingers through her long hair, brushing it back away from her face, bent over and reached past him, grabbing her jeans and the shirt. She put them on over her wet skin. She stepped over the guard, slipped her feet into her shoes, and picked up the towel again.

This time the window broke out after the first hit, and she caught as much glass as she could before it fell into the sink. She turned then, holding her breath, sure someone out there must have heard something by now—the struggle, the glass breaking. But no one did.

She picked up the iron curtain rod again and pushed against the security grill on the outside of the window. The stiff wire resisted, fought her, bent, and then one side tore out of the plaster along the edge of the window. As it did she heard voices, a door, two doors, being opened and shut.

It sounded like someone was in the front room, so close.

She froze, waiting ... listening. There was nobody in her room. She must have heard the voices coming from other rooms in the complex. She quietly went to the door of her room and made sure it was locked from the inside.

She was filled with an acute sense of urgency but knew she must not panic now.

She used the bar to push the screen away from the window as far as she could. Then she put the bar down, climbed up on the sink, and wedged herself through the window. The wire grill tore at her shirt, and then at her skin on her left side as she pulled herself through headfirst. She used her hands to try to brake her exit, felt them sliding against the dusty paint on the outer wall, and put them into the sand of the alley behind the complex as she fell out, hit, and rolled into a ball.

She got up and started to run up the alley. Her feet slid in the dirt as she realized she was running toward the front of the place. She turned and ran the other way, past the broken window, toward the water.

She would run up the beach, as far as she could go, and then cut inland. She could make it to the airport; maybe someone would help her there.

She got to the edge of the building and slid to a stop. The thin strip of pale beach was ten feet away. She looked up and all around, aware that it was the gray and deceptive dark of early evening. She heard voices again, and cautiously looked around the edge of the wall.

She caught her breath.

There, fifty yards away, was one of the Strikers, tied to the same dock they had first used. Was this the same day? And now it was just getting dark? No, she knew more time had gone by. She crouched in the corner of the wall, and brought her face around the edge as much as she dared. Now she saw who belonged to the voices.

"Just do what these men tell you to do, señor, and your trip will not be unpleasant," said the lean dark man with the hawklike face and linen suit.

"All right. Just don't dope me up again," said the other one. He sounded like an American, and in the dim light she saw that he had a blindfold over his eyes and his hands were bound in front of him.

On the other side of him walked Montilla. He carried a large bag and was silent.

Silky shuddered. With icy clarity she understood that she was seeing Ted Novak, the Lauderdale narc, being led off to his death by that lean one, with his oh-so-polite voice, and the silent, smirking Montilla. She watched them, and felt her anger overwhelming her, brushing her fear aside. She looked out at the sportfisherman again.

They had docked her stern-to this time, probably so they could march a blindfolded man out on the dock and aboard her with a minimum of exposure, she thought.

Without hesitating or thinking about it, she moved in a

slow crouch across the strip of sand and into the water. Near the dock, all eyes were on the little procession. Once in the warm water she slid outward onto her belly, feeling the salt burn her torn skin on her left side. She tried to paddle and move her hands without splashing. Where it was shallow she just dug her fingers into the sand, pulling herself along. She was glad for the darkness and the small waves, even though she took a mouthful of water as she quickly lifted her face far enough to glance to her right, toward the dock and the boat. That quick glance showed her that the group had reached the transom of the boat.

It was time.

She timed the small waves, took a deep breath, and dove under the surface. She was a strong swimmer, with good air capacity, and although it was unnerving to swim in the darkness, she knew she didn't have far to go. She pulled her arms from out in front of her and scissor-kicked her legs, moving in lunges through the water, farther and farther in the eerie green darkness, until she thought her lungs would burst.

Finally the ghostly bulk of the hull loomed into her vision and she kicked again, reaching out until her fingertips brushed the bottom of the boat. She used the flat of her palms, one under the hull and one on the side just at the waterline to hold her, while she brought her face out of the water and quietly gulped air. She rested there, realized there was no time, and moved out toward the huge bow that overhung her, shutting out the night sky.

She swam quickly now, along the side of the boat, up to the knifelike bow, and around it. Now she was between the bow and the dock, and she looked up to see the bowline still there, waiting for her.

She could not hear any voices, and the engines were not running.

Where were they? If they were still huddled around the transom, would they see her? She had to get aboard, now.

She kicked her feet, reached up, stretched, and missed the bowline. As she did the engines kicked over, sounding like a thunderous timpani. She dropped back into the water with a splash, her sob muffled by the waves.

She quickly moved to the dock piling that the line was tied to, put one foot against it, and pushed herself out of the water again. This time her fingers held the line for a moment, and then pulled away again.

Again the splash, again the muffled sob.

She let the water pull her hair out of her eyes as she raised herself again, lunged upward and grabbed the line with one hand. She swung once and using the momentum from the swing pulled herself up, turned her body, hooked one leg around a bow railing post, felt her foot hit the starboard cleat, and rolled up onto the forward deck of the Striker.

She spun around, got to her hands and knees, and reached out for the forward hatch, realizing how exposed she was on the great expanse of white bow. She looked up toward the fly bridge, and right into the eyes of the young captain, who was staring at her in shock.

Montilla had grudgingly agreed to Maximiliano's request—or was it an order?

The Cuban agent had told him that Ted Novak did not know where he was being held, or who exactly were his captors. The narc had been told he was going home and had promised to cooperate. Maximiliano did not want to have to drug the narc again for the trip. He had said he didn't want them to find any traces of that kind of tranquilizer in the narc's system, that the narc would be bound and blindfolded and would walk to the boat under his own power. Maximiliano said he understood Montilla's need to confront the narc, but wouldn't the surprise be that much more intense if it happened after a few hours of boat ride, just when the narc thought he was home free? *Then* Montilla could pull off the narc's blindfold and let him see his killer—again. This way there would be no struggle and it would be an easy thing, *sí?*

Montilla's chest was pounding when they brought Ted out of the small room, wearing plastic handcuffs and a blindfold. The Cubans had put squares of tape over the narc's eyes first, for complete security. They didn't want him to see *anything*. He had felt his mouth go dry as he fell in beside Maximiliano, who was gently leading him toward the boat.

Maximiliano had paused once, near the first room, the one nearest the beach. Montilla had been told that the girl was being held there and a guard was inside with her. He had merely grunted. But the Cuban agent had paused there, silent, and a troubled look crossed his face. Montilla had watched him shake it off, and they had walked on. Near the dock, Maximiliano had exchanged words with the narc, and Montilla had wanted very badly to say something, but he held his tongue.

When they got to *Spirit*, Maximiliano climbed aboard first, then helped the narc step unsteadily onto the gunwale and down onto the aft deck. He reached out and grabbed the heavy bag from Montilla, who then climbed aboard. Maximiliano walked across the aft deck and opened the main salon doors. He went below, threw the bag into the bottom of a closet, and led the narc through the bales to one of the bunks in the port side forward stateroom up at the bow. As Maximiliano turned to go, Montilla saw him pat the narc on the shoulder.

Once back out on the aft deck, Montilla looked at the young captain on the fly bridge and spun his hand rapidly, giving the engine run-up signal. The captain turned to the console, and the engines fired off with their pleasing throaty rumble.

Montilla then turned to have a final word with Maximiliano.

The young captain on *Spirit* stared at the still, crouching form of Silky below him on the bow deck. He saw the terror in her eyes.

What the hell was going on?

He was already very uncomfortable with the whole deal. The entire weekend had been weird, with Montilla playing all kinds of games, with that Joe character and Silky aboard. Montilla had never mentioned the smuggling of cocaine which he, the captain, had resolutely stayed away from. And Montilla hadn't discussed more pay for them either. Hey, if you're going to run coke there's got to be more for the crews.

All that was bad enough, but when he took Silky off here at South Bimini in the first place, the captain didn't like it. And now this, the place crawling with these creepy Cubans or Colombians or whatever the hell they were. And here comes Montilla la-de-da down the dock with another bag that probably wasn't full of M&M's, and a *prisoner*. A prisoner? What the hell was Montilla getting him involved in here? Is this a hit trip? They gonna kill the poor bastard halfway across the Stream, then dump him?

The captain did not like what was going on at all.

He looked quickly over his shoulder, saw the Cuban climbing out of the aft deck and onto the dock, Montilla still talking to him. The captain turned back, looked at Silky, and made his decision.

His face grim, he pointed with one stiff finger at the bow hatch, then he looked back down at the controls. He knew the bow hatch was not locked. They should have following seas and a wind at their backs on the way back to Fort Lauderdale. Not only did it mean they would make better time on the way across, but it also meant that they probably wouldn't be taking seas over the bow. He had left the hatch unlocked purposely so that he could run down later and open it, letting the pure clean air blow through the boat, keeping the stench of marijuana from becoming a permanent part of the ambience.

When he looked back, the girl was gone.

It took just a little too much time for the Cubans on South Bimini to learn that the girl was gone.

After *Spirit* made her way out of the channel into the open ocean beyond, only her navigation lights visible in the early evening darkness, there had been a flurry of activity. Another boat would be arriving in a couple of hours to take Maximiliano back to Cuba. He had told the leader of his agents there that he would have the evening meal, *la cena*, with them. They would talk over future operations, and during the meal, or over coffee later, he would decide the fate of the girl.

Maximiliano knew that a quality interrogation of the girl would take time and expertise. He did not have the time, and his men there did not have the expertise. He could not take her back with him where it could be done properly, so he would probably have to leave her in the care of the men here. He could tell them to do it quick and brutal, learn at least if she had passed information about Montilla on to some policeman somewhere, and then kill her. Or he could just order them to kill her, quickly and painlessly.

He could not decide, so he waited.

Finally, after the meal, as he took his first cup of coffee, the leader of his agents was called away by a whispering messenger. When the leader returned, his face was pale, and his voice shook slightly as he told Maximiliano, "She has escaped."

Maximiliano hurried to the room. He learned that the guard scheduled to relieve the one watching the girl during the afternoon had knocked on the locked door in vain. Finally, suspecting that the early guard might be taking advantage of being alone with the girl, he called to another of the guards, and together they broke the lock on the door. Once inside, they found that the dead bolt lock had been thrown from the inside and the guard's only key was still in the lock. It took only a moment to find the guard unconscious in the bathroom, badly beaten.

Maximiliano knelt beside the guard, closely examining his wounds. The man was alive, yes, and he might survive, if he could be taken to a modern medical facility. As the other agents crowded around the bathroom doorway, watching, Maximiliano looked around the room, reconstructing what had happened. The wet floor, the soap, the crumpled towel and broken glass, the curtain rod, and especially the fine and feather-light pair of cream-colored woman's underpants told the story.

An agent came into the main room and breathlessly told his leader that they had followed the girl's footprints in the alley behind the row of rooms. The footprints showed that she went to the beach, and then into the water. From there she could have gone in either direction, but probably south, away from the complex. How far could she have gone? A thorough search of the beach and the rest of the island would be started, and the airport would be covered.

Maximiliano listened to the plans being discussed, and somehow already knew that they would be in vain.

He looked around the room again, imagining the courage and strength that the girl must have to pull it off. He turned and spoke to the others. The guard was in critical condition. He had failed them all. He had been duped by a mere woman, an Americano piece of fluff, jeopardizing a very important operation. He, Maximiliano, was angry. The agent leader, hearing this, blanched. Maximiliano stared into the man's eyes, and then scanned the others as he said, yes, he was disappointed and very angry, so they could imagine what Fidel's reaction would be when he heard the news.

The room became very still.

Maximiliano bent, unsnapped the holster on the wounded guard's side, and pulled out the automatic. The others watched silently as he pulled the slide back slightly to check for a round in the chamber. He thumbed off the safety, bent down again, stretched out his arm so the muzzle was very close to the man's short black hair, and pulled the trigger twice in rapid succession. The roar of the two shots fired in the small room was deafening, and the concussion could be felt by the other agents. As the roar subsided, the tinkle of the shell casings could be faintly heard, bouncing on the tile floor.

Maximiliano did not look at the horrific mess the slugs had made of the guard's skull. He turned, handed the weapon to the agent leader, and walked out of the room, saying, "Clean it up, and then bury the body—deep."

He strode out of the crowded motel room, the other agents and guards making respectful way for him. Then he turned and walked out onto the dock, as far as he could go. It was not likely but it was possible that the girl could somehow tip off the Americanos to the operation.

He could take a fast boat and try to catch Montilla, he thought. Or he could begin broadcasting on the standard marine channels, calling the boat name and ordering it back. He looked out over the dark wave-tossed water, looked up into the cloudy sky, and sighed. He knew it was too late.

As he watched the sky, he saw the wind tear away a mass of clouds, exposing for a few moments the black night beyond. Some early stars took the brief opportunity to sparkle, and he found himself enveloped in a strange sadness . . . felt a cocoon of peace creeping around him, warming him in its inexplicable embrace.

Wasn't there something circular about this whole case? Something karmic? He had watched it all come around to this point, had actually been a part of it, and now it was close to coming all the way around to the point where some grand design had determined where it would eventually go.

Study that last small piece of information from home, he mused darkly, and you'll see what I'm talking about. Carmelita was being watched . . . loosely of course, so as not to alert her, but watched nonetheless. And now it was reported to him that she had disappeared. Those assigned to observe her . . . lost her. Even his contacts within the prison system had no knowledge of where she was. Had she been warned by her own apparatus? Did she feel the cold breath of the followers? Was she just laying low, hiding? Or had she finally launched herself from the world that had taken everything from her, to seek her new life in a world that would surely embrace her? He rubbed his nose. Ah, karma and coincidence, he thought, and a reason for everything.

He laughed out loud, surprised at himself. Señor Maximiliano of Fidel Castro's secret police, the philosopher.

Most likely now, somewhere out there on the Gulf Stream, Montilla would find the girl and kill her. Then he would kill the narc, Ted, and then he would smuggle our cocaine into the country for our Canadian contacts, and that would be the end of the circle . . . *sí?*

He looked out into the endless night spread out in front of him, and said to the wind, "Yes, that's probably how it will end. But perhaps not. The young policeman had been watched by a guardian angel so far, no? And the girl, the girl is magnificent, and lucky too." He smiled. "So I, Maximiliano, I say this to each of you two Americanos: *Vaya con Dios*."

Then he turned and walked back to his own world.

TWENTY-FOUR

J.B. and Fat Harry hung on, exhilarated, as the black and gray ocean racer flew across the light chop inside the turning basin of the port. The engines roared powerfully, and as he pushed forward against the twin throttles, J.B. felt that power traveling up his arm and into his heart. The aqua-dynamic hull responded smoothly to the controls, the stern and outdrives digging in through the sharp turns. J.B. admitted to himself that taking the magnificent boat out and running her hard made him feel better than he had in a long time. He scanned the red-lighted instrument panel, saw that she was in fine working order, gripped the padded wheel tightly, and hung on.

They were on a short test run, to make sure *Stiletto* was in good condition and ready for the night. The sun was going down, the day was ending, and the night waited impatiently for the last vestiges of light to disappear. The water in the basin looked metallic, bright and heavy at the same time. As the knifelike bow of *Stiletto* sliced the water, her wake turned to gold on one side and silver on the other.

J.B. eased the power back, and they rumbled under the Causeway Bridge and into the Fifteenth Street Canal. He and Fat Harry remained silent, content with the almost postcoital feeling of peace that had enveloped them after that crashing, surging, booming ride.

They idled into the police dock area, and Zaden and Maguire were there to catch a thrown line.

"Holy bilge-pumps, Barnacle Bill!" cried Reggie Maguire. "Now I know the waterways of this tropical paradise are no longer safe. Look at this—a geriatric Yankee persona non grata cop and his voluminous Sancho Panza, both in the same overpowered slice of phallic fiberglass!"

Harry, moving faster than Maguire expected, scooped him up with his big arms and held him easily out over the edge of the water, the Customs man's feet dangling precariously close to the wet surface. With his face close to Maguire's right ear, he whispered, "Keep talkin', pencil-neck—and you'll be bobbing for blowfish."

They were laughing as Harry dropped Maguire back on the dock.

Zaden stood looking down into the cockpit of a now secured *Stiletto*. He ran an appreciative eye the full length of her and whistled softly. "Man, she *is* pretty, and she really is a lady. Too bad she's Montilla's. I think in the hands of a gentleman she could really be something."

Richards looked at her too, and as he heard Zaden's words all he could think of was Silky. Then he heard a voice behind him. "So, you managed to get us a boat. Good!"

They turned to see the bulky and brooding form of William Buchanan of the CIA. He was not smiling.

With him was Scott Kelly. He waved.

Bedlam had arrived too, carrying his radio and a small cooler.

"What do you mean—we managed to get *us* a boat?" asked J.B.

"What do you think, Richards? I've watched this thing slowly come together. It looks like it will finally happen tonight, and you suppose I'm not gonna be out there?" Buchanan spread his legs, and crossed his arms over his chest. "You're wrong, buddy."

Scott Kelly said, "I told him he could work with me, J.B. We can circulate the area like Skids, listening and watching, and we can move in when either of the boats gets close to a dock or a seawall." He looked at the CIA man and shrugged. "He didn't want to hear it."

J.B. looked them over, then turned and looked at the boats at the dock. He nodded, and said, "It will be full dark soon, we know the Strikers were in Bimini this morning, and if they left there this afternoon, they'll be sliding into Port Everglades shortly. Even if we have to sit around waiting, I want to get out there and be in place. I don't want to stand around here arguing with you, Buchanan. I know you're out to nail Montilla as your own personal windup of that thing you had with Ortiz twenty years ago." He looked at the agent, his eyes icy. "Fine. I'm out to nail him because he's a killer and a cocaine cowboy and an asshole. He's probably already killed the girl, Silky. And we know he did something to Ted. He might be able to tell us where Ted is, after some coaxing, or he might even have Ted with him, for some unholy reason."

He looked at the faces of the men grouped around them. There was no question that he was in charge. He continued. "Hear this, Buchanan. Harry and I have illegally taken that boat out of storage." He pointed at *Stiletto*. "At this point I don't really care how many rules I break, but I suspect that you still do. You're not here under the umbrella of your office; you're wildcatting it for your own reasons. Okay. Here's how I see it." He pinched his nose. "Harry and I will work in *Stiletto*. Harry will have a twelve-gauge pump. Skids in my truck, radios and eyeballs and ground unit coordination. In the Customs Magnum, Zaden and Maguire, of course, and Scott Kelly and you, Buchanan. We'll have two boats and six guys on the water. We can hang back, let them come inside, then hit 'em hard."

He was punching one palm with a big fist. The others were quiet.

"Let the first one make the turn, then put two men aboard her. It should be Scott Kelly and Reggie Maguire. That way you've got a Customs man and a backup, leaving a Customs man still in the Magnum, that's Zaden, plus *his* backup—that's *you*, Buchanan. That way you'll be in on the grab."

No one said anything. The plan made sense, and they were anxious to move out. Buchanan rubbed his chin, thinking it over.

"Look, Buchanan," said J.B., his voice suddenly very soft, "you're involved in a domestic gig here, probably without your own office's knowledge. If it goes right, you'll have your revenge and you'll be a hero. If it goes wrong, wouldn't you at least prefer to be caught with your pants down on a federal boat?" He watched as Buchanan digested this. "And lastly, Buchanan, I'm a very tired and angry local cop. This gig is goin' down *tonight*, and if you or anyone else tries to screw me up, I'll take 'em *out*."

Buchanan saw J.B.'s anger, felt the desperation and conviction in his voice, took a step back, and said easily, "I won't screw you up, Richards. I've just waited too long not to have a piece of the action. Fine. I'll ride in the Customs boat, and we'll move in when you say."

The little group broke up, each man getting his personal equipment. As the others moved off, Hank Zaden said to J.B. quietly, "Just so you'll know. I agree with what you told that agent, and I think it will work out fine, but I have to tell you that once Reggie and Scott are out of the Magnum, when it comes to my backup, I'll cover my *own* ass."

J.B. looked into his eyes, and said, "I hear you, Hank."

Zaden looked up into the new nighttime sky, watched the clouds blowing by, and wondered how rough it would be offshore. He looked at Richards, saw the ice blue eyes, the tightness around the mouth, the clenched fists, and he said, "Won't be long now, J.B."

He turned to Zaden and said grimly, "Let's go take that bastard down."

Onyx Montilla made his way through the main salon, squeezed between the bales of marijuana, and went forward in the rolling and lunging boat. He had been up on the fly bridge with Joe and the captain, watching their excellent progress, and was pleased with the way things were going. Joe had jumped aboard from the other boat just outside Bimini, grinning and full of stories about the fish they caught and lost. Montilla had kept him from going below and spotting the narc, simply by mentioning how easy it would be to get sick down there, with all that smelly grass, and the stomach-churning rolls of the Striker. Joe gladly stayed topside.

Now Montilla could wait no longer. He wanted to bust the narc's balls.

Once forward, he saw that the narc had worked himself into a sitting position, his back against the bulkhead, legs stretched out on the bunk. His hands were still held tightly by the flex-cuffs, as were his ankles. The narc's face looked pale and sweaty.

"Rough ride, huh, policeman?"

Ted just nodded.

"It will help if you can see, no? And then we can share a surprise."

Ted just nodded again, the voice making him cock his head and listen closely. He couldn't be sure.

Montilla steadied himself with one hand, and with the other pulled the blindfold off the narc's head. Two small squares of tape still held the man's eyes closed. Montilla smiled, pinched a corner with his fingers as the narc jerked his head back against the bulkhead, and pulled, first one, then the other square of tape away from the eyes.

Ted felt the sharp pain of the tape tearing away from the skin, blinked his eyes rapidly, trying to get them adjusted. He brought his hands up and rubbed his face, then turned to see who belonged to the voice. His eyes flew wide, and he gasped.

"That's right, narcotics policeman . . . it's me again! Ain't life mysterious?" Montilla was taking savage glee in the narc's obvious bewilderment.

Ted hesitated, then said, "You . . . you're taking me home? You bastard. You tried to kill me."

Montilla hung on as the bow of the yacht dipped and yawed sickeningly down the face of a big wave. The gurgle of rushing water against the bow was loud, broken now and then by a hollow boom when the hull hit hard against the next wave. The smell of the marijuana was almost overpowering in the stuffy confines of the forward state-rooms, and he turned to go back outside into the air.

"Yeah, that's right, narc. I'm gonna take you home to your Uncle Richards. And won't he be surprised!"

He checked the flex-cuffs and left.

Ted Novak leaned against the bulkhead, braced himself with his legs against the bunk, and hung on. He felt an overpowering wave of fear and depression washing out all his resolve and hope. His sigh was one of despair and defeat. Had he come all this way, survived this long, just to end up back in the clutches of Onyx Montilla? Could this be happening? There was no doubt in his mind what Montilla would do with him. He knew there was no way Montilla would just bring him home as if nothing had happened. No, Montilla would kill him.

He looked down at his flex-cuffs, pulled on them, felt their resisting strength. *Could I swim like this? Could I climb out of here, make my way to the stern of this heaving and bucking bitch and just go over the side, into the water wherever the hell we are? Stay afloat long enough to get picked up by some boat?* He shook his head, and laughed. *How many times do I think I can be* that *lucky?*

Even allowing for his injured leg and his recovery time, he was unhappy with his actions to this point. He had been led around by the nose, and had let it happen, always hoping to be sent home simply because he was an American citizen. Now, it was well past time that he started fighting for himself instead of sitting around like a damsel in distress, waiting for some frigging white knight. He had to find a way to cut the cuffs off him.

He rolled off the bunk, balanced himself, and hopped toward the back of the boat. He made two hops, both times bracing himself against the wall to keep his balance. On his third hop he ran headlong into a beautiful blond-haired girl with still-wet hair hanging down the back of her T-shirt. He saw bloodstains on the left side of the girl's shirt, one on her right breast, and a look of concern and fear in her lovely eyes. She reached out and held him, using her strength to steady him against the rolling and pitching of the yacht.

"Don't tell me," he said with a grin. "I see a friendly face at last."

Her eyes widened, and she looked over her shoulder, then back at him.

"My name is Silky. I'm a friend of your uncle, J.B."

Just hearing the name warmed him and gave him strength. "Yeah? Well, you look like you've had a rough day." He paused, looked past her shoulder at the interior of the yacht, then back into her eyes. "Have you been here since we left? Hiding behind the bales?" He saw her nod. "Good deal. Now let's get out of here."

She started to say something, but turned quickly, pushed him back, and rolled over the pile of bales in the passage-way, out of sight. He arched himself back up onto the bunk as he heard Montilla yell to Joe, "You want some crackers or somethin' too, or just a Coke?"

Montilla moved around in the galley for a couple of minutes, then was gone.

Ted waited as long as he could, then rolled off the bunk again and whispered, "Silky, c'mon, we've got to find something to cut these plastic cuffs with and figure if we can stage our own little mutiny."

She stood up again, her face grim and determined.

Side by side, the two sleek, powerful boats idled out into the turning basin of Port Everglades. The Magnum, driven by Zaden, with Maguire beside him and Kelly and Buchanan behind the bolster seat, was just to the right and slightly ahead of *Stiletto*, driven by J.B. Fat Harry stood with his feet braced, tucked nicely into the bolster seat on the port side of the cockpit. His shaggy head of gray hair was whipped by the wind as he watched the outline of the Customs boat, the small navigation lights sparkling in the darkness. The water in the basin looked like undulating, brown black stainless steel. He looked to his right and saw J.B.'s intent expression as his face was faintly lit by the darkroom glow of the red instrument panel lights.

The latent power of the two boats manifested itself in the throaty, hollow pounding of the engines, the flow of water beside the graceful but solid hulls, and the sure confidence and determination on the faces of the crews.

Almost surrounding them now was the beauty of night-time Fort Lauderdale. To their right, the bright white lights of the loading docks and warehouses of the port itself, with small red lights at the top of the huge derricks near the southwest corner. Almost directly in front of them a large Spanish-style building was outlined by lights, and a warm glow came from inside. It was a large and popular restaurant at the end of the cruise ship wharf. Channel markers shone red and green, and to the left of the restaurant could be seen the lights of the Coast Guard complex. At their backs was the Causeway Bridge, both sides of it garlanded by the beckoning lights of the Marriott on the west and Pier 66 on the east. The circular top of Pier 66 was outlined in lights, and beyond it other hotels and condos could be seen. It was Saturday night in Fort Lauderdale and the city pulsated and vibrated with the energy of those who inhabited or visited it. Traffic was heavy leading toward the beach and cars could be seen and heard racing across the bridge. To their left was a quiet residential neighborhood, lights here and there on back patios, washing the trunks of palm trees. Fort Lauderdale had wrapped itself around the open water of the port, embracing it in its lovely grasp, highlighting it, and providing a beaming, sparkling, glowing backdrop for what would be their arena.

Richards pushed his hips against the bolster seat and relaxed his knees. His right hand lay on the twin throttles, and his left lay on top of the padded steering wheel. He looked through the darkness as Zaden gave a quick salute and pulled away from them, the pitch of the engines changing slightly as he headed the Magnum toward the far southwest corner of the port where the striped and red-lighted FP&L stacks stood starkly against the sky. Richards pointed the long, sharp bow of *Stiletto* toward the place where the Intracoastal Waterway ran off, south from the port in the direction of Miami. He would find a position beside one of the rusty old island freighters that tied up beyond the cruise ships.

A light wash of sprinkling rain hit them, and J.B. and

Harry both looked to the left, out toward the ocean, watching the waves roll in between the rock jetties at the entrance. They could see the channel buoys and the blackness beyond. The clouds streaming overhead seemed to brush the tops of the condos to their left, on the north side of the cut.

No night for any sailor to be out, thought J.B. Well, at least it will keep most of the weekend evening pleasure boaters tied safely to their docks—away from here, and away from the action. He pulled back on the throttles, letting her drift past the huge steel wall of a cruise ship on his right.

Both steel and fiberglass vessels, and their flesh-and-blood masters, now idled down, drifting, stalking their prey.

Two hours had gone by, and it was well after nine o'clock.

J.B. and Harry, moving slowly back and forth in the Intracoastal, with their running lights now turned off, listened to the usual Saturday night police radio traffic on Harry's hand-held unit. There had been a couple of auto accidents, one serious, and a south-end unit had called for a backup at one of the bars off State Road 84. Other than that, it was a fairly normal night from a policeman's point of view.

It changed suddenly, as it usually does.

"All units beachside, be advised . . . we have a report of a small vessel in trouble off the beach. The vessel is reported to be near the shore, just south of the Yankee Clipper and the beachside Marriott Hotel. It is reported that several persons can be seen on the vessel, and that it appears to be out of control. Any unit that can assist, come to channel three."

"Alpha twelve . . . I'm out on the beach. It's some kind of old wooden sailboat, and I can see people in it. Looks like a Haitian boat. I think you'd better contact the coasties. These people are in trouble."

Fat Harry looked at J.B., his eyes wide.

"Haitians? Now? I thought since Baby Doc had split

with his bride and his money, the refugees had stopped coming in."

J.B. rubbed his face with one hand. "Well, I guess it has slowed down some, but we're still getting them—and the Salvadorans and the Colombians and the who knows what-all. Our courts are still arguing about the difference between political asylum and economic asylum. The question is, what the hell are they doing out there in this sloppy weather . . . and what will this do to Montilla when he sees all of the action it generates?"

Harry did not get a chance to answer.

"Off duty five-one-five to four-forty-four . . . go over."

They heard Skids Bedlam's voice, and Harry switched the channel on the radio.

"Four-forty-four here. Go ahead, Skids."

"Yeah, J.B., did you hear that?"

"We got it. What great timing."

"We've been listening to other channels. There ain't no coasties here, they were all pulled south, and we know there aren't any local police boats available. Our fire department Striker went up to Pompano this morning to help them with somethin' up there. Hear me?"

"Yeah. Stand by."

J.B. saw the shadow of the Magnum coming around the corner in front of the restaurant. The Customs boat had its lights out too. He turned *Stiletto* sideways so Zaden could see him and watched as the Customs man brought his boat alongside neatly.

"You guys hear that?" yelled Maguire.

J.B. and Fat Harry shook their heads.

"Looks like we're the only boats out here."

Buchanan, holding his hat on his head, yelled, "So what, we don't have to leave our setup just to help a bunch of boat people!"

"KTU-206 to all units, be advised, any unit that can stand by on the beach should do so."

"Ten-thirty-three . . . emergency! This is alpha twelve! The boat has been turned over by a huge wave, only a couple of hundred feet from the beach! There are people in the water. Repeat, there are people in the water!" Then, "Oh God, we can hear them screaming out there."

Zaden called, "We'll take your position here, J.B. You and Harry run out there and see what you can do!"

J.B. waved, started to turn the boat, and yelled back, "My thought too, Hank! If Montilla sees flashing blue lights along the beach he might hang back anyway. We'll slide back in as soon as we know there's nothin' else we can do out there."

Buchanan was waving his arms now, calling out, "Don't get drawn off now, Richards! Let those fucking people take care of them—" But his voice was drowned out by the twin exhausts of *Stiletto* as J.B. pushed the throttles forward, pointed the bow east, and headed out of the basin.

J.B. and Harry hung on as the racer started taking the first heaving waves on the bow. J.B. pulled the throttles back slightly, so the hull would have enough power to keep pushing and cutting through the waves and the bow would point up higher than if on a plane. They took some salt spray this way, but only one or two tops of waves rolled across the deck and broke up against the windshield.

They passed the rock jetties, and J.B. turned slightly north but not too far. He would go out almost to the second buoy, avoiding the worn shallows of the old "spoil island" made by the dredging years ago. Then he would curve around all the way north and head for the beach just south of the hotels. As he drove through the wet night he could see the lights of several police vehicles on or near the beach and the jerky beams of flashlights being waved here and there along the shore.

It took only a few minutes to get to the scene, and as they did J.B. pulled back on the throttles and slowed *Stiletto* down. He and Harry strained to see if they could spot anyone struggling through the waves.

Suddenly Harry made out the bulbous shape of the sailboat's hull, floating broached in the brakers near the beach.

"Shit! There she is. She's already aground!"

They could see the rounded bottom of the hull as it was rocked violently by the crashing waves.

"She'll break up right there before the night's over! Wonder if any of the poor bastards made it to the beach."

J.B. wiped the rain off his face and hung tightly to the wheel of the racer. He kept his distance from the shore, knowing the waves would grow and steepen there. The water they were in was not to the liking of *Stiletto*. If he kept her bow on to the waves when she was slow, the pointed bow would dig in and the water would come surging over the deck. If he turned her stern-to, the outdrives and transom dug in deep and the following wave presented a frightening oncoming wall of black green water. He tried to angle her between the troughs, rolling dramatically up and over each shoulder as it passed by.

"All units on the beach . . . be advised! This is alpha twelve!"

J.B. and Harry waited, hanging on.

"All units, this is alpha twelve. I have located the leader of the group on the stricken vessel. He and I have made a head count of those that made it to the beach. He advises me . . . he advises me that everyone is accounted for, including two children! I repeat, they all made it!"

J.B. glanced up into the angry sky for a moment, then said to Harry, "Don't tell me those wretches didn't just get a big helping hand from up above!"

Harry, very pleased with the happy outcome of what could have been a tragedy, said, "No argument from me on that one, J.B."

J.B. added power and pointed the bow northeast. He wanted to get farther offshore, but he still had to take the seas at an angle. He left the running lights off. Under moderate power, they moved steadily until they were a mile from the beach. J.B. watched the waves coming from his right, timed them, and then made his turn, adding power as he did so until the bow was facing almost south, and southeast, back toward the entrance to Port Everglades.

He tried to find the horizon between the black rolling seas and the black and gray night sky, stiffening as he saw the faint outline of a ghostly shape ahead of him in the darkness. He scanned the horizon quickly again, and felt a thrill as his eyes picked up a second gray shape slightly beyond the first. He tapped Harry on the arm and pointed, turning the bow harder to port and opening the throttles a bit more. He headed the boat in order to make a large curve—out, around, and behind the two sinister forms slipping inexorably toward the cut.

Harry held the radio to his lips and keyed it, having already gone back to their own work channel. "You guys still listening?"

He heard Zaden's voice come back immediately. "Yeah, we see 'em, we see 'em!"

Bedlam broke through then. "Understand visual contact, and you're cleared from that other problem, right?"

"Ten-four."

J.B. took the radio from Harry. "One's slightly closer, I don't know if you can tell from there. I think he'll go in first, and the other will follow. Lay back and let him get well inside before you hit him. Then we'll come up from behind on the other one."

The radio crackled slightly, and he heard, "Will do, will do . . . watch your ass out there."

J.B. watched as the first gray shape seemed to hesitate, then began moving rapidly between the outside channel markers and into the cut, rolling noticeably as it entered the port. From his location he could not make out the name on the stern, and then remembered he really did not know which one Montilla was on anyway. The wind whipped some salt spray across his eyes as he looked out at the other shape, hanging there in the wet shadows. He saw how she seemed to be laying to, as if watching the progress of the first one. He watched as she rocked out there in the wind and waves and spray, and he knew. He eased the throttles forward and headed for her.

Montilla stood on the fly bridge of *Spirit* with Joe and the captain, watching as *Ghost* entered the port and sped toward the turning basin. He looked to his right again and watched the lights flashing on the beach. Joe had stayed quiet, but the captain wanted to hang offshore until the activity on the beach stopped. Montilla had pressed him on, however, somehow knowing it had nothing to do with him, knowing that whatever police units were dealing with that problem would not have the inclination to stop and check him.

Now he tapped his captain on the shoulder and pointed toward the port entrance. The boat surged forward, and Montilla let out a sigh.

Almost there.

Down below, in the forward cabin, Silky stood beside Ted Novak, watching him massage his wrists. They had managed to find a pair of fishing pliers, after much searching, and she had cut off the flex-cuffs. They had waited then, huddled together, having decided that if Onyx or one of the others came down, they would attack him and subdue him.

No one had come below.

They had been able to steal cautious glances out the side ports, and now knew they were close to land.

"I think we're getting ready to make our way right into Port Everglades," said Silky. "Maybe we could get out into the main salon, watch, and make a jump for it as we go through the cut. It won't be a very long swim to shore."

Ted nodded, and took a step forward. She saw how he favored his right leg, saw the sheen of sweat on his face, and felt growing doubt as to his ability to make it.

Quietly, in the darkened passageway of the yacht, they moved toward the stern, squeezing between the bales of marijuana, trying to keep their feet as the boat rolled with the waves. They made it to the main salon, and Silky edged forward, trying to see how close to shore they were. She saw a lighted buoy, thought she recognized it as one of the channel markers, and then heard footsteps coming down the fly bridge ladder. She turned quickly and pushed Ted down behind some of the bales, crouching beside him.

As she peered through a small crack she could see Joe standing on the aft deck, holding on to the fighting chair and looking around him.

They would have to go through him if they wanted to get off.

* * * *

Montilla watched as the gray form ahead of him moved easily into the turning basin and started to swing to starboard toward the New River. He looked to his left and saw the jetties coming abeam, and at that same moment the wind coming over his shoulder carried with it the unmistakable sound of powerful engines. He whipped his head around and stared into the night. He saw that Joe, below him on the aft deck, was looking hard behind them too.

Was that a sinister and familiar black and gray shape behind them?

The dark surging seas and the black cloudy night gave the scene behind him a smudged charcoal drawing quality, with soft and indefinite lines and shadows with hard edges. He looked forward again and stiffened as he saw the blurred outline of a small, fast boat drawing up on the Striker ahead of him. The boat was moving in from his port side, approaching the stern of *Ghost*.

He screamed, "Noooo!" and turned behind him again to see the long needlelike bow of *Stiletto*, knifing up behind him through the waves.

Silky and Ted still crouched, but dared to look over the tops of the bales now. They had heard the yell from above, and they saw how Joe's attention seemed riveted behind them. They saw him reach slowly under his shirt, on the right side, and come out with a large automatic pistol.

Ted said quietly, "We're inside the cut now, but somethin' is about to go down. Stay behind me, and I'll see if I can get this dude's gun away from him."

Silky nodded, her eyes wide. She licked her lips and prepared to move when Ted did.

Montilla reached over his captain's arms and began pulling on the wheel, yelling, "Turn . . . turn . . . take us back outside! They can't run with us out there!"

The young captain looked over and beyond his bow and saw his sister ship drifting in the basin, the small dark racer fast beside her. He looked back into the night and saw the menacing black and gray racer behind him with two men in it. He thought of all those flashing lights they had seen, the grass down below, and the prisoner. He wondered if there was some way he could make a deal with the cops later after they were all arrested, and said, "Shit, Onyx, it's the cops, man! They're all over the place!"

They struggled for the wheel for a few seconds until Harry's voice came booming through the wind over the loud-hailer.

"JUST PULL IT INTO THE BASIN AND SHUT IT DOWN, CAPTAIN . . . THIS IS THE POLICE. PULL IT INTO THE BASIN AND SHUT IT DOWN!"

The young captain looked back over his shoulder and said, "Hell, Onyx, they've got us cold! Running will just make it worse!"

Montilla screamed, "Fuck you!" He reached under the instrument panel and pulled an M-1 carbine from its clips. The weapon carried a twenty-round magazine. He brought it up and racked a round into the chamber.

The captain beside him, his eyes wide, yelled, "What are you doing . . . what are you doing, man!"

Montilla braced himself and fired three shots in quick succession down toward the boat behind them. He heard Joe, below, calling, "What the fuck is goin' on? Can't we just run from these guys?" As Joe said this he heard a roar from behind them, realizing that his eyes had already registered the flash, and instinctively ducked as the shotgun rounds impacted and ricocheted all around the port side of the sportfisherman. He crouched down behind the transom.

"Dammit!" yelled Ted, pushing Silky backward onto the carpet of the main salon. "We're in the middle of a fuckin' shoot-out! That sucker out there is locked and loaded now. We'll have to just hang back and wait for our chance!"

Silky rolled onto one hip, then got into a crouch again, breathing easily, watching and waiting. Her heart was pounding. He was *out* there, the big cop was *out* there.

Harry, who had fired the shotgun after Montilla had shot at them, racked another round into the chamber and waited. J.B. threw the throttles back and pulled the clutches into reverse. Then he added throttle again and spun the wheel hard, causing them to rapidly fall back from the Striker while they turned. He looked up on the fly bridge of the other boat and saw Montilla and the captain struggling while the big sportfisherman wallowed crazily in the troughs. The Striker was just inside the cut and the rollers were big and powerful. Richards automatically ducked as he saw Montilla turn and fire off a couple more rounds in their direction. Then he saw the young captain pull his arm back and punch Montilla in the face. Montilla fell sprawling to the deck on the fly bridge, kicking at the captain as he went down. The big boat turned slowly, the engines still pushing her, and J.B. backed *Stiletto* once more as the big bows came around and *Spirit* again headed for the open sea.

Montilla, on his back, pulled the barrel of the carbine around. As the young captain turned and shouted, "Don't!" Montilla fired twice into his belly. The young guy let go of the wheel, grabbed his bleeding waist, and backed against the port side low bulkhead. He stared at Montilla incredulously, started to say something, and slowly fell backward off the fly bridge and into the water.

As the Striker came up the port side of *Stiletto*, headed into the waves now, Joe stood up in the aft deck. He had heard the shooting above him and could see the big guy in the other boat with the shotgun. Joe may not have been much of a boat person, and he may have been young to be a bodyguard for a man like Kolin, but he had "made his bones" on the street. He had immersed himself in the role of hood, and loved all the old gangster movies. He was no boat person, but he was no coward either.

With his nine-millimeter automatic, Joe began snapping off rounds toward the cockpit of the black and gray racer passing beside them.

Richards could hear the sharp cracking of the automatic and the ripping sound the bullets made hitting the fiberglass. Harry yelled, "Watch it!" and fired the shotgun again.

Joe grunted and threw his arms into the air, the automatic flying over the side and into the water as all of the double-O load impacted his body. He tasted the blood running out of his mouth, felt the back of his head hit the fighting chair and then the deck . . . and then oblivion.

Ted had again ducked as the shotgun went off, shielding Silky as he did so. He saw Joe's automatic go flying as the hood went down, and said, "Dammit, I guess that would have been too much to ask."

Montilla struggled to his feet as he watched Joe fall. Balancing himself on the rocking fly bridge, he began firing the carbine almost straight down into the cockpit of *Stiletto* as the two boats passed in the cut. The copper shell casings rang on the deck as he fired again and again.

J.B. heard several solid thuds along with the blasts of the weapon and the tearing of fiberglass. Then he heard Harry say, "Son of a bitch!" The shotgun slipped from the big man's grip and he slumped heavily against the bolster seat, his head rolling on his chest.

Richards reached over with his left hand and tried to prop his partner up against the cushioned backrest while he yelled, "Harry! Harry! . . . are you okay, man?" Harry turned his head, his eyes half-closed, groaned, and slipped slowly to the deck between the bolster seat and the square cabin hatchway.

Richards looked up and behind him to see the Striker crashing strongly against the waves, plumes of spray flying high into the air before being scattered back by the wind. He could see Montilla on the fly bridge, at the helm, looking back over his shoulder at him. He hit the throttles and turned the wheel hard on the racer. As the pointed bow came back around after the big yacht he screamed, "Now, you bastard! Now we'll see!"

Montilla watched as the black and gray racer pulled behind him and then beside him again. He looked down into the cockpit and saw the face of the cop he knew it had to be, staring up at him, and he felt a terror deep inside. In the crazy tumult of crashing waves and whipping spray and violently rocking boats, the cop's face appeared calm. As the cop's eyes stared up at him, Montilla muttered, "No . . . oh no!" He tried to steer, fighting the seas, fumbled with the carbine, and watched fascinated as the cop slowly pulled an ugly old revolver from his belt, and pointed it at him.

Was it the same one? The same one that had killed his father?

J.B. aimed at Montilla as best he could, began to pull back on the trigger, and froze. His eyes went wide and he thought for a moment that his heart would burst. For a fleeting second nothing was important anymore. For an instant he just wanted to laugh out loud in triumph.

He saw Ted Novak come out from the main salon, grin, and wave quickly, and then turn and begin climbing steadily up the fly bridge ladder toward Montilla, who was staring intently at *Stiletto*.

Ted was alive! He was here, now! But how?

Grimly, J.B. brought his mind back to the moment. He took aim again at the fly bridge and squeezed off a shot. He doubted if he could hit Montilla with the boats rocking violently in the seas, but he wanted to distract him long enough for Ted to make the climb.

Ted made it, but his right leg was still slowing him down. As he lifted his head and shoulders over the level of the fly bridge deck, Montilla saw him, yelled, and lunged forward, trying to kick him in the face. Ted hit at Montilla's leg with one fist, and kept coming. Now Montilla kicked at him again, then brought the barrel of the carbine down. He lost his balance on the pitching deck, fired once, missed Ted's right shoulder by inches, and then swung the barrel of the weapon as he fell backward, hitting Ted across the eyes with the cold steel.

J.B., a few yards away, could only watch the struggle helplessly. He thought he saw the forward hatch up on the bow of the Striker open for a moment, but then the sportfisherman rolled away from him and he couldn't see up there anymore.

Ted pulled himself up on the ladder again and prepared to lunge forward as Montilla still struggled to regain his balance. Ted tasted his own blood, and moved.

At the same time, Montilla leaned back against the steering console, lifted the carbine, and snapped off a shot. This time he scored. The bullet hit Ted's right shoulder, lodging into the muscle. Ted reeled backward, preventing himself from falling off the ladder by hanging on grimly with his left hand. He felt a searing pain on his whole right side, and his right arm hung limply. He looked up and saw that Montilla was staring at him, grinning, the barrel of the carbine pointed right at his face.

Montilla started to squeeze the trigger when he felt his head being jerked backward by his hair, and Silky's angry voice screamed, "No, Onyx! No more . . . no more!"

She had watched Ted's struggle to get up the fly bridge ladder from below, frustrated because she could not help. Then she had turned, ducked through the interior of the boat, and raced up to the forward stateroom. She had pushed open the bow hatch, climbed out, dropped it, and almost went sliding off the wet and yawing deck before she managed to grab a rail and pull herself to the fly bridge structure on the port side. From there she was able to grab outriggers and radio antennae, swinging precariously out over the water once as the yacht rolled. She climbed over the fly bridge windshield just as Montilla shot Ted in the shoulder and prepared to finish him off.

Now she pulled Montilla's hair until he was bent back over the wheel. She saw Ted struggle onto the fly bridge deck and try to stand. Montilla got his footing and spun around, punching at Silky with his left hand, trying to bring the barrel of the carbine around with his right. Silky lunged forward at him, hoping to get in his way long enough for Ted to get there, but Montilla brought the carbine around in a wicked arc and it impacted the side of her head with a sickening sound.

Bright lights started popping off in Silky's eyes. She felt her arms swinging and her back arching, and then she was falling, out and down. The wind was knocked out of her as she hit the port side railing with the small of her back, and then suddenly she was in the water.

J.B., trying to stay with the Striker, and still on the starboard side, had seen Ted get shot and then recover enough to crawl up onto the fly bridge deck. Then, incredibly, he had seen Silky—alive and fighting with Montilla. She had

saved Ted's life, he knew, and when he saw her get hit with
the carbine he started to pull back on the throttles and
move to the other side. He had to find her before it was too
late. He pointed his revolver at Montilla again as he struggled with the wheel of *Stiletto*. If Ted didn't get up, he
would start shooting at Montilla.

"The girl just went into the water! I think it was the
girl—and it looked like she went over the port side!"
yelled Hank Zaden as he held the bow of the Magnum into
the oncoming waves. After Maguire and Kelly had boarded
Ghost he had turned the Magnum back toward the ocean.
He had seen part of the running battle, knew Harry was not
in sight, and knew the Striker could outrun either go-fast
boat in the heavy seas. They were less than fifty yards
away now—the dark, the rain, and the salt spray all combining to make visibility very bad.

Buchanan, hanging on with both hands, yelled, "The
hell with her! She's a gonner . . . we'll never find her in this
shit! Stay after that fuckin' Striker!"

But Hank Zaden ignored him. He was the captain of this
U.S. Customs Magnum, by God, and he had seen the
glimpse of a pale face and flailing arms in the waves and
wash from the runaway Striker.

He turned the bow of the Magnum toward where he
thought he had seen the girl.

J.B. looked quickly over his shoulder, saw the Magnum
moving up out of the darkness, knew that Zaden was
headed for the girl, and turned back toward the *Spirit*'s fly
bridge.

Montilla had watched the girl go over the side, had
hissed, "Fucking *bitch!*" and turned to shoot Ted again. He
was just too slow.

Ted got to him as he turned, brought his left fist up in an
uppercut, and caught Montilla in the throat. Montilla stag-
gered back, his hips hit the steering wheel, and he lunged
forward, his eyes wild. Ted, his right arm useless, kicked
out once, slipped and almost fell, and then grabbed for
Montilla with his left arm, circling the other man's waist,
and pushing him backward.

Montilla, frantic now, hissing and grunting and swear-

ing, punched Ted and kicked at him. Finally he managed to
swing the carbine around again and hit Ted in the right
shoulder with the stock. Ted winced and cried out but hung
on.

The sportfisherman, with no one at the helm, pushed and
beaten by the waves, rocked violently as the two men
struggled, flinging them this way and that across the slippery wet deck of the fly bridge. Suddenly both men were
catapulted toward the stern rail. As they hit it, Montilla
managed to swing the carbine viciously against Ted's head.
Ted went down hard. At the same time, Montilla lost his
balance, swung over the rail, hung on with one hand, and
then dropped heavily to the aft deck below, still clutching
the carbine, and missing the fighting chair by inches.

J.B. looked behind him. He saw that the Magnum had
fallen off, far behind, apparently stopped in the water.

He had seen Ted go down again, and had watched as
Montilla fell to the aft deck. Momentary elation turned to
dread when he saw that Ted was not moving. He realized
that Montilla could move inside the main salon to the interior steering station and safely operate the Striker from
there—not only out of the sloppy weather, but also away
from J.B.'s gunfire.

Stiletto followed *Spirit* in the darkness, both boats constantly battered now by the mounting seas and blowing
winds. J.B. saw the change in the waves and the deepening
color of the water, and he knew they were in the Gulf
Stream.

He knew that if he didn't stop Montilla now he might
lose him.

Montilla held on to the fighting chair, his feet straddling
Joe's sprawled body. He looked back and saw *Stiletto*
swinging around toward him again. He cursed. He looked
down into the cabin and thought of the two separate bags
of cocaine hidden below. He saw the bales of grass stacked
there, almost filling the salon, and he cursed again. He
turned, looked back at the gray racer, and in desperate fear

mixed with an overwhelming anger he shouted, "Get away
from me, *puta!* . . . leave me alone, you bastaaaard!"

He watched as the sharp bow of the racer came closer,
braced himself against the ladder, and brought the barrel of
the carbine up.

Richards could see Montilla screaming something at him
but could not hear the words as they were torn away by the
wind. He saw the carbine coming up and flinched as the
first bullets cut through the fiberglass around him. He cried
out and spun around as a bullet hit the windshield in front
of him and shattered it, rifling shards of metal and glass
and lead into his face and shoulder.

The left side of his face felt clawed and he tasted blood.
He looked down and saw the blood dripping from his face
onto his forearm and he pulled himself straight into the
bolster seat and pushed the throttles forward all the way.
He looked through the blood in his eyes, through the salt
spray, through the wind-whipped night across to the aft
deck of *Spirit*. The sportfisherman rolled violently as it
took another wave, and he could see Montilla hanging on
to the fly bridge ladder, back-dropped against the darker
shadows from inside the cabin, as if in a grainy black and
white photograph.

All of his pain and fear and anger and frustration became
instantly fused. His mind was swept clean of everything
but the present and his entire being focused on his target.

He felt the hull of the racer crashing against the waves as
he charged up on the Striker ahead of him. He could see
Montilla aiming the carbine again, and as he saw the
flashes and then heard the blasts he screamed, "Yaaaaaah!"
and drove the bow of *Stiletto* over the wide transom of
Spirit. At the same time a huge wave lifted the stern of the
Striker, while the needlelike bow of *Stiletto* slid over the
transom of the Striker—and down.

Montilla stared and screamed as the pointed bow rushed
at him with a force and power that would not be denied. He
heard and felt the fighting chair in front of him disintegrat-
ing. He dropped the carbine and reached his arms out in
front of him in terror. He backed toward the salon, his feet
slipping in Joe's blood, as the very point of the bow took

him in the chest. With a terrible grinding and crashing, *Stiletto* punched him backward until his back was thrown against the stack of heavy burlap-covered bales of marijuana. He screamed as he felt the incredible weight and force of the sharp fiberglass as the bow punched through his chest, out his back, and drove him solidly into the packed bales. He felt consuming pain as he watched the whole rear wall of the cabin collapse around the gray fiberglass bow. His fingernails ripped loose as he clawed at the deck of the racer. He looked back along the deck—straight into the ice blue eyes of the cop. He looked into those burning steel eyes, the same eyes that had seared him so long ago, and even through his agony he felt the terror.

He tried to say his father's name, blood gushed from his mouth, and he died.

Richards gripped the wheel with his bloody hands and stared down into the face of the small boy, the always-questioning face. As he watched, the face became Montilla, wide-eyed in death, mouth open in a silent scream.

He looked around at the carnage created by the two boats crashing together and was momentarily stunned. He heard a moan down by his feet, and at the same time the rough seas rocked both boats violently again and he heard an unbelievable tearing noise as fiberglass split and cracked. He felt a jolt and heard a whooshing sound as the keel broke and the stern of *Stiletto* began to break away, cracking open the fuel lines. The constant wave action, and the weight of the engines was causing the stern to break and be ripped away from the bow, which was firmly embedded in the cabin and aft deck of the Striker.

He glanced up and saw Ted getting painfully to his knees on the fly bridge, a few feet above him. He bent down behind the bolster seat to reach down for Fat Harry at his feet when, with an enormous roar, the fuel exploded and caught fire. His whole world turned to orange and he was blinded by the huge fireball and cracking explosion. As the fireball vanished into the clouds, leaving small, intense flames licking hungrily around the ruptured engine covers, another gigantic wave lifted the stern of *Spirit*. As she fell, crashing and splashing back into the trough, the stern section of *Stiletto* tore away from the Striker's transom, splashed into the blue black water, and disappeared.

Ted, who had covered his face and rolled back as the fireball mushroomed around them, got back onto his knees, looked down at the blackened carnage below him, and cried, "Jesus . . . are you still there, J.B.?" Then, ignoring the fact that the Striker was still pounding crazily through the Gulf Stream, still under power but with a free helm, he carefully eased himself down the twisted ladder to the wet glass bow of the racer.

Richards, huddled over Harry, lifted his head slowly and looked over his shoulder. From the bolster seat back, *Stiletto* was gone. He could see the torn and burned transom of the Striker, and beyond that, the sea. A wave broke over the stern and sprayed him with saltwater and the sting reminded him where he was and what he still had to do. He braced his legs, grabbed Harry under the arms, and struggled with him to a standing position. Then he draped the upper part of Harry's body over the shattered remains of the windshield, bent down, and lifted up the legs. He heard a grunt of pain, and looked up to see Ted lying on the wet deck of the racer, pulling at Harry with one hand, his face set in concentration. Richards just pushed the big man's unresisting body toward Ted, and together they slid down the fiberglass racing bow until they came to rest in a heap against part of the main cabin frame.

Ted sat up, looked at Harry, and said, "Is he still alive?"

"Yeah, but I don't know for how long," said J.B. He looked into Ted's eyes, and said, "How about you, Ted . . . you all right?"

Ted looked back, saw the bloody wounds and burns on J.B., grinned and said, "My God, Uncle, you're all banged up."

Richards grunted and crawled out of the torn cockpit and down toward the fly bridge ladder. The boat rolled violently to starboard. Richards shook himself and tried to clear his head. He grabbed the fly bridge ladder with numb hands, said to Ted in a choking voice, "Hold him, and see if you can stop the bleeding, he's hit in the chest or stom-